monday mourning

Kathy Reichs, like her character Temperance Brennan, is a forensic anthropologist, formerly for the Office of the Chief Medical Examiner in North Carolina and currently for the Laboratoire de sciences judiciaries et de médicine légale for the province of Quebec. A professor in the department of anthropology at the University of North Carolina at Charlotte, she is one of only eighty-five forensic anthropologists ever certified by the American Board of Forensic Anthropology, is past Vice President of both the American Academy of Forensic Anthropology and the American Board of Forensic Anthropology, and serves on the National Police Services Advisory Council in Canada. Reichs's first book, *Déja Dead*, catapulted her to fame when it became a *New York Times* bestseller and won the 1997 Ellis Award for Best First Novel. Her website is www.kathyreichs.com

Praise for Kathy Reichs

'Reichs is the queen of pathology thrillers' *Independent*

'Completely engrossing . . . drags the reader into a different
world where dialogue is tense, dead men tell the best tales and the ice
will freeze the bones. Read this and you'll know why the word
"thriller" was invented'
Frances Fyfield

'Reichs has proved that she is now up there with the best'
Marcel Berlins, *The Times*

'The forensic detail is harrowing, the pace relentless and the prose
assured. Kathy Reichs just gets better and better and is now the
Alpha female of the genre'
Irish Independent

'A long way from your standard forensic thriller: all the excitement
you crave, indefatigably expert. But conscience-generated and
compassionate too'
Literary Review

'A brilliant novel . . . fascinating science and dead-on psychological
portrayals, not to mention a whirlwind of a plot . . . a must-read'
Jeffery Deaver

'Tempe Brennan . . . is smart, resourceful and likeable . . .
an investigator to follow'
Daily Telegraph

'It's becoming apparent that Reichs is not just "as good as" Cornwell,
she has become the finer writer . . . the ever-accelerating unfolding of
the plot has all the élan of Kathy Reichs at her most adroit'
Daily Express

'Inevitably compared to Patricia Cornwell, Reichs is actually
in a different league. Tempe Brennan is already . . . a much
more rounded character that Cornwell's heroine Scarpetta:
more human, less driven and much better company during the time it
takes her to untangle these complex crimes'
Sunday Times

Also by Kathy Reichs

Déjà Dead
Death du Jour
Deadly Décisions
Fatal Voyage
Grave Secrets
Bare Bones
Cross Bones
Break No Bones
Bones to Ashes
Devil Bones
206 Bones
Spider Bones
(published in hardback in the UK as *Mortal Remains*)
Flash and Bones
Virals

Kathy Reichs
monday mourning

arrow books

Reissued by Arrow Books in 2011

2 4 6 8 10 9 7 5 3 1

Published by arrangement with the original publisher, Scribner, an imprint of Simon & Schuster, Inc.

First published in Great Britain in 2004 by William Heinemann

First published in paperback in 2005 by
Arrow Books
The Random House Group Limited
20 Vauxhall Bridge Road, London, SW1V 2SA

www.randomhouse.co.uk

Addresses for companies within The Random House Group Limited can be found at:
www.randomhouse.co.uk/offices.htm

The Random House Group Limited Reg. No. 954009

A CIP catalogue record for this book
is available from the British Library

ISBN 978-0-099-55655-8

The Random House Group Limited supports the Forest Stewardship Council® (FSC®), the leading international forest certification organisation. All our titles that are printed on Greenpeace approved FSC® certified paper carry the FSC® logo. Our paper procurement policy can be found at:
www.randomhouse.co.uk/environment

Typeset by SX Composing DTP, Rayleigh, Essex
Printed and bound in Great Britain by
CPI Bookmarque Ltd, Croydon, CR0 4TD

For Deborah Miner
My baby sister.
My Harry.

Thanks for always being there.

Acknowledgments

Thanks to Darden Hood, Director, Beta Analytic Inc., for advice on radiocarbon dating. W. Alan Gorman and James K. W. Lee, Department of Geological Sciences, Queens University, Kingston, Ontario, and Brian Beard, Department of Geology, University of Wisconsin, shared their knowledge of bedrock geology and strontium isotope analysis.

Michael Finnegan, Department of Anthropology, Kansas State University, provided details on aging bone with UV light. Robert B. J. Dorion, Laboratoire de Sciences Judiciaires et de Médecine Légale, supplied information on property research in Montreal. Sergeant Pierre Marineau, Special Constable, Securité Publique, guided me on a tour of the Montreal courthouse. Claude Pothel, Laboratoire de Sciences Judiciaires et de Médecine Légale, answered questions pertaining to pathology and autopsies. Michael Abel shared his knowledge of all things Jewish. Jim Junot double-checked countless details.

Paul Reichs offered advice on the qualification of an expert witness. As usual, his comments on the manuscript were greatly appreciated.

My friend Michelle Phillips graciously allowed the use of the 'Monday, Monday' lyrics.

Much gratitude to James Woodward, Chancellor of the University of North Carolina at Charlotte, for his continued support. *Merci* to André Lauzon, Chef de service, and to all of my colleagues at the Laboratoire de Sciences Judiciaires et de Médecine Légale.

My editor, Susanne Kirk, and my agent, Jennifer Walsh, were, as always, patient, understanding, and totally supportive.

monday mourning

Oh Monday mornin' you gave me no warnin' of what was to be . . .

—JOHN PHILLIPS,
The Mamas and the Papas

1

Monday, Monday . . .
Can't trust that day . . .

As the tune played inside my head, gunfire exploded in the cramped underground space around me.

My eyes flew up as muscle, bone, and guts splattered against rock just three feet from me.

The mangled body seemed glued for a moment, then slid downward, leaving a smear of blood and hair.

I felt warm droplets on my cheek, backhanded them with a gloved hand.

Still squatting, I swiveled.

'*Assez!*' Enough!

Sergeant-détective Luc Claudel's brows plunged into a V. He lowered but did not holster his nine-millimeter.

'Rats. They are the devil's spawn.' Claudel's

French was clipped and nasal, reflecting his upriver roots.

'Throw rocks,' I snapped.

'That bastard was big enough to throw them back.'

Hours of squatting in the cold and damp on a December Monday in Montreal had taken a toll. My knees protested as I rose to a standing position.

'Where is Charbonneau?' I asked, rotating one booted foot, then the other.

'Questioning the owner. I wish him luck. Moron has the IQ of pea soup.'

'The owner discovered this?' I flapped a hand at the ground behind me.

'*Non. Le plombier.*'

'What was a plumber doing in the cellar?'

'Genius spotted a trapdoor beside the commode, decided to do some underground exploration to acquaint himself with the sewage pipes.'

Remembering my own descent down the rickety staircase, I wondered why anyone would take the risk.

'The bones were lying on the surface?'

'Says he tripped on something sticking out of the ground. There.' Claudel cocked his chin at a shallow pit where the south wall met the dirt floor. 'Pulled it loose. Showed the owner. Together they checked out the local library's anatomy collection to see if the bone was human. Picked a book with nice color pictures since they probably can't read.'

I was about to ask a follow-up question when something clicked above us. Claudel and I looked up, expecting his partner.

Instead of Charbonneau, we saw a scarecrow man in a knee-length sweater, baggy jeans, and dirty blue Nikes. Pigtails wormed from the lower edge of a red bandanna wrapped his head.

The man was crouched in the doorway, pointing a throwaway Kodak in my direction.

Claudel's V narrowed and his parrot nose went a deeper red. '*Tabarnac!*'

Two more clicks, then bandanna man scrabbled sideways.

Holstering his weapon, Claudel grabbed the wooden railing. 'Until SIJ returns, throw rocks.'

SIJ—Section d'Identité Judiciaire. The Quebec equivalent of Crime Scene Recovery.

I watched Claudel's perfectly fitted buttocks disappear through the small rectangular opening. Though tempted, I pegged not a single rock.

Upstairs, muted voices, the clump of boots. Downstairs, just the hum of the generator for the portable lights.

Breath suspended, I listened to the shadows around me.

No squeaking. No scratching. No scurrying feet. Quick scan.

No beady eyes. No naked, scaly tails.

The little buggers were probably regrouping for another offensive.

Though I disagreed with Claudel's approach to the problem, I was with him on one thing: I could do without the rodents.

Satisfied that I was alone for the moment, I

refocused on the moldy crate at my feet. *Dr. Energy's Power Tonic. Dead tired? Dr. Energy's makes your bones want to get up and dance.*

Not these bones, Doc.

I gazed at the crate's grisly contents.

Though most of the skeleton remained caked, dirt had been brushed from some bones. Their outer surfaces looked chestnut under the harsh illumination of the portable lights. A clavicle. Ribs. A pelvis.

A human skull.

Damn.

Though I'd said it a half dozen times, reiteration couldn't hurt. I'd come from Charlotte to Montreal a day early to prepare for court on Tuesday. A man had been accused of killing and dismembering his wife. I'd be testifying on the saw mark analysis I'd done on her skeleton. It was complicated material and I'd wanted to review my case file. Instead, I was freezing my ass digging up the basement of a pizza parlor.

Pierre LaManche had visited my office early this morning. I'd recognized the look, correctly guessed what was coming as soon as I saw him.

Bones had been found in the cellar of a pizza-by-the-slice joint, my boss had told me. The owner had called the police. The police had called the coroner. The coroner had called the medicolegal lab.

LaManche wanted me to check it out.

'Today?'

'*S'il vous plaît.*'

'I'm on the stand tomorrow.'

'The Pétit trial?'

I nodded.

'The remains are probably those of animals,' LaManche said in his precise, Parisian French. 'It should not take you long.'

'Where?' I reached for a tablet.

LaManche read the address from a paper in his hand. Rue Ste-Catherine, a few blocks east of Centre-ville.

CUM turf.

Claudel.

The thought of working with Claudel had triggered the morning's first 'damn.'

There are some small-town departments around the island city of Montreal, but the two main players in law enforcement are the SQ and the CUM. La Sûreté du Québec is the provincial force. The SQ rules in the boonies, and in towns lacking municipal departments. The Police de la Communauté Urbaine de Montréal, or CUM, are the city cops. The island belongs to the CUM.

Luc Claudel and Michel Charbonneau are detectives with the Major Crimes Division of the CUM. As forensic anthropologist for the province of Quebec, I've worked with both over the years. With Charbonneau, the experience is always a pleasure. With his partner, the experience is always an experience. Though a good cop, Luc Claudel has the patience of a firecracker, the sensitivity of Vlad the Impaler, and a persistent skepticism as to the value of forensic anthropology.

Snappy dresser, though.

Dr. Energy's crate had already been loaded with loose bones when I'd arrived in the basement two hours earlier. Though Claudel had yet to provide many details, I assumed the bone collecting had been done by the owner, perhaps with the assistance of the hapless plumber. My job had been to determine if the remains were human.

They were.

That finding had generated the morning's second 'damn.'

My next task had been to determine whether anyone else lay in repose beneath the surface of the cellar. I'd started with three exploratory techniques.

Side lighting the floor with a flashlight beam had shown depressions in the dirt. Probing had located resistance below each depression, suggesting the presence of subsurface objects. Test trenching had produced human bones.

Bad news for a leisurely review of the Pétit file.

When I'd rendered my opinion, Claudel and Charbonneau had contributed to 'damn's three through five. A few Quebecois expletives had been added for emphasis.

SIJ had been called. The crime scene unit routine had begun. Lights had been set up. Pictures had been taken. While Claudel and Charbonneau questioned the owner and his assistant, a ground penetrating radar unit had been dragged around the cellar. The GPR showed subsurface disturbances beginning four inches down in each depression. Otherwise, the basement was clean.

Claudel and his semiautomatic manned rat patrol while the SIJ techs took a break and I laid out two simple four-square grids. I was attaching the last string to the last stake when Claudel enjoyed his Rambo moment with the rats.

Now what? Wait for the SIJ techs to return?

Right.

Using SIJ equipment, I shot prints and video. Then I rubbed circulation into my hands, replaced my gloves, folded into a squat, and began troweling soil from square 1-A.

As I dug, I felt the usual crime scene rush. The quickened senses. The intense curiosity. What if it's nothing? What if it's something?

The anxiety.

What if I smash a critically important section to hell?

I thought of other excavations. Other deaths. A wannabe saint in a burned-out church. A decapitated teen at a biker crib. Bullet-riddled dopers in a streamside grave.

I don't know how long I'd been digging when the SIJ team returned, the taller of the two carrying a Styrofoam cup. I searched my memory for his name.

Root. *Racine*. Tall and thin like a root. The mnemonic worked.

René Racine. New guy. We'd processed a handful of scenes. His shorter counterpart was Pierre Gilbert. I'd known him a decade.

Sipping tepid coffee, I explained what I'd done in their absence. Then I asked Gilbert to film and haul dirt, Racine to screen.

Back to the grid.

When I'd taken square 1-A down three inches, I moved on to 1-B. Then 1-C and 1-D.

Nothing but dirt.

OK. The GPR showed a discrepancy beginning four inches below the surface.

I kept digging.

My fingers and toes numbed. My bone marrow chilled. I lost track of time.

Gilbert carried buckets of dirt from my grid to the screen. Racine sifted. Now and then Gilbert shot a pic. When all of grid one was down a level three inches, I went back to square 1-A. At a depth of six inches I shifted squares as I had before.

I'd taken two swipes at square 1-B when I noticed a change in soil color. I asked Gilbert to reposition a light.

One glance and my diastolic ratcheted up.

'Bingo.'

Gilbert squatted by my side. Racine joined him.

'*Quoi?*' Gilbert asked. What?

I ran the tip of my trowel around the outer edge of the blob seeping into 1-B.

'The dirt's darker,' Racine observed.

'Staining indicates decomposition,' I explained.

Both techs looked at me.

I pointed to squares 1-C and 1-D. 'Someone or something's going south under there.'

'Alert Claudel?' Gilbert asked.

'Make his day.'

*

8

Four hours later all my digits were ice. Though I'd tuqued my head and scarved my neck, I was shivering inside my one-hundred-percent-microporous-polyurethane-polymerized-coated-nylon-guaranteed-to-forty-below-Celsius Kanuk parka.

Gilbert was moving around the cellar, snapping and filming from various angles. Racine was watching, gloved hands thrust into his armpits for warmth. Both looked comfy in their arctic jump-suits.

The two homicide cops, Claudel and Charbonneau, stood side by side, feet spread, hands clasped in front of their genitals. Each wore a black woolen overcoat and black leather gloves. Neither wore a happy face.

Eight dead rats adorned the base of the walls.

The plumber's pit and the two depressions were open to a depth of two feet. The former had yielded a few scattered bones left behind by the plumber and owner. The depression trenches were a different story.

The skeleton under grid one lay in a fetal curl. It was unclothed, and not a single artifact had turned up in the screen.

The individual under grid two had been bundled before burial. The parts we could see looked fully skeletal.

Flicking the last particles of dirt from the second burial, I set aside my paintbrush, stood, and stomped my feet to warm them.

'That a blanket?' Charbonneau's voice sounded husky from the cold.

'Looks more like leather,' I said.

He jabbed a thumb at Dr. Energy's crate.

'This the rest of the dude in the box?'

Sergeant-détective Michel Charbonneau was born in Chicoutimi, six hours up the St. Lawrence from Montreal, in a region known as the Saguenay. Before entering the CUM, he'd spent several years working in the West Texas oil fields. Proud of his cowboy youth, Charbonneau always addressed me in my mother tongue. His English was good, though 'de's replaced 'the's, syllables were often inappropriately accented, and his phrasing used enough slang to fill a ten-gallon hat.

'Let's hope so.'

'You hope so?' A small vapor cloud puffed from Claudel's mouth.

'Yes, Monsieur Claudel. I hope so.'

Claudel's lips tucked in, but he said nothing.

When Gilbert finished shooting the bundled burial, I dropped to my knees and tugged at a corner of the leather. It tore.

Changing from my warm woolies to surgical gloves, I leaned in and began teasing free an edge, gingerly separating, lifting, then rolling the leather backward onto itself.

With the outer layer fully peeled to the left, I began on the inner. At places, fibers adhered to the skeleton. Hands shaking from cold and nervousness, I scalpeled rotten leather from underlying bone.

10

'What's that white stuff?' Racine asked.

'Adipocere.'

'Adipocere,' he repeated.

'Grave wax,' I said, not in the mood for a chemistry lesson. 'Fatty acids and calcium soaps from muscle or fat undergoing chemical changes, usually after long burial or immersion in water.'

'Why's it not on the other skeleton?'

'I don't know.'

I heard Claudel puff air through his lips. I ignored him.

Fifteen minutes later I'd detached the inner layer and laid back the shroud, fully exposing the skeleton.

Though damaged, the skull was clearly present.

'Three heads, three people.' Charbonneau stated the obvious.

'*Tabarnouche*,' Claudel said.

'Damn,' I said.

Gilbert and Racine remained mute.

'Any idea what we've got here, Doc?' Charbonneau asked.

I creaked to my feet. Eight eyes followed me to Dr. Energy's crate.

One by one I removed and observed the two pelvic halves, then the skull.

Crossing to the first trench, I knelt, extricated, and inspected the same skeletal elements.

Dear God.

Replacing those bones, I crawled to the second trench, leaned in, and studied the skull fragments.

No. Not again. The universal victims.
I teased free the right demi-pelvis.
Breath billowed in front of five faces.
Sitting back on my heels, I cleaned dirt from the pubic symphysis.
And felt something go cold in my chest.
Three women. Barely past girl.

2

Waking to the Tuesday morning weather report, I knew I was in for killer cold. Not the occasional mid-forties damp we whine about in January in North Carolina. I mean subzero cold. Arctic cold. If-I-stop-moving-I'll-die-and-be-eaten-by-wolves cold.

I adore Montreal. I love the not-quite-eight-hundred-foot mountain, the old port, Little Italy, Chinatown, the Gay Village, the steel and glass skyscrapers of Centre-ville, the tangled neighborhoods with their alleys and gray stones and impossible staircases.

Montreal is a schizoid scrapper, continually fighting with herself. Anglophone-Francophone. Separatist-Federalist. Catholic-Protestant. Old-New. I find it fascinating. I delight in the whole *empanada*, falafel, *poutine*, Kong Pao multiculturalism of the place. Hurley's Irish Pub. Katsura. L'Express. Fairmont Bagel. Trattoria Trestevere.

I partake in the city's never-ending round of festivals: Le Festival International de Jazz, Les Fêtes Gourmandes Internationales, Le Festival des Films du Monde, the bug-tasting festival at the Insectarium. I frequent the stores on Ste-Catherine, the outdoor markets at Jean-Talon and Atwater, the antique shops along Notre-Dame. I visit the museums, picnic in the parks, bike the paths along the Lachine Canal. I relish it all.

I do not relish the climate from November to May.

I admit it. I have lived too long in the South. I hate feeling chilled. I have no patience with snow and ice. Keep your boots and ChapStick and ice hotels. Give me shorts and sandals and a thirty-blocker.

My cat, Birdie, shares this view. When I sat up he rose, arched, then tunneled back under the covers. Smiling, I watched his body compact into a tight round lump. Birdie. My sole and loyal roommate.

'I'm with you, Bird,' I said, offing the clock radio.

The lump curled tighter.

I looked at the digits. Five-thirty.

I looked at the window. Pitch-black.

I bolted for the bathroom.

Twenty minutes later I was at my kitchen table, coffee at my elbow, Pétit file spread before me.

Marie-Reine Pétit was a forty-two-year-old mother of three who worked at a *boulangerie* selling bread. Two years earlier she'd gone missing. Four

14

months later Marie-Reine's decomposed torso had been discovered in a hockey bag in a storage shed behind the Pétit home. Marie-Reine's head and limbs had been stashed nearby in matching luggage.

A search of the Pétit basement uncovered coping, hack, and carpenter's saws. I had analyzed the cut marks on Marie-Reine's bones to determine if a tool similar to one of hubby's had made them. Bingo on the hacksaw. Réjean Pétit was now on trial for the murder of his wife.

Two hours and three coffees later, I gathered my photos and papers and rechecked the subpoena.

De comparaître personnellement devant la Cour du Québec, chambre criminelle et penal, au Palais de Justice de Montréal, à 09:00 heures, le 3 décembre—

Hot diggety. *Personally* invited to testify. As personal as a summons to a tax audit. No RSVP necessary.

I noted the courtroom.

Zipping into boots and parka, I grabbed gloves, hat, and scarf, set the security alarm, and headed down to the garage. Birdie had yet to uncurl. Apparently my cat had enjoyed a predawn breakfast.

My old Mazda started on the first try. Good omen.

At the top of the ramp, I braked too quickly and swam crosswise into the lane like a kid on a Slip 'n Slide. Bad omen.

Rush hour. The streets were clogged, every vehicle spinning up slush. The early morning sun turned my salt-spattered windshield opaque. Though I applied my wipers and sprayers repeatedly, for stretches I found myself driving blind. Within blocks, I regretted not taking a taxi.

In the late sixteenth century a group of Laurentian Iroquois lived in a village they called Hochelaga, situated between a small mountain and a major river, just below the last stretch of serious rapids. In 1642, French missionaries and adventurers dropped in and stayed. The French called their outpost Ville-Marie.

Over the years, the residents of Ville-Marie prospered and built and paved. The village took on the name of the mountain behind it, Mont Real. The river was christened the St. Lawrence.

Hello, Europeans. Good-bye, First Nations.

Today the former Hochelaga–Ville-Marie turf is known as Vieux-Montréal. Tourists love it.

Stretching uphill from the river, Old Montreal oozes quaint. Gaslights. Horse-drawn carriages. Sidewalk vendors. Outdoor cafés. The solid stone buildings that were once home to colonists, stables, workshops, and warehouses now house museums, boutiques, galleries, and restaurants. The streets are narrow and cobbled.

And offer not a chance of parking.

Wishing, once again, I'd taken a taxi, I left the car in a pay lot, then hurried up boulevard St-Laurent to the Palais de Justice, located at 1 rue Notre-Dame est, on the northern perimeter of the historic district. Salt crunched underfoot. Breath froze on my scarf. Pigeons remained huddled when I passed, preferring collective body warmth to the safety of flight.

As I walked, I thought of the pizza basement skeletons. Would the bones really prove to be those of dead girls? I hoped not, but deep down I already knew.

I also thought of Marie-Reine Pétit, and felt sorrow for a life cut short by unspeakable malice. I wondered about the Pétit children. Father jailed for murdering mother. Could these kids ever recover, or were they irreparably damaged by the horror that had been thrust upon them?

Passing, I glanced at the McDonald's franchise across St-Laurent from the Palais de Justice. The owners had made a stab at colonial. They'd lost the arches and thrown up blue awnings. It didn't really work, but they had tried.

The designers of Montreal's main courthouse didn't bother with architectural harmony. The lower stories consist of an oblong box covered with vertical black bars overhanging a smaller, glass-fronted box beneath. The upper stories shoot skyward as a featureless monolith. The building blends with the neighborhood like a Hummer parked in an Amish colony.

I entered the Palais to a packed house. Old ladies in ankle-length furs. Gangsta teens in clothes big enough to accommodate armies. Men in suits. Black-robed attorneys and judges. Some waited. Others hurried. There seemed no in-between.

Winding among large planters and uprights bearing starburst lights, I crossed to a bank of elevators at the back of the lobby. Coffee smells drifted from the Café Vienne. Already wired, I considered but passed up a fourth cup.

Upstairs, the scene was similar, though tipped in favor of the waiting game. People sat on perforated red metal benches, leaned against walls, or stood conversing in hushed voices. A few conferred with counsel in small interrogation rooms lining the corridor. None looked happy.

I took a seat outside 4.01 and pulled the Pétit file from my briefcase. Ten minutes later Louise Cloutier emerged from the courtroom. With her long blonde hair and oversized glasses, the crown prosecutor looked about seventeen.

'You'll be my first witness.' Cloutier's face was tense.

'I'm ready,' I said.

'Your testimony is going to be critical.'

Cloutier's fingers twisted and untwisted a paper clip. She'd wanted to meet the previous day, but the pizza basement caper had nixed that. Our late-night phone conversation hadn't provided the degree of preparation she'd wanted. I tried to reassure her.

'I can't tie the marks on the bones to Pétit's specific hacksaw, but I can say firmly that they were made by an identical tool.'

Cloutier nodded. 'Consistent with.'

'Consistent with,' I agreed.

'Your testimony is going to be key, because in

his original statement Pétit claimed he never laid eyes on that saw. An analyst from your lab is going to testify that she removed the handle and found minute traces of blood in one of the screw grooves.' I knew all of this from the previous night's discussion. Cloutier was verbalizing the case against Pétit as much for her sake as for mine.

'A DNA expert is going to testify that the blood is Pétit's. That ties him to the saw.'

'And I tie the saw to the victim,' I said.

Cloutier nodded. 'This judge is a real pisser about qualifying experts.'

'Aren't they all?'

Cloutier flicked a nervous smile. 'The bailiff will call you in about five minutes.'

It was closer to twenty.

The courtroom was standard, nondescript modern. Gray-textured walls. Gray-textured carpet. Gray-textured fabric on long bolted benches. The only color was at center stage, inside the gates separating the spectators from the official players. Attorneys' chairs upholstered in red, yellow, and brown. The blue, red, and white of the Quebec and Canadian flags.

A dozen people occupied the public benches. Eyes followed as I walked up the center aisle and took the stand. The judge was ahead and to my left, the jury straight ahead, facing me. Monsieur Pétit was to my right.

I have testified many times. I have faced men and women accused of monstrous crimes. Murder.

Rape. Torture. Dismemberment. I am always underwhelmed by the accused.

This time was no exception. Rejean Pétit looked ordinary. Timid, even. The man could have been my uncle Frank.

The clerk swore me in. Cloutier rose and began questioning me from the prosecutor's table.

'Please state your full name.'

'Temperance Deasee Brennan.'

We spoke into microphones suspended from the ceiling, our voices the only sound in the room.

'What is your profession?'

'I am a forensic anthropologist.'

'How long have you practiced that profession?'

'Approximately twenty years.'

'Where do you practice that profession?'

'I am a full professor at the University of North Carolina at Charlotte. I am forensic anthropologist for the province of Quebec through the Laboratoire de Sciences Judiciaires et de Médecine Légale, in Montreal, and for the state of North Carolina through the Office of the Chief Medical Examiner, headquartered in Chapel Hill.'

'You are an American citizen?'

'Yes. I have a Canadian work permit. I split my time between Montreal and Charlotte.'

'Why is it that an American serves as forensic anthropologist for a Canadian province?'

'There is no Canadian citizen who is both board-certified in this field and fluent in French.'

'We'll return to the question of board

certification. Please describe your educational qualifications.'

'I hold a Bachelor of Arts degree in Anthropology from the American University in Washington, D.C. I hold MA and PhD degrees in Biological Anthropology from Northwestern University in Evanston, Illinois.'

Next followed an endless series of questions on my graduate studies, my thesis and doctoral topics, my research, my grants, my publications. Where? When? With whom? What journals? I thought she was going to ask the color of my panties the day I defended my dissertation.

'Have you authored any books, Dr. Brennan?'

I listed them.

'Do you belong to any professional associations?'

I listed them.

'Have you held office in any of those associations?'

I listed them.

'Are you certified by any regulatory body?'

'I am certified by the American Board of Forensic Anthropology.'

'Please tell the court what that means.'

I described the process of application, the examination, the ethics review, and explained the importance of certifying boards in assessing the competence of those offering themselves as experts.

'In addition to the medicolegal labs in Quebec and North Carolina, is there any other context in which you practice your profession?'

'I have worked for the United Nations, for the

United States Military Central Identification Laboratory in Honolulu, Hawaii, as an instructor at the FBI Academy in Quantico, Virginia, and as an instructor at the Royal Canadian Mounted Police Training Academy in Ottawa, Ontario. I am a member of a United States National Disaster Mortuary Response Team. On occasion I consult for private clients.'

The jury sat motionless, either fascinated or comatose. Pétit's lawyer was taking no notes.

'Please tell us, Dr. Brennan. What does a forensic anthropologist do?'

I spoke directly to the jury.

'Forensic anthropologists are specialists in the human skeleton. We are brought into cases, usually, though not always, by pathologists. Our expertise is sought when a normal autopsy, focusing on organs and soft tissue, either is not possible or is severely limited and the bones must be examined for answers to crucial questions.'

'What types of questions?'

'The questions usually focus on identity, manner of death, and postmortem mutilation or other damage.'

'How do you help with questions of identity?'

'By examining skeletal remains I am able to provide a biological profile, including the age, sex, race, and height of the deceased. In certain cases I am able to compare anatomical landmarks observed on an unknown individual with similar landmarks visible on the antemortem X-rays of a known individual.'

'Aren't most identifications accomplished using fingerprints, dental records, or DNA?'

'Yes. But to utilize dental or medical information it is first necessary to narrow the number of possibles to the smallest ascertainable sample. With the anthropological profile, an investigating officer can review missing persons reports, come up with names, and obtain individual records for comparison with the data associated with the discovered remains. We often provide the first level of analysis of a completely unknown set of remains.'

'How do you help with questions concerning manner of death?'

'By analyzing fracture patterns, forensic anthropologists are able to reconstruct events that caused particular traumas.'

'What types of trauma do you typically examine, Dr. Brennan?'

'Gunshot. Sharp instrument. Blunt instrument. Strangulation. But again, let me emphasize that this expertise would be requested only in situations in which the body was compromised to the point that those questions cannot be answered through soft tissue and organ examination solely.'

'What do you mean by compromised?'

'A body that is decomposed, burned, mummified, skeletal—'

'Dismembered?'

'Yes.'

'Thank you.'

The jury had definitely perked up. Three stared

wide-eyed. A woman in the back row held a hand to her mouth.

'Have you previously been qualified by the courts of Quebec Province and elsewhere to serve as an expert witness in criminal trials?'

'Yes. Many times.'

Cloutier turned to the judge.

'Your Honor, we tender Dr. Temperance Brennan as an expert in the field of forensic anthropology.'

The defense raised no objection.

We were off.

By mid-afternoon Cloutier had finished with me. As opposing counsel rose, I felt my stomach tighten.

Here comes rough water, I thought. Mischaracterization, incredulity, and general nastiness.

Pétit's attorney was organized and civil.

And finished by five.

As things turned out, his cross-examination was nothing compared with the nastiness I would encounter in dealing with the pizza basement bones.

3

It was dark when I emerged from the courthouse. White lights twinkled in the trees along rue Notre-Dame. A calèche clopped by, horse sporting red-tasseled ear covers and a sprig of pine. Flakes floated around faux gas lanterns.

Joyeuses fêtes! Christmas in Quebec.

Traffic was again bumper-to-bumper. I nosed in and began creeping north on St-Laurent, still high on an *après* witness stand rush.

My fingers drummed the wheel. My thoughts ricocheted from topic to topic. My testimony. The pizza basement skeletons. My daughter. The evening ahead.

What might I have told the jury that I hadn't? Could my explanations have been clearer? Had they understood? Would they convict the guilty bastard?

What would I discover at the lab tomorrow? Would the skeletons prove to be what I knew they were? Would Claudel be his usual obnoxious self?

What was making Katy unhappy? When we'd last spoken she'd hinted that all was not rosy in Charlottesville. Would my daughter complete her final year of university, or would she announce at Christmas that she was dropping out of the University of Virginia without obtaining her degree?

What would I learn at dinner tonight? Was my recently acknowledged love about to implode? *Was* it love?

At de la Gauchetière I passed under the dragon gate and entered Chinatown. The shops were closing, and the last few pedestrians were hurrying home, faces wrapped, backs hunched against the cold.

On Sundays, Chinatown takes on a bazaar atmosphere. Restaurants serve dim sum; in clement weather grocers set up outdoor stalls filled with exotic produce, potted eggs, dried fish, herbs *Chinoise*. On festival days there are dragon dances, martial arts demonstrations, fireworks. Weekdays, however, are strictly business.

My thoughts veered back to my daughter. Katy loves the place. When she visits Montreal, a trip to Chinatown is nonnegotiable.

Before turning left onto René-Lévesque, I glanced across the intersection up St-Laurent. Like rue Notre-Dame, the Main was decked in its Christmas finest.

St. Lawrence. The Main. A century ago a major commercial artery, and stopping-off point for immigrant groups. Irish. Portuguese. Italians. Jews. No matter their country of origin or ethnic affiliation, most newcomers put in time on the streets and avenues around St-Laurent.

As I waited out the traffic light at Peel, a man crossed my headlights, tall, face ruddy, hair sandy and tousled in the wind.

Mental ricochet.

Andrew Ryan, Lieutenant-détective, Section de Crimes contra la Personne, Sûreté du Québec. My first romantic sortie after the breakup of a twenty-year marriage.

My partner in history's briefest affair?

The tempo of the finger drumming sped up.

Since Ryan works homicide and I work the morgue, our professional lives often intersect. I identify the vics. Ryan collars the perps. For a decade we've investigated gangbangers, cultists, bikers, psychopaths, and people who seriously dislike their spouses.

Over the years I'd heard stories of Ryan's past. The wild youth. The conversion to the good guys. Ryan's rise within the provincial police.

I'd also heard tales about Ryan's present. The theme never varied. The guy was a player.

Often he suggested playing with me.

I have a steadfast rule against *amour* in the workplace.

But Ryan's thinking is often at odds with mine. And he likes a challenge.

He persisted, I stood firm. Moving force. Resisting object. I'd been separated two years, knew I wouldn't be returning to my husband, Pete. I liked Ryan. He was intelligent, sensitive, and sexy as hell.

Four months back. Guatemala. An emotionally battering time for us both. I decided to reassess.

I invited Ryan to North Carolina. I bought the mother lode of skimpies and a man-eater black dress. I took the plunge.

Ryan and I spent a week at the beach and hardly saw the ocean. Or the black dress.

My stomach did that flip thing it does when I think of Ryan. And that beach week.

Add another item to the list of positives. Canadian or not, the guy is Captain America in bed.

We'd been, if not 'a couple,' at least 'an item' since August. A secret item. We kept it to ourselves.

Our times together looked like the clichéd sequences in romantic comedies. Walking hand in hand. Cuddling by fires. Romping in leaves. Romping in bed.

So why the feeling that something is wrong?

Turning right onto Guy, I gave the question some thought.

There'd been long, late-night conversations following Ryan's return to Montreal from North Carolina. Recently, the frequency of those calls had diminished.

Big deal. You're in Montreal every month.

True. But Ryan had been less available on my last trip. Slammed at work, he claimed. I wondered.

28

I'd been so happy. Had I missed or misread some signals? Was Ryan distancing himself from me?

Was I imagining the whole thing, mooning like the heroine in a pulp fiction romance?

For distraction, I clicked on the radio.

Daniel Bélanger sang '*Séche Tes Pleurs.*' 'Dry Your Tears.'

Good advice, Daniel.

The snow was coming faster now. I turned on the wipers and focused on my driving.

Whether we eat at his place or mine, Ryan usually prepares the meal. Tonight I'd volunteered.

I cook well, but not instinctively. I need recipes.

Arriving home at six, I spent a few minutes recapping my day for Birdie, then took out the folder in which I stuff menus clipped from the *Gazette*.

A five-minute search produced a winner. Grilled chicken breast with melon salsa. Wild rice. Tortilla and arugula salad.

The list of ingredients was relatively short. How hard could it be?

I threw on my parka and walked to Le Faubourg Ste-Catherine.

Poultry, greens, rice, no problem.

Ever try scoring a Crenshaw melon in December in the arctic?

A discussion with the stock boy resolved the crisis. I substituted cantaloupe.

By seven-fifteen I had the salsa marinating, the

rice boiling, the chicken baking, and the salad mixed. Sinatra was flowing from a CD, and I reeked of Chanel No. 5.

I was ready. Belly-sucking size-four Christmas-red jeans. Hair tucked behind my ears and disheveled Meg Ryan style in back. Fluffed bangs. Orchid and lavender lids. Katy's idea. Hazel eyes— lavender shadow. Dazzling!

Ryan arrived at seven-thirty with a six-pack of Moosehead, a baguette, and a small white box from a patisserie. His face was flushed from the cold, and fresh snow sparkled on his hair and shoulders.

Bending, he kissed me on the mouth then wrapped me in his arms.

'You look good.' Ryan pressed me to him. I smelled Irish Spring and aftershave mingled with leather.

'Thanks.'

Releasing me, Ryan slipped off his bomber jacket and tossed it on the sofa.

Birdie rocketed to the rug and shot down the hall.

'Sorry. Didn't see the little guy.'

'He'll cope.'

'You look *really* good.' Ryan caressed my cheek with his knuckles.

My stomach did jumping jacks.

'You're not half bad, yourself, Detective.'

It's true. Ryan is tall and lanky, with sandy hair, and impossibly blue eyes. Tonight he was wearing jeans and a Galway sweater.

I come from generations of Irish farmers and fishermen. Blame DNA. Blue eyes and cable knit knock me out.

'What's in the box?' I asked.

'Surprise for the chef.'

Ryan detached a beer and placed the rest in the fridge.

'Something smells good.' He lifted the cover on the salsa bowl.

'Melon salsa. Crenshaws are tough to find in December.' I left it at that.

'Buy you a beer or mixed drink, cupcake?' Ryan flashed his brows and flicked an imaginary cigar.

'My usual.'

I checked the rice. Ryan dug a Diet Coke from the fridge. His lips twitched at the corners as he offered the can.

'Who's calling most?'

'Sorry?' I was lost.

'Agents or talent scouts?'

My hand froze in midair. I knew what was coming.

'Where?'

'*Le Journal de Montréal.*'

'Today?'

Ryan nodded. 'Above the fold.'

'Front page?' I was dismayed.

'Fourteen back. Color photo. You'll love the angle.'

'Pictures?'

An image flashed across my mind. A skinny

black man in a knee-length sweater. A trapdoor. A camera.

The little turd at the pizza parlor had sold his snapshots.

When working a case, I am adamant in my refusal to give media interviews. Many journalists think me rude. Others have described me in more colorful terms. I don't care. Over the years I have learned that statements inevitably lead to misquotes. And misquotes invariably lead to problems.

And I never look good in the pics.

'Can I open that for you?' Ryan retrieved the Coke, pulled the tab, and handed it back.

'No doubt you've brought a copy,' I said, setting the can on the counter and yanking the oven door.

'For the safety of diners, viewing will take place when all cutlery's cleared.'

During dinner I told Ryan about my day in court.

'The reviews are good,' he said.

Ryan has a spy network that makes the CIA look like a Cub Scout pack. He usually knows of my movements before I tell him. It annoys the hell out of me.

And Ryan's amusement over the *Journal* piece was lowering my threshold for irritation.

Get over it, Brennan. Don't take yourself so seriously.

'Really?' I smiled.

'Critics gave you four stars.'

Only four?

'I see.'

'Word is, Pétit's going down.'

I said nothing.

'Tell me about this pizza parlor case.' Ryan switched gears.

'Isn't the whole affair laid out in *Le Journal*?' I helped myself to more salad.

'Coverage is a bit vague. May I have that?'

I handed him the bowl.

We ate arugula for a full three minutes. Ryan broke the silence.

'Are you going to tell me about your bones?'

My eyes met his. The interest looked sincere.

I relented, but kept my account brief. When I'd finished, Ryan rose and retrieved a section of newspaper from his jacket.

Both shots had been taken from above and to my right. In the first, I was talking to Claudel, eyes angry, gloved finger jabbing the air. The caption might have read 'Attack of the Shrew.'

The second captured the shrew on all fours, ass pointing skyward.

'Any idea how the *Journal* got thesc?' Ryan asked.

'The owner's slimeball assistant.'

'Claudel caught the case?'

'Yes.' I picked bread crumbs from the tabletop.

Ryan reached out and placed his hand on mine. 'Claudel's come around a lot.'

I didn't reply.

Ryan was about to speak again when his cell phone twittered.

Giving my hand a squeeze, he pulled the unit

from his belt and checked the caller ID. His eyes flicked up in frustration. Or irritation. Or something I couldn't read.

'I've got to take this,' he said.

Pushing back from the table, he moved off down the hall.

As I cleared dishes I could hear the rhythm of the conversation. The words were muffled, but the cadence suggested agitation.

In moments, he was back.

'Sorry, babe. I've got to go.'

'You're leaving?' I was stunned.

'It's a thankless business.'

'We haven't eaten your pastry.'

The Irish blues would not meet mine.

'I'm sorry.'

A peck on the cheek.

The chef was alone with her uneaten surprise.

4

I awoke feeling down and not knowing why.

Because I was alone? Because my only bed partner was a big white cat? I hadn't planned my life that way. Pete and I had intended to grow old together. To sail married into the afterlife.

Then my forever-hubby shared Mr. Happy with a real estate agent.

And I enjoyed my own little fling with the bottle.

Whatever, as Katy would say. Life marches.

Outside, the weather was gray, blustery, and uninviting. The clock said seven-ten. Birdie was nowhere to be seen.

Pulling off my nightshirt, I took a hot shower, then blow-dried my hair. Birdie strolled in as I was brushing my teeth. I greeted him, then smiled into the mirror, considering whether it was a mascara day.

Then I remembered.

Ryan's hasty retreat. The look in his eyes.

Jamming my toothbrush back into its charger, I wandered to the bedroom and stared at the frosted window. Crystalline spirals and snowflake geometrics. So delicate. So fragile.

Like the fantasy I'd constructed of a life with Ryan?

I wondered again what was going on.

And why I was acting the featured ditz in a Doris Day comedy.

'Screw this, Doris,' I said aloud.

Birdie looked up, but kept his thoughts to himself.

'And screw you, Andrew Ryan.'

Returning to the bathroom, I layered on the Revlon.

The Laboratoire de Sciences Judiciaires et de Médecine Légale occupies the top two floors of the Édifice Wilfrid-Derome, a T-shaped building in the Hochelaga-Maissoneuve district, just east of Centre-ville. The Bureau du Coroner is on the eleventh floor, the morgue is in the basement. The remaining space belongs to the SQ.

At eight-fifteen the twelfth floor was filling with white-coated men and women. Several greeted me as I swiped my security pass, first at the lobby entrance, then at the glass doors separating the medicolegal wing from the rest of the T. I returned their 'bonjour's and continued to my office, not in the mood to chat. I was still upset from last night's encounter with Ryan. Make that nonencounter.

As at most medical examiner and coroner

facilities, each workday at the LSJML begins with a meeting of the professional staff. I'd barely removed my outerwear when the phone rang. Pierre LaManche. It had been a busy night. The chief was anxious to begin.

When I entered the conference room, only LaManche and Jean Pelletier were seated at the table. Both did that half-standing thing older men do when women enter a room.

LaManche asked about the Pétit trial. I told him I thought my testimony had gone well.

'And Monday's recovery?'

'Except for mild hypothermia, and the fact that your animal bones turned out to be three people, that also went well.'

'You will begin your analyses today?' asked LaManche in his Sorbonne French.

'Yes.' I didn't mention what I thought I already knew based on my cursory examination in the basement. I wanted to be sure.

'Detective Claudel asked me to inform you that he would come today at one-thirty.'

'Detective Claudel will have a long wait. I'll hardly have begun.'

Hearing Pelletier grunt, I looked in his direction.

Though subordinate to LaManche, Jean Pelletier had been at the lab a full decade when the chief hired on. He was a small, compact man, with thin gray hair and bags under his eyes the size of mackerels.

Pelletier was a devotee of *Le Journal*. I knew what was coming.

'*Oui.*' Pelletier's fingers were permanently yellowed from a half century of smoking Gauloises cigarettes. One of them pointed at me. 'Oui. This angle is much more flattering. Highlights your lovely green eyes.'

In answer, I rolled my lovely green eyes.

As I took a chair, Nathalie Ayers, Marcel Morin, and Emily Sant-angelo joined us. '*Bonjour*'s and '*Comment ça va*'s were exchanged. Pelletier complimented Santangelo on her haircut. Her look suggested the subject was best left alone. She was right.

After distributing copies of the day's lineup, LaManche began discussing and assigning cases.

A forty-seven-year-old man had been found hanging from a cross-beam in his garage in Laval.

A fifty-four-year-old man had been stabbed by his son following an argument over leftover sausages. Mama had called the St-Hyacinthe police.

A resident of Longueuil had slammed his all-terrain vehicle into a snowbank on a rural road in the Gatineau. Alcohol was involved.

An estranged couple had been found dead of gunshot wounds in a home in St-Léonard. Two for her, one for him. The ex-to-be went out with a nine-millimeter Glock in his mouth.

'If I can't have you no one can.' Pelletier's dentures clacked as he spoke.

'Typical.' Ayers's voice sounded bitter.

She was right. We'd seen the scenario all too often.

A young woman had been discovered behind a karaoke bar on rue Jean-Talon. A combination of overdose and hypothermia was suspected.

The pizza basement skeletons had been assigned LSJML numbers 38426, 38427, and 38428.

'Detective Claudel feels these skeletons are old and probably of little forensic interest?' LaManche said it more as a question than a statement.

'And how could Monsieur Claudel know that?' Though it was possible this would turn out to be true, it irked me that Claudel would render an opinion entirely outside his expertise.

'Monsieur Claudel is a man of many talents.' Though Pelletier's expression was deadpan, I wasn't fooled. The old pathologist knew of the friction between Claudel and me, and loved to tease.

'Claudel has studied archaeology?' I asked.

Pelletier's brows shot up. 'Monsieur Claudel puts in hours examining ancient relics.'

The others remained silent, awaiting the punch line.

'Really?' Why not play straight man?

'*Bien sûr*. Checks his pecker every morning.'

'Thank you, Dr. Pelletier.' LaManche traded deadpan for deadpan. 'Along those lines, would you please take the hanging?'

Ayers got the stabbing. The ATV accident went to Santangelo, the suicide/homicide to Morin. As each case was dispensed, LaManche marked his master sheet with the appropriate initials. Pe. Ay. Sa. Mo.

Br went onto dossiers 38426, 38427, and 38428, the pizza basement bones.

Anticipating a lengthy meeting with the board that reviews infant deaths in the province, LaManche assigned himself no autopsy.

When we dispersed, I returned to my office. LaManche stuck his head in moments later. One of the autopsy technicians was out with bronchitis. With five posts, things would be difficult. Would I mind working alone?

Great.

As I snapped three case forms onto a clipboard, I noticed that the red light on my phone was flashing.

The minutest of flutters. Ryan?

Get over it, Doris.

Responding to the prompts, I entered my mailbox and code numbers.

A journalist from *Allô Police*.

A journalist from the *Gazette*.

A journalist from the CTV evening news.

Disappointed, I deleted the messages and hurried to the women's locker room. After changing into surgical scrubs, I took a side corridor to a single elevator tucked between the secretarial office and the library. Restricted to those with special clearance, this elevator featured buttons allowing only three stops. LSJML. Coroner. Morgue. I pressed M and the doors slid shut.

Downstairs, through another secure door, a long, narrow corridor shoots the length of the building. To the left, an X-ray room and four autopsy suites, three with single tables, one with a pair. To the right, drying racks, computer stations, wheeled tubs and carts for transporting specimens to the histology, pathology, toxicology, DNA, and odontology-anthropology labs upstairs.

Through a small glass window in each door, I could see that Ayers and Morin were beginning their externals in rooms one and two. Each was working with a police photographer and an autopsy technician.

Another tech was arranging instruments in room three. He would be assisting Santangelo.

And I was on my own.

And Claudel would be here in less than four hours.

Having begun the day down, my mood was descending by the moment.

I continued on to room four. My room. A room specially ventilated for decomps, floaters, mummified corpses, and other aromatics.

As do the others, room four has double doors leading to a morgue bay. The bay is lined with refrigerated compartments, each housing a double-decker gurney.

Tossing my clipboard onto the counter, I pulled a plastic apron from one drawer, gloves and mask from another, donned them, snagged a small metal cart from the corridor, and pushed backward through the double doors.

Bed count.

Six white cards. One red sticker.

Six in residence, one HIV positive.

I located those cards with my initials. LSJML-38426. LSJML-38427. LSJML-38428. *Ossements. Inconnu*. Bones. Unknown.

Normally, I would have taken the cases sequentially, fully analyzing one before beginning another. But Detective Delightful was due at one-thirty. Anticipating Claudel's impatience, I decided to abandon protocol, and do a quick age-sex assessment of each set of remains.

It was a mistake I would later regret.

Moving from one stainless steel door to a second, then a third, I selected the same bones I'd viewed in the pizza parlor basement, and wheeled them to room four.

After jotting the relevant information onto a case form, I began with 38426, the bones from Dr. Energy's crate.

First the skull.

Gracile muscle attachments. Rounded occiput. Small mastoids. Smooth supraorbital ridges ending in sharp orbital borders.

I switched to a pelvic bone.

Broad, flaring hip blades. Elongated pubic portion with a tiny, elevated ridge coursing across the belly side. Obtuse subpubic angle. Wide sciatic notch.

I checked off these features on the 'gender evaluation' page, and penned my conclusion.

Female.

Flipping to the 'age evaluation' section, I noted that the basilar suture, the gap between the occipital and sphenoid bones at the base of the skull, had recently fused. That told me the girl was probably in her mid to late teens.

Back to the pelvis.

Throughout childhood, each pelvic half is composed of three separate elements, the ilium, the ischium, and the pubis. In early adolescence, these bones fuse within the hip socket.

This pelvis had seen puberty come and go.

I noted furrows running across the pubic symphyses, the faces where the two pelvic halves meet in front. I flipped the bone.

The superior border of the hip blade showed squiggles, indicating the absence of a finishing crescent of bone. Squiggles were also evident on the ischium, near the point at which the body is supported when sitting.

I felt the familiar cold creep into my belly. I would check the teeth and long bones, but all indicators supported my initial impression.

Dr. Energy's stowaway was a girl who had died in her mid to late teens.

Replacing 38426 on the cart, I turned to the bones I'd selected from 38427. Then 38428.

The world retreated into a different dimension. Phones. Printers. Voices. Carts. All disappeared. Nothing existed but the fragile remains on my table.

I worked straight through lunch, my sense of sadness mounting with each observation.

I am often accused of feeling more warmth toward the dead than toward the living. The charge isn't true. Yes, I grieve for those on my table. But I am also keenly aware of the sorrow visited on those left behind. This case was no exception. I felt great empathy for the families who had loved and lost these girls.

At exactly one thirty-four the phone shrilled. Lowering my mask, I crossed to the desk.

'Dr. Brennan.'

'You have finished?' Though he did not identify himself, I knew the voice.

'I have some preliminary information. Room four.'

'I am waiting in your office.'

Sure, Claudel. That's fine with me. Make yourself at home.

'Would you like to observe what I've found?'

'That will not be necessary.'

Claudel's aversion to autopsies is legendary. I used to play on this, think up ruses to force him belowdecks. I no longer bothered.

'I'll need a few minutes to clean up,' I said.

'This is probably pointless, anyway.'

'I sincerely hope so.' I hung up.

Easy. It's Claudel. The man is a throwback.

Drawing a sheet over the table, I stripped off my gloves, scrubbed, and headed upstairs, a growing dread hanging heavy on my mind.

I knew my bones. I knew I was right.

Despite his sanctimonious arrogance, I hoped to God Claudel was right, too.

5

Claudel was seated facing my desk, brows, nose, and mouth pointing south. He did not rise or greet me when I entered. I returned his cordiality.

'You have finished?'

'No, Monsieur Claudel. I have not finished. I have hardly begun.' I sat. 'But I have made some disturbing observations.'

Claudel curled his fingers in a 'give it to me' gesture.

'Based on cranial and pelvic features, I can tell you that skeleton 38426 is that of a female who died in her mid to late teens. Analysis of the long bones will allow me to narrow that age estimate, but it's obvious that the basilar suture has only recently fused, the iliac crest—'

'I do not need an anatomy lesson.'

How about my heel up your ass?

'The victim is young.' Chilly.

'Go on.'

'They're all young.'

Claudel's brows angled up in a question.

'Females. In their teens or barely past.'

'Cause of death?'

'That will require a detailed examination of each skeleton.'

'People die.'

'Not usually as kids.'

'Racial background?'

'Uncertain at this point.' Though I had yet to verify ancestry, cranio-facial details suggested all three were white.

'So it's possible we've dug up Pocahontas and her court.'

I bit back a response. I would not let Claudel goad me into a premature statement.

'While the bones from the crate and those from the northeastern depression retain no soft tissue, those from the bundled burial show traces of adipocere. Grave wax. I am not convinced these deaths took place in the distant past.'

Claudel spread both hands, palms up. 'Five years, ten, a century?'

'A determination of time since death will require further study. At this point I would not write these burials off as historic or prehistoric.'

'I do not require instruction on how to prepare my reports. What exactly are you telling me?'

'I'm telling you we just recovered three dead girls from a pizza parlor basement. At this stage of inquiry, it is not appropriate to conclude that the remains are of great antiquity.'

For several seconds Claudel and I glared at each other. Then he reached into a breast pocket, extracted a Ziploc baggie, and tossed it onto the desktop.

Slowly, I dropped my eyes.

The baggie contained three round items.

'Feel free to remove them.'

Unzipping the baggie, I dropped the objects onto my palm. Each was a flat metal disk measuring slightly over an inch in diameter. Though corroded, I could see that each disk had a female silhouette engraved on the front, an eyelet on the back. The initials ST were etched beside each eyelet.

I looked a question at Claudel.

'With some persuasion, the Prince of Pizza admitted to liberating certain items while crating the bones.'

'Buttons?'

Claudel nodded.

'They were buried with the skeleton?'

'The gentleman is a little vague on provenance. But yes, they are buttons. And it's obvious they are old.'

'How can you be certain they're old?'

'I can't. Dr. Antoinette Legault at the McCord could.'

The McCord Museum of Canadian History houses over a million artifacts, with more than sixteen thousand of those belonging to the clothing and apparel collection.

'Legault is a button expert?'

Claudel ignored my question. 'The buttons were manufactured in the nineteenth century.'

Before I could reply, Claudel's cell phone warbled. Without excusing himself, he rose and stepped into the hall.

My eyes went back to the buttons. Did they mean the skeletons had been in the ground a century or more?

In less than a minute, Claudel was back.

'Something important has come up.'

I was being dismissed.

I have a temper. I admit that. Sometimes I lose it. Claudel's condescension was prodding me toward one of those times. I had rushed through a preliminary evaluation to accommodate his schedule on the assumption that this investigation was of immediate priority, and now he was brushing me aside after a cursory inquiry.

'Meaning this case is *not* important?'

Claudel lowered his chin and looked at me, a picture of infinitely strained patience.

'I am a police officer, not a historian.'

'And I am a scientist, not a conjecturer.'

'These artifacts'—he flapped a hand at the buttons—'belong to another century.'

'Three dead girls now belong to this one.' I rose abruptly.

Claudel's body stiffened. His eyes crimped.

'A prostitute has just arrived at l'hôpital Notre-Dame with a fractured skull and a knife in her gut. Her colleague is less fortunate. She is dead. My partner and I are going to arrest a certain pimp to improve other ladies' odds of surviving.'

Claudel jabbed a finger in my direction.

'That, madame, is important.'

With that he strode out the door.

I stood a moment, face burning with anger. I despise the fact that Claudel has the power to turn me pyrotechnic, sometimes illogically so. But there it was. He'd done it again.

Dropping into my chair, I swiveled, put my feet on the sill, and leaned my head sideways against the wall. Twelve floors down, the city stretched toward the river. Miniature cars and trucks flowed across the Jacques-Cartier Bridge, motoring toward Île Ste-Hélène, the south shore suburbs, New York State.

I closed my eyes and did some Yogic breathing, Slowly, my anger dissipated. When I opened them, I felt—what?

Flattened.

Confused.

Death investigations are complex enough. Why was it always doubly difficult with Claudel? Why couldn't he and I enjoy the easy exchange that characterized my professional interactions with other homicide investigators? With Ryan?

Ryan.

Doris tapped on my shoulder for a few frames of *Pillow Talk*.

Some things were clear. Claudel's mind was made up. He didn't like rats. He didn't like the pizza parlor. He didn't think these bones were worth his attention. Whatever investigative support

I needed I would have to find through other sources.

'OK, you supercilious, knee-jerk skeptic. Scoff at my analysis without trying to understand it. We'll do this without you.'

Grabbing my clipboard, I headed back downstairs.

Three hours later I'd finished a skeletal inventory on LSJML-38426. The remains were complete save for the hyoid, a tiny U-shaped bone suspended in the soft tissue of the throat, and several of the smaller hand and foot bones.

Long bones continue to increase in length as long as their epiphyses, the small caps at each end, remain separate from the bone itself. Growth stops when a bone's epiphyses unite with its shaft. Luckily for the anthropologist, each set of epiphyses marches to its own clock.

By observing the state of development of the arm, leg, and collarbones, I was able to narrow my age estimate. I'd requested dental X-rays so I could observe molar root development, but already I had no doubt. The girl in the crate had died between the ages of sixteen and eighteen.

My case form had a dozen checks in the column indicating European ancestry. Narrow nasal opening. Sharply projecting lower nasal border. Highly angled nasal bridge. Prominent nasal spine. Cheekbones tight to the face. Every feature and measurement placed the skull squarely in the Caucasoid category. I was certain the girl was white.

And tiny. Leg bone measurements indicated she stood approximately five feet two inches tall.

Though I'd examined every bone and bone fragment, I'd found not a single mark of violence. A few scratches in the vicinity of the right auditory canal looked superficial and V-shaped under magnification. I suspected the marks were a postmortem artifact, caused by abrasion with the ground surface, or careless handling during removal to the crate.

The teeth showed evidence of poor hygiene and no dental restorations.

Now I was turning to postmortem interval. How long had she been dead? With just dry bone, PMI was going to be a bitch.

The human body is a Copernican microcosm composed of carbon, hydrogen, nitrogen, and oxygen. The heart is the daystar, providing life source to every metabolic system in the galaxy.

When the heart stops pumping, it's cytoplasmic chaos. Cellular enzymes begin a cannibalistic feast on the body's own carbohydrates and proteins. Cell membranes rupture, releasing food for armies of microorganisms. Bacteria in the gut start munching outward. Environmental bacteria, carrion insects, and scavenging animals start munching inward.

Burial, submersion, or embalming retards the process of decomposition. Certain mechanical and chemical agents boost it.

So how long are we talking for dust to dust?

With extreme heat and humidity, loss of soft

tissue can occur in as little as three days. But that's a land record. Under normal conditions, with shallow burial, a body takes six months to a year to go skeletal.

Enclosure in a basement might slow that. Enclosure in a basement in the subarctic might slow that a lot.

What facts did I have?

The bodies were found in shallow graves. Was that the original place of burial? How soon after death had they been placed there?

At least two had been flexed, knees drawn tight to the chest. At least one had been bundled, wrapped in an outer covering of leather. Beyond that, I knew squat. Moisture. Soil acidity. Temperature fluctuation.

What *could* I say?

The bones were dry, disarticulated, and completely devoid of flesh and odor. There was staining, and some soil invasion into the cranial sinuses and marrow cavities. Unless Claudel's buttons were legitimately associated, the girls had been stashed, naked and anonymous, with no accompanying artifacts.

Best estimate: more than a year and less than a millennium. Claudel would have a field day with that.

Frustrated, I packed up LSJML-38426, determined to ask a lot more questions.

I was rolling out LSJML-38427 when the phone behind me rang again. Irritated at the interruption, and expecting Claudel's arrogant cynicism, I yanked down my mask and snatched up the receiver.

'Brennan.'

'Dr. Temperance Brennan?' A female voice, quavery and uncertain.

'*Oui.*'

I looked at my watch. Five minutes until the switchboard rolled over to the night service.

'I didn't expect you to actually answer. I mean, I thought I would get another secretary. The operat—'

'Is there something I can help you with?' I matched her English.

There was a pause, as if the caller was actually considering the question. In the background I could hear what sounded like birds.

'Well, I don't know. Actually, I thought perhaps I could be of help to you.'

Great. Another citizen volunteer.

Members of crime scene recovery units are typically not scientists. They are technicians. They collect hairs, fibers, glass fragments, paint chips, blood, semen, saliva, and other physical evidence. They dust for prints. They shoot pics. When the goodies are tagged and logged, the crime scene unit's involvement is over. No high-tech magic. No heart rush surveillance. No hot lead shoot-outs. Specialists with advanced degrees do the science. Cops chase the bad guys.

But Tinsel Town has done another tap dance; the public has been conned into believing crime scene techs are scientists and detectives, and every week I am contacted by starry-eyed viewers who think they may have uncovered something. I try to be kind, but this latest Hollywood myth needs a kick in the pants.

'I'm sorry, ma'am, but to work at this lab you must submit your credentials and go through a formal hiring process.'

'Oh.' I heard a sharp intake of air.

'If you stop in the personnel office, I'm certain that printed material exists giving job descript—'

'No, no. You misunderstand. I saw your photo in *Le Journal* yesterday. I phoned your office.'

Worse than a cop show groupie. A snoopy neighbor with the tip of the century. Or some basehead looking to score a reward.

Tossing my pen to the blotter, I dropped into the chair. The call was probably a long shot, but so was Deep Throat.

'This may sound crazy.' Nervous throat clearing. 'And I know how very busy you must be.'

'Actually, I am in the middle of something, Mrs.—?'

The name was distorted by static. Gallant? Ballant? Talent?

'—bones you dug up.'

Another pause. More background whistling and squawking.

'What about them?'

The voice became stronger.

'I feel it is my moral responsibility.'

I said nothing, staring at the bones on the gurney and thinking about moral responsibilities.

'My moral duty to follow through. At least with a telephone call. Before I leave. It's the least I can do. People just don't take time anymore. No one bothers. No one wants to get involved.'

In the hall, I heard voices, doors slamming, then quiet. The autopsy techs had left for the day. I leaned back, tired, but anxious to finish the conversation and get back to work.

'What is it you would like to tell me?'

'I've lived a long time in Montreal. I know what went on in that building.'

'What building?'

'The one where those bones were hidden.'

The woman now had my full attention.

'The pizza parlor?'

'Now it is.'

'Yes?'

At that moment a bell shrilled, like those regulating movement in old school buildings.

The line went dead.

6

I jiggled the button, trying to get the switchboard operator's attention.

Nothing.

Damn!

Slamming the receiver, I raced for the elevator.

Susanne, the LSJML receptionist, lives in a small town halfway between Montreal and the Ontario border. Her daily commute involves a metro, a train, and timing more delicate than a space station linkup. At closing, Susanne is off like a shot. I hoped by some miracle to catch her in flight.

Lighted digits indicated the elevator was on thirteen.

Come on. Come on.

It took a month for the car to descend, another for the trip upstairs. On twelve, I bolted through the opening doors.

Susanne's desk was deserted.

Praying that the informant had phoned back, and that the call had been rolled by the automatic night service to my voice mail, I rushed to my office.

The red light was flashing.

Yes!

A mechanical voice announced five messages.

My friend Anne in South Carolina.

Allô Police. Again.

The *Gazette*. Again.

A newcomer from CFCF news.

Ryan.

Mixed emotions. Curiosity that Anne had called. Relief that Ryan had tried to contact me. Frustration that my mysterious tipster had not. Fear that I'd lost the woman forever.

What was her name? Gallant? Ballant? Talent? Why hadn't I asked that she spell it?

Flopping into my chair, I stared at the phone, willing the little square to light up and tell me a call had come into the system. I drummed the desktop. Pulled the phone cord. Allowed the spirals to curl back into place.

Why wasn't the woman trying to reconnect? She had the number. Wait. Hadn't she referred to an earlier call? Did she think I'd blown her off? That I'd hung up on her? Had she given up?

I opened the desk drawer. Rooted for a pen. Closed the drawer.

Hadn't the caller mentioned something about leaving? Leaving home? The city? The province? For the day? For good?

I was dividing triangles into smaller triangles, berating myself for my carelessness, when my cell phone sounded. I flew to my purse and dug it out.

'Mrs. Gallant?'

'I've been called gallant, but never Mrs.'

Ryan.

'I thought you were someone else.'

I knew that was stupid as soon as I said it. Mrs. Gallant/Ballant/Talent had phoned through the switchboard. She couldn't possibly know my private number.

'It shatters me to hear such disappointment in your voice.'

Resuming my seat, I smiled the first smile of the day. 'You're dazzling, Ryan. My disappointment has to do with a case.'

'What case?'

'The pizza basement skeletons.'

As we spoke I kept watch on the message light. One twinkle and I'd leap back into my voice mail.

'Did today bring the pleasure of Claudel's company?'

'He was here.'

'Alone?'

'The rest of the Waffen SS couldn't make it.'

'Claudel can be a little rigid.'

'Claudel is a Neanderthal. No. I sell the Paleolithic short. Neanderthals had fully sapient brains.'

'There's nothing wrong with Claudel's brain. He just tends to put a lot of weight on past experience and usual patterns. Where was Charbonneau?'

58

'Two prostitutes were assaulted. One died. The other is hanging on at the Notre-Dame Hospital.'

'I heard about that,' Ryan said.

Of course. A twinge of irritation.

'I believe the ladies' business manager was invited in for questioning.'

'You would know.'

Ryan either ignored or missed the annoyance in my voice.

'What does Claudel want to do with your bones?'

'Unfortunately, very little.'

'I know what I'd like to do with your bones.'

'That didn't top your agenda last night,' Doris piped up before I could stop her.

Ryan did not reply.

'All three skeletons are the remains of young girls,' I segued back.

'Recent?'

'Claudel relieved the owner of some buttons he claimed to have found with one set of bones. An expert at the McCord assessed them as nineteenth century.'

'Let me guess. Claudel's not interested in what he sees as prehistoric?'

'Odd, since his head's been up his ass since the Neolithic.'

'Having a bad day, sunshine?' The amusement in Ryan's voice irked me. His failure to explain last night's hasty departure irked me. My desire for an explanation irked me.

What was Anne's philosophy? Never explain, never complain.

Right on, Annie.

'This week has not been a picnic,' I said, still staring at my desk phone. The little square remained frustratingly dark.

'Claudel's a good cop,' Ryan said. 'Sometimes he needs more convincing than we intuitively brighter types.'

'His mind is made up.'

'Change it.'

'I hadn't thought of that.'

A moment of silence. Ryan broke it.

'How old do you think these bones are?'

'I'm not sure. I'm not even sure all three girls died at the same time.'

'Dental work?'

'None that I've noticed.'

More silence.

'Gut feeling?'

'The burials haven't been in the basement that long.'

'Meaning?'

'We should be taking them seriously.'

Again, Ryan ignored my churlishness.

'On what do you base your gut feeling?'

I'd been asking myself that question for three days.

'Experience.'

I didn't mention my recent mysterious inform-ant. Or the brainless indifference with which I'd treated her.

'Well, sunshine—'

'Yes, cupcake.' I cut him off.

60

Pause.

'You must find evidence to convince Claudel that he's wrong.' Patient, a teacher reprimanding a kindergartner.

Long pause, filled with my irritated breathing. Again, Ryan spoke first.

'I'm guessing tonight is not good for you.'

'What does that mean?'

'I understand how tired and frustrated you are. Go home and take one of your famous bubble baths. Things'll serve up better in the morning.'

When we'd disconnected, I sat listening to the hum of the empty building.

There was no denying it. I'd been in Montreal three full days. And nights. Ryan had been his usual amiable and charming self.

And almost totally unavailable.

I didn't need a burning bush. Officer Studmuffin was moving on.

And I was stuck with Detective Dickhead.

I tottered toward tears, yanked myself back.

I'd lived without Ryan. I would do so again.

I'd coexisted with Claudel. I would do so again.

But was the problem with Ryan of my own making? Why had I been so short with him just now?

Outside, the wind gusted. Downstairs, three young women lay silent on stainless steel.

I glanced at the phone. Mrs. Gallant/Ballant/ Talent wasn't hitting her redial button.

'Screw bubbles,' I said, rocketing from my chair.

'And screw you, Andrew Ryan. Wherever you are.'

By nine I'd finished with LSJML-38427, the skeleton from the first depression.

Female. White. Age fifteen to seventeen. Sixty-four to sixty-seven inches tall. No odor, no hair, not a shred of soft tissue. Bones well preserved, but dry and discolored, with some soil infiltration. Postmortem cranial damage, including fragmentation of the right temporal area, right facial bones, and right mandibular ramus. No perimortem skeletal trauma. No dental work. No associated clothing or possessions. 38427 was a carbon copy of 38426.

With one difference. I'd seen this young lady *in situ* and knew something about burial context. LSJML-38427 had been placed naked in a pit in a fetal curl.

We of the Judeo-Christian persuasion send our dead packing in their Sunday best. We literally lay them out, legs extended, hands on the belly or straight down at the sides. The tucked sleeping posture is more typical of our precontact native brethren.

So. Did the curled posture support Claudel's assumption of antiquity?

Not that simple.

A flexed body requires a smaller hole. Less digging. Less time and energy. Pit burial is also popular with those in a hurry.

Like murderers.

Exhausted, I wheeled the bones to their bay, changed, returned to my office, and rechecked the phone.

No messages.

By the time I clocked out, it was well past ten. Wind whipped around the corner of Wilfrid-Derome, slicing through my clothes like a blade. My breath billowed as I scurried to my car.

Throughout the drive, I could think of nothing but the girls in the morgue.

Had they died of illness? Had they been killed in a manner leaving no mark on their bones? Poisoning? Smothering?

Hypothermia?

At the Viger traffic light, two teenagers emerged from the shadow of the Jacques-Cartier Bridge. Tattooed, pierced, and spiked, they raised squeegees with tense nonchalance. Nodding a go-ahead, I dug a dollar from my purse and watched as they scraped dirty water down my windshield.

Had the pizza basement girls been young rebels like these, marching toward nonconformity down prescribed paths? Had they been loners, abused by family tyrants? Runaways struggling to survive on the streets?

I'd found not a single indicator of clothing. Granted, natural fibers such as cotton, linen, and wool deteriorate quickly. But why no zipper tooth? Eyelet? Bodice fastener? Bra hook? These girls had been stripped before being hidden in anonymous graves.

Had they died together? Over a span of months? Years?

And always, the central question: When? A decade ago? A century?

By the time I reached home, a headache was cranking into high gear, and I was hungry enough to eat Lithuania. Except for granola bars and diet sodas, I'd consumed nothing all day.

After showering, I nuked a frozen Mexican dinner. As I dined with Letterman, I thought about Anne. Anne would understand. Let me vent. Say comforting things. I'd just collected the handset, when it rang in my hand.

'How's Birdie?' Anne.

'You're calling about my cat?'

'I don't think the little guy gets enough attention.'

The little guy was beside me on the couch, staring at the sour cream oozing from my burrito remains.

'I'm sure Bird would agree.'

Setting my dinner on the coffee table, I scooped a dollop of cream and offered a finger. Birdie licked it clean and refocused on the plate.

'How about you?'

I was lost. 'How about me what?'

'Are you getting enough attention?'

Though Anne has the instincts of a NAVSAT, she couldn't have known of my anxiety over Ryan.

'I was just about to call you,' I said.

'I'm not,' she continued, not really listening to my answer.

'What are you talking about?'

'Tom-Ted.'

Anne is married to an attorney named Tom Turnip. When Tom was a second-year associate with his firm, a senior partner had addressed him as Ted for an entire month. He'd been Tom-Ted ever since.

'What about TT?'

'Guess?'

Though I wanted to be sympathetic, I was far too exhausted for puzzles.

'Please just tell me.'

'Good idea. I'll be there tomorrow.'

7

Eight hours later my state of mind was much improved. The headache was gone. The sun was shining. My best friend was coming.

Maybe. Anne has a way of changing her mind.

Speaking of changing minds, Ryan was right. Evidence as to postmortem interval, or PMI, was at the heart of the debate with Claudel.

Crunching cornflakes, I considered the problem.

At this point I knew 38426 and 38427 had come from shallow graves in a dry basement. The skeletons were devoid of flesh but well preserved, with no surface cracking or flaking.

Mental checklist. What other data are useful for pinpointing PMI with dry bones?

Deterioration of associated materials. I had none.

Analysis of insect inclusions. I had none.

Bird nosed toward my cereal, hoping to score milk. I displaced him to a chair.

Should I move on to 38428, or should I focus on establishing PMI?

Birdie oozed back onto the table. Again, I lifted him down.

If I found evidence that the burials were old, I could relax and notify the archaeologists. On the other hand, if I found evidence that the deaths were recent, as I suspected, the coroner would insist on an investigation, and Claudel would have no choice. He and Charbonneau could start the legwork while I analyzed the third set of remains.

As I poured coffee, Birdie launched a third sortie. I relocated him again, somewhat less gently.

OK. I had no artifacts or bugs. What options did that leave?

I knew that the elemental composition of bone changes over time. The amount of nitrogen decreases, the amount of fluoride increases. But these shifts are too slow to be of use in evaluating the age of modern remains.

I'd read studies that focused on radiography, histology, chemical reaction, and isotope content. I was aware of research that pointed to amino acids as useful in distinguishing recent from ancient bone.

But a myriad of factors influence biochemical and physical processes. Temperature. Ground moisture. Oxygen tension. Microbial activity. Soil pH. No technique is reliably accurate. Once the flesh and bugs move on, PMI becomes the Bermuda Triangle of forensic anthropology.

I could think of only one test that might yield

definitive results. But it would take time and cost money, and only a handful of labs performed it. Given the current financial climate, I knew it would be a hard sell to LaManche.

But it was worth a shot.

Placing my bowl on the floor, I gathered my purse and laptop and set off.

In my office, the message light remained obstinately dark.

The morning meeting was routine. A man dead of fumes from a malfunctioning space heater. An alcohol-related traffic death. An autoerotic with a faulty escape knot in his noose. A charred body in a burned-out motor home.

Pelletier caught the fire victim. Though the remains were thought to be those of the trailer's owner, he asked that I be available in case things got dicey.

As the others filed out, I turned to LaManche.

'May I speak with you a moment?'

'*Mais, oui.*' LaManche folded back into his seat.

'I've examined two of the skeletons from the pizza parlor basement.'

When LaManche raised his brows, the lines in his flesh elongated and deepened. He seemed suddenly older, more worn than I remembered. Was it the cold morning light from the windows behind me? Was LaManche unwell? Had I simply not noticed until this moment?

'The two victims I've examined are young and female,' I said. 'I'm certain the third is a young woman as well.'

'You use the word "victim."'

'They're kids and they're dead.'

LaManche's melancholy eyes did not flinch at my sharpness.

'But I've found no signs of violence,' I admitted.

'Monsieur Claudel feels these remains are probably not recent.'

'The restaurant owner found buttons that could be nineteenth century.'

'Could be?' The brows rose again.

'Claudel took them to the McCord.'

'You are unconvinced?'

'Even if the buttons are genuine, it's unclear whether they were associated with any of the skeletons. Their presence in the basement could have any number of explanations.'

LaManche sighed and pulled his ear. 'Monsieur Claudel also told me that the building is more than a hundred years old.'

'Claudel has researched the property?' I felt heat flush my face. 'He has not shared that information with me.'

'Construction took place over a century ago.'

I have a flash point temper. My father's temper. Along with drink, Daddy's fury sometimes ruled him. I grew up with the impact of those outbursts.

Like Daddy, I succumbed to the lure of the bottle. Unlike him, I walked away from booze. Also unlike him, I learned to control my temper. When fire simmers inside, outside I grow deadly calm.

'Did Monsieur Claudel not realize that such

information is relevant to my task?' I asked, my voice glacial.

'I am certain he will inform you in detail.'

'During my lifetime?'

'Do not grow defensive. I am not fighting you.'

I drew a deep breath.

'There is one test which might resolve the question.'

'Tell me.'

'You've heard of Carbon 14 dating?'

'I know it is used to assign age to organic materials, including human bone. I do not know how it works.'

'Radiocarbon, or Carbon 14, is an unstable isotope. Like all radioactive substances, it decays by releasing subatomic particles at a uniform rate.'

LaManche's eyes stayed heavy on mine.

'In about 5,730 years half of a population of radiocarbon atoms will have reverted to nitrogen.'

'That is the half-life.'

I nodded. 'After 11,460 years, a fourth of the original amount of radiocarbon remains. After another 5,730 years, only an eighth remains, and so on.'

LaManche did not interrupt.

'The amount of radiocarbon in the atmosphere is really tiny. There's only about one radiocarbon atom for every trillion stable carbon atoms. Radiocarbon is constantly being created in the upper atmosphere by cosmic bombardment of nitrogen. Some of the nitrogen converts to radiocarbon, which immediately oxidizes to CO_2. That

CO_2 works its way down into the biosphere, where it's taken up by plants. Since humans, animals, and plants comprise the same food chain, as long as they are alive they have a constant amount of radiocarbon in them. The actual amount is gradually decreasing due to radioactive decay, but is being replenished through food intake, or through photosynthesis in the case of plants. This equilibrium exists as long as an organism is alive. When it dies, decay becomes the only active process. Radiocarbon dating is a method that determines the point in time at which this disequilibrium started.'

LaManche raised both palms in a gesture of skepticism. 'Five-thousand-plus years. How can such a slow process be of value with recent remains?'

'A fair question. It's true that Carbon 14 dating has been used primarily by archaeologists, and has been shown to be quite reliable. But the technique is based on a number of assumptions, one of which is that the atmospheric level of radiocarbon has remained constant over time. Data inconsistent with that assumption can actually be used to give the process wider applicability.'

'How so?'

'That's where it gets interesting. Studies have documented significant anomalies in radiocarbon data for certain time periods. Two perturbations have taken place over the past eighty years, both of which were caused by human activity.'

LaManche leaned back, interlaced his fingers,

and laid his hands on his chest. A hint for brevity? I did some mental abridgment.

'The period from about 1910 to 1950 is characterized by a decrease of atmospheric radiocarbon, probably due to the release into the atmosphere of the products of combustion of fossil fuels such as oil, coal, and natural gas.'

'Why?'

'Because of their great age, fossil fuels contain no detectable radiocarbon. They are said to be dead. Since the combustion of these fuels releases carbon dioxide devoid of radiocarbon, the relative amount of Carbon 14 in the atmosphere drops.'

'*Oui.*'

'But beginning about 1950, the atmospheric testing of thermonuclear weapons reversed this downward trend.'

'The radiocarbon in living things increased.'

'Dramatically. From 1950 to 1963, the values rose to about 85 percent above contemporary reference levels. In 1963, an international agreement halted atmospheric nuclear testing by most nations, and biospheric radiocarbon levels began settling into a new equilibrium.'

'Such folly.' LaManche wagged his head sadly.

'These permutations are known as the fossil fuel and atomic bomb effects.'

LaManche stole a glance at his watch.

'The bottom line is that artificial or "bomb" Carbon 14 can be used to determine if someone died before or after the period of atmos-pheric nuclear testing.'

'How is this test done?'

'There are actually two methods. With the standard radiometric technique, materials are analyzed by synthesizing the sample carbon to benzene, then measuring the Carbon 14 content in a scintillation spectrometer.'

'And the other method?'

'With the other method results are derived from reduction of the sample carbon to graphite. The graphite is then tested for Carbon 14 content in an accelerator mass spectrometer.'

For several seconds LaManche said nothing. Then, 'How much bone is required?'

'For conventional decay counting, two hundred fifty grams. For accelerator mass spectrometry, just a gram or even less.'

'AMS testing costs more?'

'Yes.'

'How much?'

I told him.

LaManche removed his glasses and squeezed the bridge of his nose with a thumb and forefinger.

'Is there no intermediate step to determine that such an expenditure is justified?'

'There's one thing I could try. The technique isn't terribly reliable, but it's simple and might show if death occurred more or less than a hundred years ago.'

LaManche started to speak.

'And free,' I added. 'I can do it myself. But again, it will yield only a very rough indication of

73

whether the bones are more or less than a century old.'

'Please.' LaManche repositioned his glasses and rose. 'In the meantime I will discuss your proposal with Dr. Authier.'

Jean-François Authier, the chief coroner, considered all requests for exceptional expenditures. Few were granted.

Grabbing a lab coat from my office, I headed to the morgue. Morin and Ayers were already cutting Y incisions in room two. I requested a UV light, and waited while the tech got it. Then I hurried to the appropriate bay and pulled the left femora from skeletons 38426, 38427, and 38428.

In autopsy room four, I wrote the respective case numbers on the proximal and distal ends of the leg bones, and placed them on the autopsy table. Each made a soft thunk in the stillness.

After masking, I plugged in and revved a Stryker saw. White powder coned on the stainless steel as I bisected each femoral shaft. A hot, acrid odor filled the air.

I wondered again about the young women whose bones I was cutting. Had they died surrounded by family? Probably not. Alone and frightened? More likely. Hopeful of rescue? Desperate? Angry? Relieved? All possible. They never get to say.

When I'd finished sawing, I gathered the femoral segments and the UV light, and carried them to a storage closet at the end of the hall.

Come on. Let this work.

Entering the closet, I located an outlet and

plugged in the UV. Then I set the femoral halves on a shelf with their freshly sawn surfaces facing outward.

When I closed the door, it was pitch-black.

Barely breathing, I pointed the UV and thumbed the switch.

8

'Yes!' My free hand pumped the air.

Limb bones of up to a century in age may fluoresce when viewed under UV light. This fluorescence diminishes over time, the dead zone progressing outward from the marrow cavity and inward from the external surface. A century postmortem, the yellow-green glow is absent altogether.

These babies were smoking like neon doughnuts.

OK, Claudel. That's step one.

Returning the femora to their respective body bags, I went in search of my boss.

LaManche was slicing a brain in the histo lab. He looked up when I entered, knife in one hand, plastic apron tied behind his neck and waist. I explained what I'd done.

'And?'

'The cut surfaces lit up like novas.'

'Indicating?'

'The presence of organic constituents.'

LaManche laid his knife on the corkboard. 'So these are not native burials.'

'These girls died after 1900.'

'Definitely?'

'Probably.' Less vehement.

'The building was constructed around the turn of the century.'

I did not reply.

'Do you recall the remains found near le Cathédral Marie-Reine-du-Monde?'

LaManche was referring to a time he'd sent me downtown to investigate 'bodies' discovered by a water main crew. I'd arrived to find backhoes, dump trucks, and an enormous hole in boulevard René-Lévesque. Skull, rib, and long-bone fragments lined the pavement and lay at the bottom of the freshly dug trench. Mingled with the human bits I could see wood slivers and corroded nails.

Easy one. Coffin burials.

Archaeologists later confirmed my opinion. Until a cholera epidemic forced its closure in the mid-eighteenth century, a cemetery had occupied the land where the cathedral now oversees rush hour on René-Lévesque. The repair crew had stumbled on a few souls overlooked during the graveyard's relocation.

'You think the bloody building was constructed over unmarked graves?' I asked. 'I found no evidence of coffins.'

French Canadians are virtuosos of the shrug,

using subtle nuances of hands, eyes, shoulders, and lips to convey countless meanings. I agree. I disagree. I don't care. What can I do? Who knows? You are a fool. Do as you like.

LaManche raised one shoulder and both brows. A 'maybe, maybe not' shrug.

'Have you discussed radiocarbon dating with Authier?' I asked.

'Dr. Authier is hosting visitors from the Moroccan Institute of Legal Medicine. I left a message asking that he call me.'

'The testing will take time.' I didn't mask my agitation.

'Temperance.' LaManche was the only person on the planet to address me thus. On his tongue *mon nom* had perky little accent marks and rhymed with 'sconce.' 'You are becoming much too personally involved.'

'I don't believe these bones are ancient. They don't have that feel, that look. The context seems wrong. I—'

'Did these girls die last week?' The hound dog face sagged with patience.

'No.'

'Is there great urgency?'

I said nothing.

LaManche gazed at me so long I thought his mind had wandered. Then, 'Send off your samples. I will deal with Dr. Authier.'

'Thank you.' I resisted the impulse to hug him.

'In the meantime, perhaps the third skeleton will yield useful information.' With that not so subtle hint, LaManche turned back to his brain.

Elated, I headed downstairs and changed into scrubs.

Lisa stopped me on my way to autopsy room four. The trailer fire victim had no teeth, no dentures, and no printable digits. Identification had become problematical, and Dr. Pelletier wanted my opinion.

I told her I would join Pelletier in half an hour.

Working quickly, I cut a one-inch plug from the midshaft of each femur, raced upstairs, logged onto the Web, and entered the address of the Florida lab that would perform the analyses. Clicking onto the sample data sheet, I filled in the required information, and requested testing by accelerated mass spectrometry.

I paused at the section concerning delivery. Standard service took two to four weeks. With advanced service, results could be available in as little as six days.

At a significantly higher price.

Screw it. If Authier balked, I'd pay.

I checked the second box and hit SEND.

After completing transfer-of-evidence forms, I gave Denis the address, and asked that he package and FedEx the specimens immediately.

Back downstairs.

I had to agree with Pelletier. The owner of the motor home was a sixty-four-year-old white male. The body on the table was wearing the charred remains of a Wonder Bra and handcuffs.

OK. So the guy was kinky.

Nope. X-rays showed a diaphragm center stage in the pelvis.

It was late afternoon when we finally got it sorted.

The fire victim was female, white, and toothless, with healed fractures of the right radius and both nasal bones. She'd been walking the earth thirty-five to fifty years.

Where was Trailer Man? That problem now belonged to the cops.

At three-forty, I washed, changed, and returned topside, grabbing a Diet Coke and two powdered sugar doughnuts on the way to my office.

The phone was flashing like a sale light at Kmart. Bolting from the door, I grabbed the receiver.

Anne. Her flight would arrive at five twenty-five.

Arthur Holliday, the man who would perform the Carbon 14 test. His message asked that I contact him before sending the samples.

Racing to the secretarial office, I checked the mound of outgoing mail. FedEx had yet to collect my package. I dug it out, returned to my office, and dialed the lab in Florida, puzzled as to what the problem could be.

'Tempe, good, good. I called as soon as I got your e-mail. Have you sent off the bone samples?'

'They're ready, but still here. Is there a problem?'

'No, no. Not at all. Terrific. Good. Listen, do your unknowns have teeth?'

'Yes.'

'Good. Good. Listen, we've got a little research

80

project going down here, and we wondered if place of birth might be of interest in your case.'

'I hadn't considered that angle, but yes, that information might be useful. Can you *do* that?'

'Is there a lot of groundwater in that basement?'

'No, it's fairly dry.'

'I can't promise anything, but we're getting some pretty good results with our strontium isotope analyses. If you'll allow us to store the results in our database, then get back to us when your unknowns are eventually identified, I'll be glad to perform this experimental test on your samples gratis.'

'Gratis?'

'We need to expand our reference database.'

'What should I send?'

He told me and started to expound on the reasons for needing both bone and tooth speci-mens. The clock said three-fifty. I cut him off.

'Art, could you explain this when we discuss results? If I want these specimens to go out with today's FedEx pickup, I have to get back to the skeletons and pull the teeth within the next thirty minutes.'

'Yes, yes. Of course. We'll talk then. Tempe, this may go nowhere, but, well, you never know.'

Disconnecting, I descended to the morgue, cut another plug of bone from the femur of each set of remains, replaced the bone, removed the jaw, returned to my lab, photographed the jaw, removed the right second molar from each, repacked everything, and returned the parcel to the mound of uncollected mail, thankful that I'd already had dental X-rays made.

By four-thirty, I'd resettled in my office.

Crossing my ankles on the window ledge, I sipped diet soda, nibbled my first doughnut, and forced my thoughts to subjects other than the pizza basement girls.

Katy.

What about Katy? I had no idea what my daughter was doing at that moment. Or even her specific whereabouts. Call? I looked at my watch. She was probably out, studying at the library or in class. Right.

Presumably, Katy was diligently attending classes and planning her future beyond university. I was not being kept advised. Had my little girl slipped into an adulthood in which I would play only minor walk-ons?

That smiley-face thought cranked my mind back to the girls who were now skeletons.

Why no single shred of clothing? Had I missed something? Should I have used a finer mesh screen? Had the owner gathered more than buttons? What could explain three girls buried naked in a basement?

Diet Coke. Mental right turn.

Anne.

Why the unexpected visit? What was behind the funny sound in her voice?

With the second doughnut, my mind took another go at the skeletons.

If all three girls died at the same time, why

adipocere only with the third set of remains? OK. The wrapping. But why just that one burial?

Nope. New topic.

A sweater I'd seen in Ogilvy's window. A ratchety noise in my car's engine. An odd brown spot on my right shoulder.

At the end of the second doughnut, my mind made another hard run at the skeletons.

The bodies had been less than six inches down. Why so close to the surface? Native burials typically lie much deeper. So do historic graves.

What if Art really could tell me where each of the girls had been born? Would that be helpful? Or would his analysis merely indicate that they were locals?

Maybe LaManche had a point. Maybe I was becoming obsessed. I was jumpy and defensive. I wasn't sleeping well. The case had even entered my dreams.

My mind veered down another alley.

Could work dissatisfaction be at the root of my problem with Ryan? Were anxiety and frustration transferring to him and firing my own destruction in that arena?

Ryan.

As though triggered by some errant electron escaping that synapse, the phone rang. I swiveled and snatched the receiver, this time nearly upsetting my drink.

'Dr. Brennan.'

Susanne informed me that a detective was on his way to my office.

Claudel. Just what I needed.

Only it wasn't.

Standing six feet two, wearing khakis, fawn linen, and a tweed jacket, Ryan looked like a cross between Pierce Brosnan and the older guy in an Adidas ad. He shook his head at the Diet Coke in my hand and the sugar powdering my desk blotter.

'The woman is a swirling mass of contradiction.'

'I have eclectic tastes.'

'Your tastes must confuse the hell out of your pancreas.'

'It's *my* pancreas.'

Ryan looked surprised at the sharpness of my response.

'Catching you at a bad time, cupcake?'

'I was expecting someone else.' I set down the can. '*Honey bun.*'

'I'm hearing that a lot lately.'

'Honey bun?'

'That I am other than your expectations.'

'I thought someone might be calling with information on a case.'

'Once more I've dashed hopes of which I know nothing.'

'You sound like Winston Churchill,' I said, slumping back in my chair.

'That is nonsense up with which I will not put.'

'A for grammar, D-minus for clarity.' I pressed powdered sugar onto the tip of my finger.

'Winnie said it.'

'You repeated it.'

'How are things going with Claudel?' Ryan leaned against the doorjamb and crossed arms and ankles. As usual, I found my eyes drawn to his. No matter how often I experienced it, the intensity of the blue always caught me off guard.

'Claudel's running on a limited supply of brain cells. The few he has need to e-mail each other regularly to maintain contact.'

'And the system is down?'

'I haven't heard from Claudel today. Actually, I'm looking forward to sharing something with him.'

I licked sugar from my finger and dipped more from the blotter.

'You going to share it with Honey Bun?'

'LaManche authorized expenditure for a special test I requested.'

'Without passing it by Authier?'

I nodded.

'LaManche can be a rascal. What test?'

'Carbon 14.'

'As in mummies and mastodons?'

I walked Ryan through the short course I'd given LaManche, but decided against mentioning the strontium isotope analysis. Too iffy.

'How far out for results?'

'Hopefully, no more than a week. LaManche suggested I move on to the third skeleton. Basically, he's telling me to forget about PMI for now.'

'Not bad advice.'

'It's frustrating.'

'Goes with the job.'

Ryan's beeper sounded. He checked the number and clipped the gizmo back on his belt.

'Granted, these kids didn't die last week, or even last month,' I went on. 'But I can't shake the thought that time is being wasted. I just have a bad feeling about this case.'

'Why?'

I told Ryan about Mrs. Gallant/Ballant/Talent.

'What exactly did she say?'

'That she knew what had gone on in that building.'

'Which was?'

'We didn't get that far.'

'She could be a crackpot.'

'She could be.'

'You say she sounded old.'

'Yes.'

'It's possib—'

'I've thought of that, Ryan. But what if she is sharp and she is on the level? And she *does* know something?'

'She'll ring back.'

'She hasn't.'

'Are you having her call tracked?'

'Yes.'

'Want me to see what I can find out?'

'I can handle it.'

'What threat could an old lady pose to anybody?'

'This woman knows about our little field trip to the basement. God knows who else read or heard about it. You saw *Le Journal*. The media were on the thing like cats on a fish wagon.'

'Other than its age, what do you know about this building?'

'Three dead girls were buried in its basement.'

'You can be a pain in the ass, Brennan.'

'I work at it.'

'Have dinner with me tonight?' Ryan asked.

'I'm busy.'

Deafening quiet slipped across the office. Thirty seconds. A full minute.

Uncrossing his ankles, Ryan straightened from the wall. The ice blue eyes looked straight into mine. It was not a happy look.

'We need to talk.'

'Yes,' I said.

Adios, cowboy, I thought, watching Ryan disappear through the door.

9

Midweek, late afternoon is not a good time for motoring in Montreal. Through the Ville-Marie Tunnel and onto the 20, I flew along at a clip that reached thirty-five mph at its peak. At the Turcot Interchange, my progress could be measured in spastic movements of car lengths.

A bumper sticker glimmered in the tail-lights ahead of me. *The beatings will continue until morale improves.* The first reading drew a chuckle. By the tenth, the humor had bled out. Translate: The traffic snarl will continue until impatience subsides.

To ease the boredom, I scanned billboards. Slogans in mangled English and French hawked cell phones and Hondas and sitcoms and hair spray.

With darkness, a hard wind had kicked up. Now and then the car rocked, as though toed at one end by a giant sneaker. A winter city crept by my windshield. Lamp-lit windows in the high hills of Westmount. The blackened rail yards. Suburban bungalows electric with discount store Christmas schlock.

Past Ville St-Pierre, congestion eased, and I gunned it back up to a blistering thirty. My fingers drummed the wheel. The dashboard clock said five-thirty. Anne's flight had probably landed.

A full hour after leaving the lab, I entered the terminal at Dorval Airport. Anne had cleared customs and was standing at the end of a chute of people awaiting arrivals.

I did the windmill thing with my arms. Catching sight of me, Anne grasped the pull-handle of a boxcar-sized suitcase and wheeled it in my direction. A laptop hung from one shoulder, an enormous leather purse from the other.

Sudden flashback. My sister, Harry, surrounded by enough Louis Vuitton for a world tour. She'd come for a week. She'd stayed a month.

Oh boy.

Anne is very tall and very blonde. More eyes than mine followed as she muscled her Pullman through the crowd of greeters. Reaching me, she bent and threw both arms around my neck. The laptop slid forward and gouged my ribs.

'Traffic was a nightmare,' I said, relieving Anne of her shoulder gear.

'You're a darlin' to come for me.'

'I'm thrilled you're here.'

'The pilot claimed it was eighteen below. Can that be true?' Anne's drawl sounded as out of place in the quebecois hubbub as the *Rawhide* theme at a PETA benefit.

'That's Celsius.' I didn't point out that the reading was only a hair above zero in her worldview.

'I hope there's a blizzard. Snow would be a kick.'

'Did you bring warm clothing?'

Anne spread both arms in a check-it-out gesture.

My friend wore a cable-knit sweater, suede jacket, green cords, and pink angora muffler with matching hat. I was certain her purse contained fuzzy pink mittens to complete the accessorizing. I knew her thinking. 'Winter *chic*.'

Though Anne was born in Alabama and schooled in Mississippi, she had traveled North, and, like many Southerners, gained a theoretical understanding of the concept of cold. But the mind is an overprotective parent. What it doesn't care for, it hides. Like many inhabiting the subtropics, Anne had repressed the reality of subzero mercury.

This was Quebec. Anne was dressed for autumn cool in the Blue Ridge Mountains.

Exiting the terminal, I heard Ms. Winter *Chic* suck in her breath. Smiling, I hurried her toward the car. I really couldn't fault Anne. Though I commute regularly between Charlotte and Montreal, that first winter blast clotheslines even me.

Anne talked around topics on the drive to Centre-ville. Her cats, Regis and Kathie Lee. The twins, Josh and Lola. Her youngest son, Stuart, who'd become a spokesman for gay rights. Between bursts, she'd stop, and a moody silence would fill the small space around us.

Now and then I'd sneak a sideways glance. Anne's face flickered in a mosaic of neon and brake lights. I could take nothing from it. She uttered not a word about the reason for her visit.

OK, old friend. Tell the tale when you will.

An hour and a half later Anne began meandering through an explanation. As she talked, I sensed vacillation, as though she were testing ideas as she spoke them.

We'd stopped at home to deposit Anne's things, and were now in the Trattoria Trestevere on lower Crescent. The waiter had just delivered Caesar salads. I was drinking Perrier. Anne was working on her third chardonnay.

And the chardonnay was working on Anne.

'I'm forty-six years old, Tempe. If I don't search for some meaning now, there's going to be nothing out there for me to find later.' She tapped a manicured nail to her breast. 'Or in here.'

Again, I thought of my sister. Harry had come to Montreal questing for inner peace. She'd hooked up with apocalyptic crazies who were going to take her on a voyage to permanent peace. As in dead. Fortunately, she'd survived. Anne's discourse sounded like flotsom straight down the same self-help psychobabble pipeline.

'So the kids are all right?'

'Peachy.'

'Tom didn't do anything to piss you off?'

The nail pointed at me. 'Tom didn't *do* anything. Ever. Unless you count defending asshole developers who want to rid the world of trees, and spending the rest of the time seeking the grail of a hole in one. Guess it's my own fault marrying someone with a name like Turnip.'

Tom-Ted's surname had also been a source of much amusement over the years.

'The tuber is terminated.'

'You've left him?' I couldn't believe it.

'Yes.'

'After twenty-four years and three kids?'

'This does not concern the kids.'

My fork stopped in midair. Anne and I froze eye to eye.

'You know that's not what I mean,' she said. 'The kids are grown. Josh and Lola have graduated college. Stuart's off doing whatever it is Stuart does.' She jabbed at a lettuce leaf. 'They're moving on with their lives and I'm left with selling real estate and cultivating fucking azaleas.'

Upon completion of my doctorate at Northwestern, Pete joined a Charlotte law firm, and I accepted an appointment at UNCC. I was thrilled to leave Chicago and return to my beloved North Carolina. But the move had its downside.

By day, I was surrounded by academics. Dedicated. Compassionate. Bright. And as socially sophisticated as the Burpee seed catalog. Katy was an infant. My colleagues were childless and clueless concerning the demands of parenthood.

Each evening, I collected my baby at child care and transitioned to a picture perfect ad for country club living. Manicured lawns. Upmarket cars.

Stepford wives with stay-at-home mind-sets. Female conversation focused on tennis, golf, and car pools.

I was despairing of ever developing meaningful female friendships when I spotted Anne at a neighborhood charity tea. Or heard her, to be more precise. Steel magnolia meets the drunken sailor.

I zeroed in. Instant connection.

Anne and I have seen each other's kids through broken bones and broken hearts. Our families have shared two decades of camping and ski trips, Thanksgiving dinners, christenings, and funerals. Until the collapse of my marriage, the Turnips and the Petersonses hadn't missed a summer at the ocean. Now Anne and I made the beach trips alone.

'What have you told the kids?'

'Nothing. I haven't actually moved out of the house. I'm on a leave of absence. Traveling.'

'But—'

'Let's not talk about me, darlin'. Let's talk about you. What are you working on these days?'

There is no pursuing an issue with Anne when she closes down.

I summarized the pizza basement case, and told her of my frustration with my pal Claudel.

'You'll bring him around. You always have before. Get to the good stuff. Are you seeing anyone?'

'Sort of.'

The waiter replaced our salads with entrées. Lasagna for Anne. Veal piccata for me. Anne ordered another wine, then snatched up the grinder and screwed cheese onto her pasta. I decided to try another run at the Tom thing.

'What exactly is the focus of this new personal outreach program?' I tried to keep the cynicism from my voice.

'Fulfillment. Self-esteem. Appreciation.' She smacked the grinder onto the tabletop. 'And don't even suggest it. I'm not signing up for one more puking course.'

We ate in silence for a few moments. When Anne spoke again her tone sounded lighter, but forced, somehow.

'I got more attention from the hunk in 3C than I have from Tom Turnip in the past twelve months. Boy's probably out buying me gardenias right now.' Anne knocked back a swig of wine. 'Hell, messages are probably piling up on your answering machine as we speak.'

'What boy in 3C?'

'A sweet little stud I met on the plane.'

'You gave him my phone number?'

'He's harmless.'

'How do you know he's harmless?'

'He was in first class.'

'So were the nice lads who torpedoed the Trade Center.'

My friend looked at me as though I'd suggested she cut off a foot.

'Don't get your panties in a bunch, Tempe. I'm not actually going to see the guy.'

I wasn't believing this. I use extreme caution in

94

giving out my home number. Anne had blithely shared it with a complete stranger, who might be calling my home looking for her.

'I'd had a couple of Manhattans,' she continued, oblivious to the extent of my annoyance. 'We talked. He asked where he could reach me. I jotted the stuff on a napkin—'

'Stuff? Meaning address, too?'

Anne gave an Academy Award orbital roll.

'I'm sure the guy tossed it as he exited the Jetway. How's your veal?'

In contrast to the conversation, my meat was perfect.

'Good,' I mumbled. So the guy might not call. He could show up on my doorstep.

'Mine is *parfait*. See what I mean? Already I'm in a different galaxy from Clover, South Carolina.' Anne circled her fork in the air. '*Québec! La belle province! C'est magnifique!*'

I have been accused of speaking Southern French. Anne's accent left me in the Dixie dust.

'This is just a cooling-off period, right? A marital sabbatical?'

When I was married to Pete, Anne and I often joked about the 'marital sabbatical.' It was our code phrase for 'road trip, no men allowed.'

'I could be dead a week and Tom Turnip wouldn't notice I was gone.' The fork came back up, this time pointed at me. 'No. That may be harsh. If Tom ran out of toilet paper he might holler to inquire as to my whereabouts.'

Anne gave one of her full, throaty laughs.

'There's a pretty picture, darlin'. The great barrister, caught midstep taking a dum—'

'Annie.'

'Hon, the boy is history.'

For a few moments we ate in silence. When I'd finished, I gave the topic one last shot.

'Annie, this is Tempe. I know you. I know Tom. I've seen you two together for twenty years. Tell me what's really going on.'

Anne laid down her fork and began working the paper napkin under her wineglass. A full minute passed before she spoke.

'Things were amazing when Tom and I first met. The March of the Toreadors every night. And things stayed great. The books and talk shows tell you that married couples go from towering inferno to not so hot, and that that's normal. But it didn't happen with Tom and me.'

Jagged scallops were appearing along the napkin's edge.

'Not until a couple of years ago.'

'Are you talking about sex?'

'I'm talking about a major, total downshift. Tom stopped smoldering and began focusing on anything that wasn't me. I began settling for less and less of him. Last week it struck me. Our paths were barely crossing.'

'Nothing terrible had happened?'

'That's just it. *Nothing* had happened. Nothing *was* happening. Nothing was *about* to happen. I'd begun to feel numb. And I'd begun to think numb wasn't so bad. Numb began to feel normal.'

Anne gathered the napkin scraps into a tiny mound.

'Life's too short, Tempe. I don't want my obituary to read, "Here lies a woman who sold houses."'

'Isn't it a bit soon to just pull the plug?'

With a sweep of the hand, Anne sent the scraps spiraling to the floor.

'I have aspired to be the perfect wife more than half my life. The result has been deep disappointment. Cut and run. That's my new philosophy.'

'Have you considered counseling?'

'When hell and the golf courses freeze over.'

'You know Tom loves you.'

'Does he?'

'We meet very few people in this life who truly care.'

'Right you are, darling.' Anne drained her fourth chardonnay with a quick, jerky move, and set the glass onto the mutilated napkin. 'And those are the folks who hurt us the most.'

'Annie.' I forced my friend's eyes to mine. They were a deep, dusky green, the pupils shining with an alcohol buzz. 'Are you sure?'

Anne curled the fingers of both hands and placed her forehead on her fists. A hesitation, then her face came back up.

'No.'

The unhappiness in her voice stopped my heart.

During dinner the wind had blustered up for a personal best, and the temperature had dropped in opposition. Negotiating the quarter mile home felt like mushing the Iditarod from Anchorage to Nome.

Gusts moaned up Ste-Catherine, manhandling our clothing and sandblasting our faces with ice and snow. Anne and I ran hunched like soldiers on a bunker charge.

Rounding the corner of my block, I noticed oddly drifted snow against the outer door of my building. Though cold teared my eyes, something about the white mound looked very wrong.

As I blinked my vision into focus, the drift expanded, changed shape, contracted again.

I stopped, frowned. Could it be?

An appendage snaked out, was drawn back.

What the hell was going on?

I dashed across the street and up the outer stairs.

'Birdie!'

My cat raised his chin slightly and rolled his eyes up. Seeing me, he shot forward without seeming to flex a limb. A small cloud puffed from my mouth as my chest caught his catapulted weight.

Birdie clawed upward, laid his chin on my shoulder, and pressed his belly to my jacket. His fur smelled wet. His body shivered from cold or fear.

'What's he doing out here?' A gust snatched Anne's question and whipped it up the street.

'I don't know.'

'Can he let himself out?'

'Someone had to have opened a door.'

'You tight enough with anyone to give out a key?'

'No.'

'So who's been inside?'

'I have no idea.'

'Well, we better find out.'

Pulling off her mittens, Anne produced a Mace dispenser from her shoulder bag.

'I think that's illegal here,' I said.

'So shoot me.' Anne yanked the outer door.

Entering the vestibule was like stepping from a vortex into a vacuum.

Handing off Birdie, I removed my mittens, reached into a pocket, and took out my keys. Palms sweaty, I unlocked the interior door.

The lobby was graveyard quiet. No snow residue or wet prints marred the runners or the marble floor. Heart hammering, I crossed and made a hard right. Anne followed.

Faux brass wall sconces light the interior lobby and corridors. Normally, the low-level illumination is sufficient. Tonight, two candles were out, leaving murky pools of darkness between the islands of yellow dotting my hallway.

Had the bulbs been out when we left? I couldn't remember.

My condo lay straight ahead. Seeing it, I stopped dead, totally unnerved.

Black space gaped between the open door and jamb.

10

Through the gap, I could make out disordered shadows and an odd luminescence, like moonlight on water.

I glanced over my shoulder. Anne stood with one arm wrapping the cat, the other upraised, Mace at the ready. Birdie clung to her chest, head twisted one-eighty to stare at his home.

I turned back to the door, straining to hear sounds on the far side. A footfall. A cough. The whisper of a sleeve.

Behind me, Anne's ragged breathing. Beyond the door, intimidating silence.

The three of us held stock-still, eyes wide, a triptych in trepidation.

A heartbeat. A lifetime.

Then Birdie made his move. Scrabbling upward, he gave a 'Rrrp,' rocketed off Anne's chest, and shot toward the opening. In a lunge to grab him, Anne only managed to divert his flight path.

Paws slammed the door, sending it backward into the wall. Birdie sped inside as the door ricocheted back from the wall and shut.

Blood drained from my brain. Options kaleidoscoped.

Retreat? Call out? Dial 911?

I find cell phones in restaurants annoying beyond tolerance. I hadn't brought mine to dinner.

Damn!

I turned to Anne. Her face was a tense white oval in the dim light.

I pantomimed punching numbers on a cell phone. Anne shook her head, canister on high. Lady Liberty with Mace, but no phone.

We traded looks of indecision. I spoke first, barely a whisper.

'Could the latch have failed to catch?'

'I pulled it tight. But it's your damn door.' Barely a sibilant, but she managed to hiss. 'Besides, that doesn't explain Birdie being outside.'

'If someone was waiting to assault us, the door wouldn't be open.'

'Assault us?' Anne's eyes saucered. 'Oh, sweet Jesus. Are you talking about some homicidal crazoid you've pissed off through your work?'

'That's not what I meant.' It was exactly what I meant. 'I meant some random intruder.'

Anne's eyes ballooned. 'Great. Some crazoid *rapist*.'

'That's not the point. Leaving the door open would be a dead giveaway of a break-in.'

'Excellent choice of wording.'

Under stress, Anne's sarcasm keeps its cool.

'If it's a routine burglary, they wouldn't announce their presence with an open door. The door makes no sense if anyone's inside.'

Lady Liberty relaxed her arm a fraction, but said nothing.

Creeping forward, I placed my ear to the door.

No noise.

But something else.

Squatting, I held my hand to the crack. Cold air was seeping out.

'What?' Anne was still using her church voice.

I straightened.

'There's a door or window open inside.'

'Meaning the Ripper has split? Or settled in for a Guinness and garroting?'

At that moment the lobby door opened. We both went rigid.

Voices. Male.

Anne's Mace arm shot skyward.

Footsteps retreated down the wing opposite mine. A door opened, closed.

Silence.

Then more footsteps. Coming in our direction!

I motioned Anne into the stairwell hallway parallel to my door. We shrank sideways as one.

A figure filled the frame of the main entrance to my corridor, tuque pulled low to his eyes. Dimness and the hat obscured the man's face. All I could make out was body form. Tall. Lean.

The figure hesitated, then pulled off the tuque and strode toward us.

Anne's knuckles went white around her canister.

The figure passed under a sconce. Sandy hair. Bomber jacket.

Relief flooded through me. Followed by embarrassment. And feelings of which I was uncertain.

Defusing Anne with a gesture, I stepped forward.

'What are you doing here?' Whispered, but shrill, thanks to the adrenaline pumping through me.

Ryan's smile sagged, but held on. 'I've come to view that greeting as a sign of affection.'

'I'm always *saying* that because you're always showing up unexpectedly.'

Ryan placed both hands on his chest. 'I am a man smitten.' He spread the hands wide. 'I cannot stay away.'

Anne lowered her arm, a look of confusion crimping her features.

Ryan turned, preparing to beam charm in Anne's direction. Seeing the Mace, his smile wavered. He looked a question at me.

Annoyance and embarrassment began a full-court press against fear and relief. If the break-in wasn't real, I didn't want to look like a fool. If the break-in was real, I didn't want to need Ryan's help. Or his protection.

Unfortunately, at that moment, I suspected I needed both.

'Someone may have broken into my place.'

Ryan didn't question what I'd said. He spoke without moving.

'How long were you away?'

'A couple of hours. We've been back five minutes or less.'

'Did you set the alarm when you left?'

Normally I am good about security. Tonight, Anne and I had been intent on catch-up.

'Probably.' I wasn't sure.

Pocketing gloves and tuque, Ryan unzipped his jacket, drew his Glock, and gestured us back toward the stairwell.

Anne slid left, back pressed to the wall. I moved behind Ryan.

Ryan twisted sideways against the wall and rapped the door with his gun butt.

'*Police! On entre!*'

No answer. No movement.

Ryan barked again, in French, then English.

Silence.

Ryan pointed at the lock.

I stepped forward and used my key. Sweeping me back behind him with one arm, Ryan nudged the door open with his foot.

'Stay here.'

Gun gripped in both hands, barrel angled skyward, Ryan crossed the threshold. I followed.

Something crunched underfoot.

One step. Two.

The mirrored wall in the foyer gaped densely black. Courtyard light sparked like phosphorous off the marble floor.

Three.

A saffron trapezoid gleamed from the glass-topped table in the dining room ahead. Other shapes formed out of the darkness. The writing desk. A corner of the sideboard.

A sudden sense of foreboding. I'd left lights burning.

Again, Ryan called out.

Again, no answer.

Ryan and I crept through the darkness, predators testing the air.

Sounds of emptiness. The refrigerator. The humidifier.

Cold, from the direction of the living room.

At the side hall Ryan reached out and flicked the switch. Motioning me to stay put, he made a hard right and disappeared. Lights went on in the bedroom, the bath, the study.

No one bolted. No one rushed past me. Ryan's movements were the only sounds.

Backtracking to the main hall, Ryan moved forward and probed the kitchen, then the living room. In seconds he reappeared.

'Clean.'

I took my first real breath since entering the apartment.

Seeing my terror, Ryan reengaged the safety and holstered his gun, then wrapped his arms around me.

'Someone cut the glass in the French door.'

'But the alarm?' My voice sounded stretched and quavery, like an overused cassette.

'Wasn't breached. Do you have a motion detector?'

'Disabled.'

I felt Ryan's chin tap the crown of my head.

'Birdie kept triggering the damn thing,' I said defensively.

'What the hell?'

Ryan and I turned. Anne was standing in the doorway, Mace aloft, eyes wide.

'*Bienvenue à Montréal,*' said Ryan.

Anne's brows shot skyward.

'He's a cop,' I said.

'Serve and protect,' Ryan said.

Anne lowered brows and Mace. 'My kind of community policing.'

Ryan released me and I made introductions.

Hearing voices, Birdie fired from the bedroom and raced a figure eight around my ankles, fur erect with agitation.

'Detective Ryan would be the "sort of" referred to at dinner?' Anne floated one brow in query.

'Someone's been in here,' I said, shooting her a 'not now' look.

'Holy shit,' Anne said, crunching into the foyer.

As Ryan phoned burglary, Anne and I assessed the damage.

While the French door pane had been cleanly cut, without damage to the security-system trip wires, glass had been shattered in the foyer, dining room, and bathroom mirrors, and in every picture frame in the place. Fragments glittered from furniture, sinks, countertops, and floors.

A few books and papers had been tossed here and there, but otherwise, the main living areas were unharmed.

In contrast, the bedrooms were chaos. Bed pillows were shredded, drawers pulled out and upended, closets ransacked.

A hasty inventory turned up two losses. Anne's digital camera. Anne's laptop. Otherwise, nothing seemed to be missing.

'Thank God,' said Anne, drawing out the deity's name.

'I'm so sorry,' I said, gesturing lamely at her belongings.

Tossing the jewelry pouch onto the dresser, Anne shot out a hip and placed a hand on it. 'Guess the little pricks didn't care for Tom Turnip's taste in gems.'

It took an hour to do the paperwork. The officers promised that crime scene would check for prints, shoe impressions, and tool marks in the morning.

Anne and I thanked them. No one had much enthusiasm. We all knew that her belongings had disappeared into the black hole of petty theft.

Ryan stayed. Perhaps to inspire diligence on the part of the CUM. Perhaps to buoy my flagging spirits.

When the cops had gone, Ryan offered his place as refuge. I looked at Anne. She shook her head no. Her eyes told me the adrenaline was yielding to the alcohol.

Anne and I did some rough cleanup while Ryan went in search of duct tape, cardboard, and plastic. When he returned, we watched him construct a temporary patch on the French door. Then Anne excused herself and disappeared into the bathroom.

Watching Ryan drop the extra tape into a paper bag, I realized I hadn't a clue why he'd come.

'I don't know how to thank you,' I began.

'No thanks required.'

'I've been so caught up in this'—I waved an arm at the mess behind me—'circus, I haven't even asked why you stopped by.'

Ryan laid the bag on the coffee table, straightened, and placed a hand on each of my shoulders. For a long moment, he said nothing. Then his face softened, he brushed hair from my cheek, and his hand went back to my shoulder.

When I thought I could bear his silence no longer, he spoke.

'I'm going to be scarce for a while.'

Stomach clutch. Here it comes. The end of the end.

'I can't go into details, but it's big—CUM, SQ, RCMP, even the Americans are involved. Op's been under way for several months.'

A moment went by before I got it.

'You're talking about a police sting?'

'Claudel's in, so's Charbonneau. I'm not compromising anything by telling you that.'

My mind was just not forming the links.

'Why *are* you telling me that?'

'Claudel's lack of interest in your pizza bones. I know it's been grinding at you.'

'You'll be away?'

'It's not what I want.' The hint of a smile. 'Comes with the glamour and the big bucks.'

I looked down at my hands.

'I hate to leave you alone with this.'

'I didn't call for backup, Ryan. You dropped in.'

'I don't like the look of this, Tempe.' Ryan's voice was gentle.

'It's not a big deal.'

I could feel cobalt eyes roving my features.

'I'm requesting stepped-up surveillance.'

'I'll be fine.'

Ryan raised my chin with one finger.

'I'm not sure what went down here, but I intend to find out.'

'It's a pissant B and E.'

The finger went to my lips.

'Think about it. What was taken? What was left behind? Why the slick entry, then all the smashed glass?'

Ryan squeezed my hands in his, a gesture intended to calm. Instead, it increased my agitation.

'I really would like to stay, Tempe.'

I searched his face, hoping for words that would comfort. Instead Ryan released me and slipped into his jacket. Grabbing the tape, he reached out, touched my cheek, and was gone.

I stood a moment, pondering his comment.

Stay what, Andrew Ryan? The course? The night? Cool? Free?

Not a sound from the bathroom. Not a sound from the study. Anne's light was off.

After cranking up the heat, I checked the lock on every door and window, set the alarm, and tested the phone. Then I headed toward my room.

I hadn't noticed earlier. As I crossed the threshold, it drew my attention like some malignant phantom.

My legs gridlocked in shock at the macabre outrage above my bed.

11

'No!'

Rushing forward, I jumped onto the bed, yanked a long, jagged shard from the painting above the headboard, and hurled it to the far side of the room.

Glass shattered. Fragments bounced from the wall and dropped onto others swept to the baseboard during our hasty cleanup.

'You low-life son of a bitch!'

My heart hammered. Tears burned the backs of my lids.

Stripping off my clothes, I flung them one by one after the shard. Then I threw myself under the covers, naked and trembling.

As an entering freshman at UVA, Katy chose a studio arts major. Her interest was short-lived, but during that brief blossoming, my daughter was as passionate about *les beaux arts* as any Montmartre aspirant. In one semester she produced four prints, fourteen drawings, and six oils, her style a lyrical blend of fauvist gaudiness and Barbizon realism.

On my fortieth, my only-born presented me with a Katy Petersons oil original, a raucous Matisse-meets-Rousseau interpretation of a Charlottesville hillside. I treasure that canvas. It is one of the few possessions I have transported from Carolina to Quebec to make a home out of my condo. Katy's landscape is my last sight as I pull back the covers each night, and regularly catches my eye whenever I move through the room.

Why couldn't you just take whatever it was you wanted? Why ruin Katy's painting? Why ruin my daughter's beautiful goddamned painting?

I squeezed my eyelids, too angry to cry, too angry not to. My fingers bunched and rebunched the blanket.

Minutes clicked by.

One.

Two.

Tears trickled to my temples.

Three.

Four.

Eventually, my breathing steadied and my death grip on the blanket relaxed.

I opened my eyes to blackness, and the soft orange glow of the clock radio. I stared at the digits, willing back rational thought.

Eventually, the anger abated. I began picking apart the mosaic of the last three hours.

What had gone on here? Had Anne and I merely interrupted a burglary in progress, or had we climbed into something more sinister? B and E didn't figure.

Again, my fingers grip-locked. A stranger had violated my personal space.

Who? A very selective thief looking for particular items of value? A junkie looking for anything that could be fenced to fund a buy? Thrill-seeking kids?

Why? Most important, why the gratuitous violence?

I remembered Ryan's words.

What was stolen?

Anne's laptop and camera.

What was wrong there?

The jewelry case had been in full view. It contained items of value and was portable. Why not take that? The TV? The DVD player? Less portable. My laptop? In the excitement of Anne's arrival, I'd left it in the trunk of my car.

Had the intruder been spooked before scoring the good stuff? Not likely. He had taken the time to break things. Assuming it was a he. Gratuitous damage is more characteristic of the male of the species.

The main door was open when we arrived. The courtyard doors were locked from the inside. Escape through the French doors would have necessitated scaling the backyard fence.

So? That's how he'd come in. Had the front door been opened simply for the effect when I returned? Had Bird been thrown out or had he bolted through the French door when things were being smashed?

I rolled over. Punched the pillow. Rolled back.

Why so much damage? Where were my neighbors? Had no one heard the noise?

Was Ryan right? Was the episode more than a simple B and E? Burglars work in silence.

Why cut cleanly through the French door then smash mirrors and pictures?

Why mutilate the painting?

Another blast of anger.

Was the act a threat? A warning?

If so, to whom? Me? Anne?

From whom? One of my schizoid crazies? A random schizoid crazy? Anne's buddy from the plane?

Thoughts winged and collided in my head.

I heard soft crunching, like whispered footsteps in sand. A weight hit the bed, then Birdie curled by my knee.

I reached down and stroked him.

'I love you, Bird boy.'

Birdie stretched full length against my leg.

'As for you, you loathsome son of a bitch. Yes, you've gotten to me, but one day we may have a reckoning.'

I was talking aloud over the gentle purring.

I awoke with a sense that something was wrong. Not full memory, just a nagging from the lower centers.

Then recollection.

I opened my eyes. Sunlight sparkled from flecks on the carpet and dresser top.

Birdie was gone. Through my partially open door I could hear a radio.

I found Anne drinking coffee in the kitchen, working a crossword and humming David Bowie.

Hearing me, she sang out aloud.

'Ch- ch- ch—changes!'

'Is that a suggestion?' I asked.

Anne glanced at my hair over the pink and green floral frames of her reading glasses, one of a dozen pairs she purchases each year at Steinmart.

'That do's gotta go.'

'You're not exactly the Suave girl, yourself.'

Anne's hair was twisted upward and clipped with a barrette. A spray winged from her head like the crown on Katy's cockatiel.

'I considered more tidying, but wasn't sure how much I should touch.' Anne stood, dug a mug from a cabinet, filled, and handed it to me.

'Thanks.'

'What's on the rail for the lizard?'

Anne had many expressions deriving from her Mississippi childhood. This was one I hadn't heard before.

'Translation?'

'What are your plans for today?'

'I have a date with the last of those pizza basement skeletons. Yours?'

'Contemporary Art Museum. That's the Place-des-Arts metro stop, right?'

'Correct.'

I poured cream into my coffee, then dropped two halves of an English muffin into the toaster.

'Did you know that twenty-five hundred morons bared their fat asses in the rain for a Spencer Tunick photo in that plaza?'

'How do you know they were all rump heavy?'

'Ever been to a nude beach?'

Anne had a point. Those who shouldn't are often those who most willingly flaunt it.

'Then St-Denise for lunch and shopping,' she went on.

'Alone?' I asked, remembering the hunk in 3C.

'Yes, Mom. Alone.'

'Annie, do you suppose that man could have broken in here?'

'Why in the world would he do that? He probably doesn't know you, and that is no way to impress me. Why would he do something so totally crazy?'

'Someone did.'

'I don't think it could be him, really I don't. The guy looked perfectly normal. But . . .' Her voice trailed off. 'I'm sorry, Tempe. It was stupid.'

I was spreading blackberry jam when Anne spoke again.

'What's a seven-letter word for "insensitive"?'

'Hurtful.'

'Beginning with C.'

'Claudel.'

Anne's eyes rolled up over the flowery frames.

'I think I'll go with "callous,"' she said.

Anne refocused on her puzzle. I settled opposite her and listened to the news. A fire in St-Léonard. Another Habs loss. More snow on the way.

I'd just finished my muffin when Anne tossed down her glasses and pen.

'Is this Claudel a good detective?'

I sheeshed air through my lips.

'I take that as a negative.'

'Claudel's thorough, but narrow-minded, opinionated, and stubborn. He also sees no need for forensic anthropologists in general, and female ones in particular. He views every suggestion as interfering.'

'Let me guess. And he's not making much of an effort on your skeleton case?'

'He's not even humoring me. And he considers it to be his skeleton case, not mine.'

'You've had that problem with him before, haven't you?'

'Oh, yeah. Often-wrong-but-never-in-doubt Claudel.'

'So he's not your favorite?'

'Claudel's not a laugh riot. His questions are curt to the point of rudeness, and he rarely explains why particular facts are of interest to him, or why my opinions are not.'

'What would it take to get him to listen?'

'I could sing the Hallelujah Chorus naked.' I got up and popped a second muffin into the toaster.

'You still have the bod, but you never had the voice. I was thinking along more professional lines,' Anne said.

'The point of controversy is postmortem interval. Claudel believes the bones are old. I don't. I've sent off samples for Carbon 14 testing, but I won't get results for at least a week.'

'What else might get his attention?'

'Six or seven dead preschoolers.'

'You're starting to piss me off, Tempe. I'm asking a serious question.' Anne held out her empty mug. 'What would inspire Claudel to show more interest in your bones?'

'Proof that the deaths were recent.'

I poured two refills and gave her one.

'There you go.' Anne proffered her coffee-free hand, palm up.

'Claudel believes such proof is lacking.'

'Don't wait for the Carbon 14. Change his mind.'

'He refuses to explore the possibility.'

'So give him more to chew on.'

'What am I supposed to do? Hire thugs and have him beaten until he agrees?'

'Agrees to what?'

'To investigate.'

'Meaning?'

'What is this, twenty questions?' I sat back down with my second muffin.

'What is it you would like Claudel to do?'

I gave that a few moments' thought.

'Canvas the neighborhood. Learn more about the building. Research previous residents. Find out who owned the place. Who lived there. How long the first floor has been commercial. What businesses have occupied the premises. What building permits were issued and to whom.'

'There you go.' Again, the upraised palm.

'That's the second time you've said that.'

'Don't force me to three.'

'Where do I go?'

'To the solution to your problem.'

It was too early. I wasn't making the bridges.

'Which is?'

'Do it yourself.'

'Claudel would go ballistic.'

'How could he? He says the bones are old. He sees no reason to explore further. You're doing additional research.'

'It's not my job.'

'Apparently Claudel thinks it's not his either.'

'Claudel has no interest in my suggestions, but if I do anything that even loosely resembles detective work, he gets overtly hostile.'

'Look. You don't have to make a TV series out of it. Just poke down the burrow and see what crawls out.'

I thought about that while Anne entered, erased, then reentered thirty-four down in her puzzle. She had a point. What could it hurt to check out old deeds, tax records, and building permits? If Claudel was right, I'd be working with the archaeologists anyway. Besides, he was going to be tied up with this sting Ryan had mentioned. Also, when Claudel was free again and heard I was looking into things, though furious, he might feel obligated to do more investigating himself, just to guard against my finding things that he had not.

At that moment, the doorbell chirped. When I

answered, SIJ announced its presence. I buzzed the team in, pointed out the damaged French door, Anne's room, and Katy's painting, and asked if they'd mind starting in the living room.

While the techs shot photos and dusted for prints, Anne and I retreated to our respective quarters to dress and brush and apply whatever makeup each deemed essential. During my toilette, I considered options.

It was Friday. Public offices were closed on weekends. If I examined the third skeleton today, I wouldn't have access to the courthouse or City Hall until Monday.

I could work at the lab anytime, over the weekend if absolutely necessary. I couldn't research records anytime.

Decision.

Once again, full analysis of the third skeleton was being deferred.

After replenishing Birdie's food and water, I checked with the SIJ techs. So far, zip.

I was reaching for the phone when Anne swept into my bedroom. She wore boots and the jacket she'd declined the evening before. The angora scarf was in place, the hat and mittens clutched in one hand.

'Setting off?' I asked.

'We're setting off,' Anne said.

'What about the museum?'

'Art is eternal. It will be there tomorrow. Today I sleuth. See? Already my life is multidimensional. You and I. Cagney and Lacey. It'll be a gas.'

'You're sure?'

'I'm sure.'

'Cagney and Lacey were trained detectives with badges and guns. We'll be more like Miss Marple and one of her friends from the garden club. But, OK, let's give it a go. The crime scene techs will let themselves out. I'll check my messages and we're on our way.'

I dialed the lab, punched in my mailbox number and access code. One message. Nine forty-three the previous evening.

The woman's words started a holocaust of possibilities whirling through my head, each uglier than the next.

12

Frantically, I jabbed at a pen on my dresser. Anne darted and handed it to me.

'Dr. Brennan. I feel I must give this one last try or I will not be able to live with myself.'

I logged details of the voice. Old. Female.

'I called the day before yesterday about the story in *Le Journal*.'

A pause. As before, I heard chirping in the background, vaguely familiar chirping.

'I believe I know who is dead and why.' Shot through with desolation and doubt.

'Come on,' I urged under my breath. 'Who are you?'

'You have my name.'

'No. I don't!'

Anne's head snapped up in surprise at my outcry.

'You may reach me at 514-937—'

'Atta girl!'

Anne watched as I scribbled the number, clicked off, and dialed.

Somewhere on the island a phone rang ten, eleven, twelve times.

I cut the connection and repunched the digits.

A dozen more unanswered rings.

'Damn!'

I clicked off and tossed the handset onto the bed, my whole body taut with frustration. I rose and paced the room, then snatched up the handset and dialed again.

No answer.

'Pick up your goddamn phone!'

What to do? Call Claudel or Charbonneau and give him the number? Call Ryan? All three of them were probably fully occupied with this massive joint operation they were on and didn't have time for phone numbers.

Disconnecting, I grabbed my keys, raced to the basement, and retrieved my laptop from the trunk of my car. When I returned to the bedroom Anne was sitting on the bed, arms crossed, one foot flicking up and down. She watched without comment as I booted the computer, and typed the phone number into a browser.

No results. The browser suggested I check my spelling or try different words. 'How do you spell a number, you ignorant twit?'

I tried another browser. Then another.

No matches. Same useful tips.

'What good are you!'

Snatching the handset again, I punched another

number, requested an individual, and made an inquiry.

No. Wednesday's call to the lab had not yet been traced. Why not? These things take time. Well, then, write down this number and see if you get a match.

I sailed the handset back onto the bed, crossed to the dresser, dug for gloves, and slammed the drawer.

While jamming my right hand into one glove, I let go of the other. I bent to pick it up, dropped it again, kicked it to the wall, retrieved it, and yanked it onto my left hand.

When I turned Anne was gazing up at me, arms still folded, an amused expression on her face.

'Is this our resident forensic specialist demonstrating the art of a tantrum?' Anne asked in a Mr. Rogers voice.

'You think *that* was a tantrum? Piss me off and I'll show you a gorilla.'

'I haven't seen you stage a nutty like that since you caught Pete screwing the travel agent.'

'It was a Realtor.' I had to smile. 'And *she* definitely had a fat ass.'

'Let me guess. We aren't pleased with our phone message?'

'No. We aren't.'

I summarized the tale of Mrs. Gallant/Ballant/Talent's calls.

'*That* brought out the Diva of Dachau?'

I didn't respond.

'The nice lady is probably out buying her weekly

124

Metamucil. She has called twice. She will call a third time.' Again, the patient schoolmarm. 'If not, you have the number and you will reach her later. Or you must have resources downtown that can identify the listing that goes with that number. Hell, some everyman directory assistance systems will give you the name and address if you have a number.'

I could not mask my agitation.

'Anne, the woman said she knew who was dead and why. If she's legit she can break this investigation wide open. Of course, she may not be legit. I'd like to talk to her before I set Claudel off on a false trail You're right, I need to make some more efforts to talk to her myself. She called me, not the police.'

'I do have one other question.'

I raised my hands in a go-ahead gesture.

'How do you plan to button your jacket?'

I yanked off both gloves and pegged them at her.

For the second time that week I pulled into a pay lot in the old quarter. The sky was gunmetal, the air heavy with unborn snow.

'Bundle up,' I told Anne, zipping my parka.

'Where are we going?'

'Hôtel de Ville.'

'We're booking a room?' Muffled through angora scarving.

'City Hall. It's a four-block walk.'

Perched atop place Jacques-Cartier, Montreal's City Hall is a Victorian extravagance in copper and stone. Built between 1872 and 1878, the place looks as though its designer didn't quite know when to call it a day. Mansard roof? *Très Parisien*. Columns? Of course. Porticos? *Bien sûr*. Eaves, dormer windows, balconies, cupola, clock? Yes. Yes. Yes. Yes. And yes.

Though devastated by fire in 1922, Hôtel de Ville remained structurally sound, was rejuvenated, and today is a favorite with both natives and visitors, one of Montreal's most charming landmarks.

'One would not confuse this with the Clover City Hall,' Anne said as we climbed the front steps.

I pointed to a balcony over the front door. 'See that?'

Anne nodded.

'Charles de Gaulle made his famous or infamous *Vive le Québec Libre* speech from that balcony.'

'When?'

'Sixty-seven.' (1967?)

'And?'

'The separatists liked it.'

Despite its modern status as a tourist attraction, Hôtel de Ville remains the city's main administrative center. And the repository of the information I was seeking. I hoped.

Anne and I entered to the smell of radiator heat and wet wool. Across the lobby, a kiosk offered *Renseignements*. Information.

A woman looked up when I approached. She

was about twenty, with towering blonde hair that added inches to her height.

The woman stifled a yawn as I explained what I wanted. Before I'd finished, she pointed to a wallboard listing offices and locations, her bony arm clattering with plastic bracelets.

'*Accès Montréal*,' she said.

'*Merci*,' I said.

'I think she could have been less interested,' Anne said, trailing me to the office directory. 'But not without a heavy dose of Lithium.'

In the Access Montreal office we encountered an older, heavier, and decidedly friendlier version of Ms. Information. The woman greeted us in typical Montreal Franglais.

'*Bonjour*. Hi.'

I explained my objective in French.

The woman dropped chained glasses to her bosom and replied in English.

'If you have a civic address, I can look up the cadastral and lot numbers.'

I must have looked confused.

'The cadastral number describes the parcel of land. The important one is the lot number. With that you can research the history of the property at the Registre Foncier du Québec office in the Bureau d'Enregistrement.'

'Is that located here?'

'Palais de Justice. Second floor. Room 2.175.'

I jotted the address of the pizza parlor building and handed it across the counter.

'Shouldn't be long.'

It wasn't. In ten minutes the woman returned with the numbers. I thanked her, and Anne and I set off.

Montreal's three courthouses lie just west of its City Hall. As we scurried along rue Notre-Dame, Anne's eyes probed gallery, café, and boutique windows. She hung back to pat a horse, gushed over the beauty of the Château Ramezay, laughed at cars snowbanked in by plows.

Architecturally, City Hall and the modern courthouse have little in common aside from the fact that each is a building. Anne did not comment on the charm of the latter.

Before entering, I pulled out my cellular and tried Mrs. Gallant/Ballant/Talent's number.

Nope.

As on the day of my testimony, the courthouse was busy with lawyers, judges, journalists, security guards, and worried-looking people. The lobby was controlled confusion, each face looking like it would rather be elsewhere.

Anne and I rode an elevator to the second floor and went directly to room 2.175. When my turn came, I explained my mission, this time to a short, bald clerk shaped like a cookie jar.

'There's a fee,' Cookie Jar said.

'How much?'

He told me.

I forked over the money. Cookie Jar handed me a receipt.

'That allows you to research all day.'

I presented my lot and cadastral numbers.

Cookie Jar studied the paper. Then he looked up, a pudgy finger jabbing black-framed glasses up the bridge of his nose.

'These numbers go pretty far back. Anything prior to 1974 can't be researched online. Depending on how often the property changed hands, this could take time.'

'But I can find out who owned the building?'

Cookie Jar nodded. 'Every deed transfer is recorded with the provincial government.' He held up the paper. 'What's at this location now?'

'The building has residential units upstairs, small businesses below. The address that interests me is a pizza-by-the-slice joint.'

Cookie Jar shook his head. 'If the property is commercial, you won't learn what businesses have occupied it unless the owner has included such information.'

'How could I find that out?'

'Tax records maybe. Or business permits.'

'But I can determine who the owners have been?'

Cookie Jar nodded. In some irrational way, looking at him made me think of Don Ho and tiny bubbles.

'That's a start,' I said.

Cookie Jar pointed to the one unoccupied computer in the room. 'If you need something prior to 1974, I'll explain how to use the books.'

I crossed to the terminal, took off my jacket, and hung it on the chair back. Anne followed.

Slinging my purse strap over the jacket, I turned to her.

'There's no reason for you to sit and watch me punch a keyboard and dig through old books.'

'I don't mind.'

'Right. The diversions for which you flew twelve hundred miles are not found in this registry.'

'Beats cooking and freezing casseroles for surgeries and funerals.'

'Wouldn't you rather shop?'

'Fuck shopping.'

Anne was in the Mariana Trench of doldrums. Sitting here watching me was not going to cheer her.

'Go to the basilica. Scout out a place to eat. When I've finished, I'll phone your cell.'

'You won't get frustrated and throw another hissy?'

I put a hand on her shoulder.

'Go forth and shop with the mighty. Your work here is done.'

Three hours later, I was still at it.

The online research had taken forty minutes, thirty-seven figuring out what I was doing, three printing out information on the building's current owner.

Digging backward through the tomes of bound deeds had taken somewhere in the vicinity of an eon.

Cookie Jar had been polite and helpful, patiently taking my money and photocopying the record of each transaction as I found it.

In the course of my research, I discovered several things.

Claudel was correct about the building's age. Prior to construction, the land had been part of the CNR train yards. Since then, the property had changed hands several times.

I was studying my collection of photocopies when one name leaped out.

I knew that name.

Why?

A local politician? A singer?

I stared at the name, willing a synapse.

A television personality? A case I'd worked? Someone I knew?

The date of transfer was before my time in Montreal. So why the subliminal ring-a-ding?

Then, recognition.

'Sweet mother of Mary!'

Jamming the printouts and photocopies into my purse, I grabbed my jacket, and bolted.

13

Outside, snow was powdering the stairs and handrails, and adding to mounds lining the sidewalks and streets. I didn't care. As soon as I cleared the doors I phoned Claudel.

The CUM operator told me Claudel was out. I asked for Charbonneau. Out.

'This is Dr. Brennan from medicolegal. Do you know when either will be back?'

'No.' Distracted. 'Tried their beepers?'

'Numbers, please?'

She gave them to me. I dialed and left my cellular as a numeric page for each detective. But I had little hope of an immediate response. Claudel, in particular, was not likely to be diverted from a major operation to call me back on a case in which he had almost no interest.

Next I tried Mrs. Gallant/Ballant/Talent.

No answer.

Working hard to calm myself, I phoned Anne.

She was buying ornaments at a Christmas shop.

Anne suggested Le Jardin Nelson for lunch, and started to give directions.

'I know where it is,' I cut her off.

A metered silence, then, 'Did we have a bad search?'

'I think I've found something. See you in ten.'

Hunching against the snow, I hurried toward place Jacques-Cartier, a pedestrian playground stretching from rue Notre-Dame riverward to rue de la Commune. Lined with restaurants, cafés, and kitschy T-shirt and souvenir shops, *la place* teems with life during mild weather. Today I shared the square with a handful of tourists, one street artist, and a scraggy yellow terrier pissing on a lamppost.

Flakes were obliterating the cobblestones, the street signs, the pillar memorializing Admiral Nelson, the Englishman who spanked the French at the battle of Trafalgar. Never a favorite with the separatists. Beyond the square, I could see the gauzy blur of the silver-domed Bonsecours Market, City Hall until mothballed by the mansarded Parisian at my back.

Quebec. The Twin Solitudes. One French and Catholic, the other English and Calvinist. The two languages and cultures have butted heads in the province since the Brits seized Montreal in 1760. Place Jacques-Cartier is a microcosm in stone of the linguistic tribalism.

Le Jardin Nelson is located halfway down the east side of the square. The restaurant is squat and solid, with plaza-side terraces under bright blue awnings. A parasoled courtyard with infrared heaters keeps the eatery *Montréal chic* many months of the year.

This was not one of them. When I entered, Anne looked up over her menu and tracked me across the room.

'It's really coming down,' I said, removing my parka, then shaking flakes.

'Will it stick?'

'Snow always sticks in Montreal.'

'Excellent.'

'Hm.' I placed my cellular on the tabletop.

A young woman filled water glasses. Anne ordered Crêpes Forestiers and a glass of chardonnay. I went for Crêpes Argenteuil and a Diet Coke.

'Find any treasures?' I asked when the waitress had gone.

Even in a state of apathy, Anne is a commando shopper. She showed me her purchases.

Tangerine wool sweater. Hand-painted Provençal bowl. Six pewter frogs on red satin ribbons.

'Odd choice for the unfettered life,' I said, gesturing at the ornaments.

'I can use them as gifts,' Anne said, rewrapping the tissue.

The waitress delivered drinks. I sipped my Coke, unwound my napkin, positioned my utensils. Adjusted the fork. Aligned the spoon and knife. Repositioned the fork. Checked my cell phone to be sure it was on.

More Coke.

Then I flattened the edges of my place mat with

both palms. Straightened the fringe. Picked up the phone. Laid it back down.

Anne raised one analytical brow.

'Expecting a call?'

'I left messages for Claudel and his partner.'

'Are you going to tell me what you discovered?'

I pulled the photocopies and printouts from my purse and stacked them on the side of my mat.

'I'll spare you a Michener saga on the land. The building went up in 1901 and was owned by a man named Yves Sauriol. At that time it was all residential. Sauriol's son, Jacques, inherited in twenty-eight, then his son, Yves, got the place in thirty-nine.

'In 1947, Yves Sauriol, Jr., sold the property to Éric-Emmanuel Gratton. That's when the first floor went commercial. A small printing company occupied the space until 1970.

'Éric-Emmanuel Gratton died in 1958, and his wife, Marie, inherited. Marie went to her reward in sixty-three, and the place transferred to their son, Gille. Gille Gratton sold the property in 1970.'

'Is this going to have a punch line?'

'To Nicolò Cataneo.'

Anne's expression indicated the name meant nothing.

'Nick "the Knife" Cataneo.'

The green eyes went wide. 'Mafia?'

I nodded.

'The Knife?'

I nodded again.

135

'That explains the manic moves with your flatware.'

'I don't know much about the mob, but Nicolò Cataneo is a name I've heard over the years.'

'The Mafia operates here?'

'Since the turn of the century.'

'I thought you had bikers.'

'We do. And right now they're the biggest game in town. But the biker boys are just one element in the wonderful world of organized crime in Montreal. The Mafia, the West End Gang, and the Hells Angels make up what's known as the "Consortium."'

'Like New York's "Commission"?'

'Exactly.'

'Do the sunny peninsula folk here get along with the sunny peninsula folk south of the border? Or are they island folk?'

'As in Italy versus Sicily? I'm not privy to the details of ancestral geography. I do know that at one time Montreal was virtually a branch office for New York City.'

'The Bonanno family? I read a book on that.'

I nodded. 'The Montreal organization was led by a fellow named Vic "the Egg" Cotroni. I think Cotroni died in the mideighties.'

I checked my cell. Still on. Still no messages.

'What's the West End Gang?' Anne asked.

'Predominantly Irish.'

'Your people.'

'We Irish are but foot soldiers in the Army of the Lord.'

'More like poets and barflies, in reverse order of diligence.'

'Careful.'

'What's this Consortium into?'

'Prostitution. Gambling. Illegal substances. The Consortium determines things like drug prices, quantities to be imported, the names of lucky buyers. Cotroni's network is thought to have smuggled millions of dollars' worth of narcotics into the American market over the years. The profits from illicit activities are then laundered through legitimate businesses.'

'Typical pattern, from what I read.'

'Same one the biker gangs have adopted. They must teach it in the business schools.'

At that moment the waitress arrived with our food. Another phone check. Still humming. Still no messages.

'Getting back to the building,' I said, after a few crepe moments. 'Nick the Knife bought the place in 1970, and held on to it for ten years.'

'How is all this relevant to your skeletons?'

'I'm talking wiseguys, not choirboys, Anne. Anyone could have been buried in that basement.'

'Aren't we being a bit melodramatic?'

'People were whacked left and right in those days.'

'Teenaged girls?'

'Strip clubs? Prostitution? Life's pretty cheap to these thugs.'

Especially female life, I thought, flashing on the gutted hooker now at the Notre-Dame Hospital.

Anne focused on her crepes until their completion. Then, 'What was on the ground floor when this Knife guy owned the building?'

'That information wasn't available.'

'Who bought the property?'

I checked my printout.

'In 1980 the building was purchased by Richard Cyr. According to records, Cyr still owns it.'

'What does Cyr have on the ground floor?'

'There are four separate businesses.'

'Including a pizza parlor.'

'Yes.'

'Where does Monsieur Cyr live?'

Back to the printout.

'Notre-Dame-de-Grâce.'

'How far is that from Montreal?'

'It's a neighborhood just west of Centre-ville.'

Anne's wineglass froze in midair. As in my kitchen that morning, the other hand came up, palm skyward.

'There you go.'

'That's three, Annie.'

Exasperated look.

'Your next step. Give Cyr a call. Better yet. If he's that close, how 'bout a surprise drop-in? The Cagney and Lacey thing's been kind of a bust for me so far. Let's solve this case.'

My eyes swung to the phone by my plate. The little screen offered nothing but my name and the time.

It was obvious neither Claudel nor Charbonneau was answering my page.

138

I raised my Coke. Anne raised her wine.

'Archaeological research,' I said, clinking my glass to hers.

'With one slight modification.' Anne drained her chardonnay. 'We're digging *for* dirt instead of in it.'

Notre-Dame-de-Grâce, or NDG, is a quiet residential neighborhood two circles out from Centre-ville. Not the Westmount of the well-heeled English, or the Outremont of their hotsy-totsy French counterparts, but nice. Middle-class. A good place to raise kids and collies.

Richard Cyr lived in a redbrick duplex on Coronation, within spitting distance of the Loyola Campus of Concordia University. It took twenty minutes to get there, another five to size the place up.

Faded metal awning over a small front porch. Postage-stamp yards in front and back. Driveway leading nowhere. Blue Ford Falcon.

'Monsieur Cyr doesn't step and fetch to the call of the shovel,' Anne noted.

In winter, Montreal homeowners either clear their own walks or hire a company or neighborhood kid for the task. Cyr did neither. The afternoon's snowfall was blanketing a sidewalk already two inches deep in packed snow and ice from earlier accumulations.

Anne and I had to watch our footing as we made our way to the steps and up onto the porch. When I pressed the bell, an elaborate chime sounded somewhere deep in the house.

A full minute later, no one had answered.

I rang again.

Nothing but chimes.

'Cyr must be physically impaired and the tightest miser on the planet,' Anne observed, almost losing her footing.

'Maybe he spends his money on other things.'

'There's a happy thought. This peckerhead's on his yacht in Barbados while we're trying not to kill ourselves navigating his front steps.'

'Car's here,' I observed.

Anne turned to look. 'Guess he doesn't drop the bucks on glitzy wheels.'

I was raising my hand for another go at the chimes, when the inner door opened. A man peered out through the aluminum and glass storm door.

The man did not look happy, but his expression was not what alarmed us.

Anne and I started easing back off the porch.

14

The man watching us was short and wiry, with yellowed white hair and an elaborate gray mustache. He wore grease-smeared glasses and gold chains around his neck.

Nothing else. Just glasses and chains.

The man's scowl turned to self-satisfaction at the sight of Anne and me backpedaling unsteadily across his porch. Then the expression went fierce again.

'*Je suis catholique!*'

My boots slithered and angled on the uneven ice.

Cyr grabbed his penis and waggled it at us.

Beside me, Anne grabbed the railing and made a one-eighty toward the steps.

'*Catholique!*' the man shouted.

Catholic?

I stopped. I'd seen Harry use the same ploy. Dressed.

'We're not missionaries, Monsieur Cyr.'

The scowl wavered, then reaffixed itself.

'And I'm not Pee-wee Herman.' The name sounded strange in joual French.

I reached into my purse.

Cyr made a feint at the door. 'Get lost!'

I pulled out one of my cards.

'And don't leave none of your damn pamphlets, *tabarnouche!!'*

'We're not with any church.'

Realizing what was happening, Anne used the handrail to turn herself back toward the house.

Cyr repeated his penile threat, this time in Anne's direction.

'Oh, horror,' Anne said, sotto voce. 'Assault with a dead weapon.'

The grimy lenses froze on my companion. A smile did a slow crawl across the wrinkled lips.

Cyr waggled again.

Anne replied with the old standard. 'What do you think, Tempe? Looks like a penis, only smaller.'

Cyr waggled.

Anne opened her mouth to counter.

I truncated the exchange. 'Monsieur Cyr, I'm part of an investigation concerning property you own and I need to ask some questions about your building.'

Cyr reoriented to me, fingers of one hand still wrapping his merchandise.

'You girls ain't storm trooping to save my damn soul?'

'Sir, we're here to discuss the property you own.'

'You with the city?'

I hesitated. 'Yes.' After all, I was with the province, and Cyr hadn't asked to see identification.

'Some pissant tenant lodge a complaint?'

'Not that I'm aware of.'

'She with the city?' Cyr tipped his head at Anne.

'She's with me.'

'She's a looker, that one.'

'Yes. Sir, we really need to ask you some questions.'

Cyr opened the storm door. Anne and I picked our way forward and stepped inside. When Cyr closed the inner door, the small foyer dimmed. The air felt hot and dry and smelled of smoke and decades of unventilated cooking.

'You're a looker, all right.' Cyr winked up at Anne, who stood a good foot taller than he. He seemed to have forgotten that he was naked.

'You want to throw a blanket on ole Hopalong?' Anne suggested.

'I thought you was Watchtower,' said Cyr in English. 'Those folks ain't got the common sense God gave a parsnip. But they leave you alone if you're naked.' It came out *nek-kid*. 'Or tell 'em you're Catholic.' It came out *cat-lick*.

Anne pointed at Cyr's genitalia.

Cyr led us through leaded glass doors and gestured to a living room on the right.

'Gimme a minute.'

Cyr began climbing a central stairway, placing one foot on a riser, then joining it with the other, one blue-veined hand gripping the banister. His body looked frog-belly white against the dark wood paneling covering the stairwell, and his ascending derriere was hairy black.

Plastic crackled as Anne and I settled on opposite ends of a rose brocade sofa. I unzipped and removed my parka. Anne remained fully clothed.

'I never saw this on *Cagney and Lacey*.'

I grinned in response. My eyes took a visual tour. Opposite the sofa, a La-Z-Boy and a plastic-coated armchair. Stage right, a fireplace, the bricks painted brown. Stage left, a small organ, a large TV with a shabby armchair pulled close to the screen. No plastic.

Everywhere, velvety quiet.

I wondered if the old man had added the vinyl slipcovers, or simply left them in place when the furniture was delivered.

I doubted there was a Mrs. Cyr. There were no figurines, photo-graphs, or souvenirs of holidays past. Ashtrays overflowed. Stacks of *Playboy* and *National Geographic* filled the fireplace enclosure.

I noticed Anne was also checking the place out.

'This could all be yours,' I said in a low voice. 'I think Cyr's in love.'

'I think ole Hopalong is harmless,' Anne whispered back.

'You said you craved life in the fast lane.'

'The little guy *is* a biscuit.'

I wondered if she meant ole Hopalong or Cyr, but didn't ask.

Moments later we heard footfalls.

Cyr reappeared wearing sneakers, a green plaid shirt, and gray wool pants hiked up to his nipples.

'You girls want a drink?'

We both declined.

'Nice nip on a snowy day?'

'No thank you.'

'Speak up if you change your minds.'

Cyr shuffled to the recliner and lowered himself, a tsunami of Old Spice following in his wake.

'You've got a damn fine head of hair, young lady.' Cyr spoke to Anne.

'Thank you,' Anne said.

It was true. By some bizarre fluke of genetics Anne's hair is blonde *and* thick *and* willing to grow as long as she'll let it. Right now she wasn't letting it, but the fact remains, it will. While I try never to hold such perfection against her, there have been times this has proven difficult. Today was not one of them.

'You're a tall one.' Cyr breathed nasally, firing out words between short puffs. 'You married?'

'Yes.'

'Let me know if things bottom out.' Cyr turned to me. 'I'm a sucker for blondes.'

I wanted to get matters on a more official footing.

'Mr. Cyr—'

'How's my English?'

'Excellent.' Though heavily accented, it *was* good.

Cyr cocked his chin at the fireplace.

'Keep it sharp reading.'

145

'Aren't you annoyed by all those naked women breaking up the text?' Anne asked, undermining my efforts at official inquiry.

Cyr made a wheezing noise I took to be a chuckle. 'She's a pistol, that one, yes?'

'Annie Oakley herself.' I rose and handed Cyr my printout.

'Records indicate you own this property.'

Cyr raised the printout to within inches of his face, and read in silence for almost a minute.

'*Oui*.' The inhaled joual *oui*. 'She's mine.'

'You've owned it since 1980?'

'Four-karat pain in the ass.' Cyr thrust the paper back at me.

I took the printout and resumed my seat.

'You purchased the property from Nicolò Cataneo?'

'I did.'

'Do you know why Mr. Cataneo sold it?'

'Didn't ask. Property was listed for sale.'

'Isn't that a standard question when making such a large investment?'

'To Nicolò Cataneo?'

Cyr had a point.

'May I ask what was on the ground floor at the time of your purchase?'

Cyr answered without hesitation.

'Bakery. Le Boulangerie Lugano. Cleared out before I took possession.'

'What replaced the bakery?'

'I subdivided. Put four businesses in the same space. More cost-effective.'

'One of those businesses is a pizza parlor?'

'Le Pizza Paradis Express.'

'How long has that been there?'

'Since 2001.' Cyr puffed air out through his lips. 'Better it should be called "rat hairs and cockroaches by the slice." Damn ethnics wouldn't know hygiene if it punched 'em in the face.' Like a former prime minister, Cyr pronounced the word *et-nicks*. 'But I got no gripe with Matoub. Pays his rent right on time.'

'Said Matoub is the current tenant?' I'd learned that from Claudel on the day of the recovery.

Cyr twisted a finger in his ear and inspected it absently.

'Do you remember any tenants previous to Mr. Matoub?' I went on.

'Course I remember the previous tenants. Remember every damn one of 'em. I look like I'm short-listed for assisted living?'

Expectations often grow from stereotypes, and, though loath to admit it, I'm as guilty as the next. Because Cyr was old, I'd assumed his memory would be less than spot-on. I was quickly revising that view. Though eccentric, ole Hopalong was nobody's fool.

'No, sir—'

'Had more tenants than Blondie's got hairs on that pretty head.'

Cyr gave Anne an eyebrow flash.

Anne tipped her pretty head and Groucho-ed back.

'Before the pizza parlor, place was a nail salon,'

Cyr said to me. 'Vietnamese named Truong had a half dozen little ladies painting nails in there. Didn't make a go, I guess. Only lasted a year or two.'

'And before that?'

'Liked the nail ladies. Looked like little china dolls. Covered their teeth when they laughed.'

'Before the nail salon?'

'Before the nail salon place was a pawnshop. Guy named Ménard.' Cyr pointed one gnarled finger. 'Stéphane. Sébastien. Sylvain. Something like that. Bought and sold junk. Must have been pretty good at it, 'cause he hung in nine years. Eighty-nine to ninety-eight.'

I did some quick math. 'Did the place sit empty awhile between the pawnshop and the nail salon?'

'Couple of months.'

'And before the pawnshop?'

'Let's see. Eighty to eighty-nine there was a luggage store, a butcher shop, and some kind of travel agency. I'd have to go to my records for names and dates.'

'Please do that, sir.'

Cyr's eyes narrowed behind their greasy lenses. 'Would you mind *my* asking why *you're* asking all this, young lady?'

I was expecting the question, was surprised Cyr hadn't posed it sooner. What to tell him? What to hold back?

'Something has been found in the basement of your building which is being investigated.'

If I wanted a reaction, I didn't get one, nor did he ask who was investigating.

'May I ask about access to the pizza parlor basement?' I went on.

'Used to have a stairway leading up to a street-level door. Lost that entrance with the renovation.'

'Is access possible from elsewhere in the building?'

Cyr shook his head. 'Basement hasn't been used in years. The only way down is through a trapdoor in the crapper.' He turned to Anne. 'Pardon my rowdy tongue.'

'A perfectly acceptable historic reference.'

'Eh?'

'Thomas Crapper.'

Blank stares from Cyr and me.

'Inventor of the silent, valveless water-waste preventer.'

Blank.

'Someone else got the patent, but Crapper invented the toilet.'

Where did she come up with this stuff?

Cyr gave a laugh that sounded like one of Crapper's brainchildren. '*Sacrifice*. You are a pip. That husband of yours loses playground privileges, you give old Richard Cyr a call.'

'You're as good as on my speed dial.'

Cyr pushed to his feet using both hands.

'May take me a few minutes to dig through my files. Want some scotch that'll curl your toenails?'

Again, Anne and I declined.

A half hour later Cyr shuffled back clutching a sheet from a spiral tablet.

Anne and I stood.

'How 'bout you ladies stay for dinner? We could order out, maybe knock back some enchiladas and margaritas?'

'That's very kind,' I said. 'But I'm working right now, not socializing.'

'You know where to find me.'

I zipped into my jacket and Cyr led us to the foyer.

At the door, I handed him my card.

'Please phone if you think of anything.'

Cyr held out his paper. 'As I recall, these folks was about as sinister as mushroom soup.'

'*Merci, Monsieur Cyr.*'

'Someone got killed, I had nothing to do with it.' Low and without a trace of humor.

'What makes you think someone was killed?' Since Cyr hadn't mentioned *Le Journal*, I assumed he hadn't seen the article.

'That detective told me what was down in that cellar.'

So Claudel had interviewed Cyr. Damn him. Again, he'd left me out of the loop.

'Is that a fact?'

'Pompous little shitass.'

'Detective Claudel?'

'Little prick acted like I wasn't quite bright. I didn't tell him shit.'

'Tell me, Mr. Cyr. How do you think three people ended up buried in your basement?'

'Something bad went down, it was before my time.'

'How can you be so certain?'

'You ever meet Nicolò Cataneo?' The old man's voice could have sharpened a razor.

I shook my head no.

'Watch yourself.'

15

The storm had its sleeves rolled up, its collar unbuttoned, and its tie hanging loose. Going for a two-footer.

Anne didn't say a word as we picked our way to the car. She watched impassively as I dialed into my voice mail.

No messages.

I tried Mrs. Gallant/Ballant/Talent's number.

No answer.

I checked to see if her call to the lab on Wednesday had been traced, or if the number she'd left Thursday had been tied to a name or address.

Working on it.

'Damn!' Why didn't they at least give me the name on the listing for the number I'd given them? They could compare the earlier call when they finished their trace. Were they just putting me behind any and all requests from detectives?

Ramming the cellular into my purse, I dug a scraper from the backseat, got out, cleared the windows, slid back behind the wheel, and slammed the door.

After starting the engine, I rocked the Mazda by shifting between forward and reverse. At the first hint of traction, I accelerated, and we fishtailed from the curb. White-knuckling, I turtled forward, squinting to see through the blanket of white.

We'd gone two blocks when Anne broke the silence.

'We could try old newspapers, pull up stories on missing girls.'

'English or French?'

'Wouldn't disappearances be reported in both?'

'Not necessarily.' My attention was focused on holding to the tracks created by previous traffic. 'And Montreal has several French papers today, has had godzillions in both languages over the years.'

The car's rear winged left. I steered into the spin and straightened.

'We could start with the English papers.'

'What years? The building went up at the turn of the century.'

The snow was winning out over the wipers. I maxed the defroster.

'The UV fluorescence tells me the bones are probably not older than the building. Beyond that, I can't narrow it.'

'OK. We won't search newspaper archives.'

'Without knowing language and time frame,

we'd be at it all winter. Also, the girls were found here, but may not have gone missing here.'

We crept another block.

'What about that button?' Anne asked.

'What about that button?' I snapped, again coaxing the rear wheels back behind the front.

Loosening her scarf, Anne leaned back in an attitude that suggested I was now to be ignored.

'Sorry.' I was playing Claudel to Anne's Tempe.

The silence lengthened. Clearly, it was going to be up to me to end it.

'I apologize. Driving in blizzards makes me tense. What was your button idea?'

After a few more moments of 'you're being an asshole' muteness, Anne rephrased her suggestion.

'Maybe you could talk to another expert. Try to develop more information.'

Gently pumping the brakes, I brought the car to a stop. Across Sherbrooke, an old woman walked an old dog. Both wore boots. Both had their eyes crimped against the snow.

I looked at Anne.

Maybe I could.

Depressing the gas pedal slowly, I crawled into the intersection and turned left.

Jesus, of course I could. I'd been ignoring the buttons, accepting Claudel's opinion concerning their age. Maybe his McCord source was less than a quiz kid.

Suddenly, I was in a froth to get another opinion.

'Annie, you're a rock star.'

'I shimmer.'

'You up for a couple more stops before dinner?'

'Mush on.'

Anne waited in the car while I dashed up to the lab, made a quick call, and grabbed the buttons. When I rejoined her, she was listening to Zachary Richard on a local French station.

'What's he singing about?'

'Someone named Marjolaine.'

'I think he misses her.'

'So he says.'

'Local talent?'

'Louisiana Cajun. Your part of the world.'

Anne leaned back and closed her eyes. 'That boy can sing about me any ole day.'

It took twice the normal drive time to return to the old quarter. Though it was just past five, night was in full command. Streetlights were on, shops were closing, pedestrians were hurrying, heads bent, purses and packages pressed to their chests.

Leaving boulevard René-Lévesque, I followed rue Berri to its southern end, then turned west and crept along rue de la Commune. The narrow lanes of Vieux-Montréal crisscrossed the hill. To our right lay le Marché Bonsecours, le Pavillon Jacques-Cartier, les Centre de Sciences de Montréal, beyond them the St. Lawrence, its water a black sheen like ebony ice.

'It's beautiful,' Anne said. 'In an arctic tundra sort of way.'

'Cue the caribou.'

In the ice-free months ships belly up to quays jutting from the river's edge, and cyclists, skateboarders, picnickers, and tourists throng the adjacent parklands and promenades. This evening the riverfront was still and dark.

At the head of place d'Youville, I turned onto a small side street, and parked opposite the old customs house. Anne followed as I trudged downhill, threading her way drunkenly in my tracks.

Glancing across the river, my gaze fell on the snow-misted outline of Habitat '67. Built for World Expo, the complex is a pile of geometric cubes that challenges the delicate art of balance. Born more of imagination than architectural pragmatism, Habitat's walkways and patios are a delight in summer, an invitation to hypothermia in winter.

Andrew Ryan lived in Habitat.

A multitude of questions sidetracked my concentration.

Where was Ryan? What was he feeling? What was I feeling? What had he meant? The need to talk. Agreed. But about what? Commitment? Compromise? Conclusion?

I pushed the questions aside. Ryan was working an operation and not thinking or feeling anything having to do with me.

At de la Commune, we entered a futuristic gray stone building, all corners and angles. High up, a banner draped one tower. *ICI NAQUIT MONTRÉAL.* 'Where Montreal Was Born.'

'What is this place?' Anne stomped snow onto the green tile floor.

'Pointe-à-Callière, Montreal's Museum of Archaeology and History.'

A man's face rose from below a circular desk at the far end of the lobby. It was gaunt and pale, and needed a shave.

'Sorry.' Rising, the man pointed to a sign. He was wearing an army surplus overcoat, and holding a boot in one hand. 'The museum is closed.'

'I have an appointment with Dr. Mousseau.'

Surprise. 'Your name, please?'

'Tempe Brennan.'

The man punched a number, spoke a few words, then cradled the receiver.

'Dr. Mousseau is in the crypt. Do you know the way?'

'Yes, thank you.'

Crossing the lobby, I led Anne past a small theater, down a set of iron stairs, and into a long, narrow, softly lit hall, its walls and floor made completely of stone.

'I feel like Alice tunnel-chasing the hatter,' said Anne.

'This point of land was the site of Montreal's first settlement. The exhibit demonstrates how the city has grown and changed over the past three centuries.'

Anne flapped her gloves at a truncated wall rising from the floor. 'The original foundations?'

'No, but old.' I pointed to the far end of the hall. 'That walkway lies directly below place d'Youville, near where we parked. What's now street was once a sewage dump, before that a river.'

'*Tempe?*' The voice rang hollowly off rock and mortar. '*Est-ce toi, Tempe?*'

'*C'est moi.*'

'*Ici.*' Over here.

'Who's Mousseau?' Anne whispered.

'The staff archaeologist.'

'I'll bet the woman's got buttons.'

'More buttons than a political primary.'

Monique Mousseau was working at one of several dozen glass cases lining the corridors spidering off from the main chamber. At her side, a metal cart held a camera, a magnifying glass, a laptop, a loose-leaf binder, and several books.

Seeing us, Mousseau reshelved an object, closed and locked the cabinet, dropped Harry Potter glasses to her chest, and hurried toward us.

'*Bonjour, Tempe. Comment ça va?*'

Mousseau kissed each of my cheeks, then stepped back and beamed up at me, hands still clasping my upper arms.

'You're good, my friend?'

'I'm good,' I replied in English, then introduced Anne.

'A very great pleasure to meet you.' Mousseau cranked Anne's arm as one would a pump handle.

'Likewise.' Anne stepped back, overwhelmed by the tiny cyclone working her limb.

The two women looked like members of different species. Anne was tall and blonde. Mousseau stood four foot eleven and had curly black hair. Anne was swathed in pink angora. The archaeologist wore a khaki boy's shirt, black jeans, and lumberjack boots. An enormous wad of keys dangled from one belt loop.

'Thanks for agreeing to see us so late on a snowy Friday,' I said.

'Is it snowing?' Mousseau released Anne and swiveled to me, bouncing like someone jiggered on speed.

I'd met Monique Mousseau a decade back, soon after my first sortie to Montreal. I'd worked with her often over the years, and understood that her energy did not come from a chemical high. The woman's extraordinary vigor came from love of life and vocation. Give Mousseau a trowel and she'd dig up New England.

'Gangbusters,' I said.

'How wonderful. I've been underground so long today I've lost touch with the outside world. How does it look?'

'Very white.'

Mousseau's laugh echoed louder than a sound someone her size should. 'So. Tell me about these buttons.'

I described the skeletons and the basement.

'Fascinating.' Every utterance owned an exclamation point. 'Let's take a look.'

I dug out and handed her the Ziploc.

Mousseau slid the Harry Potters onto her nose and examined the buttons, turning the baggie over and over in her hands. A full minute passed. Then another.

Mousseau's face took on a puzzled expression.

Anne and I looked at each other.

Mousseau raised round lenses toward me.

'May I remove them?'

'Of course.'

Unzipping the baggie, Mousseau shook the buttons onto her palm, crossed to the cart, and studied each with the magnifying glass. Using a fingertip, she rolled the buttons, observed, righted them, and observed some more. With each move the perplexed expression deepened.

Anne and I exchanged another glance.

Mousseau's examination seemed to go on forever. Then, 'Will you excuse me one moment?'

I nodded.

Mousseau hurried off, leaving two of the three buttons on her cart.

Around us, an eerie silence. Outside, the occasional honking of a horn.

The waiting played hell with my nerves. Why the confusion? What was Mousseau seeing?

A lifetime later the archaeologist returned, picked up the abandoned buttons, and resumed her inspection. Finally, she looked up, eyes enormous behind their lenses.

'Antoinette Legault looked at these?'

'A detective showed them to her at the McCord.'

'Legault felt they were nineteenth century?'

'Yes.'

'She's right.'

My heart plummeted.

Mousseau crossed to me, held up her palm, and manipulated two buttons with the tip of her pen.

'These are sterling silver, produced by a jeweler and watchmaker named R. L. Christie.'

'Where?'

'Edinburgh, Scotland.'

'When?'

'Sometime between 1890 and 1900.'

'You're certain?'

'I was pretty sure I recognized Christie's work, but I looked them up just to be sure.'

I nodded, too deflated to think of something to say.

'But this'—Mousseau flipped the third button with her pen—'is a copy, and a poor copy at that.'

I stared at her blankly.

Mousseau handed me the lens. 'Compare this one,' she indicated one of the Christie buttons, 'to this one.' The pen moved to the forgery.

Under magnification, details of the Christie woman's face were clear. Eyes. Nose. Curls. In contrast, the silhouette on the fake was a featureless outline.

Mousseau flipped the buttons. 'Notice the initials etched beside the eyelet.'

Even to an amateur, the difference was obvious. Christie had engraved his letters with smooth, flowing motions. On the forgery, the S had been gouged as a series of intersecting cuts.

I was perplexed and somewhat taken aback.

But not as taken aback as I would be come Monday morning.

16

My condo is a ground-floor unit in a four-story low-rise wrapping a central courtyard. Two bedrooms. Two baths. Living and dining rooms. Narrow-gauge kitchen. Foyer.

From the long hall running between the front entrance and the dining room, just opposite the kitchen, French doors open onto a patio bordering the central courtyard. From the living room, another set of French doors gives access to a tiny patch of lawn.

In summer, I plant herbs along the edge of the grass. In winter, I watch snow build on the red-wood fence, and on the boughs of the pine within its confines. Five square yards. Acreage *extra-ordinaire* in a downtown flat.

That night, the dark little yard triggered feelings of exposure and vulnerability. No matter that the patrol car Ryan had requested was passing frequently. His makeshift patch on the door was a constant reminder of my unbidden caller and the point of entry he had chosen. What other choices had been available to him? I had to admit that having Anne there was a comfort.

After a quick meal of carry-out Thai, Anne and I cleaned. Anger wormed inside me as I swept and vacuumed.

Again, I fell asleep with my thoughts brawling.

Had some coked-out ragnose violated my refuge? That seemed most likely. Someone desperate for cash for a fix who turned destructive when he didn't find it. No B and E felon would have been that messy. But what about a scare scenario? Some greaseball ordered to divert me from long-hidden mob secrets leaving a 'we know where you live' message. Or was it some malevolent sociopath with an issue specifically related to me?

What did the buttons mean?

Why hadn't Claudel or Charbonneau returned my calls?

Where was Ryan? Why hadn't he phoned?

Did I give a rat's ass? Of course I did.

Saturday morning Anne made a trip to Le Faubourg while I dealt with the glass repairman. By noon a new pane was in, the refrigerator was stocked, and the place was reasonably clean.

For reasons my subconscious chooses not share with me, there are certain items I am incapable of discarding. Prescription medicines. *National Geographics*. American Academy of Forensic Sciences directories. Phone books.

Hey, you never know.

After tomato, cheese, and mayo sandwiches with Anne, I collected every phone book in the house and stacked them beside my computer. Then I pulled out Cyr's list. Where to begin locating tenants? Work backward or forward?

I started with Cyr's earliest renters.

From 1976 until 1982 a luggage shop had occupied the space currently in use by Matoub's pizzeria. The proprietor had been a woman named Sylvie Vasco.

The number on Cyr's list was answered by a college student living in the McGill ghetto. He had no idea what I was talking about.

Neither the computer nor any directory listed a Sylvie, but together they coughed up seven S. Vascos. One number had been disconnected. Two went unanswered. My fourth call got me a lawyer's office. My last three were picked up by women. None was named Sylvie or knew of a Vasco named Sylvie or Sylvia.

Circling the two unanswered numbers, I moved on.

From 1982 until 1987 the pizza parlor space had been occupied by a butcher shop named Boucherie Lehaim. Cyr had written the name Abraham Cohen, then made a notation 'sp?'

The White Pages listed a zillion Cohens in and around Montreal. They too suggested alternate spellings, including Coen, Cohen, Cohn, Kohen, and Kohn.

Great.

The Yellow Pages listed a Boucherie Lehaim in Hampstead.

No one answered the *Boucherie*'s phone.

Back to Cyr's list.

Patrick Ockleman and Ilya Fabian had been Cyr's tenants from 1987 to 1988. The old man had penned the words 'queer' and 'travel' next to their names.

I found nothing in any directory for the name Ockleman.

Ilya Fabian was listed at an Amherst address in the Gay Village. The phone was answered on the first ring.

I introduced myself and asked if I was speaking with Ilya Fabian.

I was.

I asked if the gentleman was the same Ilya Fabian who had operated a travel agency on Ste-Catherine in the late eighties.

'Yes.' Wary.

I asked if Ockleman and his partner had used or visited the basement of the property during their tenancy.

'You said you're with the coroner?' Wariness now edged with distaste.

'Yes, sir.'

'Oh my God. Was someone dead down there? Was there a body in that cellar?'

What to tell him?

'I'm investigating bones found buried below the floor.'

'Oh my Gawd!'

'The material is probably quite old.'

'Oh my Gawd! Like *The Exorcist*. No, no. What was that movie with the little girl? The one where they built the house over the cemetery? Yes! *Poltergeist*.'

'Mr. Fabian—'

'I'm not surprised about that basement. Patrick and I took one look at that wretched, stinking, filthy cesspool and never set foot in it again. Made my skin crawl every time I thought about all that creeping and breeding going on below my feet.' Fabian gave 'creeping' and 'breeding' at least four e's each. 'That basement was alive with vermin.' Four i's to 'alive.' 'And now you're telling me there were corpses down there?'

'Did you ever use the cellar for storage?'

'God forbid.' In my mind I saw a theatrical shudder.

Bit squeamish for a tour operator, I thought.

'Did your agency specialize in any particular world area, Mr. Fabian?'

'Patrick and I arranged gay travel packages to sacred places.' Sniff. 'The era was a bear market for spiritual journeys. We folded in eighteen months.'

'Patrick Ockleman?'

'Yes.'

'Where is Mr. Ockleman now?'

'Dead.'

I waited for Fabian to elaborate. He didn't.

'May I ask how and when your partner died?'

'He was run over by a bus, of all things. A tour bus.' Whiny. 'In Stowe, Vermont, four years ago.

Wheels squashed his head like an overripe—'

'Thank you, Mr. Fabian. If follow-up is needed we'll be back in touch.'

I disconnected. Fabian and Ockleman seemed unlikely candidates for serial killers, but I underlined the number and made a few notes.

The next name listed was S. Ménard. Beside it Cyr had written 'pawnshop' and the dates 1989 to 1998.

I found four pages of Ménards in the Montreal phone book, seventy-eight listed with the initial S.

After forty-two calls I decided Ménard was a job for a detective.

Next.

Phan Loc Truong's nail salon had occupied Cyr's property from 1998 until 1999.

Not as discouraging as Ménard, but the White Pages alone listed 227 Truongs. No Phan Loc. Two P's.

Neither of the P's listed was a Phan Loc. Neither knew a Phan Loc who had operated a nail salon.

I started working my way through the rest of the Truongs. Many spoke little English or French. Many had affiliations to nail salons, but none knew anything about the shop once located in Richard Cyr's building.

I was dialing my twenty-ninth Truong when a voice interrupted me.

'Find anything?'

Anne was standing in the doorway. The room had gone dark without my noticing.

'A lot of ladies willing to do my nails.'

Discouraged, I turned off the computer.

Together Anne and I cooked steaks, potatoes, and asparagus. As we ate, I told her about my fruitless afternoon.

After dinner we watched two Inspector Clouseau movies while Birdie dozed between us. None of us laughed much. We all turned in early.

Around noon on Sunday I tried the Boucherie Lehaim again.

No go.

At two p.m. my call was answered.

'Shalom.' Voice like a baritone oboe.

I introduced myself.

The man said his name was Harry Cohen.

'Is this the same Boucherie Lehaim that was located on Ste-Catherine during the eighties?'

'It is. The shop belonged to my father then.'

'Abraham?'

'Yes. We moved in eighty-seven.'

'May I ask why?'

'We cater to a strictly kosher crowd. This neighborhood seemed a better fit.'

'I know this may sound like an odd question, Mr. Cohen, but can you remember anything about the basement of that building?'

'The cellar was accessed through our shop. We kept nothing there, and I don't remember anyone ever entering or leaving it.'

'Might other tenants have used the basement for storage?'

'We would not have permitted that kind of use of

our space, and the only way down was through a trapdoor in our bathroom. My father kept that door padlocked at all times.'

'Do you know his reason for doing that?'

'My father is extremely conscientious about security.'

'Why is that?'

'He was born Jewish in Ukraine in 1927.'

'Of course.'

I was grasping at straws. What to ask?

'Did you know the tenants that preceded or followed you?'

'No.'

'You were in that location for almost six years. Did anything in particular trigger your move?'

'That neighborhood became'—Cohen hesitated —'unpleasant.'

'Unpleasant?'

'We are Chabad-Lubavitch, Dr. Brennan. Ultra-Orthodox Jews. Even in Montreal we are not always understood.'

I thanked Cohen and disconnected.

A small spruce is rooted in a stone planter at courtyard central. Each December our caretaker strings the scraggly thing with lights. No tasteful Presbyterian-in-Connecticut-Christmas-white for Winston. It's rainbow natty, or nothing at all.

My cat is especially appreciative. Birdie puts in hours curled by the fireplace, eyes shifting from the flames to Winston's miracle in the snow.

Anne and I idled away Sunday afternoon following Birdie's lead. We spent long stretches by the fire, heads pillowed, ankles crossed on the hearth. Over endless cups of coffee and tea, I whined about Claudel and Ryan. Anne whined about Tom. We laughed at our neediness. We were somber over our neediness.

Through the hours of talk and tide of words I came to understand the true depth of Anne's unhappiness. The shopping and banter had been 'game face.' Slap on the greasepaint and raise the curtain. The show must go on. Win one for the team. Do it for the kids. Do it for Tempe.

Anne had always been unflappable. I found her intense sadness deeply disturbing. I prayed it wasn't a permanent sadness.

As we talked, I tried to think of encouraging things to say. Or comforting. Or at least distracting. But everything I came up with sounded clichéd and worn. In the end, I simply tried to show my support. But I feared for my friend.

Mostly, Anne and I shared memories. The night we swam naked at the lake. The party where Anne did a bunny-hop pratfall. The beach trip on which we misplaced two-year-old Stuart. The day I showed up drunk at Katy's recital.

The year I showed up drunk at everything.

Between chats, we'd check our messages.

Many from Tom.

None from Ryan.

Though I dialed every few hours, Mrs. Gallant/ Ballant/Talent persisted in not answering. She was equally unswerving in not phoning again.

Now and then conversation veered to Claudel's

buttons. Monique Mousseau had ventured no opinion as to the age or meaning of the forgery. Anne and I cooked up countless scenarios. None made sense. Birdie offered little input.

Sunday evening I finally persuaded Anne to accept a call from Tom. Later she drank a great deal of wine. Quietly.

17

Anne was still sleeping when I left for the lab Monday morning. I jotted a note asking her to phone when she woke. I didn't expect a call before noon.

Exiting the garage, I was almost blinded. The sky was immaculate, the sun brilliant off the weekend's snow.

Once again the city's armada of plows had prevailed. All roads were clear in Centre-ville. Farther east, most side streets were passable, though bordered by vehicles buried to their roofs. The cars looked like hippos frozen in rivers of milk.

Here and there I passed frustrated commuters, shovels pumping, breath mimicking the exhaust from their half-hidden vehicles.

The lesser streets surrounding the lab were impossible, so I parked in Wilfrid-Derome's pay lot. Crossing to the building's back entrance, I wove between snowbanks and circled a small sidewalk plow, its amber light pulsing in the crystalline air.

My footfalls sounded sharp and crunchy. In the distance, tow trucks jolted residents awake with their brain-piercing two-toned *whrrps*. Out of bed! Move your ass! Move your car!

The day's first surprise ambled in as I was reaching to check my voice mail.

Michel Charbonneau is a large man whose size isn't diminishing any with age. His bull neck, beefy face, and spiky hair give him the look of an electrified football tackle.

Unlike Claudel, who favors designer silks and wools, Charbonneau has taste that runs to polyesters and markdowns. Today he wore a burnt-orange shirt, black pants, and a tie that looked like a street fight at the south end of a color wheel. His jacket was an unfortunate brown and tan plaid.

Dropping into a chair, Charbonneau draped his overcoat across his lap. I noticed an abrasion on his left cheek.

Charbonneau noticed me noticing.

'You should see the other guy.'

He grinned.

I didn't.

'Sorry I didn't get back to you. Claudel and I were last-minute loan-overs to narco, and the bust came down on Friday. I suppose you read about it?'

'No. I haven't gotten to the news.' Anne and I had dispensed with all forms of journalism over the weekend, opting for videos and oldies on the Movie Channel.

'Task force had been backgrounding the thing for months.'

I let him go on.

'Couple of pharmaceutical pinstripes were pipelining pseudo-ephedrine under the counter. Stuff's used in the production of methamphetamines. Product was warehoused in Quebec and Ontario, then trucked all over Canada and the lower forty-eight.'

Charbonneau hunched forward, rested elbows on thighs, and let his hands dangle.

'These bozos were supplying cookers from Halifax to Houston. Dragged forty-three to the bag on Friday, eleven more on Saturday. A lot of lawyers will be banking retainers.'

'Was Andrew Ryan involved in the sting?'

Charbonneau smiled and wagged his head.

'Even if he is SQ, that guy's the stuff of legend.'

To say some rivalry exists between the SQ and the CUM would be like saying the Palestinians have some issues with the Israelis.

'Why is that?' I picked up a pen and began drawing squares inside squares.

'Saturday morning Ryan almost gets his lights blown out, right? That night I see him cool as an ice slick, squiring a number half his age.' Charbonneau leaned back and curved a figure eight in the air with his hands. 'Very little spandex, acres of skin. Ryan's what, forty-five? Forty-seven? Chick's barely out of braces.'

I subdivided a square. Disinterested.

'The señorita's hanging in, so I guess the guy's still got what it takes.'

Ryan and I had been discreet. Beyond discreet. Charbonneau had no way of knowing we'd been lovers.

'Hanging in?' Casual.

Charbonneau shrugged. 'I've seen them together before.'

'Really.'

'Let's see, when was that?' Charbonneau sailed on, unaware of the reaction his words were having. 'August? Yeah. August. It was hotter than a friggin' banana boat.'

A meaty finger pointed in my direction.

'I came by here to ask about a case. You were down South. I had to testify, and the preliminary took place in early August. I spotted Ryan and the prom queen as I was leaving the courthouse. Yep. It was the first week of August.'

The first week of August. Ryan in Charlotte. An urgent phone call. Trouble with his niece. An unscheduled return to Canada.

I tossed the pen and buckled down my face.

'Monsieur Charbonneau, I called Friday because I've found information relevant to the pizza basement skeletons.'

Charbonneau slumped back and thrust out both feet. 'I'm listening.'

'I got a second opinion on the buttons found by Said Matoub.'

Charabonneau looked blank.

'The owner of the pizza parlor.'

'The guy who found the skeletons.'

'Actually that was the plumber, but close enough. Matoub admitted to having pocketed three silver buttons while collecting the bones.'

'Right.'

'Your partner took the buttons to the McCord for evaluation.'

'Lady there said they were old.'

'Antoinette Legault. She was only partially correct.'

'Oh, yeah?'

'According to Monique Mousseau at Pointe-à-Callière, only two of the buttons are nineteenth century in age. The third is a forgery.'

'Meaning what?'

'She didn't know.'

'How old is the fake?'

'She couldn't assign an age, but doubted it was of much antiquity.'

'OK. So maybe the buttons don't go with the bones. That ain't exactly a smoking gun.'

'Have you heard of a man named Nicolò Cataneo?'

'Nick the Knife? Who hasn't?'

'The building housing Matoub's pizzeria currently belongs to Richard Cyr. Cyr purchased the property from Nicolò Cataneo.'

'Yeah? When?'

'In 1980.'

Charbonneau retracted his feet and sat up.

'How long did Cataneo own the place?'

'Ten years.'

Charbonneau frowned.

'Does that mean something, Detective?'

'Might.'

'I know Cataneo was connected.'

Charbonneau began picking at the cuticle on his right thumb.

'What is it you're not telling me?'

Charbonneau looked undecided a moment, then slumped back.

'Things exploded here in the late seventies. The Calabrian and Sicilian factions went at each other big-time. Power struggle ended with the assassination of a boss named Paolo Violi.'

'And?'

'A new boss took over.'

Down the hall I heard one phone ring, then another, and another. LaManche was gathering his troops for the morning meeting.

'And?'

'New boss broke with the Bonannos in New York and established ties between the Montreal family and the Caruana/Cuntrera family.'

'Your point?' I made a show of checking my watch.

'It was a wild ride.' Charbonneau shrugged. 'Bunch of guys got killed.'

'And maybe some girls?'

Charbonneau shrugged again. 'You didn't say anything about trauma to those bones.'

'I didn't find any. You'll speak to your partner?'

Charbonneau tugged an earlobe, rolled his eyes

sideways, then back to me. He hesitated a moment, then seemed to arrive at some private decision.

'Luc's spoken to Cyr.'

'I know.'

'Guess he didn't tell you.'

'No.'

'We probably should have.'

'That would have been nice.'

'The old geezer never mentioned Cataneo.'

'Perhaps that has to do with your partner's social skills.'

'You learn anything else?'

I told him about Cyr's list of tenants, and about the phone calls I'd made.

'So who do you like? The drag queen or the guy in the side curls and hat?'

'Chabad-Lubavitch men don't wear the *payot* or the *streimel*.'

'Just having some fun with you, Doc. You think either could be a player?'

'You're asking my opinion?'

Charbonneau nodded.

'Not likely.' I rose.

Charbonneau lumbered to his feet, flipped his coat over one arm, and dug a paper from a pocket. 'I'm supposed to give you this.'

The note contained the telephone number left by Mrs. Ballant/Gallant/Talent, the name Alban Fisher, and an address in Candiac.

'That a phone trace?'

I nodded.

'Someone giving you a hard time?'

'Besides the freak that broke into my condo?'

'Oh, yeah?' Charbonneau's face tensed.

Mistake.

'It's nothing. Anyway, Ryan's got stepped-up surveillance on my place.'

I glanced at the paper Charbonneau had handed me.

'This woman called claiming to know something about the pizza parlor bones.'

'What?'

'Beats me. She said she knew what had gone on in Cyr's building.'

'You let me know what this lady says as soon as you talk to her. If you don't reach her today I'll take a spin out there. And you let me know if anyone hassles you, Doc. I mean it.'

Again, Charbonneau hesitated, longer this time.

'Don't let Luc get under your skin. He'll come around. And, Doc, he won't stand for you being hassled either. You can believe that.'

I wondered.

Having survived the minefield of Charbonneau's conversation, I should have been prepared for my next surprise. I wasn't.

When I arrived in the conference room, the five pathologists were deep in discussion.

I mumbled an apology for my late arrival. LaManche slid a photocopy across the table.

Three autopsies had already been assigned. Pelletier got two crack addicts found in the Lionel-Groulx Metro. Morin drew a cyclist crushed by a fire truck.

179

I flipped a page and glanced quickly through the last two cases.

A man had been discovered facedown below the staircase at the Mont Royal end of Drummond.

Nom de décédé: Inconnu. Unknown.

A woman had been found dead in her bed.

Nom de décédé: Louise Parent
Date de naissance: 1943/6/18
Info.: Mort suspecte

My eyes dropped to the next line.
My heart dropped like a rock.

18

LaManche's voice grew distant. The room receded around me.

Jamming one hand into the pocket of my lab coat, I yanked out Charbonneau's note.

Sweet Jesus!

The address on the phone trace matched the address on the case file.

As I stared at the name, LaManche spoke it.

'Louise Parent.'

Ballant. Gallant. Talent. Parent.

Bands of tension squeezed my chest.

'Who discovered her?'

Everyone turned, surprised at my vehemence.

Wordlessly, LaManche pulled out the police report.

'Claudia Bastillo. The victim's niece.'

'What happened?'

LaManche read silently for several seconds.

'Madame Bastillo was in the habit of talking

regularly with her mother. The mother, Rose Fisher, and the victim, Louise Parent, were sisters, sharing a residence in Candiac.'

LaManche filtered the pertinent facts.

'Over the weekend, Bastillo's calls went unanswered. Early this morning she went to check and found her aunt dead in bed.'

Dear God! I'd been trying to reach Parent during the same period as her niece!

'Rose Fisher is all right?'

LaManche finished skimming.

'The report says nothing concerning the whereabouts of Madame Fisher. I assume the lady is among the living since she is not on her way here.'

'Cause of death?' I knew it was stupid as soon as I asked it.

LaManche looked up over his glasses.

'That is why Madame Parent is coming to us.'

Questions swirled and tilted.

Foul play or ghastly coincidence? Had Parent been killed, or had she died of natural causes? Was her death related to the calls made to me?

Had the calls been placed by Louise Parent?

Say something? Hold off?

I glanced at the box indicating police jurisdiction.

SQ.

I decided to wait until I'd spoken to the investigating officers. Until LaManche had completed his autopsy.

'Dr. Santangelo, please take the staircase gentleman,' LaManche continued.

Santangelo marked her list.

'I will take Madame Parent when she arrives,' LaManche said.

LaManche jotted 'La' next to Louise Parent's name. Business concluded, everyone rose and filed out.

Back in my office I wasted no time dialing Ryan's number. He answered on the first ring.

'Who'll be working the Louise Parent case?'

'Yes, it is nice to hear your voice. Yes, it is a bit warmer today. Yes, it was a bitch of a weekend,' Ryan said.

'How was your weekend?'

'A bitch.'

'The big sting?'

'All wrapped up.'

'They've cut you loose?'

'Yes.'

I waited. He did not elaborate.

'Who'll be working the Louise Parent case?'

Squad room noises indicated Ryan was a few floors below me.

'Candiac?' I prodded. 'Sixty-year-old woman found dead in her bed this morning. Who'll catch the case?'

'You're looking at him, kid.'

'They didn't give you much downtime.'

'Seems I was missed here.'

'Find anyone who'll pal around with you yet?'

Several years earlier Ryan's partner had died in a plane crash while escorting a prisoner from Georgia to Montreal. Since then Ryan had been working alone, shifting from one special assignment to another.

'The charisma is simply too overpowering.'

'Could be the aftershave.'

'I like flying solo.'

'Why did Parent come in as a *mort suspecte*?'

'My guess would be the death looked suspicious.'

'You're a laugh riot, Ryan.'

'Vic was in good health, not that old. No malfunctioning space heater. No leaking gas or carbon monoxide. No history of depression. No suicide note. Vic's sixty-four-year-old sister's in the wind. Disappeared. Candiac cops thought it called for a look-see by the big boys.'

'LaManche is doing the autopsy this morning.'

I pictured Ryan shoulder-cradling the phone, ankles crossed on his desk.

I pictured Ryan lying in my bed.

I pictured Ryan strutting with a prom queen.

'Vic's niece found the body. Claims it's out of character for her mother to take off without telling her.'

'Rose Fisher.'

I heard paper rustle.

'Bingo.'

'You're trying to locate her?'

'Yes, ma'am.'

'Who's Alban Fisher?'

Hitch of hesitation. 'I can find out. Why?'

'Remember the woman who phoned about the pizza parlor skeletons?'

'Yes.'

'Remember I thought her name was Ballant or Gallant or something like that?'

'Yes.'

'Both calls came from Rose Fisher's house in Candiac.'

'Parent.'

'Sounds similar over a bad connection.'

'The phone account's in the name of Alban Fisher?' Ryan guessed.

'Yes.'

'Alban in the directory?'

'Hold on.'

I laid down the receiver, pulled out the phone book, and thumbed to the F's. Sometimes detecting doesn't take much genius. Alban Fisher was listed at the Candiac address.

'He's there.'

'The niece didn't put anyone else in the picture. Said the women lived alone. I'll give her a call.'

'I'll get back to you when LaManche finishes.'

'Could be a simple heart attack.'

'Could be.'

'Happens all the time.'

'Second leading cause of death.'

'You sure the ticker isn't *numero uno*?'

'No.'

'Anything else breaking?'

'Actually, yes.'

I told him about the forged button. He asked what it meant. I told him I hadn't a clue.

Then I told him about Nicolò Cataneo.

There was a pause, after which Ryan's voice sounded different. Harder, somehow.

'I don't like the sound of that, Tempe. Wiseguys value life about as much as they value used dental floss. You watch your back.'

'I always do.'

'Window fixed?'

'Yes.'

'I missed you this weekend.'

'Did you?'

'Your friend still there?'

'Yes.'

'We'll talk when she's gone.'

'Anne doesn't bite.'

Long pause. Ryan broke it.

'Let me know what LaManche says. Page me if I'm out.'

Before launching into my analysis of the third skeleton, I made a detour to the main autopsy room. Pelletier had the first of the crack twins on table one. LaManche had Louise Parent on table two.

Parent had arrived wearing a granny gown. The long flannel nightie lay spread on the counter. Red roses on pink. Lace-trimmed yoke with tiny pearl buttons.

Flashbulb memory. Gran, shuffling to bed with her Dearfoam slippers and her chamomile tea.

My gaze shifted to the body.

Parent looked small and pitiful on the perforated steel. So alone. So dead.

Stab of sorrow.

I pushed it down.

LaManche gently twisted the dead woman's head. Opened her jaw. Levered one shoulder. The wrinkled back and buttocks were purple with livor.

LaManche pushed a finger into the discolored flesh. The pressure point did not blanch.

LaManche allowed the body to resettle onto its back, then lifted a lifeless hand. Paper-thin peelings were loosening from the underlying dermis.

'Lividity is fixed. Rigor mortis has come and gone. Skin slippage has barely begun.'

As LaManche jotted his observations, my eyes roamed the geography of Parent's corpse.

The woman's muscles were withered, her hair gray, her skin pale to the point of translucence. Her shriveled breasts lay limp on her bony chest. Her belly was going green.

'How long do you think she's been dead?' I asked.

'I see no marbling, no bloating, only minimal putrefaction. The house was warm, but not excessively hot. I will of course check her stomach contents and eye fluids, but at this point I'd say forty-eight to seventy-two hours.'

Another stab of pain.

I had blown this woman off on Wednesday. She had phoned me again on Thursday. LaManche's estimate placed her death on Friday or Saturday.

I noticed a thin white line on her abdomen.

'Looks like she's had some sort of surgery.'

LaManche was already sketching the scar onto a diagram.

My eyes moved to Parent's face.

Both eyes were half open and covered with dark bands.

In death, the eyelid muscles relax, exposing the corneas, and allowing the epithelial tissue to dry. *Tache noir sclerotique*. Normal. But the change gave Parent the macabre look of yesterday's roadkill.

I leaned in and inspected Parent's teeth. Though worn, they were clean and only moderately discolored. The gums showed little swelling or resorption. Dental hygiene had been good.

I was straightening when my eye fell on something lodged between the right lateral incisor and canine. I drew closer.

Something was definitely there.

Digging a handheld lens from a drawer, I returned to the table.

Under magnification, details were clearer.

'Dr. LaManche,' I said. 'Take a look at this.'

19

LaManche circled the table and I handed him the lens. He studied Parent's dentition, then spoke without straightening.

'A feather.'

'Yes,' I agreed.

LaManche used forceps to transfer the feather to a plastic vial. Then he spread Parent's jaws and examined her back teeth.

'I see no others.' Muffled through his mask.

'Luma-Lite?'

'Please.' He turned to the autopsy technician. 'Lisa?'

As I dug the apparatus from a closet, Lisa transferred Parent to a gurney and rolled her next door to the X-ray room. By the time I rejoined them, she had also collected the granny gown and spread it on the X-ray table.

While LaManche and I donned orange-tinted plastic goggles, Lisa hooked up the Luma-Lite, an alternate light source composed of a black box and an enhanced blue fiber-optic cable. With it, we would be able to see trace evidence invisible to the naked eye.

'Ready?' Lisa asked.

LaManche nodded.

Lisa slipped on her goggles and hit the light switch.

In the dark, the pathologist began scanning Parent's nightie. Here and there hairs lit up like tiny white wires. Lisa tweezed and transferred them into a plastic vial.

When we'd finished with the gown, LaManche turned to the corpse. Slowly, the light crept over Parent's feet and legs. It probed the hills and valleys of her pubis, belly, rib cage, and breasts. Lit the hollow at the base of her throat.

Nothing glowed but a few more hairs.

'They look identical to her head hair,' I said.

'Yes,' LaManche agreed.

Parent's hands and fingernails yielded nothing. Her eyes, nostrils, and ears were clean.

Then the beam entered the dark recess of the woman's mouth.

'*Bonjour,*' Lisa said in the darkness.

One molar sparked like phosphorous along the gum line.

'That's not a hair,' I said.

Lisa withdrew the thing with forceps.

Though we worked another thirty minutes in the dark, our efforts produced only two more hairs, both fine and wavy like those of the victim.

When Lisa restored the lights, LaManche and I headed back to the autopsy room. There he opened the molar vial and examined the contents under magnification. It seemed a decade until he spoke.

'It is another feather fragment.'

LaManche and I exchanged glances, identical suspicions crossing our minds.

At that moment, Lisa reappeared with Mrs. Parent. LaManche crossed to the gurney. I followed.

Grasping the tissue firmly, LaManche rolled the woman's upper lip upward. The inner surface appeared normal.

When LaManche pulled Parent's lower lip downward, I could see tiny horizontal lacerations marring the smooth purple flesh. Each corresponded to the position of a lower incisor.

Using thumb and forefinger, the pathologist spread Parent's left eyelids. Then her right. Both eyes showed petechia, pinpoint red dots and blotching of the sclera and conjunctiva.

'Asphyxia,' I said, terrible images filling my thoughts.

I pictured this woman alone in her bed. Her safe place. Her refuge. A silhouette looming in the darkness. Fingers wrapping her throat. Oxygen hunger. Heart-pounding terror.

'Petechial hemorrhage can be caused by many things, Temperance. Its presence indicates little more than capillary rupture.'

'Resulting from sudden increase in vascular congestion in the head,' I said.

'Yes,' LaManche said.

'As in strangulation,' I said.

'Petechiae can occur due to coughing, sneezing, vomiting, straining at stool, laboring in child-birth—'

'I doubt this woman was having a baby.'

LaManche continued speaking as he probed Parent's throat with a gloved finger.

'—foreign object obstruction, gagging, swelling of the airway linings.'

'Are you seeing indications of any of those?'

LaManche raised his eyes to mine.

'I have barely begun my external exam.'

'She could have been smothered.'

'There are no scratches, no broken nails, no signs of violence or of a defensive struggle.' More to himself than to me.

'She could have been smothered in her sleep. With a pillow.' I was verbalizing thoughts as they were forming in my head. 'A pillow would leave no marks. A pillow would explain the feathers in her mouth and the cuts on her lip.'

'Coarse petechiae aren't uncommon in corpses found prone with the head at a level lower than the rest of the body.'

'The lividity on her back and shoulders suggests she died face up.'

LaManche straightened. 'Detective Ryan promised scene photos this afternoon.'

For a moment our gazes locked. Then I lowered my mask and told LaManche the story of Mrs. Parent.

The sad old eyes held mine. Then, 'I appreciate your bringing the victim's involvement with you to my attention. I will take extra care in performing my internal examination.'

The statement was unnecessary. I knew LaManche would be as meticulous with Mrs. Parent as he was with every corpse he studied, prime minister or petty thief. Pierre LaManche refused to acknowledge unexplained death.

By ten-thirty I'd unwrapped the bundled remains recovered from the second depression in the pizza parlor basement.

By eleven-thirty I'd disengaged the bones from their leather shroud, removed their matrix of dirt and adipocere, and arranged them anatomically on the autopsy table.

By three-forty I'd completed my inventory and examination.

The skeleton designated LSJML-38428 was that of a white female, sixty-five to sixty-eight inches in height, who had died between the ages of eighteen and twenty-two. She had poor dental hygiene, no restorations, and a well-healed Colles' fracture of the right radius. Her skeleton showed only minimal postmortem damage, and bore no evidence of trauma occurring at or near the time of her death.

My preliminary conclusions had been correct. Though slightly older, this third girl was disturbingly similar to the other two.

I was jotting a few last notes when I heard the door to the outer office open and close. Seconds later LaManche appeared. His expression told me he hadn't come to report an aneurysm.

'I found excess deoxygenated hemoglobin in the venous blood, indicating cyanosis.'

'Asphyxia.'

'Yes.'

'Anything else?'

'Nothing atypical for a woman in her seventh decade of life.'

'So she may have been smothered.'

'I fear that is a possibility.'

'Any injuries?'

LaManche wagged his head. 'No fractures. No hemorrhage. No scratches or claw marks. No tissue under her nails. Nothing to suggest a struggle.'

'She could have been attacked while sleeping. Or drugged.'

'I will request a full toxicology screen.'

Again, the outer door opened then clicked shut. Booted footsteps crossed the ante-office.

Ryan was doing detective casual that day. Denim shirt, jeans, tan wool blazer with elbow patches.

Ryan and LaManche exchanged '*Bonjour*'s.

Ryan and I exchanged nods.

LaManche filled Ryan in on his findings.

'Time of death?' Ryan asked.

'Did you observe any evidence of a last meal?'

'Saucepan, spoon, and cup in the dish rack. Empty soup can in the trash. Garden vegetable.'

'The stomach contents were completely evacuated. That would have occurred within three hours of consumption of the soup.'

'Niece says the ladies usually ate supper around seven, turned in around nine or ten.'

'If the soup was her supper, and not her lunch.' LaManche raised a finger. 'And keep in mind that gastric physiology is extremely variable. Nervous stress and certain diseases can delay stomach emptying.'

I remembered the shaky voice at the other end of the line. Parent's agitation had been evident even at a distance.

'I'll request a warrant to pull up the phone records.'

'But the state of decomposition suggests death probably occurred on Friday. And now.' LaManche clasped his hands behind his back. 'What have you brought us, Detective?'

Ryan slid a brown envelope from a jacket pocket, and spread color photos on the counter.

One by one, the five-by-sevens took us to Louise Parent's final day.

Exterior views of a blond brick bungalow. Ice-free walks. Front porch, window strung with multicolored lights. Blue wooden door. Wreath with *Joyeuses Fêtes!* on a red velvet ribbon. Front lawn with plastic reindeer.

Enclosed backyard, a child's sled leaning on the far side of chain-link fencing. Ice-free cement stoop. Snow shovel.

Wordlessly, LaManche and I worked our way through the photos.

Close-ups of the rear and front doors showing undamaged knobs and latches.

A kitchen, shot from the right, then the left. Stove, refrigerator, wraparound counter with stainless steel sink. Freestanding butcher block.

Single spoon, mug, and pan in the dish rack.

'Looks very tidy,' I said.

'Not a thing out of place,' Ryan agreed. 'No signs of a break-in. No signs of company.'

'The doors were locked?' LaManche.

'Bastillo thinks so, but can't swear to it.'

'That is the niece?'

Ryan nodded. 'Bastillo got a call on her cellular just as she arrived at her mother's door. She remembers having trouble with her key, but figured it was because she was holding the phone in one hand and trying to unlock the door with the other. She admits that if the door was open, she could have unwittingly locked it then unlocked it again.'

'Did the home have a security system?' LaManche.

Ryan shook his head no, then pulled a snapshot from his pocket and handed it to LaManche. LaManche passed it on to me.

The snapshot showed a plump woman with apricot hair and Jackson Pollock makeup. She looked to be somewhere just north of sixty.

'Rose Fisher?' I asked.

Ryan nodded.

I returned the snapshot and went back to the crime scene photos.

Living room with doilied sofa and love seat. Picture window. Lace curtains. Closed venetian blinds. Birdcage on an ornate metal stand.

I remembered the background twittering during Parent's calls.

'What kind of bird?' I asked dismally.

'Cockatiel.'

Like Katy's. Those were the sounds I'd tried to place over the phone.

'Who's caring for it?'

Ryan gave me an odd look. 'Bastillo.'

'Has the victim's sister turned up?' LaManche asked.

'Rose Fisher. No.'

'What do you make of that?'

'Bastillo says her mother and aunt liked to take off on road trips, but normally gave her a heads-up.'

'So she could feed the bird,' I guessed.

Ryan nodded.

'These ladies, they went by car?' LaManche asked.

'Fisher's. A ninety-four Pontiac Grand Prix.'

'Is that vehicle now missing?'

'It's not at Fisher's house. I've put out an APB. If it's out there, someone should spot the plate.'

'Who's Alban Fisher?' I asked.

'Fisher's husband. Tax accountant. Died in ninety-four. Rose never bothered to change the name on the phone.'

'Can Bastillo think of anyone who might have wanted to harm her mother or aunt?'

'The two had an ongoing beef with some neighbor about parking an SUV too close to their driveway. Bastillo insists we should check this guy out.'

'Bastillo seem credible?' I asked.

'I doubt she'll be recruited by the Berkeley Roundtable, but she comes off sincere enough.' Ryan did a head nod toward LaManche. 'Doc says homicide, I'll start digging on the lady's background.'

LaManche and Ryan became disembodied voices as I continued down the row of photos.

A corridor. A bedroom. A bathroom. A second bedroom, slightly smaller than the first. Maple dresser, nightstand, four-poster.

Dead body.

Louise Parent was a child-sized bulge under pale pink bedding. She lay facing the door, right arm thrown upward, head angled oddly on a rumpled pillow. Her eyes were black and empty crescents. Gray hair trailed limply across her face.

A pink floral quilt lay neatly drawn back across the foot of the bed. A second pillow sat atop the folded quilt. This one had no pillow slip.

'Bastillo moved the body?' I asked of no one in particular.

'Says she found her aunt unconscious and tried to rouse her.'

'Did she touch the pillow?'

'She doesn't remember.'

Beneath the bed, I could see two neatly aligned slippers. On the nightstand, a folded pair of eyeglasses, a mug, and a vial of prescription pills.

'That is the Ambien that was sent to us?' LaManche asked.

'Yes. Labeled for thirty, filled last Wednesday. Eight missing.'

'Do you know the contents of the mug?'

'Water. Bastillo filled it when she couldn't rouse her aunt. Says she got rattled. Didn't know what to do.'

'Had she found it empty?'

'She thinks so. Remember, this Bastillo isn't the sharpest knife in the set.'

'Did you find medications other than those that came in with the body?' LaManche asked.

'Vioxx for arthritis. You've got that. Otherwise, just the standard medicine cabinet collection. Calcium. Aspirin. Preparation H. Half-used tube of Neosporin. Over-the-counter allergy meds.'

'Anything unusual about the mug being in the bedroom?' I asked.

'According to Bastillo, her mother's snoring registers a seven on the Richter. Parent was a light sleeper so when she hit the sack her habit was to knock back a couple of Ambien with herbal tea. If the mug held anything, and she isn't sure that it did, Bastillo says she would have figured it was tea and tossed it.'

'Probably a good idea to get that mug,' I said.

'Yes, ma'am.' Ryan nodded solemnly.

My cheeks flamed. Of course they'd collected the mug.

'We can do amylase testing for Parent's saliva on the pillowcase, but that won't be particularly useful,' said LaManche.

'Old ladies drool,' I said.

'They're known for doing it,' Ryan agreed.

'Did you find any indication when Rose Fisher last slept at home?' LaManche asked.

'Bed was made. Nightdress was on a hook on the bathroom door.' Ryan pointed a finger at me. 'No mug on the nightstand.'

No snappy answer catapulted to mind.

'Bastillo said her mother often retired later than her aunt,' Ryan added.

For a full minute we all studied the photos. Then Ryan spoke to LaManche.

'What's the word, Doc? We got a homicide?'

LaManche straightened, hands still clasped behind his back.

'Continue your investigation, Detective. This is definitely suspicious. I will inform you when I have toxicology results.'

When LaManche had gone Ryan and I spent a few more moments scanning the photos. A leaden feeling was settling in the pit of my stomach.

I broke the silence.

'She was murdered.'

'LaManche isn't totally convinced.' Ryan's voice was resonant with sensibleness.

'Parent made calls claiming to have information about three dead girls. Four days later she's found dead in her bed with feathers in her mouth.'

'Old ladies die.'

'So where's her sister?'

'That's a mystery.'

'What did Parent want to tell me about the bones?'

'That's another mystery.'

Ryan winked.

My stomach tried a flip, landed on its backside.

I took a breath.

'What's up with us, Andy?'

Ryan regarded me with eyes as blue as a Bahamian bay.

A debating team took their seats in my head. Pro: Confront him with Charbonneau's prom queen sighting. Con: Keep it to myself.

Prize to the Con side. Wiser to hold back.

Wisdom also did a pratfall.

'Charbonneau mentioned an odd thing this morning.'

'If you're talking about Saturday's shooting, it was no big deal.'

'He saw you at the courthouse last August.'

'I'm a hardworking boy.' Boyish grin.

'The week you left Charlotte.'

The Bahamian bay showed nary a ripple.

'For a family crisis in Nova Scotia.'

Calm waters.

'You weren't alone.'

'It's not what you think.'

'What *do* I think?'

Ryan's smile wavered, recovered. His fingertips brushed my cheek. Then he scooped the photos from the counter and handed me the envelope. For a long time his eyes held mine. Then, 'I love you, you know.'

I looked at my shoes, emotions cannonballing in my chest.

I closed my eyes.
The anteroom door clicked, clicked again.
When I opened my eyes, Ryan was gone.
Nothing much happened for the next three days.
Then I caught my first break.
And my second.
And my third.

20

For back-to-back days no provincial dead required a look-see by the anthropologist. There were no boxcar decomps. No attic mummies. Not a single Popsicle body part.

Tuesday I tried calling a few more Ménards and Truongs, then caught up on case reports, e-mail, and correspondence. Anne slept until two, then listlessly watched soaps and reruns. She initiated very little conversation even though I'd taken the afternoon off from the lab to be with her. At dinner she drank three quarters of a bottle of Lindemans, professed great fatigue, then dragged off to bed at ten. How tired can one get being up only eight hours and doing nothing? I wondered.

Each December, artisans from across the province gather to sell their wares at the Salon des métiers d'art du Québec. On Wednesday I roused Anne at noon and suggested an arts and crafts Christmas-shopping blitz.

She declined.

I insisted.

Only a few million people were at place Bonaventure. I bought a ceramic bowl for Katy, a carved oak pipe stand for Pete, a lama wool scarf for Harry. Birdie and Boyd, Pete's canine house-mate in Charlotte, got spiffy suede collars. Apricot for the cat. Forest green for the chow.

A display featuring hand-painted silk jerked Ryan to mind. Necktie? No sale.

Anne dragged lethargically from booth to booth, showing the level of interest of a control group lab rat. I bought her fudge, tried on funny hats. Tried on the dog collar. She would attempt to show interest, then lapse into nonresponsiveness, almost as though I were not there. Nothing amused her. She made not a single purchase.

Anne's depression had plunged to depths greater than the Marianas Trench.

All day, I gave her hugs and said soothing things. Otherwise, I had no idea what to do. She was not talkative, which for her is an unnatural state.

At dinner, Anne barely picked at her sushi, focused instead on more alcohol poisoning. Once home, she again pleaded weariness and withdrew to her room.

I'd never seen my friend so down, couldn't judge the seriousness of her condition. I knew something was terribly wrong, but to what extent could I interfere? Maybe the mood slump would just play itself out.

I fell asleep troubled and dreamed of Anne on a dark, empty beach.

My Thursday morning e-mail contained the Carbon 14 results from Arthur Holliday.

I stared at the subject line, fingers frozen over the keyboard.

I'd been anxious for the report. Why the hesitation?

Easy one. I didn't really want confirmation of yet more malignant brutality overtaking innocent young women.

I didn't want to know that lives barely past childhood had again been taken by—what? Some freak with a head full of porn who can find sexual gratification only through physical submission? Some psycho-creep with a video camera who then needs to destroy the evidence? Or mutated macho-scum who view women as disposable items, to be discarded after perverse abuse? They were all out there.

I almost wanted Claudel to be right. I wanted the bones to belong to the past. To daughters laid to rest by grieving families in another era. But I knew better, and I knew I had to face the evidence if I was to help identify the victims.

Deep breath.

I hit the download command, then opened the Acrobat file.

The transmission consisted of five pages: a cover letter, the report of radiocarbon analyses, and three graphs calibrating the individual radiocarbon ages to calendar years.

I looked at the measured and conventional radiocarbon ages, then scrolled through the calibrations curves.

Images flooded my brain.

I printed the report, and headed for the lab.

LaManche was in his office. Since our last meeting either he or his secretary had added a ceramic Christmas tree to the chaos on his desk.

I tapped the door lightly with my knuckles.

LaManche looked up.

'Temperance. Please come in. You have heard the news?'

I gave him a puzzled look.

'The jury found Monsieur Pétit guilty on all counts.'

'When?'

'Yesterday.'

'That was fast.'

'When she called, the crown prosecutor said she was certain your testimony was instrumental.' LaManche looked at the papers in my hand. 'But that is obviously not why you are here.'

'I have the Carbon 14 results.'

'That, too, was fast.' Surprised.

'This lab is very efficient.' I didn't mention the additional fee.

LaManche rose and joined me at the small oval table beside his desk. I spread the printout and we both bent over it.

'Two variables matter,' I began. 'The radioactivity of a known standard, and the radioactivity of our unknown sample. We've already discussed the phenomenon of atmospheric nuclear testing and its effect on Carbon 14 levels, so, to simplify, just assume that the standard value for Carbon 14 in 1950 is one hundred percent. Any value over that represents "bomb," or modern carbon, and indicates a death date more recent than 1950.'

I pointed to the last figure in a column labeled 'Measured Radiocarbon Age.'

'The pMC for LSJML-38428 is 120.5, plus or minus .5.'

'A percent modern carbon significantly higher than one hundred percent.'

'Yes.'

'Meaning this girl died since 1950?'

'Yes.'

'How long after 1950?'

'It's tricky. By the time atmospheric testing was banned in 1963, pMC values had elevated to one hundred ninety percent. But what goes up must come down. So a pMC value of one hundred twenty percent could indicate a point on the upside of the curve, when levels were increasing, or a point on the downside, when levels were dropping.'

'Meaning?'

'Death could have occurred in the late fifties or in the mid to late eighties.'

LaManche's face sagged visibly.

'It gets worse. The present pMC value is around one hundred seven percent.' I pointed to the figures for LSJML-38426 and LSJML-38427.

'*Mon Dieu.*'

'These girls died as long ago as the early fifties, or as recently as the early nineties.'

'You will inform Monsieur Claudel of these results?'

'Oh yes,' I said. With feeling.

LaManche steepled his fingers, tapped them against his lower lip.

'If these girls disappeared during the past twenty years, it is possible they will be in the system. Descriptors must be sent to CPIC.'

LaManche referred to the Canadian Police Information Centre, the equivalent of NCIC, the National Crime Information Center in the United States.

CPIC and NCIC, maintained by the RCMP and the FBI respectively, are computerized indexes of information, including criminal record histories, details on fugitives and stolen properties, and data on missing persons. The databases are available to law enforcement and to other criminal justice agencies twenty-four hours a day, 365 days a year.

As we rose, LaManche laid a hand on my shoulder.

'We must apply ourselves, Temperance. We have to get to the bottom of this.'

'Oh yes,' I repeated with equal feeling.

Thirty seconds later I was in my office talking to Claudel. He was making only minor contribution to the dialogue.

'Not so quickly.'

'Three-eight-four-two-six,' I repeated at the

208

pace a sloth might have employed if speaking French. 'Female.' Pause. 'White.' Pause. 'Age sixteen to eighteen.' Pause. 'Height fifty-eight to sixty-two inches.'

'Dentals?' You could have used Claudel's voice to scythe wheat.

'No restorations. But of course I have post-mortem X-rays.'

'These are the bones from the crate?'

'Yes.'

'Next.'

'Three-eight-four-two-seven. Female. White. Age fifteen to seventeen. Height sixty-four to sixty-seven inches. No dental work.'

'The bones recovered from the first depression?'

'Yes.'

'Go on.'

'Three-eight-four-two-eight. Female, white, age eighteen to twenty-two, sixty-five to sixty-eight inches in height. Healed Colles' fracture of the distal right radius.'

'Meaning?'

'She fractured her right wrist several years before death. Colles' fractures often occur when the hands are thrown out to break a fall.'

'The bones from the second depression?'

'Yes.'

'There are no distinguishing features on any of these individuals?'

'One was quite short. One broke her arm.'

'If these people died in the fifties this is a waste of time.'

'Their families might disagree.'

'Any relatives will be scattered. Or dead.'

'These girls were stripped naked and buried in a basement.'

'If these girls were associated with Cataneo, they were probably hookers.'

Deep breath. The man is a troll.

'Yes, they may have been prostitutes, guilty of the sins of ignorance and need. They may have been runaways, guilty of the sins of poor judgment and bad luck. They may have been random innocents, yanked from their lives and guilty of nothing. Whoever they were, Monsieur Claudel, they deserve more than a forgotten grave in a moldy cellar. We could not help these girls when they died, but perhaps we can prevent others from joining them in the future.'

Now the pause was of Claudel's making.

'You've said the skeletons show no signs of violence.'

I ignored this. 'As we both discovered'—pause to let Claudel know that I knew of his visit—'that building presently belongs to Richard Cyr. As *I* discovered, the previous owner was Nick Cataneo, and Cataneo's period of ownership comes damn close to one of the Carbon 14 ranges.'

The silence that followed was long and hostile.

'You do realize the number of hits this may produce?'

I did.

'I'll reexamine the bones to see if there's anything else I might possibly help you with.'

'That would be appropriate.'

Dial tone.

Over many years I'd come to think of Claudel as obstinate and rigid, rather than outright loathing his attitude. This case was threatening a reversal in that trend.

Quick trip downstairs for coffee.

Quick call to Anne suggesting lunch.

As feared, she begged off.

I told her about the Carbon 14 results.

'You have at it with your bones, Tempe. I'll just hang here.'

'OK, but let me know if you change your mind. I'm flexible.'

When we'd disconnected, I cleared the two worktables and the side counter in the lab, and laid out each of the skeletons. I was examining the Dr. Energy girl's tibia when Marc Bergeron appeared.

To say Bergeron is peculiar-looking is like saying fudge contains a wee bit of sugar. Standing six feet three, perpetually stooped, and weighing in on the downside of one sixty, Bergeron has all the grace and coordination of a wading stork.

Bergeron is Quebec's forensic odontologist. For thirty years he has drilled and filled the living Monday through Thursday, and examined the teeth of the dead each Friday.

We exchanged greetings. I expressed surprise at seeing Bergeron at the lab on a Thursday.

'Family wedding. Tomorrow I must be in Ottawa.'

Bergeron walked to the closet, freed a lab coat

from a hanger, and slipped into it. The coat hung on him like a bedsheet on an unstuffed scarecrow.

'Who are these folks?' Bergeron flapped a hand at the skeletons.

'Found in the basement of a pizzeria.'

'Reflection on the food?'

'I don't think so.'

'Old?'

'All I know is that they died after 1950. Ideas?'

Bergeron adjusted his collar and fluffed his hair. It is extraordinary hair, white and frizzy, starting a mile north of his brows. Against all fashion logic, Bergeron lets it grow long enough to halo wildly around his head.

'Carbon 14 dates suggest death occurred either during the fifties or during the eighties and nineties.'

Bergeron stick-walked to a drawer, withdrew a penlight, picked up the Dr. Energy skull, and peered at the dentition.

'Very poor hygiene. You pulled a molar for sampling?'

I nodded.

'I assume you'd first requested X-rays.'

I unclipped a brown envelope from the LSJML-38426 case file, and slid ten small films onto the light box. Bergeron studied them, the dandelion hair electrified by the fluorescence.

'Besides extensive decay, there's little of note. A slightly rotated upper right canine.' He tapped one X-ray with a bony finger.

'Age estimate?' I asked.

'Sixteen, maybe as old as eighteen.'

'That was my thought.'

Bergeron had shifted to LSJML-38428.

'That one was buried wrapped in a leather shroud.'

'Was this body autopsied?'

'What do you mean?' His question threw me.

'These cuts on her temporal bone. Could they have been made during retraction of the scalp?'

'I hadn't considered that.'

Carrying the skull to the dissecting scope, I viewed the marks under low, then higher-power magnification. Bergeron continued along his train of thought.

'Perhaps these are old biological specimens or teaching skeletons. Perhaps someone kept them as curiosities, later lost interest, or decided possession was risky.'

I had considered that. It was not an uncommon scenario.

'There are no drilled holes, no wire fragments, no signs of chemical treatment or mechanical modification. The bones were not assembled for display purposes.'

Magnified, the temporal marks looked like broad V-shaped valleys. Some ran parallel to the ear opening, others were scattered at angles around it. Micro-chipping along the edges suggested the damage had occurred when the bone was dry and defleshed.

'These marks weren't made by a scalpel. They're too wide in cross section. Also, the alignment is more random than I'd expect as a result of an autopsy. I think they're postmortem artifacts.'

An ill-formed thought tapped gently on a mental shoulder.

Why the V-shape? That's not typical of abrasion damage.

'This one had considerably fewer dental problems.'

I looked up. Bergeron was at the second worktable, examining the jaw fragments belonging to LSJML-38427.

'The apicals are in the file.' I pointed at a yellow folder beside the bones.

Bergeron spread the dental X-rays on the light box.

'Could be a bit younger, I'd say fifteen to seventeen.'

'Do you see anything at all distinctive?'

Bergeron shook his head. The frizz wobbled.

Replacing the mandibular fragments of 38427, Bergeron moved back to 38428, picked up the skull, and aimed his penlight.

'There was something on this one . . .' Bergeron's voice trailed off.

'What?'

Bergeron swapped the skull for the jaw, and aimed his beam at the lower dentition.

'Yes.'

Abandoning the scope, I joined him.

'What?'

'This should clarify the uncertainty on your dates.'

Bergeron handed me the skull and penlight.

21

'Tip the cranium, then move the light back and forth over the molars.'

I did as Bergeron instructed.

'Do you see a glossiness in the folds of the enamel?'

I didn't.

'Angle the beam.'

Bergeron was right. The shine was subtle but present, way down in the grooves.

'What is it?'

'If I'm not mistaken, the molars have been treated with a pit and fissure sealant.'

When I looked up, Bergeron was gangling his way to the scope. The man was definitely not poetry in motion.

'Sealant is a thin coating of plastic resin that's applied to the chewing surface of a bicuspid or molar. It's painted on as a liquid, and in roughly a minute it hardens to form a protective shield.'

'What's the purpose?'

'To prevent occlusal caries. Tooth decay.'

Bergeron slipped the lower jaw of LSJML-38428 under the lens, peered through the eyepieces, and adjusted focus.

'*Oui, madame*. That's a sealant.'

Hope did a little moth-flutter in my chest.

'When did these sealants come into use?'

'The first commercially available sealants were marketed to dentists in the early 1970s. They've been in widespread use since the eighties.' Bergeron spoke without looking up.

The moth exploded into a hummingbird.

The girl in the leather shroud couldn't have died in the fifties! By elimination, that jumped her to the late eighties!

I tried to keep my voice calm.

'How common are these sealants?'

'Unfortunately for forensic purposes, very. Most pediatric dentists recommend application once the permanent molars erupt. School-based programs have been under way in a majority of American states for at least twenty years. Canada's a bit behind in that, but sealants have been very popular here since the mid-eighties.'

Bergeron clicked off the fiber-optic light.

'Didn't help this young lady much.' He thrust his chin at Dr. Energy's girl. 'She's got more decay than that one over there.'

'So she was seeing a dentist at one point, then quit caring for her teeth.'

'Typical pattern for runaways. The parents

provide dental care while they're growing up, then the kids hit the streets, their diets and hygiene go to hell, and their teeth suffer.'

'How old was she?'

Bergeron returned to the light table and examined the dental X-rays for 38428.

'A little older than the others. I'd give her eighteen to twenty-one.'

Again, Bergeron's estimate was consistent with what I'd seen in the bones.

'Any evidence of sealant on the other two?'

Bergeron reexamined the teeth of 38426 and 38427. Neither had been treated.

'A pity there are no restorations on any of them. Let me know if there's anything else I can help you with.'

'You've helped plenty.'

I flew to my office and dialed Claudel.

He and Charbonneau were tied up in an interview and couldn't be disturbed. I left a message requesting they call me as quickly as possible.

Returning to my lab, I picked up a fractured segment of jaw that Bergeron had left beside the scope. As I was returning it to LSJML-38427, I noticed a tiny nick on the right mandibular condyle.

Back to the scope.

By angling the fiber-optic light across the bone, I found two more nicks on the ascending ramus, and a minuscule groove at the mandibular angle.

I checked the left portion of the mandible.

No nicks or grooves.

The skull.

No nicks or grooves.

One by one I examined the isolated shards broken from the right cheek and temporal bones.

The light picked out six superficial grooves, each roughly five millimeters in length, grouped in three sets of two.

Another shoulder tap from my hindbrain.

I increased the magnification.

The nicks and grooves, though clearly not natural, looked different from those on 38428. Though V-shaped, these were much narrower in cross section and cleaner at the edges.

Like marks left by a scalpel. In fresh bone.

I leaned back, thinking through what that could mean.

In my mind I reconstructed the skull fragments and articulated the jaw.

The cuts circled the ear opening.

What the hell had gone on?

Coincidence? Something more sinister?

I was about to reexamine the skull and mandible of Dr. Energy's girl when I spotted Charbonneau through the window over the sink. Gesturing him to my office, I stripped off my gloves, washed, and crossed the hall.

Charbonneau had assumed his usual legs-splayed, shoulder-slumped position in the chair facing my desk. Today's jacket was cranberry and as glossy as the dental sealant.

'Monsieur Claudel is meeting with the Nobel committee this morning?'

Charbonneau dipped his chin, rolled his eyes up, and raised both palms.

'What? I'm not cool enough? Luc really is busy.'

'Being fitted for another Ermenegildo Zegna?'

Charbonneau looked at me as though I'd spoken Etruscan.

'They make suits,' I said.

Charbonneau suppressed a grin. 'He's going through Cyr's tenant list.'

'Really?' My brows shot up in surprise.

'Authier phoned.'

LaManche must have spoken with the chief coroner, who then ordered Claudel to get serious about the pizza basement case.

'Not a lot of jolliness in Authier's message?'

'Luc is viewing the comments as suggested guidelines.'

I explained Bergeron's discovery.

'Bergeron's convinced it's this sealant stuff?'

'Absolutely. I believe that's what journalists call independent corroboration.'

'So at least one of the three died in the seventies or later.'

'Carbon 14 analysis bracketed this girl's death in the fifties or in the eighties.'

'Guess we're talking the eighties.'

'Guess we are.'

'The kid with the broken wrist?'

I nodded. 'The skeleton wrapped in the leather shroud.'

'Son of a bitch.' Charbonneau pushed to his feet. 'I'll get her stats into the system right away.'

Charbonneau had barely cleared the door when the phone rang. It was Art Holliday, calling from Florida.

'You got the Carbon 14 report?'

'Yes, thank you. I appreciate your turning it around so quickly.'

'We aim to please. Listen, I may have something else for you.'

I'd forgotten Holliday's offer to perform additional testing.

'For prosecutorial purposes, strontium isotope analysis is still experimental. But we have applied the technique to forensic questions. In one case, we nailed the point of origin of six white-tail deer. Used the antlers. Course, we knew the animals had to have come from one of two states, so we had isotopically distinct geographic localities from which to measure control groups. That made the job easier.'

Over the years I've learned that it is impossible to hurry Art Holliday. You go with the flow, half listen to the buildup, and focus on the conclusions.

'We're getting good results looking at immigration and settlement patterns with ancient populations.'

That rang an archaeological bell.

'Yours is the group analyzing the pueblo materials from Arizona?'

'Thirteenth- and fourteenth-century burials. Construction and occupation of some of the grander pueblos spanned many generations. Hundreds of people occupied them, probably a mixture of longtime residents and immigrants from outside. We're trying to sort that out.'

'Strontium isotope analysis can separate newcomers from lifelong inhabitants of a place?'

'Yep.'

The hummingbird revved up again.

'The technique can tell you where someone lived?'

'If you have reference samples. In some circumstances, if a subject moved from one geographic region to another, Sr analysis can tell where they were born, and where they spent the last six to ten years of their life.'

The hummingbird gunned it to red-line.

'Drop back and start from the beginning.' I grabbed pen and paper. 'Using no word having more than three syllables.'

'There are four stable isotopes of strontium, and one isotope, 87Sr is produced by the radioactive decay of 87Rb. The half-life's forty-eight point eight billion years.'

'Much slower than Carbon 14.'

'Much slower than my old dog Spud.'

Spud?

'The geology of North America shows tremendous age variation,' Art sailed on, oblivious to my confusion over the dog reference. 'For example, the age of the crust varies from less than a million years in Hawaii, to just over four billion years in parts of the Northwest Territories of Canada.'

'Resulting in differences in Sr values in the soil and rock of different regions.'

'Yes. But such differences are also due to variations in bedrock composition.'

'When you use the term value, do you mean the ratio of the unstable strontium to its stable counterpart?'

'Exactly. It's the ratio of the strontium 87 isotope to the strontium 86 isotope that's important, not the absolute level of each.'

I let him go on.

'For example, basaltic lavas, limestone, and marble all have very low Sr ratios, whereas those of sandstone, shale, and granite are commonly high. Clay minerals have some of the highest.'

'So differences in geologic age and/or bedrock composition produce variations in Sr isotope ratios in different geographic regions.'

'Precisely. But one final thing to keep in mind is that because ratios are so messy to remember, with all those decimals, we usually compare a measured Sr ratio to the average Sr ratio of the whole Earth. If the measured ratio is greater than this, it yields a positive value. If it's less than this, it gives you a negative value.'

'What does this have to do with establishing where someone was born?'

'Strontium is an alkaline-earth metal, chemically similar to calcium.'

I made the link. 'Strontium is absorbed by plants from the soil and water. Herbivores eat the plants, and on up the food chain.'

'You are what you eat.'

'So the Sr isotope composition of an organism's

bones and teeth will reflect the Sr composition of its diet during the period those body parts were forming.'

'You've got it.'

'My grandmother used to worry about strontium in her food.'

'Your granny wasn't alone. The biological processing of strontium was studied extensively in the 1950s because of the potential for radioactive 90Sr ingestion due to aboveground testing of nuclear weapons.'

A light was going on.

'You're saying strontium is incorporated into a person's bones and teeth, much like calcium.'

'Right.'

'And calcium in the human skeleton is replaced on roughly a six-year cycle.'

'Yep.'

'So, like skeletal Ca, skeletal Sr reflects an individual's diet over the last six years of life.'

'Six to ten,' Art said.

'But Ca levels don't change in tooth enamel as they do in bone. Once laid down, enamel is stable.'

'And the same is true of Sr. So dental enamel continues to reflect the average dietary Sr isotope composition ingested when the tooth was formed.'

'So if someone relocated from the place in which she was living when her teeth were forming, that individual's dental and skeletal Sr levels would differ. If she stayed put, those levels would remain similar.'

'Precisely. Enamel values suggest place of birth

and early childhood. Bone values suggest place of residence during the last years of life.'

A thought stopped me in midscribble.

'Doesn't our food come through national and international networks these days?'

'We drink local water, at least most of the time.'

'True. Tell me what you did with my specimens.'

'After removing all extraneous materials, we ground them. Then we separated out the Sr by ion-exchange chromatography, analyzed the purified Sr using thermal ionization mass spectrometry, and collected the Sr ratios by multicollector dynamic analys—'

'Art.'

'Yes?'

'What did you find?'

'One of your three saw a bit of the world.'

22

'Go on.'

'First, let's talk teeth. Two of your individuals overlap in their dental Sr values.'

'Which two?'

Paper rustling.

'Let's see . . . 38426 and 38427. For them I'd expect a childhood diet with an average Sr value of plus ninety to plus one hundred five. But 38428 is statistically distinct. The Sr isotope composition of that individual's dental sample suggests a childhood diet with an average Sr value of plus fifty to plus sixty.'

'Meaning 38428 was not born in the same region as the other two?'

'Correct.'

'Can you tell where she's from?'

'That's where it gets interesting. Last year we had a case of jumbled remains from a barrel found in some hophead's basement in Detroit. Police knew the victims were business associates of the drug dealer who owned the house, but wanted the bones sorted into individuals. None had dental work, all were black, in their mid-twenties, and about the same size. One of the three was born in north-central California, one was from Kansas, and the other was local Michigan talent.

'We didn't have control groups from the three areas in question, so we had to infer the isotope composition of the dietary Sr from the bedrock geology in each region, then work back to the various bones in the barrel. You still there?'

'I'm here.'

'Someone who spent their childhood in north-central California should have Sr values in the range of plus thirty to plus sixty.' Rustle. 'That's exactly where 38428 falls.'

For a moment I was taken aback.

'Meaning my girl's from California?'

'Meaning she could be. If you have no other ideas, it's as good a starting point as any. Of course, she could be from another region with similar bedrock geology.'

'And my other unknowns?'

'A couple of years back we had a case involving commingled remains recovered from a common grave in Vietnam. The army had IDs for the two soldiers, but wanted the bones separated into individuals. One soldier had grown up in northeastern Vermont. The other was from Utah.'

Art gave me no chance to interrupt.

'A study of the Sr isotope composition of the

groundwater near St. Johnsbury in Vermont suggested values in the range of plus eighty-four to plus ninety-four. The teeth from one of the soldiers produced Sr values smack-dab in that range.'

'The Vermonter.'

'Yes. The teeth of 38426 and 38427 produced identical values.'

'Meaning these girls were from Vermont?'

'Not so fast. The same rock formations extend across the border into Quebec. What I'm suggesting is that the Sr values of your other two girls are consistent with what I'd expect from people born in the region where the remains were found.'

'The Montreal area.'

'Yes. Now let's talk bones. For 38426 and 38427, the Sr values in their teeth are similar to the Sr values in their bones.'

'Suggesting they didn't stray too far from home.'

'Right. But 38428 is a different story.'

I waited.

'Her skeletal Sr values are higher than her dental Sr values. What's more, her skeletal Sr values are very similar to the skeletal Sr values for 38426 and 38427.'

'The Quebec stay-at-homes.'

'Yes.'

I took several moments to digest that.

'You're suggesting 38428 was raised in one place, but spent the last few years of her life in another.'

'Looks that way.'

'That she may have grown up in north-central California.'

'Or in an isotopically similar region.'

'But later she may have moved to Quebec or Vermont.'

'Or to an isotopically similar region.'

I couldn't wait to phone Charbonneau.

'This is terrific, Art.'

'We aim to please. Let me know when you get these ladies ID'd.'

I was so excited I misdialed and had to punch the numbers a second time.

Charbonneau was out. So was Claudel.

Were they ever in?

I left a verbal message with the receptionist, then a numeric one on Charbonneau's pager.

Back to my lab.

Anticipating what I might find, I carried the Dr. Energy girl's skull and jaw to the scope.

There they were. Five tiny grooves, two above and three posterior to the auditory canal on the right temporal bone. Magnified, the cuts looked like those on 38427.

I could see nothing on the jaw or on any of the other cranial bones.

Sweet Jesus. What had been done to these girls?

Anne phoned at one-fifteen, her voice sounding listless and flat. After apologizing for being lousy company all week, she told me she was thinking of leaving. Said she didn't want to impose on my hospitality any longer.

I assured her that she was not imposing. I also assured her that I was enjoying her company tremendously. Given her current mood, the latter was a stretch, but I encouraged her to think in terms of staying until she decided on a better place to go.

Charbonneau phoned at one-forty.

'*Cibole!* It's colder than a witch's tit out there.'

Not all of Charbonneau's expressions were Texan in origin.

'You ran the CPIC search?'

'I did.'

I heard cellophane.

'Since we don't know if the two without dental sealant died before or after the one with the sealant, I ran those cases two ways. First I searched disappearances reported in the nineties.'

'Makes sense, given the Carbon 14.'

'Some came close, but no cigars.'

Charbonneau sounded like he was eating something involving caramel or taffy.

'Then I left the date of disappearance open. Got what I expected, given no dentals, no details, and no dates.'

'Lots of hits?'

'List from here to East Bumfuck.'

'What about 38428?'

'Pulled up everything back to 1980. Broken wrist cut the numbers down. Again, a few came close, but no matches. Sure would help to know where the kid lived.'

'How about north-central California?'

'Yeah. Like that.'

'I'm serious.'

All crinkling and chewing stopped.

'You're kiddin'.'

Simplifying the biochemistry and geophysics, I told Charbonneau what I'd learned from Art Holliday.

'Luc's gonna shit his Fruit of the Looms.'

'You've got to send her descriptors south of the border.'

'NCIC. Done. I'll also roll them by the Vermont and California State Police.'

'It's a long shot.'

'Can't hurt anything.'

'Except your partner's shorts.'

Charbonneau laughed. 'I'll tell him you said that.'

'There's something else.'

'Make my day.'

I described the nicks and grooves.

'And you think the marks were made by a scalpel?'

'Or an extremely sharp, fine-edged blade.'

'You're talking all three skeletons?'

'Yes. Though the marks on the shrouded burial differ from those on the other two.'

'Differ how?'

'They're cruder. And there's more chipping along the edges.'

'Meaning they were made by a different tool?'

'Maybe. Or maybe they were made after the bone had dried out. Or maybe they're not the result of cutting at all. Maybe they're postmortem artifacts mimicking cut marks.'

'Scratches caused by dragging or rolling or something?'

'Maybe.'

'You don't sound convinced.'

'There seems to be a pattern.' I stopped, picturing the skulls and jaws in my mind. 'The marks circle the right ear opening.'

'On which skeleton?'

'On all three.'

'And nothing anywhere else?'

'No.'

'Holy crap. You think someone was slicing off ears?'

The thought had occurred to me.

'I don't know.'

After telling LaManche what I'd learned from Art Holliday, I spent the rest of the afternoon with my pizza basement girls. That's how I'd come to think of them. My girls. My lost girls.

I reexamined every bone, bone fragment, and tooth. I studied the dental and skeletal X-rays. I rescreened the soil. I pored over the buttons.

When at last I sat back, the windows were dark and the halls were quiet. The clock said five-twenty.

I'd learned not one damn additional thing.

I closed my eyes.

I felt sadness over my failure to give names to these girls. Anger over my failure to satisfy Claudel. Frustration over my failure to understand the buttons. Guilt over my failure to spot the cut marks before Bergeron pointed them out.

How could I have missed those marks? Yes, I'd been interrupted many times. Yes, I'd been working on different aspects of the case. Yes, the marks were almost invisible. Yes, at least one skull was fragmented. But how could something that important have escaped my attention?

Failure, failure everywhere and not a drop to drink.

Failure with Anne.

Failure with Ryan.

'Ryan,' I snorted.

'Yes?'

My eyes flew open.

Ryan was standing in the doorway, coat finger-hooked over one shoulder. He was regarding me with an expression I couldn't interpret.

Ryan raised his free hand, palm out.

'I know. What are *you* doing here? Right?'

I started to speak. Ryan cut me off.

'I work downstairs.' Ryan grinned. 'I'm a cop.'

I sat forward and tucked my hair behind my ears.

'Do you have news on Louise Parent?'

'No.'

'Have you found Rose Fisher?'

The grin evaporated. 'No. It doesn't look good.'

'You think she's dead?'

'She's sixty-four. She's been missing almost a week.'

'What kind of mutant murders elderly women?'

Ryan took my question as rhetorical. 'Is the extra surveillance still on your place?'

'Yes.' If you came to visit you'd know. 'Are you suggesting I'm elderly?'

'I want you to keep your eyes open, Tempe.'

'They're rarely closed these days, Andy.'

Ryan ignored that.

'I'm going to swing by Fisher's house. Thought you might like to ride along.'

I did.

I waved a hand in the direction of the skeletons. 'I'm pretty busy.'

'They're not going anywhere.' Another boyish grin.

Again the debate. Confrontation? Avoidance?

I decided on vague. Give Ryan the opening. Let him tackle or dodge.

'Do you ever ask yourself questions, Ryan?'

'Sure. What ever happened to Alice Cooper?'

'Important questions?'

'What *was* Alice Cooper?'

'I'm serious.'

'I'm serious, too.' Ryan's voice was calm and quiet. 'Do you want to ride along?'

The hell with relationships. The hell with Ryan. Cauterize the pain. Do your job.

Stripping off my lab coat, I jammed my keys into my purse and jerked my coat from its hook.

'Let's go.'

Ryan and I crawled through rush-hour traffic,

the atmosphere in the car as relaxed as a coiled snake. Conversation was nonexistent.

Familiar images galloped through my brain. Ryan at the beach. Ryan and me in Guatemala. Ryan in my bed.

Ryan and his prom queen.

At one point Ryan's hand brushed my knee. A missile rocketed straight to my libido.

Closing my eyes, I made a conscious effort to take control. Deep breathing.

By the time we arrived in Candiac, my neck muscles were taut as guitar strings.

Blinds were drawn across every window in Rose Fisher's house. Soft yellow light oozed through one set.

'Hm.' Ryan slid to the curb and killed the engine.

'What?'

'I don't remember leaving a light on.'

'Is the place still sealed?'

'No point. Crime scene finished processing days ago. Took the tape down.' Ryan opened the driver's side door. 'Stay here.'

I gave Ryan a few seconds, then followed him up the front walk and onto the porch. The wreath still wished everyone *Joyeuses Fêtes!*

Ryan rang the bell.

Inside, chimes sounded faintly.

Wind flapped my scarf.

Ryan rang again.

Seconds ticked by. Another gust. One tear cut loose. I pulled my hat lower.

Ryan was sorting through keys when a light went on in the living room. Locks rattled, then the knob turned. The door opened a crack, and a face peered out.

It was the last face I expected to see.

23

'Who are you?' The words sounded wet and slushy, like someone speaking with a mouth full of peas.

Ryan held out his badge.

'Polishe?' Fearful.

'May we come in, Mrs. Fisher?'

'Where'sh Louishe? Where'sh my shishter?'

Dear God. She didn't know.

'We'd like to talk to you about that.' Ryan's voice was calm and reassuring.

The crack widened. I saw a pumpkin face, oddly concave around the mouth.

'Wait.'

The door closed.

The raw wind whipped my collar and scarf. I lowered my head, stomped my feet.

I felt leaden. Ryan and I would be the bearers of bad news. Our words would change Rose Fisher's life forever. I hated what I was about to see. It was not ordinarily part of my job, and I was thankful for that, but when involved, I hated it.

Minutes later the door reopened, and Ryan and I stepped into the house. The warmth made the skin on my face feel soft and loose.

Rose Fisher was not plump. She was enormous. A bad dye job and perm gave her swollen face a clownish look. An overabundance of cosmetics didn't help.

'Where is my sister?' The fear lingered, but the slush was gone. Though wrinkled and coated with lipstick, Fisher's mouth now looked normal.

The leaden feeling intensified. Sweet Jesus. The woman had inserted dentures and applied makeup. For strangers.

Ryan laid a hand on Fisher's shoulder. 'May we sit down?'

A pudgy hand flew to the fire engine mouth. 'Oh my God. Something's happened to Louise.' Mascaraed eyes darted from Ryan to me. 'You've come to tell me something's happened to Louise. Where is she?'

Ryan guided Fisher to the living room sofa and sat beside her. From the corner, a gray and yellow cockatiel with bright orange cheeks chirped, then whistled six notes of 'Edelweiss.'

Positioning myself to Fisher's left, I took one chubby hand in mine.

Ryan tipped his chin, indicating I should take the lead.

The cockatiel said, *'Bonjour.'* Repeated itself. Chirped.

'Mrs. Fisher, we do have bad news.'

Fisher's eyes closed. Her fingers tightened into a death grip.

'I'm so sorry, but your sister has died.'

Chirp. Chirp. Chirp.

Fisher began throwing her head back and forth, eyes squeezed so tightly they disappeared into the fat surrounding the orbits. With each oscillation a high, thin note rose from her throat, then choked off behind the carefully placed dentures.

I placed an arm around the woman's shoulders.

'I'm so sorry,' I repeated.

Fisher continued her keening, mascara and eye shadow flowing to mix with the orange-rose blusher.

The cockatiel went silent.

Ryan patted Fisher's right shoulder. His eyes met mine. They mirrored the sadness I was feeling.

The cockatiel regarded its mistress, crown raised, head frozen at a forty-degree angle.

Seconds ticked by on a sideboard clock. The cockatiel tried a few notes of 'Alouette,' gave up.

Fisher wailed and bobbed.

One minute. Two.

Ryan slipped from the room, returned with a box of tissues.

Three.

Gradually, the terrible sobbing diminished.

'*I love you.*' Chirp. '*Je t'aime.*'

The porcine eyes opened and Fisher's head swiveled toward the bird.

'I love you, too, 'Tit Ange.'

Little Angel cocked his head, but said nothing.

'My sister adores that silly bird.' Almost inaudible. 'Adored.'

Ryan offered tissues. Fisher took several, and turned to me, her face a rainbow popsicle left to melt in the mud.

'Who are you?'

'Dr. Temperance Brennan. I work with the coroner.'

Beneath the clown makeup, Fisher's face went white.

'It was some kind of allergic reaction, right?'

'Cause of death isn't totally clear at this point.'

Fisher wiped at the chaos on her face.

'I should never have left Louise alone when she was feeling poorly.'

Fisher slumped back.

'Your sister was unwell?' Ryan asked gently.

'Allergies. Wheezy, itchy eyes, runny nose.' The massive body collapsed into itself. 'I never dreamed—'

Fisher's chest heaved with another involuntary spasm. I plucked tissues and handed them to her.

'I know this is terribly difficult,' I said in the most soothing voice I could muster. 'And I'm so sorry to have to ask you these questions. But a great many people have been trying to find you this week. Would you mind telling Detective Ryan and me where you've been?'

'Louise and I signed up for a ceramics workshop in Pointe-aux-Pics. We thought it would be fun to learn how to make pottery—'

Heave. Heave.

'—stay in a B and B, do our Christmas shopping in the Charlevoix region.'

'Your sister didn't feel up to going?'

When Fisher nodded an upper chin plunged into the fat of its lower counterpart.

'Louise insisted she'd be fine. Said if she needed anything, she'd call Claudia. That's my daughter.' Fisher's throat seemed to clench. 'Oh God. Does Claudia know?'

'Yes, ma'am. Claudia's been very worried about you.'

'We should have told her. *I* should have told her. When Louise decided to stay behind, it didn't seem necessary. Claudia's always fussing at me about driving during the winter. Treats me like I'm a doddering old fool. Wants me to stay home all the time.'

'When did you get back from Charlevoix?' Ryan asked.

'Not long before you arrived. I thought Louise was over to the church. They do bingo on Thursday nights. I was tired from the drive, so I was about to leave her a note and turn in.'

Fisher was wadding and unwadding the saturated tissue.

'Louise's bed is unmade. That's not like her.'

The corpulent bosom heaved again.

'Let me get you some water.'

As I filled a glass from the kitchen tap, Ryan and Fisher talked on in the living room. Now and then the cockatiel chirped or sang a fragment of song.

Before returning, I made a quick pass by Louise Parent's room. The scene differed little from the SIJ photos. The bed was now stripped, exposing a stain on the mattress where Parent's bladder had voided at death. A single pillow lay by the headboard.

I returned to the living room and handed Fisher the water.

Ryan caught my eye and gave a subtle head shake, indicating Fisher was too distraught for meaningful questioning.

'I'm going to call your daughter now,' Ryan said.

Fisher made disjointed slurping sounds as she drank.

'We'll talk tomorrow, when you're feeling better.'

'When can I see Louise?'

Ryan looked at me.

'A viewing can be arranged, if that's what you'd like.'

'What a terrible Christmas.' Fisher's lips trembled. Tears glistened on each of her cheeks.

I squeezed the woman's hand. 'It's so very hard when we lose someone we love.'

'I'll have to plan the funeral.'

'I'm sure Claudia will be a great help.'

'I know just what Louise would want.'

'That's good,' I said.

'We told each other everything.'

That's good, I thought.

Claudia arrived within minutes.

Before leaving, I had one last question.

'Mrs. Fisher, did your sister sleep on a feather pillow?'

'Never. Louise was allergic.'

'Do you use a feather pillow?'

'Goose down.' Fisher's face clouded. 'Why? Was my pillow on Louise's bed?'

My eyes met Ryan's.

'Seems like a nice lady,' I said, as Ryan shifted into drive.

'More important, a living lady.'

'No wonder no one spotted her car.'

'Not likely, parked behind some pissant B and B in Pointe-aux-Pics.'

We drove in silence, bare branches cutting odd patterns in the streetlight bouncing off the windshield. Within minutes Ryan pulled onto the Pont Victoria. The wheels made the sound of a thumb rubbing the rim of a very large glass. Below us, the St. Lawrence looked black and still.

'Parent was murdered,' I said grimly.

'It's looking that way.'

'With Fisher's pillow.'

'Fiber guys should be able to match the feathers.'

'Some coldhearted bastard slipped into the house, took a pillow from Fisher's bed, and used it to smother Parent.'

'While she was dead to the world on Ambien.'

'How could someone break in without leaving a trace of evidence?'

'I intend to discuss that with Fisher.'

'And Bastillo.'

'And Bastillo.'

'Do you suppose Fisher knew about Parent's phone calls to me?'

'Another topic for discussion.'

That was it for conversation.

Fine.

I didn't want to think about Rose Fisher. Louise Parent. Ryan. Anne. My lost girls.

Leaning my head against the seat, I closed my eyes and occupied my mind making up phrases to describe the silence in the car.

The silence of a walled tomb. An abandoned library in a Vatican basement. A black hole at the terminus of a spiral galaxy. A startled cockatiel.

Ryan dropped me at my car.

'You on for tomorrow?'

'Tomorrow?'

'Rose Fisher?'

'What time?'

'I'll phone after I've checked with Bastillo.'

By the time I drove from the lab to Centre-ville, it was seven thirty-five. Anne was dozing, floral glasses on her nose, a paperback on her chest. Birdie was beside her.

Anne had made pot roast. We chatted as she thickened gravy and I tossed a salad.

During dinner, Anne described her book, the subject of which was death. She was finding the author's perspective enlightening. I found her choice of topic unsettling.

'Why the morbid interest in death?'

'You sound like Annie Hall.'

'You're acting like Woody Allen.'

Anne thought a moment.

'To move forward it is often necessary to change.'

'Move toward what and change how?'

'In substance.'

'What are you talking about?'

'Cycles.'

As I pondered that enigmatic comment, the phone rang. It was Katy.

'Hi, Mom.'

'Hi, sweetheart. Where are you?'

'Charlottesville, but I'm heading home tomorrow.'

'Exams went well?'

'Of course. I'm checking to make sure you'll be in Charlotte on the twenty-second.'

The twenty-second?

'Hannah's shower? You promised you'd help me?'

What demented moron would plan a wedding at Christmas?

'Of course I'll be there.'

'I'm counting on your years and years of experience.'

'Cute.'

'I sent you a couple of e-mails. Ho! Ho! Ho! 'Tis the season, and all that. I especially crave that sweater from Anthropologie. And the tranquillity fountain would help me chill.'

'What do you need to chill about?'

'Help me study, I mean.'

'Um. Hm.'

'Love you, *ma mère*. Gotta go.' Katy's voice sounded strung with mistletoe and holly.

'What are you so bubbly about?'

''Tis the season.'

'Ho. Ho. Ho.'

'Hold on to that thought.'

When we'd disconnected I went looking for Anne. She'd already retired. No further explanation of fulfillment or substance. I had the sense she'd used the phone call as an escape opportunity.

I undressed, washed my face, brushed and flossed, all the time worrying over my promise to Katy. I'd been so wrapped up in Louise Parent and my pizza basement girls I'd virtually forgotten Christmas. And totally forgotten Hannah's shower.

Could I resolve the case in a week, or would I be forced to put my lost girls on hold for the holidays?

Back in my room, I reached to set the alarm, stopped. Had Ryan given me a pickup time? I remembered asking, but couldn't recall his reply.

Ten-thirty. He'd probably be at home.

I hit Ryan's button on my speed dial. The phone was answered after two rings.

'Yes?' The voice was female.

Something hot-wired through my stomach and lungs.

'Andrew Ryan, please.'

'Who's calling?' Young and female.

'Dr. Brennan.'

'You.' Young and female and edged like a saw. 'Why don't you leave him alone?'

'Excuse me?'

'Quit screwing with his head.'

'Is this Danielle?'

Long silence.

My mind raced. Was that the right name?

'Is this Detective Ryan's niece?'

The woman snorted. 'Niece? That's what he told you? And you believed him? You're dumber than I thought.'

The truth dropped into place like a guillotine blade.

'Just leave him alone.'

I was listening to a dial tone.

24

After lying awake most of the night feeling more despondent than Anne, I began to sleep in fitful intervals.

Toward morning, I dreamed Ryan and I were in a long, dark tunnel. As we spoke, Ryan receded farther and farther from me, until his body was a hazy silhouette at the tunnel's mouth.

I tried to follow, but my legs were tar. I shouted again and again, but my mouth was mute.

Something skittered past me in the dark, dry and spidery like the wing of a bat.

I tried to raise my arm. It wouldn't move.

The thing brushed my cheek.

I flailed at it.

And awoke to find Birdie licking my face.

The tunnel *monsieur* phoned as I was crunching cornflakes and toast. I'd resolved I would go to Candiac with him as planned. I wanted to talk with Rose Fisher. After that, it was sayonara.

247

Too much heartache. Too many sleepless nights.

Too many prom queens.

I'd considered, but decided against a confrontation concerning the woman at Ryan's home. I'd been betrayed once. I'd played out that drama. The teary accusations. The hostile denials. The heart-splintering admissions. I wouldn't go there again.

Birdie supported my decision.

'Sleep well, sunshine?'

'Like igneous rock.'

'Bastillo is taking Fisher to visit her priest at ten. She suggested we swing by the house at eleven.' I heard what sounded like a match, then the exhalation of smoke. 'Pick you up around ten-thirty?'

'I'll be at home.'

Claudel phoned as I was blow-drying my hair.

As usual, there was no greeting, no formulaic query about my health or my day.

'Detective Charbonneau suggested I contact you, though I am uncertain why.' From most tongues, the French language glides like silk. From Claudel's, it thuds like potatoes down a chute. 'I have nothing to report.'

'Meaning?'

'No smoking gun on Cyr's list of renters. No hits with CPIC. No hits with NCIC. No hits in Vermont or California.'

'Not a single missing person even came close?'

'One kid in California. Broken right wrist. Tickled the lower end of your height range.'

'How tall?'

'Five-four.'

I felt a buzz of electricity.

'Close enough. When was she reported missing?'

'Eighty-five.'

'What's the problem?'

'Kid was fourteen.'

The current fizzled.

'The skeleton with the fractured radius had to be closer to twenty.' I pictured the bones of the girl in the leather shroud, the molar root closure on her dental X-rays. 'Maybe as young as eighteen, but there's no way she was fifteen.'

'My point precisely.'

'Of course date of disappearance need not be the date of death. Did you learn anything else?'

'Battalions of girls go missing each year.'

Hang up, a voice warned. Hang up now or Claudel's going to suffer another direct hit.

My doorbell doesn't ring. It twitters. At that moment, it did so.

'I'd like a printout of every female aged fifteen to twenty-two reported missing in Quebec over the past twenty years.'

'You're talking dozens. Most'll turn out to be runaways who eventually slunk back to Mommy or Daddy when they got tired of eating beanie weenies and sleeping on the floor.'

Easy.

'It would be helpful to me to know which ones didn't.'

More twittering.

'Madame, th—'

'Detective Ryan is here. I have to go.'

'Andrew Ryan?'

'We are going to interview Louise Parent's sister.'

'The DOA in Candiac?'

'Yes.'

'The old lady that was burning up your phone line?'

'She called me.'

'Wanting what?'

'That is exactly what I intend to find out.'

'When did the sister surface?'

'Yesterday.'

'Where?'

'At her home.'

'Where was the old biddy hiding out?'

'Pointe-aux-Pics.' Icy. 'I'd like that printout as soon as it's ready.'

'*Sacrifice.*'

'*Merci.*' Asshole.

I shot to the bathroom. One side of my hair was fine. The other hung in damp spirals. I reached for the dryer.

Twittering. With talons.

'Terrific.'

Birdie was watching from the doorway. At the sound of my voice he rose, stretched one leg backward, and moved on. No time to leave a note for Anne.

I jammed the dryer into its holder, pulled on a tuque, and headed out.

Ryan was waiting in the outer lobby, face ruddy

from the cold. Brown-tinted shades. Bomber jacket.

Libido liftoff.

Though the previous night's call still held a stranglehold on my emotions, apparently lust had pulled a Houdini.

'Did I wake you, cupcake?' Big Ryan grin.

'You did not wake me.' I tried to keep the hostility from my voice.

'Are we testy this morning?'

'Are we smoking this morning?'

'Minor setback.' Ryan jammed his cigarette into an urn of sand beside the door.

Outside, the cold hit me like an icy explosion. Sun roared down from a clear blue sky.

Ryan's car was idling at the curb.

I got in and buckled my seat belt.

Ryan got in, turned to me, and raised the shades up onto his head. A dark crescent hung below each azure eye.

'Something's on your mind.'

I said nothing.

'It's obvious you're upset.'

I said nothing, louder this time.

'I suspect you're unhappy with me.' Though he smiled, there was tension in his jaw and around his eyes.

'I know you consider yourself a hot property, Ryan, but I have other things to think about besides you.'

And your niece. I felt like one raw nerve.

'Do you want to talk?' Ryan asked.

'I want to drive,' I said, not trusting my voice with anything more.

We did.

In brittle silence.

Claudia Bastillo answered the bell at the Candiac house. Slapping on a fraudulent smile, I greeted her warmly.

Rose Fisher was sitting alone, staring at the venetian blinds. She wore a green rayon dress dotted with poppies. The orange hair was pushed up in back with a plastic clip-comb. If possible, the makeup was more extravagant than on the previous evening.

'Tit Ange was on a roll with 'Frère Jacques.'

Fisher didn't stir when we entered the living room. Hearing her daughter's voice, she turned and looked at us, puzzled, as if trying to figure out who we might be.

'It's the cop. And the coroner.'

With that less than accurate introduction, Bastillo withdrew.

Ryan and I assumed our positions flanking Fisher. 'The cop' gestured to 'the coroner' to proceed.

'I hope you're feeling better today, ma'am.'

Fisher nodded almost imperceptibly.

'Mrs. Fisher, I'm wondering about some calls your sister placed to me at my lab.'

The garish eyes dropped.

'When?'

'Last week.'

'About what?' Fisher's focus remained down-wardly fixed.

'Mrs. Parent—'

'Louise never married.'

'Miss Parent spoke of a building on rue Ste-Catherine.'

The sausage fingers closed and opened.

'She said she was bothered by events that had taken place there.'

Fisher's fidgeting intensified.

'Your sister stated that she felt morally obligated to share certain information with the authorities.'

'She called you?' Fisher looked up, eyes wide in the artlessly re-created face.

'Twice. Do you know why?'

'I didn't think she'd actually do it.'

'What did your sister want to discuss with me?'

At that moment Bastillo arrived and took the chair opposite the couch. The cockatiel shifted from chirping to shrilling short, strident notes.

''Tit Ange!' Bastillo barked.

The cockatiel did another series of power shrills.

'Cut it out!'

The cockatiel said 'pretty bird' in English and French, then began investigating the contents of its seed basin.

'He's mimicking the smoke detector,' Bastilllo explained. 'Little cretin picked it up when he was alone one weekend and the batteries failed.'

'He's very talented,' I said. 'And bilingual.'

'He's a pip.' Bastillo was clearly not fond of the bird.

'Trilingual.'

We all looked at Fisher.

'English, French, and Cockatiel. Louise used to laugh about that.' Fisher's voice made abrupt stops and starts as her chest clutched. 'She was a translator, you know.'

'No, ma'am. I didn't.'

Fisher nodded and the chins joined hands.

'Translated books from French to English. And the other way round.'

'That's very difficult work,' I said, then turned to Bastillo.

'We were asking your mother about calls your aunt placed to my lab shortly before she died.'

'There's a connection?'

'We're not sure.'

'Are you suggesting my aunt's death may not have been natural?'

'We want to investigate every possibility,' Ryan said.

'Do you suspect us?' Shrill as the bird.

'Of course not.' Ryan's voice was reassurance itself. 'We'd simply like to know what was on your aunt's mind.'

Ryan addressed Fisher.

'Do you know what Miss Parent intended to tell Dr. Brennan?'

When Fisher nodded, lattice bands of sunlight slid over her cheek.

'Tit Ange whistled a line from *Camelot*.

Rose Fisher drew a deep breath.

'Louise lived on Ste-Catherine for almost seventeen years. When my husband passed away in ninety-four, I persuaded her to move in with me. Her building was one of those big things, with businesses on the street level and people living on the floors above. Too noisy for me, but Louise liked it. She had a two-bedroom apartment overlooking the street, loved looking out the window as she worked at her desk. Called herself the neighborhood snoop.'

'What kind of businesses occupied the building?' I urged gently.

'There was a whole string. A luggage lady. A butcher. Then this guy opened a pawnshop.'

Fisher looked down.

'Louise didn't like him. *Really* didn't like him.'

'What was his name?'

'Started with an M. Maynard? Martin? Louise might have said he was American. I don't remember. This was years ago.'

Stéphane Ménard. The guy on Cyr's list. The guy who'd rented space in Cyr's building from eighty-nine to ninety-eight.

'Why did your sister dislike this man?'

'Don't get me wrong. Louise usually liked everybody. But she had a bad feeling about this guy.'

'Do you know why?'

Fisher looked at Bastillo. Bastillo nodded.

'She saw him carry a sleeping girl into his shop one night. Louise said he was kinda cradling her, like a baby.'

'A child?'

'Teenager.'

'His daughter?'

'Louise said he'd told her he regretted never marrying and having kids. My sister had a real knack for getting people to open up. Five minutes and Louise knew your whole life story.'

'Anything else?' My heart was picking up extra beats.

'There was this other time Louise saw a girl run out of the shop. This pawnbroker fellow shot into the street and dragged her back inside.'

'When was this?'

Fisher misunderstood my question. 'Late at night.'

I looked at Ryan. He looked as keyed up as I felt.

'Louise kept it to herself until she moved here, then her conscience began bothering her and she told me what she'd seen.'

'Did your sister ever speak to the pawnbroker about these incidents?'

Fisher nodded. 'Louise said she asked about the girls several times, you know, not right out, but kinda subtle. She said this pawnbroker always side-stepped her questions, eventually got pretty hostile over the whole thing. So she dropped it.'

Fisher's eyes came up and fastened on mine.

'Louise kept agonizing over whether she should call the cops. You know, so someone could check it out. I told her to mind her own business. Not get involved.'

'These incidents took place before 1994?'

Fisher nodded. 'Do you think I gave my sister bad advice?'

'Tit Ange chirped and rang his bell.

25

Ryan continued his interrogation of Rose Fisher. Bastillo hovered nearby. I slipped outside and dialed Claudel.

Astoundingly, he picked up on the second ring.

I repeated Fisher's story.

'I've already run him while working Cyr's list of tenants. Ménard's a saint.'

'No record at all?'

'Officially, the guy never even spit on the street.'

'Is he still in Montreal?'

'Owns a house in Pointe-St-Charles.'

'What does he do now?'

'Nothing, as far as I can tell.'

'Ménard operated the pawnshop from eighty-nine until ninety-eight. What was he into before that?'

Slight pause.

'The record is unclear.'

'Unclear?'

'It stops in eighty-nine.'

'What do you mean, it stops?'

'There is nothing on Stéphane Ménard before 1989.'

'No birth certificate, tax return, credit report, medical record? Nothing?'

Silence.

'Rose Fisher thought her sister said Ménard was American. Did you send the name south?'

I waited for Claudel to speak. When he didn't I said, 'I'll phone Monsieur Authier and tell him we have a lead.'

Explain your lack of enthusiasm to the chief coroner, Monsieur Claudel.

After disconnecting, I returned to the living room. While Ryan spent another thirty minutes questioning Fisher, I observed quietly.

In my absence, tears had again wreaked havoc on the vivid maquillage. Fisher's anguish was heart-breaking.

Bastillo was another story. Her spine remained rigid, her stare fixed and devoid of compassion for her mother's grief. From time to time the younger woman would recross her legs, or refold her arms across her chest. Otherwise, she sat motionless and without comment.

At last Ryan finished.

We both rose, repeated our regrets to Fisher and her daughter, and took our leave.

Back in the car, Ryan suggested we grab a sandwich.

'No, thank you.'

My stomach chose that moment to growl.

'I'll take that as a metabolic veto of your decision not to lunch.'

Without further discussion, Ryan pulled into the parking lot of a Lafleur, Montreal's answer to fast food. Rounding the car, he opened my door, bowed at the waist, and made a sweeping gesture with his free hand.

What the hell. I was hungry.

Lafleur is famous for its steamed hot dogs and fries. Steamé et frites. Though regulars register blood cholesterol counts that would classify them as solids, now and then every Montrealer eats at Lafleurs.

Minutes later Ryan and I were seated at a Formica-topped table, four weenies and twenty pounds of fries between us.

My cell rang as I was starting my second dog. As usual Claudel wasted no time on greetings.

'*Vous avez raison.*'

I almost choked. Claudel was admitting I'd been right about something?

Ryan mouthed 'Heimlich?' and stretched out his arms. I flapped a hand at him.

'Monsieur Stéphane Ménard was born Stephen Timothy Menard. Parents were Vermonters, Genevieve Rose Corneau and Simon Timothy Menard.'

'Fisher remembered correctly.'

'The Menards were schoolteachers who also owned and operated a small truck farm about fifteen miles outside of St. Johnsbury. Papa died in

260

sixty-seven when the kid was five. Mama died in eighty-two.'

'How did Menard end up in Canada?'

'Legally. Corneau was born in Montreal. After hooking up with Menard she moved to Vermont, married, and became a U.S. citizen. Conveniently, Genevieve Rose was visiting the folks back home when little Stephen signaled his entrance.'

'Menard has dual citizenship.'

'Yes.'

'But he didn't take up residence in Canada until eighty-nine?'

'When Corneau died in 1982 Menard inherited the truck farm. Three acres and a two-bedroom house.'

I did a quick calculation. 'Menard was twenty.'

'Yes.'

Ryan was dousing his fries with vinegar, but listening attentively.

'Did Menard remain in Vermont?'

'Charbonneau is clarifying that with the St. Johnsbury PD. I've established that Menard's grandparents died in an auto crash here in Montreal in 1988.'

'Let me guess. Menard inherited Grand-mère and Grand-père Corneau's home, said *au revoir* to Vermont, added accents to his name, and headed north.'

'He took possession of the Corneau home in November 1988.'

'In Pointe-St-Charles.'

Claudel read off an address.

I gestured to Ryan. He handed me a pen and I jotted it on a napkin.

'He a loner?'

'No record of anyone else living there.'

'Does Menard have a jacket in the States?' I asked.

'DWI at age seventeen. Otherwise the young man was a paragon of virtue.'

Claudel's cavalier attitude was doing its usual number on my disposition.

'Look, up to this point we've been focusing on the victims, working the case from the bottom up. It's time to rethink that, go at it from the top down. Look at who might have put them in that basement.'

'And you think this Menard is your shovel man.'

'Do you have any better ideas, Monsieur Claudel?'

We disconnected simultaneously.

Between bites of my second hot dog, I relayed Claudel's information. If Ryan had doubts about my suspicions concerning Menard, he kept them to himself.

'Menard must be in his forties now,' he said, crumpling his waxed paper wrappers into the grease-stained carton that had held our food.

'With no obvious means of support for the past several years.'

'But real estate holdings in Vermont and Quebec.'

'And a lot of dead relatives,' I said.

Charbonneau phoned as we were paying our bill.

'How's it hanging, Doc?'

'Good.'

'Did some interesting chin wagging with several of our Green Mountain neighbors. Seems your boy was a college grad.'

'Where?'

'University of Vermont. Class of 1984. Nice lady in the registrar's office even faxed me a yearbook photo. Kid looks like every mama's dream. Howdy Doody hair and freckles, Clark Kent glasses, and a Donny Osmond smile.'

'Redhead?'

'Looked like Opie in specs. Oh, and you're going to love this, Doc. Menard earned a BA in anthropology.'

'You're kidding.'

'Story gets better. Menard went on to graduate school. Enrolled in a master's program in archaeology at some place called—' Pause. 'Wait. I got it. Chico.' My heart rate shot into the stratosphere.

'California State University at Chico?'

Ryan's head whipped around at the sharpness of my tone.

'Yep. Long way from home for a kid from Vermont.'

I reminded Charbonneau about the strontium isotope testing Art Holliday had done on the skeletons.

'Her dental strontium ratios suggest the girl in the leather shroud may have grown up in north-central California, remember?'

'Right.'

'Chico is in north-central California.'

'I'll be damned.'

'And remember too, her skeletal strontium ratios suggest she may have lived the last years of her life in Vermont.'

'Sonovabitch.'

'What else did you get?'

'Apparently Menard's scholarship left something to be desired. He either dropped out or got booted after one year in the program. *Hasta la vista*. No degree.'

'Where did he go?'

'Showed up at Mama's farm in Vermont in January eighty-six.'

'If he dropped out of Chico after one academic year, that leaves a gap from the end of spring term in eighty-five until January eighty-six. Where was he during that period?'

'I'll make some calls to Chico.'

'What did Menard do when he landed back in Vermont?'

'Grew vegetables, I guess. Lived off his inheritance. Paid no Social Security, filed no tax returns.'

'Did you talk to the locals?'

'I managed to scare up a couple of neighbors who remembered him. Most people in the area are newcomers since Menard left, but a few old-timers remembered Genevieve Rose and her son. Apparently Mama was one tough lady. Kept the kid on a very short rein.'

'Corneau never remarried?'

'Nope. Single parent. Folks remember Menard as a quiet kid who stayed in a lot. Didn't participate in sports or the usual extracurricular school stuff. One or two said they recalled seeing him during the year following his return from Chico. Guy must have had some sort of epiphany in grad school. Made an impression back home with the dreadlocks and beard.'

'It's Vermont.'

'Meaning?'

'They're conservative. What else did these neighbors say?'

'Not much. Apparently Menard kept to himself, only ventured out to buy groceries or fill up on gas.'

'Talk to Chico. Dig up everything you can on this guy. And get a list of every female aged fifteen to twenty-five who went missing in the area while Menard was out there.'

'You really liking Menard for these pizza skeletons?'

'It's the classic profile. Dominating mother. Failed ambition. A loner. An isolated location.'

'I don't know.'

'Connect the dots, Charbonneau. Three girls were buried in the basement of a property Menard rented for nine years. Carbon 14 dating suggests that the timing of their deaths coincides with the period of Menard's tenancy. Louise Parent was sufficiently suspicious of Menard to phone me twice.'

I was summarizing as much for Ryan's sake as for Charbonneau's.

'According to her sister, what Parent wanted to tell me was that on one occasion she had observed Menard carrying an unconscious teenaged girl into his shop. On another occasion she had observed Menard dragging a fleeing girl back into his shop. Both incidents took place late at night.'

'And Parent is now dead,' Charbonneau said.

I looked at Ryan. He was following every word.

'And Parent is now dead,' I said.

'Bring out the party hats. We may all be working the same patch.'

'Looks that way.'

'Ryan there?'

'Yes.'

'Put him on.'

I handed Ryan the phone, then watched as he listened to Charbonneau. Though my nerves were high-stepping, I kept my face neutral. No hint of the jolt Charbonneau had just given me. No hint of the pain Charbonneau had triggered on Monday. No hint of the torture last night's phone call had been.

I'd vowed to distance myself from Ryan, but all the threads were starting to connect. With the Parent and pizza basement investigations merging, professional separation would not yet be possible.

C'est la vie. I would be a pro. I would do my job. Then I would wish Ryan well and move on.

'Yeah, she is.' Ryan chuckled the chuckle men use when sharing a joke about women.

Paranoia roared. She is *what*? *Which* she?

Forget it, Brennan. Focus on the case. Keep your energy pointed there.

I pictured the bones in their anonymous cellar graves, Menard buying and selling above in his shop. Electronics stolen for a drug hit. Family heirlooms tendered with regret.

I pictured Menard in Vermont, hoeing peas and potatoes. Menard in California, studying Struever, Binford, Buikstra, Fagan.

An ill-defined thought tried to get my attention. Chico.

'—got it right here.' Ryan rotated the napkin to read Menard's address.

Chico is in north-central California. I know that. So why the heads-up from my hindbrain?

That wasn't it. There was something more. What?

'Will do,' Ryan said.

Charbonneau said something.

'Yeah. Squeeze the squirrel a little. See how he reacts.'

Ryan clicked off and handed me my phone.

'You up for a little chat with this guy?'

'Menard?'

Ryan nodded.

'Definitely.'

The hindbrain thought seemed to relax slightly.

As Ryan and I left the restaurant we had no idea we were being watched.

26

The map of Montreal makes me think of a foot, with Dorval Airport and the west island suburbs forming the ankle, the toes pointing east, and the heel dropping down into the Fleuve St-Laurent. Verdun forms the fatty pad of the heel, with Pointe-St-Charles as a tiny toeward bunion.

The Point is topped off by the Lachine Canal, and bottoms out in the CP rail yards. Vieux-Montréal and its port lie to the east. Originally inhabited by immigrants working construction on Montreal's bridges, the Point has street names that reflect a strong Irish presence. Rue St-Patrick. Sullivan. Dublin. Mullins.

But that's history. Today the Point is largely French.

Less than twenty minutes after leaving Lafleur, Ryan turned onto rue Wellington, the neighborhood's main east-west artery. We passed sporting goods stores, tattoo parlors, the MH Grover clothing shop, a Wellington institution for decades. Here and there, a perky café interrupted the drab little strip.

Ryan paused where rue Dublin tied into Wellington on the left. On the right, a row of Victorians looked incongruously playful, styling out in pastels, ornate woodwork, brick arches, and leaded glass. I could read the name *Dr. George Hall* scripted in milky glass above one front door.

Ryan noticed my gaze.

'Doctor's Row,' he said. 'Built in the nineteenth century by a group of fat-cat physicians looking for prestigious addresses. The hood's changed a bit since then.'

'Are they still private homes?'

'They're divided into condos, I think.'

'Where's rue de Sébastopol?'

Ryan tipped his head left. 'It's a rabbit warren in there, lot of dead ends and one-ways. I think de Sébastopol skims the edge of the rail yard.'

As Ryan turned onto Dublin, I noticed a historic marker out my window.

'What's Parc Marguerite-Bourgeoys?'

'*Mon Dieu, Madame la docteure*, you're referring to one of Quebec's best-loved ladies. Sister Maggie set up schools for little girls back in the seventeenth century. Pretty rad idea for Quebec at the time. She also founded the Soeurs de la Congrégation de Notre-Dame. A few years ago the church upped her pay grade to saint.'

'Why the sign?' I asked.

'In the mid-sixteen hundreds Bourgeoys was

given a hefty hunk of this little peninsula. Bit by bit, the nuns sold the land off, and Pointe St-Charles now covers most of the acreage, but Bourgeoys's original school and parts of the farm are up ahead. Site's now a museum.'

'Maison St-Gabriel?'

Ryan nodded.

Snow removal in the area had been sketchy at best. Sidewalks were mounded and parked cars jutted into the traffic lanes. Ryan drove slowly, pulling far to the right for oncoming traffic. As we moved deeper into the Point I assessed my surroundings.

The architecture was a jumble of nineteenth- and twentieth-century housing, most of which appeared to have been built for the working-class poor. Many streets were lined with two-story redbrick row houses whose front doors opened right at the curb. Other streets tended toward rough-hewn limestone. While most residences were starkly plain, a few sported a cornice, a false mansard, or a carved wooden dormer.

Mixed in with the previous century's efforts were three-story tri- or six-plexes built during the early years of this one. Their creators favored more generous setbacks allowing tiny front gardens, recessed entrances, yellow, chamois, or brown brick facing, and exterior staircases twisting to second-floor balconies.

Near the entrance to the Maison St-Gabriel, we passed several four-story postwar monstrosities with entrances canopied under concrete or plastic.

The designers of these eyesores obviously placed efficiency well before style. So much for feng shui.

After several turns, Ryan made a right, and rue de Sébastopol stretched before us. To our left sprawled the rail yards, half-hidden by six-foot fencing and evergreen shrubbery. Through the branches and chain-linking, I could see row after row of rusted tanker cars.

Snow crunched under our tires as Ryan rolled to a stop. Wordlessly, we each made a visual tour.

At midblock, a series of redbrick row houses elbowed up to the curb, the run-down little dwellings seeming to huddle together for support. Or warmth.

Beyond the row houses, I could see a gap, then a hodgepodge of cement structures with graffiti scarring their exterior walls. To our right stood a seedy barn enclosed within a dilapidated fence. Inside the fence, a mongrel dog took issue with our presence.

Bare trees fingered up through the power lines. Previously plowed snow sat mounded and blackened with grime.

Rue de Sébastopol looked like many other streets in the Point.

Yet somehow more bleak.

More isolated.

To our left yawned the vast uninhabited rail yard. Behind us lay the only vehicle access to the lane.

As I stared the length of the block, I felt a deep sense of foreboding.

Ryan nodded toward the row houses. 'That's

Sébastopol Row, built in the 1850s by the Grand Trunk Railway.'

'Apparently Big Railroad didn't pony up for aesthetics.'

Ryan pulled the napkin from his pocket, checked the address, then advanced so he could see the digits on the first row house.

The dog stopped barking, rose with forepaws on the fence, and watched our progress.

'What's the number?'

Ryan told me.

'Must be farther down.'

As Ryan crept forward, I read off the addresses. The numbers on the row houses didn't go high enough, but that on the first cement structure indicated we'd gone too far.

'Maybe it's farther off the pavement, back in that vacant area,' I suggested.

Ryan reversed up the block and parked opposite the last of the row houses. A silhouette was faintly visible through bare trees and heavy pines.

'Ready?' Ryan scooped his gloves from the backseat.

'Ready.'

I pulled on my mittens and got out. At the thunk-thunk of our doors, the dog reengaged.

Ryan proceeded up an ice-crusted walkway six feet beyond the outer wall of the last row house. Needled boughs and bare branches blocked the sky, creating a gloomy tunnel effect.

The air smelled of pine, coal smoke, and something organic.

'What's that odor?' I hissed.

'Horse manure.' Ryan was also whispering. 'Old Yeller is guarding a *calèche* horse stable.'

'The horses that pull the carriages in Old Montreal?'

'The very ones.'

I took another whiff.

Maybe. But there was something else there.

Ryan and I picked our way carefully along the uneven walk, breaths billowing, collars up to ward off the cold.

Ten yards off de Sébastopol the path took a sharp left, and Ryan and I found ourselves facing a weathered brick building. We both stopped and read the rusted numbers above the door.

'Bingo,' Ryan said.

The building's entrance was recessed, the door rough and aged, but ornately carved. The windows were opaque, some black, others white with frost and windblown snow.

Dead vines spiderwebbed across the roof and walls, and one wooden sill angled down from its frame. The pines were thicker here, keeping the house and its small yard in even deeper shadow.

Irrationally, small hairs rose on the back of my neck.

Drawing a deep breath, I worked myself just calm enough.

Ryan stepped up to the door. I followed.

The bell was dull brass, the old-fashioned kind that sounded when the knob was turned clockwise. Ryan reached out and gave it a twist.

Deep in the house, a bell shrilled.

Ryan waited a full minute, then rang again.

Seconds later, locks rattled, then the door creaked open four inches.

Ryan extended his badge to the crack.

'Mr. Menard?' he asked in English.

The crack didn't widen. The person peering through it was hidden from me.

'Stephen Menard?' Ryan repeated.

'*Qu'est-ce que voulez-vous?*' What do you want? Heavily accented. American.

'Police, Mr. Menard. We'd like to talk to you,' Ryan persisted in English.

'*Laissez-moi tranquille.*' Leave me alone.

The door moved toward its frame. Ryan palmed it back with jackrabbit quickness.

'Are you Stephen Menard?'

'*Je m'appelle Stéphane Ménard.*' Menard pronounced the name in the French manner. '*Qui êtes-vous?*' Who are you?

'Detective Andrew Ryan.' Ryan flicked a hand in my direction. 'Dr. Temperance Brennan. We need to speak with you.'

'*Allez-vous en.*' The voice sounded dry and almost frail. I still couldn't make out its owner.

'We're not going to go away, Mr. Menard. Cooperate and our questions should take only a few minutes of your time.'

Menard didn't reply.

'Or we could do this at headquarters.' Ryan's tone was tempered steel.

'*Tabarnac!*'

The door closed. A chain rattled, then the door reopened.

Ryan entered and I followed. The floor was linoleum, the walls a color way too dark for the windowless room. The air smelled of mothballs, old wallpaper, and musty fabric.

The tiny foyer was lit by one small china lamp. Menard stood shadowed by the door, one hand on the knob, the other pressing a brass letter opener flat to his chest.

When Menard closed the door and turned to us, I got my first look at him.

Stephen Menard had to be six foot four. With his freckled face and bald, toad-shaped head, he was one of the most peculiar men I'd ever laid eyes on. He could have been a worn forty or a well-preserved sixty.

'*Qu'est-ce que vous voulez?*' Menard asked again. What do you want?

'May we sit down?' Ryan unzipped his jacket.

A shrug. '*Peu importe.*' Whatever.

Menard led us into a parlor as dim as the foyer. Heavy red drapes, mahogany secretary, coffee and end tables. Dark floral wallpaper. Deep cranberry upholstered pieces.

Laying the letter opener on the secretary, Menard dropped onto the sofa and crossed his legs. I removed my jacket and took the armchair to his right.

Ryan circled the room, turning on the overhead chandelier and a pair of crystal and brass lamps flanking the couch. The improved lighting allowed a better evaluation of the man of the house.

Stephen Menard was not just bald, he was totally hairless. No whiskers. No eyelashes. No body or head hair. The trait made him look smooth and oddly pale. I wondered if Menard's lack of hair was a genetic condition, or some bizarre fashion statement intentionally created.

Ryan lifted a Windsor chair from beside the secretary and parked it in front of Menard with body language clearly not intended to calm. Sitting, he placed elbows on knees, and leaned forward to within a yard of Menard's face.

Our reluctant host wore slippers, jeans, and a sweatshirt with the sleeves pushed above the elbows. Drawing back from Ryan, Menard tugged the sleeves to his wrists, shoved them back up, adjusted his glasses, and waited.

'I'm going to be honest with you, Mr. Menard. You've caught our interest.'

'*Je suis*—'

'My understanding is that you're American, so English shouldn't be any problem for you, right?'

Menard's chin tucked in a bit, but he said nothing.

'Richard Cyr tells us you ran a pawnshop out of his property on rue Ste-Catherine a few years back.'

Menard's lips went needle thin, and a wrinkle formed above the place his brows should have been.

'You got a problem with my asking about that?'

Menard ran a hand across his jaw, readjusted his glasses.

'Pretty successful operation. Lasted, what? Nine years? You're a young man. What made you decide to call the pawn business quits?'

'I was not a mere pawnbroker. I traded in collectibles.'

'Please explain that to me.'

'I helped collectors locate hard-to-find items. Stamps. Coins. Toy soldiers.'

I'd seen Ryan interrogate suspects in the past. He was good with silence. The person being interrogated would complete an answer, but instead of putting another question Ryan would look up expectantly and wait. He did so now.

Menard swallowed.

Ryan waited.

'It was a legitimate business,' Menard mumbled.

Somewhere in the house I thought I heard a door open and close.

'Things grew complicated. Business was dropping off. The lease came up. I decided not to renew.'

'Complicated how?'

'Just complicated. Look, I'm a Canadian citizen. I have rights.'

'I'm just asking a few questions, Mr. Menard.'

Eye contact had become noticeably difficult for Menard. His gaze kept shifting from his hands to Ryan, then darting back down.

Ryan allowed another long pause. Then, 'Why the switch from archaeology?'

'What are you talking about?'

'What happened out in Chico?'

An idea hared through my mind. I didn't chase it.

'You got a warrant?' Menard asked, again adjusting the glasses.

'No, sir,' Ryan said.

Menard's gaze drifted to a point over Ryan's left shoulder. We both turned.

A woman stood in the doorway. She was tall and thin, with ivory skin and a long black braid. I guessed her age as mid to late twenties.

The crow's-feet cornering Menard's eyes constricted.

The woman tensed so visibly she seemed to flinch. Then her arms wrapped her waist, and she scurried out of sight.

Menard pushed to his feet.

'I'm not answering any more questions. Either arrest me, or leave my home.'

Ryan took his time rising.

'Is there a reason we should be arresting you, Mr. Menard?'

'Of course not.'

'Good.'

Ryan zipped his jacket. I slipped into mine and started toward the foyer. Pausing near the secretary, I noticed the letter opener.

Out of the corner of my eye I saw Ryan put his face to Menard's.

'We'll play it your way for now, sir. But if you're withholding information from me, I'll make certain you come to regret that.'

This time Menard met Ryan's gaze. The two stood eyeball-to-eyeball.

Turning my back to the face-off, I quietly scooped the letter opener into my purse.

27

'Thoughts?' Ryan was turning off the far end of de Sébastopol.

'If they ever bring back the Inquisition, you'll be their first hire.'

'I view that as a compliment. What's your take on Menard?'

'Guy gave me the creeps. Do you think the hairlessness is a medical condition?'

Ryan shook his head no. 'I could see nicks on his scalp.'

'Why would a man shave and pluck every hair?'

'Telly Savalas fan?'

'His whole body?'

'Cut cost on shampoo?'

'Ryan.'

'Training to swim in the next Olympics?'

That one got no reply.

'I don't know. Zonked-out stylist? Lice? Some kind of hair phobia?'

'Did you notice how strangely that woman acted?'

'Didn't jump in to offer us tea.'

'She seemed terrified.'

Ryan shrugged. 'Maybe. Maybe the lady disapproves of uninvited guests.'

'Claudel said there's no record of anyone else living at that address. Who do you suppose she is?'

'I intend to find out.'

I told him about the letter opener.

'Illegal seizure.'

'Yep,' I agreed.

'A judge would exclude any information gained from it.'

'Yep,' I agreed again. 'But a print might ID the woman.'

'Might.'

'Look. It was an impulse. The opener was lying there. I figured the woman might have handled it. I borrowed the thing.'

'Uh. Huh.'

'I'll return it.'

'I never doubted that.'

The sun was arcing down, turning the windshield opaque with salty slush thrown up by the cars ahead. We fell silent as Ryan concentrated on driving.

'Could explain the antique buttons,' I said, as we crossed the Lachine Canal and wound onto de la Montagne.

'Could.'

I had a sudden thought.

'The forgery,' I said, turning to Ryan.

'You think Menard was helping customers round out their collections by doing a little manufacturing on his own?'

'Maybe that's what he thinks we're investigating. Maybe that's why he was so nervous.'

'It's a possibility,' Ryan said.

I had another thought.

'Or maybe Menard stumbled onto the skeletons but kept it to himself, thinking he might sell the bones to a collector someday. I'm pretty sure it's illegal to trade in human skeletal parts in Canada.'

'Another possibility.'

I settled back. 'My gut tells me it's more than that.'

'If the guy's got baggage, I'll find it.'

'Menard was definitely not glad to see us.'

'Exuded all the warmth of an autopsy room. Which reminds me. Where would you like to go?'

'The lab.'

I dialed my condo to check on Anne's schedule but got no answer. I left a message for her to call me.

Twenty minutes later I was at my desk.

Ryan had promised to take the letter opener to SIJ. Either he or a tech would call if they were able to pull up latents.

For as long as I've known her, Anne has steadfastly insisted she dislikes Indian cuisine. I called again to propose dinner at La Maison du Cari, certain their lamb korma would change her mind.

Still no answer. Second message.

Two printouts lay on my blotter. The longer was Claudel's list of girls who'd gone missing in Quebec. The shorter was Charbonneau's list of those who'd disappeared in north-central California.

I started with the former.

One by one I worked my way through the names, excluding any girl whose profile was inconsistent with the pizza basement skeletons. A serious headache was kicking in by the time I came to Manon Violette.

Manon Violette had a rotated upper right canine and no restorations.

I sat forward, feeling a sudden rush of excitement.

The girl in Dr. Energy's crate had a rotated upper right canine and no restorations.

Barely breathing, I read the details.

Manon Violette had disappeared nine years earlier after leaving her home in Longueuil to take a bus to Centre-ville.

Violette was white.

Violette was fifteen years old.

The next entry punched me in the sternum.

Manon Violette stood only fifty-eight inches tall.

Damn!

I'd estimated the Dr. Energy girl's stature at sixty-two inches.

Could I have been that far off?

I fired into the lab and checked.

Nope. Dr. Energy's girl was tiny. But not that

tiny. Even considering the error factor, 38426 was too tall.

What about 38427? I'd estimated her age at fifteen to seventeen, her height at sixty-four to sixty-seven inches.

I pulled out the skull and checked the teeth.

An orthodontist's dream. Perfect alignment. No rotations.

Back to the list.

An hour later I sat back, frustrated.

I hated to admit it, but Claudel was right. There were no matches. If height fit, age didn't. If age and height were consistent with one of the skeletons, racial background or some other trait excluded the candidate.

None of the MPs from Quebec and only one from California had suffered a Colles' fracture of the right radius.

Claudel had referenced the girl from California in our earlier conversation. I read through her stats.

In 1985, Leonard Alexander Robinson filed a missing person report with the Tehama County Sheriff's Department. Robinson's daughter, Angela, a white female, age fourteen years and nine months, left home on the night of October 21 and was never seen again. Friends said she'd intended to hitchhike to a party.

Angela Robinson, 'Angie,' had fallen from a swing at age eight, fracturing her right wrist.

Angie stood five foot two.

Back to the lab to double-check myself.

Angie Robinson was too young to be the girl in the leather shroud.

And too short.

I was discouraged, and my headache could have pounded the golden spike in Ogden. What if Angie had lived for a time after her disappearance? She would have aged. Perhaps grown.

Again, my subconscious seemed to be crooking a finger.

What?

The clock said five-ten. I decided to call it a day.

Returning to my office, I again tried Anne.

Still no answer.

I was replacing the receiver, when someone tapped on my door.

'Hey, Doc.' Charbonneau was in polyester from stem to stern. And cowboy boots.

'Hi.'

'I was on my way out, thought I'd pop up and give you the current lore.'

With what remained of my brain, I tried to decipher that.

'Lore?'

Charbonneau took a pink wad from his mouth, studied it, rolled his eyes up, and tipped his head toward my wastebasket.

I handed him a Post-it.

Charbonneau wrapped the Bazooka and arced it into the bin.

'Ryan told me about your drop-in at Menard's crib on de Sébastopol. Sounds like the guy's a real piece of work.'

'Yeah.'

I rubbed circles on my temples with the balls of my fingers.

'Headache?'

I nodded.

'Try eating something real spicy. That works for me.'

'Thanks.'

'Not much news from my end. Menard's got no jacket in California. One correction on his academic career, though. Squirrel wasn't tossed. He actually registered for the second year at Chico.'

'And?'

'No show.'

I stopped rubbing. 'Menard paid tuition, enrolled in classes, then never showed up?'

'Yep.'

'Why?'

Charbonneau shrugged. 'Squirrel didn't RSVP. Just never showed up.'

'Did he terminate his lease? Close out his accounts?'

'I'm working on that.'

'Where was he until he landed in Vermont in January?'

Charbonneau grinned. 'I'm working on that, too.'

The condo was dark when I arrived. Birdie was sleeping on the sofa back. He raised his head and blinked when I turned on a lamp.

'Anne?' I called out.

No answer.

Birdie stretched, dropped to the floor, and went belly up.

'Anne?' I called again as I rubbed Birdie's tummy.

Silence.

'Where is she, Bird?'

The cat rolled to all fours, stretched each back leg, then strolled to the kitchen. In seconds I heard the crunch of Science Diet nuggets.

'Annie?'

Her bedroom door was still closed. I knocked and went in.

And my heart sank.

Anne's belongings were gone. A note lay on the desk.

I stared at it a moment, then reached out and unfolded the paper.

Dearest Tempe,

I can't tell you how much I appreciate your kindness and patience. Not just this past week, but throughout the entire course of our wonderful, joyful, precious friendship. You have been my buttress, the wind beneath my wings. (Remember 'our' movie?)

We're alike in so very many ways, Tempe. I'm not good at talking about my feelings. I'm not even good at thinking about my feelings. You were perfect for me.

Now it's time to wrap this up. Though I can never say it to you, know that I love you so very

very much. Please don't be angry with me for doing it this way.

Anne

A whole catalog of emotions gripped me.

Love. I knew my friend and understood how hard those words had been for her.

Guilt. Engrossed in my own problems, I'd not really focused on Anne's. How could I have been so selfish?

Anger. She'd just packed and split for home without telling me? How could she be so insensitive?

Then fear barreled in like a locomotive.

Had she gone home? Wrap what up? For doing what this way? What way?

I remembered Anne's book and our dinner conversation the night before. She hadn't mentioned leaving.

What had she said? Something about cycles and changing in substance. I'd blown her off.

Sweet Jesus! Was she talking about death? Surely not. Depressed or not, Anne was not the suicidal type. But did we ever really know?

Memory collage. Another friend who'd stayed in that room. Left. Turned up dead in a shallow grave. Could Anne have undertaken some risky odyssey?

I tried calling her cell. No answer.

I dialed Tom.

'Hello.'

'Is Anne there?'

'Tempe?'

'Has Anne come home?'

'I thought she was with you.'

'She left.' I read Tom the note.

'What's she talking about?'

'I'm not sure.'

'She was pretty upset with me.'

'Yes.'

'You don't think she'd do something crazy, do you?'

The same question had been winging through my skull.

'She hasn't phoned?'

'No.'

'Call the airlines. See if she's booked on a flight to Charlotte.'

'I don't think they'll tell me.'

'Fake it, Tom!' I was almost crying. 'Lie! Think of something.'

'OK.'

'Call me the instant you know anything.'

'You, too.'

Standing with the phone in one hand, I caught a snapshot of myself in the newly replaced dining room mirror.

Body tense, face a frightened white oval.

Like Anne in my corridor the night of the break-in.

Dear God! Let her be all right.

What to do? Phone the airlines? Tom was doing that. Car rental companies? Cab companies? The police?

Was I overreacting? Had Anne simply taken off

to be by herself? Should I do nothing and wait?

But Anne left a note. She had some plan in mind. But what plan?

I jumped when the phone shrilled in my hand.

'Anne?'

'It's me.' Ryan must have picked up on the tension in my voice. 'What's wrong?'

I told him about Anne's abrupt departure.

'Does the note say she's going home?'

'Not in so many words.'

'Did she phone anyone?'

'This phone doesn't record outgoing calls.'

'Or incoming. Or have caller ID. You really need to upgrade.'

'Thanks for the technical advice.'

'I'll make some inquiries.'

'Thanks. Ryan?'

'Yeah.'

'She was very down.'

'She took her things. That's a good sign.'

'Yes.' I hadn't thought of that.

Pause.

'Do you want me to come over there?'

I did. 'I'll be all right. Why are you calling?'

'SIJ was able to lift prints from the letter opener. Two sets.'

'Menard and the woman.'

'You're probably half right.'

'Half?'

'The guy's not Menard.'

28

'The prints were left by two different people. Neither is Menard.'

'You're sure?'

'I sent everything down to Vermont. Their lab compared the latents from our letter opener to those taken when Menard was busted on the DWI charge.'

'But Menard was all over that letter opener.' I wasn't believing this.

'The guy in the house was. But he's not Menard.'

'Any hit on the second set?'

'No. We're running them up here, and sending them through AFIS in the States.'

AFIS is the Automated Fingerprint Information System.

'If the guy's not Menard, who is he?'

'An exceptionally perceptive question, Dr. Brennan.'

This was not making sense. 'Maybe there's a screwup on the prints.'

'It happens.'

'Charbonneau's got a college yearbook photo of Menard. Let's roll it by Cyr and see what he says.'

'Can't hurt,' Ryan agreed.

I waited, half hoping Ryan would reiterate his offer to come over. He didn't.

'I'll get the photo from Char—' Ryan started.

I heard what could have been a female voice in the background, then the muffled sound of a covered mouthpiece.

'Sorry.' Ryan's voice was pitched lower. 'I'll get the photo from Charbonneau and pick you up at eight.'

I held it together through a Friday night macaroni and cheese dinner for one. Through a long, hot bath. Through the eleven o'clock news.

In bed, in the dark, unbidden images bombarded my mind.

A dingy basement. Bones in a crate. Bones in trenches.

A woman in bed, gray hair trailing across her face. A stained mattress. A lifeless body on stainless steel.

Shattered mirrors. A shard in a painting.

Anne with her luggage. Anne peering over her floral frames.

I felt a scream in my belly, streams of hot wetness on my face.

The last time I'd felt this overwhelmed I'd been with Ryan. I remembered how he'd wrapped his arms around me and stroked my head. How I'd felt his heart beating. How he'd made me feel so strong, so beautiful, so everything-would-be-all-right.

My chest heaved and a sob muscled up my throat.

Sucking air deep into my lungs, I drew my knees to my chest, and let go.

A good cry is more therapeutic than a one-hour bump with a shrink.

I awoke purged of all the grief and pent-up frustration.

Rejuvenated.

In control.

Until I made a jackass of myself twelve hours later.

Tom called at seven to ask if I'd heard from Anne. I hadn't.

He'd established that his wife had made no reservations for a flight from Montreal to Charlotte for any day that week. I told him I'd talked to an SQ officer.

Tom suggested Anne had probably gone off by herself to think and we would hear from her soon. I agreed. We both needed to believe it.

Hanging up, my eye once again fell on the mirror. Nine days since the break-in and the cops had found zip.

Flash recall.

Anne's hunk in 3C.

Mother of God! Had she gone off with some

stranger she'd met on an airplane? Could that stranger be the same person who had vandalized my home?

Another flash.

Ryan's surveillance order.

Were there still stepped-up patrols past my place? Might a passing squad car have seen Anne's departure?

Unlikely, but worth a shot.

Bundling up, I headed out.

It was another immaculate day. The radio had predicted a high of minus thirty Celsius. At seven fifty-five, we weren't even close.

Within ten minutes a squad car rolled up the block. I walked to the curb and waved them over.

Yes, they were still passing frequently. Yes, this team had been working days all week. No, they hadn't seen a towering blonde with a lot of luggage. They promised to ask the guys on the other shifts.

Back to the lobby, where it was at least warm enough for blood to circulate.

Ryan pulled up at eight-ten. I got in. The car smelled of cigarette smoke.

'*Bonjour.*'

'*Bonjour.*'

Ryan handed me the faxed photo from Menard's senior yearbook. The shot was small and dark, with all color and some contrast lost in transmission. But the face was reasonably clear.

'Looks like Menard,' I said.

'And a thousand other guys with red hair, glasses, and freckles.'

I had to agree.

'Any word from your friend?'

'No.'

I shifted my feet. Unzipped my parka. I didn't know what to do with my eyes. My legs. My arms. I felt awkward and uncomfortable with Ryan. I wasn't sure I could manage conversation with him.

'Rough night?' Ryan asked.

'Why the sudden interest in my sleep patterns?'

'You look tired.'

I looked at Ryan. The shadows under his eyes seemed deeper, his whole face more clenched.

What the hell's going on with you? I wanted to ask.

'I've got a number of things on my plate,' I said.

Ryan put a finger to the tip of my nose. 'Don't we all.'

Twenty minutes later we were on Cyr's porch.

Ryan had phoned ahead, and Cyr answered on the first ring. This time the old coot was fully clothed.

In the living room, Cyr took the same recliner he'd occupied during my visit with Anne.

Ole Hopalong.

Put it away, Brennan.

I introduced Ryan and let him do the talking.

'*Monsieur Cyr, nous avon—*'

'Speak English for the little lady.' Cyr grinned at me. 'Where's that good-looking friend of yours?'

'Anne's gone home.'

Cyr cocked his head. 'She's a pistol, that one.'

'This will just take a moment.' Ryan pulled the fax from his pocket and handed it to Cyr. 'Is that Stephen Menard?'

'Who?'

'Stéphane Ménard. The man who ran the pawnshop in your building.'

Cyr glanced at the fax.

'*Tabarnouche!* I may look like Bogie, but I'm eighty-two years old.'

Cyr pushed to his feet, shuffled across the room, and turned on the TV. Picking up a large, boxy lens attached by a cord to the back of the set, he flipped a button and scanned the fax.

Menard's face filled the screen.

'That's terrific,' I said.

'Videolupe. Great little gadget. Magnifies so I can read just about everything.'

Cyr moved the lens casually over the photo, then focused on Menard's ear. The image zoomed until the upper edge of the helix almost filled the screen.

'Nope.' Cyr straightened. 'That's not your boy.'

'How do you know?' I was astonished at his certainty.

Cyr lay down the lens, shuffled back, and crooked a finger at me.

I stood.

'See that?' Cyr fingered a small bump of cartilage on the upper part of his ear's outer rim.

'A Darwin's tubercle,' I said.

Cyr straightened. 'Smart lady.'

Ryan was watching us, a look of confusion on his face.

'Never knew anybody had bumps like mine, so one time I showed them to my doctor. He told me it was a recessive trait, gave me some articles.' Cyr flicked his ear. 'Know how these little buggers got their name?'

'They were once thought to be a vestige of pointed ears on quadrupeds.'

Cyr bounced on his toes, delighted.

'What does this have to do with Menard?' Ryan asked.

'Menard had the biggest bastards I've ever seen. I teased him about it. Told him one day I'd find him grazing on trees or eating small furry things in the basement. He wasn't amused.'

Ryan rose. 'And the man in the photo?'

Cyr held out the fax. 'No bumps.'

At the door, Ryan paused.

'One last question, sir. Did you and Menard part on good terms?'

'Hell no. I threw his ass out.'

'Why was that?'

'Got tired of complaints from other tenants.'

'Complaints about what?'

'Unsavory clientele, mostly. Some about noise late at night.'

'What kind of noise?'

'Damned if I know. But I'd heard enough carping. Is that a word? Carping?'

'Yes.'

'Sounds like a fish.'

Ryan dropped me at home, apologized, said he'd be on duty all weekend. He promised to phone if he heard anything on Menard or the other set of prints. Or anything on Anne.

I didn't ask if his work schedule extended into Saturday night.

Screw it. Who cares?

My answering machine held no messages.

Katy wanted me in Charlotte by the twenty-second, so I tried busying myself with tasks that had to be done before my departure.

Bed linen. Plants. Gift wrapping of packages for the caretaker, the techs at the lab.

Ryan?

I set that one aside.

I also busied myself with tasks that just had to be done.

Laundry. Cat litter. Mail.

I blasted Christmas music, hoping jingling bells or heralding angels might kick-start me into a holiday mood.

No go. All I could think about were the bones on my lab tables, the printouts on my blotter, and where the hell was Anne.

At three, I gave in and headed to Wilfrid-Derome.

Typical Saturday afternoon. The lab was empty and still as a tomb.

One *Demande d'expertise* form lay on my desk.

Four months earlier an elevator worker had disappeared from an inspection job at a building in

Côte St-Luc. Thursday his decomposed body was found in Parc Angrignon in LaSalle. X-rays showed multiple fractures. Pelletier wanted me to analyze the trauma when the bones were cleaned.

Setting the form aside, I again took up Claudel's list.

Overhead, the fluorescents hummed. Outside, gusts whined around the window casings. Now and then some frozen windborne particle ticked a pane.

Simone Badeau. Too old.

Isabelle Lemieux. Dental work.

Marie-Lucille d'Aquin. Black.

Micheline Thibault. Too young.

Tawny McGee. Way too young.

Céline Dallaire. Broken collarbone at age fourteen.

The names went on and on.

After an hour I switched to Charbonneau's list.

Jennifer Kay. Esther Anne Pigeon. Elaine Masse. Amy Fish. Theresa Perez.

Now and then I crossed to the lab to recheck a bone, hoping to find some detail I'd overlooked. Each time I returned disappointed.

When I'd finished with the names, I went back through the lists by age. Then height. Date of disappearance.

I knew I was grasping at straws, but it was like a compulsion. I couldn't stop myself.

Down the corridor, I heard the security doors swoosh.

Place of disappearance.

Terrebonne. Anjou. Gatineau. Beaconsfield.

Butte County. Tehama County. San Mateo County.

At six I sat back, thoroughly discouraged. Two and a half hours, and I'd accomplished nothing.

Footsteps sounded hollow in the empty hall. Probably LaManche. Besides me, the chief would be the only one punching in on a Saturday night.

Congratulations, Brennan. You have the same social life as a sexagenarian with seven grandchildren.

Back to the lists.

I still had the persistent feeling I was missing some connection.

What?

The cut marks?

All three skulls bore evidence of sharp instrument trauma. With the girl in the leather shroud, the cuts appeared to have been made postmortem. With the others, the cuts appeared to have been made to fresh bone. With all three, the cuts were limited to the ear region.

Death sequence?

Carbon 14 dating suggested the girl in the leather shroud died in the eighties, the other two in the nineties.

Place of origin?

Strontium isotope analysis suggested the girl in the leather shroud might have been born or lived her early childhood in north-central California, then moved to Vermont or Quebec. The others might have lived their whole lives in Quebec.

Might have.

Maybe I was hanging too much on the strontium. Maybe the California angle was a dead end.

Another swoosh, then the sound of voices.

But Menard attended grad school in Chico. Chico is in north-central California. Menard was a renter where the dead girls were found. The period of his tenancy coincided with the timing of at least two of the deaths. Louise Parent saw him with young girls on two occasions. One running. One unconscious.

Was the California link mere coincidence?

My hindbrain thought sat up, settled back.

What?

Try as I might, I couldn't lure the thought from its lair.

Back to Menard.

Menard took possession of his grandparents' home in Montreal in 1988.

But the guy living there now isn't Menard, though he's using Menard's name.

I threw my pen on the blotter.

'So who the hell is he?'

'I don't know.'

I jumped at the voice.

Looking up, I saw Ryan standing in my doorway.

'But we got a hit on his girlfriend.'

29

'Anique Pomerleau.'

I curled my fingers in a give-it-to-me gesture.

'Went missing in 1990.'

'Age?'

'Fifteen.'

That fit. The woman at Menard's house appeared to be in her mid to late twenties.

'From where?'

'Mascouche.'

'What happened?'

'Kid told her parents she was spending the weekend with a friend. Turned out the girls had cooked up a story so Pomerleau could bunk in with her new squeeze. When she didn't turn up on Sunday, the parents started checking. On Monday they filed the MP report. At that point Anique had been gone for almost sixty hours.'

'She never made it to the boyfriend's place?'

'She made it all right. The two hit a couple of

bars Friday night, got into a fight, Anique stormed out. Lover boy got lucky, spent the weekend with bachelorette number two.'

'Cops believed his story?'

'The bartender and the lucky lady backed him up. Pomerleau was a troubled kid with a history of runaways. The parents insisted she'd been abducted, but the cops figured she'd taken off.'

'Did they pursue the case?'

'Until the leads went cold.'

'That was it?'

'Not quite. Three years later the Pomerleaus got a call from little Anique. Said she was fine, wouldn't divulge her whereabouts.'

'That must have been a shock.'

'Couple years go by, the phone rings again. Same deal. Anique tells them she's OK, but not a word about where she's living. Last call came in ninety-seven. Father's dead by then. Mother's living in a bottle of Bombay Sapphire.'

'Pomerleau's prints were on file here in Quebec?'

Ryan nodded. 'She's got a jacket full of petty stuff. Vandalism. Shoplifting. One incident involving a stolen auto. Probably joyriding. Last entry was four months before her disappearance.'

I felt agitation bubbling to the surface. Here was another twist that didn't fit. 'What on God's earth is Anique Pomerleau doing with Stephen Menard?'

'He's not Menard.'

'Don't patronize me, Ryan.' I picked up my pen,

tossed it back on the blotter. 'Mister X. *Monsieur X.* How'd she end up with the guy?'

I snatched up the pen and pointed it at Ryan.

'And why can't we find out who this toad is? And where's the real Stephen Menard? And when did the identity switch take place?'

'Would you like some dinner?'

'What?'

'Dinner.'

'Why?'

'I have some things I want to tell you.'

'Right. You and Claudel keep a hotline to my phone for all breaking news. Where the hell is Claudel, anyway?'

Ryan started to speak. I cut him off.

'I'm sick to death of Claudel and his fuck-you-if-you-don't-like-it attitude. Charbonneau's the only one who treats me with any respect.'

'Claudel's got his own way of doing things.'

'So do echinoderms.'

'You're judging Claudel harshly. What are echinoderms?'

That tripped the switch.

'*I'm* judging *him* harshly? From the outset I've had to fight that narcissistic little prig to get him to take me seriously. To get *anyone* to take me seriously.'

I considered crushing the pen.

'The bones are too old. Carbon 14 is too expensive. The girls were hookers. Louise Parent died in her sleep. Old ladies do that. They're known for doing it.'

'I was referring to drooling.'

'See!' I jabbed the pen at Ryan. 'Your flip attitude doesn't help.'

'Tempe—' Ryan reached out to touch me. I drew back.

'Of course. I forgot. You love me. But you love a lot of things. Goat cheese. Parakeets. The Weeki-Wachee Mermaids.'

Ryan's mouth opened to say something. I cut him off.

'Right. You love me. You just can't find time to be with me.'

I stormed on, all the pent-up frustration rolling in one powerful surge.

'Now, suddenly you're free for dinner! On Saturday night! What a lucky girl I am!'

The words spewed like water through a sluice gate.

'What about duty? What about your'—I hooked my index fingers to bracket the word—'niece?'

The pen ricocheted off the blotter and winged toward Ryan. Throwing up a hand, he deflected it.

I shot to my feet.

'Oh God, I'm sorry. I didn't mean to hit you.'

Dropping into my chair, I put my face in my palms. My cheeks felt warm and damp.

'Christ. What's wrong with me?'

I felt a hand on my shoulder.

Palming away wetness, I did an ear-tuck with my hair and raised my head.

Ryan was gazing down at me, the travel-poster eyes filled with concern.

Or pity?

Or what?

'I'm sorry,' I said. 'I'm not sure where all that came from.'

'Everyone's under pressure.'

'Everyone's not turning into Il Duce.'

I was aware of LaManche before actually seeing him. Movement in my peripheral vision. The smell of pipe tobacco and drugstore cologne.

Throat clearing.

Ryan and I turned. LaManche was in my doorway.

'I thought you both might like to know. The coroner has officially ruled Louise Parent's death a homicide.'

'She was smothered?' I asked.

'I believe so.'

'Have you gotten the tox results?' Ryan asked.

'Traces of sleeping medication, Ambien, were detected in the blood and urine. Levels were consistent with the ingestion of ten milligrams several hours before death.'

'What about timing?' Ryan asked.

'Did you establish whether Parent ate that soup for lunch or for dinner?'

'Phone records indicate calls were made from the Fisher home at three fifty-five, four-fourteen, and five-nineteen P.M. that Friday. The first was to Parent's priest, the second to a pharmacy two blocks away. The third was to a cell phone. We're working on that.'

I shot Ryan a look. No one had told me that.

'So Parent's last meal must have been dinner.'

'The soup would have been evacuated from the stomach after three hours, the Ambien after two,' LaManche said. 'The sleeping aid would have been dissolved in the tea.'

'According to the niece, Parent usually ate around seven. Assuming she did so on Friday, that brings us up to ten P.M.,' Ryan calculated. 'Assuming she took the Ambien at bedtime, that brings us up to eleven or midnight. So death must have occurred in the early hours of Saturday morning.'

'That is consistent with the state of decomposition,' LaManche said.

'My offer's still on the table,' Ryan said, when LaManche had gone.

'When did you learn about the phone calls?' I asked.

'Today. It's one of the things I was going to tell you. Hurley's?'

I looked at Ryan a long, long time, then wrenched my lips into a smile.

'With one condition.'

Ryan spread his palms.

'The check's mine.'

'Hee-haw!' Ryan said.

Hurley's Irish Pub is on rue Crescent just below rue Ste-Catherine. Driving there, I debated my choices: Park at home and risk hypothermia walking. Die of old age searching for a place to leave the car.

I opted for parking over thermal equilibrium.

Scurrying along Ste-Catherine, I questioned the wisdom of that decision.

Ryan was seated in the snug when I arrived, a half-drunk pint on the table in front of him. I ordered lamb stew and a Perrier with lemon. He ordered chicken St-Ambroise.

While awaiting our food, Ryan and I circled each other warily. We both tried jokes. Most fell flat.

Around us swirled the usual Saturday night throng of drinkers. Some looked happy. Others desperate. Others merely blank. I couldn't imagine their myriad problems and relationships.

Beside us, a young couple sat pressed together closer than socks from a dryer. He wore red felt reindeer antlers. She wore a Christmas sweater.

As I stared, reindeer antlers nuzzled Christmas sweater's neck. She laughed.

They looked so happy, so comfortable with each other.

Christmas sweater's eyes met mine. I looked away quickly, to a sign above Ryan's head.

Bienvenue. Welcome. Fáilte. Someone had draped a pine garland across the top edge.

A girl wormed past our table, moving with the exaggerated care one uses to mask inebriation. She had pale skin and a long black braid.

I thought of Anique Pomerleau. Where had she been for almost fifteen years? Why was she now with the man who was using Menard's name?

The waitress brought our dinners. Ryan ordered another pint. I ordered another Perrier.

As we ate, the conversation turned to work. Safe ground.

'Claudel's gone to Vermont.'

My brows shot up. 'To research the real Menard?'

Ryan nodded.

'Whose idea?'

'Claudel is a good cop.'

'Who thinks I'm a moron.'

'I don't hang with morons.'

You don't hang with me. I didn't say it.

'Do you suppose this Menard impostor killed Louise Parent?' I asked.

'It's a possibility.'

'Pretty good possibility, don't you think? Parent calls me about Menard. Within days, some guy tunes her up with a pillow.'

Ryan didn't comment.

'But how could this Menard impostor have known that Parent called me?'

'How could anyone have known?'

I had no answer for that.

'Have you talked to the neighbor with the SUV?'

'He's clean.'

'I keep thinking about Parent's final night. Her last feelings and thoughts. Do you suppose she knew?'

'There were no signs of a struggle. She was lubed on Ambien.'

'Some cold-blooded psycho found a way into that house in the middle of the night and smothered Parent with her sister's pillow. Do you suppose she sensed pressure against her face? Smelled the fabric softener? Tasted the feathers? Felt terror at some level?'

'Don't do this to yourself, Tempe.'

'I just keep wondering about her last sensations.'

To keep myself from imagining those of three dead girls. I didn't say that either.

'There's something I haven't told you yet.'

I waited for Ryan to continue.

'Louise Parent left an estate worth almost a half million dollars. She was insured for another quarter million.'

'The beneficiary?' I asked.

'Her sister. Rose Fisher.'

Ryan dropped me off around nine-thirty. He didn't ask to come in. I didn't invite him.

The answering machine was dark and still.

Where the hell was Anne?

Shower. Teeth. Face.

Into bed. Birdie hopped up and curled beside me.

I tried reading. Too agitated.

Closing my book, I turned off the light.

Subliminal gnawing.

I rolled from my right side to my left. To my right.

Birdie shifted to the corner of the bed.

I'd never wanted a drink so badly in my life. Could one tiny cabernet hurt?

You're an alkie. Alkies can't do booze.

I punched the pillow. Rolled to my back.

Giving up on sleep, I groped for the remote, clicked on the TV, and found a mindless sitcom.

What was it I was missing?

Anique Pomerleau disappeared from Mascouche in 1990. She was fifteen. Today she's alive and living in Montreal.

Two of the pizza basement girls were around fifteen. The leather shroud girl was older.

Angie Robinson disappeared in 1985. She was almost fifteen. Unlike Pomerleau, she's never turned up.

The actors became shadowbox puppets. The dialogue and laugh track receded to background.

Angie Robinson broke her wrist. The leather shroud girl broke her wrist. But their ages don't match. Neither do their heights.

What was I missing?

Angie Robinson disappeared in north-central California. I couldn't remember the name of the place. Conners? Corners? Cornero?

Was that Butte County?

No. Butte County was Chico.

Menard spent at least a year in Chico. But which Menard? The real one?

Angie Robinson's father filed his MP report with the Tehama County Sheriff's Department.

Throwing back the covers, I got up, booted my computer, logged onto Yahoo!, and asked for a map of north-central California.

Tehama County lay directly northwest of Butte.

I found Chico, and almost directly above it, the little village of Corning.

I zoomed in on the region.

Towns and secondary highways appeared. Hamilton City. Willows. Orland.

I clicked on an arrow, moved north.

Red Bluff.

The thought lurking in my subconscious lumbered toward focus, receded.

Red Bluff.

What?

Think, Brennan. Think.

The most minuscule atom of an idea sparked.

When had Red Bluff been in the news?

Ten years ago? Twenty?

Why?

Think!

I got up and killed the TV. Tossing the remote, I paced the room, desperate to get into the back-country of my subconscious.

Silence filled the condo. Not the comforting, I'm-alone-enjoying-my-solitude kind. A pressing silence.

Back and forth. Back and forth.

Red Bluff. Red Bluff.

Finally, a neural pathway fired. I froze.

Dear God! Was that it?

I flew to the computer.

Who was that victim?

Using multiple search engines, most of which sent me through infuriating, labyrinthine back alley cyberloops, I finally found the name.

More searching.

Archives of the *Red Bluff Daily News*.

Archives of the *Chico Examiner*.

The normal sounds of night receded to the edge of my hearing. Birdie slumbered on.

Hours later, I sat back, numb with the horror of what I was unraveling.

I understood what was going on.

30

I lasted until seven A.M. before phoning Ryan. He answered quickly, sounding alert but tired.

'Am I waking you?'

'I had to get up anyway to answer the phone.'

'Old joke, Ryan.'

'You sound wired. What's up?'

I laid out my theory and told him what I'd discovered in my cyber research.

'Holy shit.'

'We need to get into that house, Ryan.'

'The pizza parlor bust isn't my case.'

'The Louise Parent homicide is. Menard-whoever probably killed Parent to keep her from talking to me.'

I heard a match, then slow exhalation.

'I want Claudel and Charbonneau to hear this. You going to be there awhile?'

'I'll wait.'

Ryan called back at nine to tell me they'd rendezvous at my place at eleven.

'Claudel agreed?'

'Luc's a good cop.'

'With all the charisma of the Night Stalker. I'll make coffee.'

Knowing Claudel would be hard to convince, I spent the next hour online arming myself with as much information as possible.

Claudel arrived first, wearing his usual arrogant frown.

'*Bonjour*,' I said, gesturing him to the sofa.

'*Bonjour*.'

Claudel removed his overcoat. I took it.

Claudel tugged each Armani sleeve to cover each antiseptically white Burberry cuff, then sat and crossed his legs.

'*Café?*' I offered.

'No.' Claudel made a show of checking his watch. '*Merci*.'

Ryan and Charbonneau showed up within minutes of each other, each in faded jeans and sweater. Ryan had hit a pâtisserie on his way.

I filled mugs of coffee for Ryan and Charbonneau, then the three of us helped ourselves to pastries. Throughout, Claudel maintained his this-better-be-good detachment.

Ryan kick-started the meeting.

'Tempe, tell these guys what you told me.' He turned to Claudel. 'Luc, I want you to hear her out.'

I started churning out the words.

'On May 19, 1977, a twenty-year-old woman named Colleen Stan set out to hitchhike from Eugene, Oregon, to Westwood, California. After several rides she was picked up by Cameron Hooker and his wife, Jan. The Hookers drove Stan to the Lassen National Forest, handcuffed, blindfolded, bound, and gagged her, and took her to their home.'

Birdie strolled in, sniffed two pairs of boots and one pair of loafers, made his choice.

'The little guy likes you, Luc.' Charbonneau winked at his partner.

'Sorry.' I jumped up and removed my cat from Claudel's lap.

Birdie, in as much as cats are capable, looked offended.

'Cameron Hooker kept Colleen Stan sealed in total darkness, subjected to complete sensory deprivation, for up to twenty-three hours per day. For seven years.'

'Sonovabitch,' Charbonneau said.

'Hooker imprisoned Stan in a series of boxes he designed specifically for that purpose. When it suited him, he took her out, hung her from pipes, stretched her on a rack, whipped her, shocked her with electrical wires, starved, raped, and terrorized her.'

Claudel picked a cat hair from his sleeve.

'Hooker's wife ultimately set Stan free. Hooker was arrested in November 1984. The following fall he was convicted of kidnap, rape, sodomy, and a number of other charges. Media

316

coverage turned into blood sport.'

'What is the relevance of this?' Claudel sighed.

'Colleen Stan's ordeal took place in Red Bluff, California. Red Bluff is forty miles from Chico.'

'Stephen Menard was a grad student in Chico in 1985,' Charbonneau said, reaching for his second doughnut.

I nodded.

Birdie sidled to the couch, arched, then brushed Claudel's leg. Going bipedal, he placed both forepaws on Claudel's knee.

Again apologizing, I scooped the cat up and secured him in my bedroom.

'But the mutt here in Montreal isn't Menard,' Charbonneau said when I returned.

'I'm using the name for convenience.'

'So where's the real Menard?'

'I don't know. Maybe he was killed by the man living in Pointe-St-Charles. That's your job.'

'Go on,' Ryan urged.

'The Stan case was all over the news from the fall of eighty-four through the fall of eighty-five. The press loved it, called it the Girl in the Box Case. Then the Sex Slave Case.'

Claudel looked at his watch.

'In 1985 a fourteen-year-old girl named Angie Robinson disappeared from Corning, California. Corning is located between Chico and Red Bluff.' I paused for emphasis. 'I have reason to believe one of the three pizza basement skeletons is that of Angie Robinson.'

Charbonneau's doughnut stopped in its trajectory to his mouth. 'The kid in the leather shroud?'

'Yes.'

'The one with the broken wrist,' Claudel jumped in. 'You were certain the ages are incompatible.'

'I said Angie Robinson was too young and too short to be a match with skeleton 38428. But if Angie lived for some time after her disappearance, that would account for the discrepancies.'

'Explain the strontium and Carbon 14 results to Luc,' Ryan said.

I did.

'And explain the dental sealant again.'

I did.

'Holy shit,' said Charbonneau. 'You think Menard followed the news coverage and was inspired by this head case Hooker?'

'Yes. But there's more. Anique Pomerleau disappeared from Mascouche in 1990 at age fifteen. Friday, Ryan and I saw Pomerleau in Menard's house.'

'Menard's been here since eighty-eight,' Charbonneau said.

Claudel tipped back his head and spoke down his nose.

'So based on this story about a girl in a box—'

'The girl has a name.' Claudel's cynicism was jiggling my switch. 'Colleen Stan.'

Claudel's nostrils tightened.

'So you believe Menard has been holding Anique Pomerleau against her will for a decade and a half? That Angela Robinson and the other females buried in the cellar were also his captives?'

I nodded.

For a few moments no one spoke. Claudel broke the silence.

'Did Anique Pomerleau attempt to escape?'

'No.'

'Did she signal to you in any way that she wanted to leave Menard's house?'

'She wasn't wearing a banner that said "Help Me," if that's what you mean.'

Claudel arced an eyebrow at Ryan.

'Pomerleau looked pretty scared,' Ryan said.

'She looked terrified,' I said.

'What exactly did she do?' Charbonneau asked.

'She ducked out of sight as soon as Menard looked at her. Acted like an abused puppy.'

'You think Menard's holding Pomerleau as some kind of sex slave?' Charbonneau.

'I am not suggesting motive.'

'Bull snakes.' Claudel snorted.

'I'm a little hazy on herpetology, Detective. What exactly does that mean?'

Claudel raised both shoulders and spread his hands. 'Any healthy adult capable of doing so would reach out for help.'

'Psychologists disagree,' I snapped. 'Apparently you're not familiar with the Stockholm syndrome.'

Claudel's outstretched palms turned skyward.

'It's an adaptation to extreme stress experienced under conditions of captivity and torture.'

The hands dropped to Claudel's lap. His chin dipped.

'The Stockholm syndrome is seen in kidnap victims, prisoners, cult members, hostages, even abused spouses and kids. Victims seem to consent to, and may even express fond feelings for, their captors or abusers.'

'Weird label,' Charbonneau said.

'The syndrome's name came from a hostage situation in Stockholm, Sweden, in 1973. Three women and a man were held for six days by two ex-cons robbing a bank. The hostages came to believe the robbers were protecting them from the police. Following their release, one of the women became engaged to one of the captors, another started a defense fund.'

'The defining characteristic is to react to a threatening circumstance with passivity,' Ryan said.

'Lie down and take it.' Charbonneau shook his head.

'It goes beyond that,' I said. 'Persons with Stockholm syndrome come to bond with their captors, even identify with them. They may act grateful or even loving toward them.'

'Under what circumstances does this syndrome develop?' Claudel asked.

'Psychologists agree there are four factors that must be present.' I ticked them off on my fingers. 'One, the victim feels his or her survival is threatened by the captor, and believes the captor will carry through on the threat. Two, the victim is given small kindnesses, at the captor's whim.'

'Like letting the poor bastard live,' Charbonneau interjected.

'Could be. Could be brief respites from torture, short periods of freedom, a decent meal, a bath.'

'*Sacrament.*' Charbonneau again shook his head.

'Three, the victim is completely isolated from perspectives other than those of the captor. And four, the victim is convinced, rightly or wrongly, that there is no way to escape.'

Neither Charbonneau nor Claudel said a word.

'Cameron Hooker was a master at this game,' I said. 'He kept Stan entombed in a coffin under his bed and usually took her out simply to brutalize her. But now and then he'd allow her periods of freedom. At times she was permitted to jog, to work in the garden, to attend church. Once Hooker even drove her to Riverside to visit her family.'

'Why wouldn't she just split?' Charbonneau jabbed a hand through his hair, sending the crown vertical.

'Hooker also had Stan convinced he owned her.'

'Owned her?' Charbonneau.

'He showed her a cooked-up contract and told her he'd purchased her as a slave from an outfit called the Company. He told her she was under constant surveillance, that if she tried to escape members of the Company would hunt her down and kill her, along with members of her family.'

'*Cibole!*' Charbonneau threw up his hands.

'Hooker traumatizes Stan, she feels totally isolated, has to look to him for her slightest need, and she ends up bonding with the freak?'

'You've got it,' I said. 'Some of the most damaging defense testimony focused on a love letter Stan wrote to Hooker.'

Charbonneau looked appalled.

'Elizabeth Smart was held by crazies for almost a year,' I said. 'At times she could hear searchers calling out to her, even recognized her own uncle's voice on one occasion. She never really tried to escape.'

'Smart was a fourteen-year-old kid,' Charbonneau said.

'Remember Patty Hearst?' Ryan asked. 'Symbionese Liberation Army grabbed her and kept her locked in a closet. She ended up robbing a bank with her captors.'

'That was political.' Charbonneau shot to his feet and started pacing the room. 'This Hooker had to be some kind of psychotic mutant. People don't go around snatching up girls and stashing them in boxes.'

'The phenomenon may be more common than we know,' I said.

Charbonneau stopped pacing. He and Claudel looked at me.

'In 2003, John Jamelske pleaded guilty to holding five women as sex slaves in a concrete bunker he'd constructed under his backyard.'

'Right down the road,' Claudel said, at last switching to English. 'Syracuse, New York.'

'Oh, man.' Charbonneau again did the hair thing. 'Remember Lake and Ng?'

Leonard Lake and Charles Ng were a pair of pathological misogynists who built a torture chamber on a remote ranch in Calaveras County, California. At least two women were videotaped while being tormented by the pair. The tape was labeled *M Ladies*, M standing for murdered.

'Whatever happened to those assholes?' Claudel's voice dripped with disgust.

'Lake was collared for shoplifting and offed himself with a couple of cyanide capsules. Ng was nailed in Calgary, then fought extradition to the U.S. for about a decade, right, Doc?'

'It took six years of legal wrangling, but Ng was finally returned to California for trial. In 1998, a jury found him guilty of murdering three women, seven men, and two babies.'

'Enough.' The chill had gone from Claudel's voice. 'You believe Menard brought his freak show to Montreal?'

'According to Rose Fisher, Louise Parent phoned to tell me she'd seen Menard twice with young girls. We found three buried in a basement under space he rented.'

'You think Menard transported Angie Robinson from Corning, California, to Montreal?'

'Angie or her body.'

'And that he abducted and subjugated Anique Pomerleau?'

'I do.'

Claudel voiced my fear.

'And, if threatened, Menard might kill Pomerleau.'

'Yes.'

Claudel's eyes pinched. He looked at his partner, then rose.

'A judge should consider this probable cause.'

'You'll get a warrant?'

'When his ass hits the bench.'

'I want to go with you to Pointe-St-Charles.'

'Out of the question.'

'Why?'

'If all this is true, Menard will be dangerous.'

'I'm a big girl.'

Claudel looked at me so long I thought he wasn't going to reply. Then he hitched a shoulder at Ryan.

'Ride shotgun for the cowboy. No one else will.'

I was stunned. The humorously challenged had attempted a joke.

The rest of that Sunday was agony. Puttering through tasks, I felt sadness mixed with deep disappointment in myself. Why hadn't I realized earlier that the bones might have been those of girls held captive? Why hadn't I understood why my profiles failed to fit the descriptions on the MP lists? Again and again, I wondered: Would it have made a difference?

Disturbing images kept welling in my head. Anique Pomerleau, with her pale white face and long dark braid. Angie Robinson in a leather shroud in a cellar grave.

Riding with Ryan.

Anne. Where the hell was Anne? Should I be doing more to find her? What?

I tried Christmas carols. They cheered me as effectively as a Salvation Army Santa.

I went to the gym, pounded out three miles with CDs of old favorites cranked in my earphones.

The Lovin' Spoonful. Donovan. The Mamas and the Papas. The Supremes.

Tossing and turning in bed that night, one refrain kept looping through my brain.

Monday, Monday . . .

Two Mondays back I'd excavated the bones of three young girls.

One Monday back I'd tweezed feathers from Louise Parent's mouth.

Tomorrow I might be exploring the house of horrors.

Can't trust that day . . .

I shuddered over what the next Monday would bring.

31

Claudel had a warrant by nine. Ryan was at my place at quarter past.

When I got into his Jeep, Ryan handed me coffee. Caffeine was not what I needed. I was wired enough to recaulk the Pentagon.

Thanking him, I pulled off my mittens, wrapped my fingers around the Styrofoam, and worked on slowing my heartbeat even as I sipped.

Five minutes out, Ryan cracked his window and lit up a Player's. Normally he would have asked if I minded. Today, he didn't. I assumed he was feeling as jittery as I was.

The streets were clogged with the remnants of Monday morning rush hour. A decade and twenty minutes later we entered the Point.

Turning onto de Sébastopol, I could see two cruisers and an unmarked Impala positioned at intervals along the block. Exhaust floated from all three tailpipes.

Ryan slid behind the nearest cruiser. Killing the engine, he turned to me.

'If Menard so much as frowns in your direction, you're out of there. Do you understand?'

'We're going to search the place, not assault it.'

'Things could turn ugly.'

'There are seven cops here, Ryan. If Menard's uncooperative, cuff him.'

'Any threatening move, you hit the deck.'

I saluted smartly.

Ryan's voice hardened. 'I'm serious, damn it. If I say split, you're gone.'

I rolled my eyes.

'That's it.' Ryan's hand moved to restart the engine.

'All right,' I said, pulling on my mittens. 'I'll obey orders. *Sir*.'

'No nonsense. This is dangerous work.'

Ryan and I got out and quietly closed our doors.

Overnight the weather had changed. The air felt moist and icy, and heavy gray clouds hung low in the sky.

Seeing us, the stable dog started in. Otherwise, there wasn't a sign of life on de Sébastopol. No kids sticking pucks. No housewives hauling groceries. No pensioners gossiping on balconies or stoops.

Typical Montreal winter day. Stay indoors, stay in the metro, stay underground. Hunker in and remain sane until spring. The barking sounded all the louder in the overall stillness.

Ryan and I angled across the street. As we

approached the Impala, the dynamic duo got out.

Claudel was wearing a tan cashmere overcoat. Charbonneau was in a big shaggy jacket, the composition of which I couldn't have guessed.

We exchanged nods.

'What's the plan?' Ryan asked in English.

Claudel spread his feet. Charbonneau leaned his fanny on the Impala.

'One unit will stay here.' Claudel jerked a thumb toward the cruiser at the far end of the block. 'I'll send the other around to de la Congrégation.'

Charbonneau unzipped his parka, shoved his hands in his pockets, jiggled his change.

'Michel's going to take the back door.'

A walkie-talkie screeched from Charbonneau's hip. Reaching back, he fiddled with a button.

Claudel's eyes flicked to me, back to Ryan.

'Brennan knows what to do,' Ryan said.

Claudel's lips thinned, but he said nothing.

'We'll show Menard the judge's Christmas greeting, order him to sit, then toss the place.'

Charbonneau rested a hand on his gun butt. 'Wouldn't ruin my holiday if this pogue decided to pull a Schwarzenegger.'

'All set?' Claudel slipped a two-way from his waistband, rebuttoned his coat.

Nods around.

'*Allons-y,*' Claudel said.

'Let's go,' his partner echoed.

Pushing off the Impala, Charbonneau strode

toward the far end of de Sébastopol. He spoke to the driver, then the cruiser disappeared around the corner. Charbonneau reversed direction and cut diagonally across the vacant lot.

Thirty seconds later, Charbonneau's voice came across Claudel's walkie-talkie. He was at Menard's back door.

Claudel waved a 'come on' to the other team of uniforms.

As we picked our way up the icy walk, Claudel in the lead, Ryan and I following, the second cruiser slid to the curb behind us.

Stumbling along, I felt the same formless dread I'd felt on Friday. Heightened. My heart was now thumping like a conga drum.

At the turn, Claudel stopped and spoke into his walkie-talkie.

I stared at Menard's house, wondering what it had been like when the real Menard's grand-parents, the Corneaus, owned it. The place was so dark, so menacing. It was hard to imagine chicken being fried, baseball being watched, or kittens chasing balls in its gloomy interior.

Claudel's radio sputtered. Charbonneau was in position.

We stepped onto the stoop. Ryan twisted the brass knob. The bell shrilled as it had on Friday.

A full minute passed with no response.

Ryan twisted again.

I thought I heard movement inside. Ryan tensed, and one hand drifted toward his Glock.

Claudel unbuttoned his coat.

Still no one appeared.

Ryan twisted the bell a third time.

Absolute stillness.

Ryan pounded on the door.

'Open up! Police!'

Ryan was raising his fist for another go when a muffled shot spit through the silence. Blue-white light popped around the curtain edges in the window to my right.

Claudel and Ryan dropped to identical crouches, weapons drawn. Grabbing my wrist, Ryan pulled me to the ground.

Claudel screamed into his walkie-talkie.

'*Michel! Es-tu là? Répet. Es-tu là?*'

In a heartbeat Charbonneau's voice crackled back, 'I'm here. Was that gunfire?'

'Inside the house.'

'Who's shooting?'

'Can't tell. Any movement back there?'

'Nothing.'

'Hold position. We're going in.'

'Move!' Ryan gestured me back.

I scrambled to the spot he indicated.

Claudel and Ryan rocketed to their feet and began battering the door, first with their shoulders, then with their boots. It held firm.

In the distance the stable dog flew into a frenzy.

The men kicked harder.

Splinters flew. Slivers of yellowed varnish skittered in the air. The weathered boards held.

More kicking. More cursing. Claudel's face went raspberry. Ryan's hairline grew damp.

Eventually I saw movement where the faceplate of the lock screwed into the wood.

Waving Claudel back, Ryan braced, flexed one leg, and thrust it forward in a karate kick. His boot slammed home, the latch bolt gave, and the door flew inward.

'Stay here,' Ryan panted in my direction.

Breathing hard, guns crooked two-handed to their noses, Claudel and Ryan entered the house, one moving left, the other right.

I slipped inside and pressed my back against the wall to the right of the door.

The foyer was dim and still and smelled faintly of gunpowder.

Claudel and Ryan crept down the hall, weapons arcing, eyes and bodies moving in sync.

Empty.

They moved into the parlor.

I moved to the far side of the foyer.

In seconds my eyes adjusted.

My hand flew to my mouth.

'*Este!*' Claudel lowered his weapon.

Wordlessly, Ryan dropped his elbow and angled his Glock toward the ceiling.

Menard was seated where he'd been on Friday, his body slumped left, his head twisted strangely against the sofa back. His left hand dangled over the armrest. His right lay palm up in his lap, the fingers loosely curled around a nine-millimeter Smith & Wesson.

Charbonneau's voice sputtered on the two-way. Claudel answered.

Ryan and I moved closer to Menard.

Claudel and Charbonneau exchanged excited words. I heard 'suicide,' 'SIJ,' 'coroner.' The rest of their conversation didn't register. I was mesmerized by the Menard-thing on the sofa.

Menard had a dime-sized hole in his right temple. A stream of blood trickled from its puckered white border.

The exit wound was at Menard's left temple. Most of that side of his head was gone, spattered on the brass lamp, the dangling crystals, and the floral wallpaper of the hideous room. Mingled with Menard's cranial wreckage was a macabre gumbo of blood and brain matter.

I felt a tremor under my tongue.

Ryan dragged the Windsor chair as far as from the body as possible, led me to it, and pressed gently on my shoulders. I sat and lowered my head.

I heard the uniformed cops storm in.

I heard Ryan's voice, shouted orders.

I heard Charbonneau. The word 'ambulance.' The name Pomerleau.

I heard doors kicked open as Ryan and the others moved through the house.

To escape the present, I tried to focus on all I would have to do in the future. Reassess the MP lists. Resubmit skeletal descriptors with open age estimates. Obtain DNA samples from Angie Robinson's family.

It was no good. I couldn't think. My attention kept drifting back across the room. My eyes roved the hands, the splayed legs, the gun.

The face.

Menard's freckles stood out like dark little kidneys against the pallid skin. Though his eyes were open, the expression was blank. No pain. No surprise. No fear. Just the empty stare of death.

My own mind was a combat zone. Relief that Menard would hurt no one else. Anger that he'd escaped so easily. Pity for a life so grotesquely twisted. Anxiety for Anique Pomerleau.

Concern that we still did not have the answers.

This wasn't Menard. Who *was* this guy? Where was Menard?

Fingers caressed my hair.

I looked up.

'You OK?'

I nodded, touched by the tenderness in Ryan's expression. 'Have you found Pomerleau?'

'House is empty.' Ryan's voice was heavy as a coffin lid. 'There are things here you might want to see.'

I followed him through a hallway, into a back room, and down a narrow stairway to a poorly lit cellar. The walls were brick and windowless, the floor cement. The air was damp and smelled of mold, dust, and dry rot.

Around me I could see the usual assortment of basement junk. A metal washtub. Garden implements. Stacks of cardboard boxes. An old sewing machine.

I heard voices, then a muffled expletive ahead and to my right.

Passing through an open door, Ryan led me into

a second room. Though similar in construction to the outer basement, this one was smaller and brightly lit. Its walls and ceiling were covered with polyurethane panels.

Claudel and Charbonneau were standing by a counter that might once have served as a workbench. Both wore latex surgical gloves.

Hearing us enter, Charbonneau turned. His face looked like something in the claret family.

Ryan left to do another sweep of the basement.

'The little troll had himself a really special place down here.' Charbonneau swept a hand around the room. 'Soundproofing and all.'

My eyes followed the arc of Charbonneau's motion.

In one corner two sets of handcuffs dangled from a pair of rings imbedded in the ceiling. A crude table hugged the adjacent wall. I crossed to it, a cold numbness in my gut.

The table was sturdily built, of plywood and two-by-fours. Eye-hooks had been screwed into each corner, then a leather cuff attached to each hook. Four chains lay coiled beside the cuffs.

'This table isn't old,' I said.

'Table?' Charbonneau's voice trembled with anger. 'It's a goddamn rack!'

I walked to the workbench. Claudel looked at me, then shifted left, his face a shrink-wrapped mask of control.

The numbness made the rounds of my innards.

A bullwhip. A cat-o'-nine-tails. A riding crop. A

hide-covered paddle. A noose with an enormous knot at midloop.

'All the tricks needed to show your slave who's boss.' A vein throbbed in Charbonneau's temple. I saw fury in his eyes.

'*Calme-toi, Michel.*' Claudel's voice was a flat line.

'And this asshole was real creative.'

Charbonneau jabbed at a horse bit, a curling iron, a crudely made gag with a ball in the center.

'Check out his reading material.'

Charbonneau's rage made him hyperactive. He snatched up a magazine, tossed it down. 'Porn. Bondage. S and M.' He grabbed a videotape. *The Story of O.*

As the video hit the workbench, Ryan charged in, his jaw muscles tightened all the way to his sternum.

'I've found something.'

We moved as one, out the door, through the outer basement, around an ancient furnace, and into a chamber much like the one we'd just left.

Floor-to-ceiling shelves wrapped three sides of this room. A single bare bulb hung from its ceiling.

Ryan strode to the far wall. We followed. Behind the shelving I could see polyurethane similar to that lining the other room. The edge of one panel had been pried free.

'This wall isn't brick. It's plywood.'

Ryan ran his fingertips vertically along the newly exposed plywood, just beyond the shelving.

'There's a discontinuity.'

Claudel removed one glove, mimicked Ryan's move, then nodded.

Ryan pointed to the door through which we'd entered.

'Check out the lights.'

We all turned. One switch plate looked shiny and new, the other dingy and cracked.

'The older one works the overhead.'

He left the rest unsaid.

Claudel yanked off his remaining glove. Wordlessly, he and Ryan began ripping polyurethane.

Charbonneau hurried to the outer basement. I heard clattering and scraping, then he was back with a rusted crowbar.

Within minutes Ryan and Claudel had bared a six-inch swath. In it I could see a crack and two hinges. Through the crack, not a sliver of light.

Gauging door width, they attacked the other side of the shelving where two polyurethane panels met. Their efforts revealed another hairline fissure between sheets of plywood.

'Let me at it.' Charbonneau moved forward.

Ryan and Claudel stepped aside.

Charbonneau inserted the tip of the crowbar into the gap and levered.

A section of wall and shelving jigged forward.

Charbonneau slid the tip of the crowbar farther and heaved.

Plywood, batting, and shelving popped free.

Charbonneau grabbed a shelf and yanked. The false wall swung wide, revealing an opening approximately five by two feet.

The overhead bulb illuminated the first eighteen inches of the cavity behind the wall. Beyond that, the chamber was pitch-black.

Dashing to the door, I flicked the shiny switch, and spun.

My teeth clamped my lower lip as my throat clenched.

32

The room had begun life as a fruit cellar or storage bin. It was approximately eight by ten, and, like Menard's little fun house, entirely soundproofed. The interior smelled of mold and old earth overlain by chemicals and something organic.

The furnishings were grimly stark. A naked bulb on a frayed wire. A portable camp toilet. A crudely built wooden platform. Two tattered blankets.

On the platform sat a pair of women, heads down, backs rounded against the polyurethane paneling. Each wore a studded leather collar. Nothing else.

The women's skin looked bitter white, the shadows defining their ribs and vertebrae dark and sinuous. A long braid snaked from the nape of each neck.

Charbonneau let forth a curse charged with the full lexicon of anger and abhorrence.

One face snapped up. Haggard. Eyes like those

of some wild creature startled in the night.

Anique Pomerleau.

Her companion remained motionless, head down, bony arms clutching her bony knees.

Claudel spun and disappeared into the outer basement. I heard boots cross cement then thunder up stairs.

'It's all right, Anique,' I said, as gently as I knew how.

Pomerleau's eyes flinched. The other woman hugged her legs harder to her chest.

'We're here to help you.'

Pomerleau's gaze darted between Ryan and Charbonneau.

Motioning the men back, I stepped into the chamber.

'These men are detectives.'

Pomerleau watched me, eyes wide black pools.

'It's over now, Anique. It's all over.'

Moving slowly, I crossed to the platform and laid a hand on Pomerleau's shoulder. She recoiled from my touch.

'He can't hurt you anymore, Anique.'

'*Je m'appelle "Q."*' Pomerleau's voice was flat and lifeless.

Removing my parka, I draped Pomerleau's shoulders. She made no attempt to hold the garment in place.

'I'm "Q." She's "D."' Accented English. Pomerleau was Francophone.

Ryan shrugged off his jacket and handed it to me.

I took a cautious step toward 'D,' gently touched her hair.

The woman tucked tighter and curled her hands into fists.

Enveloping 'D' in Ryan's jacket, I squatted to her level.

'He's dead,' I said in French. 'He can never harm you again.'

The woman rolled her head from side to side, not wanting to see me, not wanting to hear me.

I didn't press. There would be time to talk.

'I'll stay with you.' My voice cracked. 'I won't leave.'

Stroking her foot, I rose and withdrew.

While Charbonneau remained in the antechamber, I retreated to the outer basement. Ryan followed.

The honest truth? I didn't trust my own treacherous emotions. My mind was paralyzed by shock and by anguish for these women, my gut curdled by loathing for the monster who'd subjected them to this.

'You OK?' Ryan asked.

'Yes,' I said in the calmest voice possible. It was a lie. I was flailing, and feared an enormous coming apart.

Folding my arms to mask the tremors in my chest, I waited.

A lifetime later distant sirens split the stillness, then grew into a screaming presence. Boots pounded overhead, then down the staircase.

Pomerleau panicked at the sight of the paramedics. Darting to the toilet, she hopped up, wedged herself into the corner, and held both arms straight out in front of her. Neither the EMTs nor I could coax her down. The more we reassured, the more she resisted. In the end, force was required.

The other woman went fetal as she was placed on a gurney, covered, and removed from the cell.

Ryan and I accompanied the ambulance to the Montreal General. Claudel and Charbonneau remained to greet LaManche and the coroner's van, and to oversee the SIJ techs in processing the house.

Ryan smoked as he drove. I kept my eyes on the city sliding by my window.

At the ER, Ryan paced while I sat. Around us swirled a cacophony of bronchial coughs, colicky wails, exhausted moans, and anxious conversation. In one corner Dr. Phil chastised a couple who'd been sexless for years.

Now and then Ryan would drop next to me and we'd exchange whispered comments.

'These women don't even know their names.'

'Or they're too terrified to use them.'

'They look starved.'

'Yes.'

'"D" looks worse.'

'I think she's younger.'

'I never saw her face.'

'Sonovabitch.'

'Sonovabitch.'

We'd been there an hour when Ryan's cell vibrated. He stepped outside. In minutes he was back.

'That was Claudel. The prick made home movies.'

I nodded numbly.

'I'm to call Charbonneau when we leave here.'

Twenty minutes later a frizzy-haired woman entered through sliding doors that led to the ER. She wore a white lab coat and carried two clipboards and one of those plastic bags used for patient possessions.

A huge black woman with swollen breasts and a bawling newborn lumbered to her feet and zeroed in. The doctor led the mother back to her chair, glanced at her infant, then spoke a few words. The woman shouldered her baby and patted its back.

The doctor wove toward us through the obstacle course of human misery. Scores of eyes followed her, some frightened, some angry, all nervous.

Again, her progress was blocked, this time by a burly man with a towel-wrapped hand. As before, the doctor took the time to reassure.

Ryan and I rose.

'I'm Dr. Feldman.' Feldman's eyes were bloodshot. She looked exhausted. 'I'm treating the two women brought in a short time ago.'

Ryan made introductions.

'The older—'

'Anique Pomerleau,' I cut in.

Feldman made a notation on the top chart.

'Ms. Pomerleau has minor bruising, but otherwise looks pretty good. Her lungs are clear. Her X-rays are normal. We're waiting for results on bloodwork. Just to be sure, we'll run her through the scanner when it's free.'

'Is she talking?' I asked.

'No.' Clipped. I have a hundred others waiting to be seen.

'Any signs of sexual assault?' Ryan asked.

'No. But the kid's a different story.'

'Kid?' I popped.

Feldman exchanged the bottom chart for Pomerleau's. 'Do you have a name?'

Ryan and I both shook our heads.

'I'd say the younger one's fifteen, maybe sixteen, although she's so emaciated I could be under-estimating. Someone's used this kid as a punching bag for a very long time.'

I felt white heat invading my brain.

Feldman flipped a page and read from her notes. 'Old and new bruising. Poorly healed fractures of the left ulna and several ribs. Scarring around the anus and genitals. Burns on the breasts and limbs from some sort of—'

'Curling iron?' I kept my voice even, my face neutral.

'That would do it.' Feldman wrist-flipped the pages of the chart into place.

'Is she lucid?' I asked.

'She's practically catatonic. Unresponsive. Stone-flat eyes. I'm no psychiatrist.' The harried face went from Ryan to me. 'But this kid may never be lucid.'

'Where are they now?' Ryan asked.

'On their way upstairs.'

An orderly appeared at the sliding doors. Catching Feldman's attention, he waggled a chart. She waved in his direction.

'When can we talk to them?' Ryan asked.

'I'm not sure.' The orderly threw up both hands. Feldman gave him a hold-on gesture. 'What about security? Is some psycho papa or ex-hubby going to bluster in and try to reclaim his possessions?'

'The psycho in this case just blew his brains out.'

'Pity.'

We gave Feldman our cards. She pocketed them.

'I'll call.' She held out the bag. 'Here are their outfits.'

I could see metal studs poking through the plastic.

Ryan and I met Charbonneau at Schwartz's deli on boulevard St-Laurent. Though I had no appetite, Ryan insisted food would sharpen our minds.

We placed three identical orders. Smoked meat sandwich, lean. Pickle. Fries. Cott's cherry soda.

We updated one another as we ate.

'Doc LaManche lifted prints from the corpse that ain't Menard. They're a match for the ones from the letter opener. Luc's ringing the land of fruits and nuts.'

'When did the latents go into the California system?' Ryan asked.

'Late Friday.' Charbonneau took a bite of his sandwich, knuckled mustard from a corner of his mouth. 'If California's a bust, Luc'll shoot the prints through Canada and the rest of the States.'

Ryan told Charbonneau what Feldman had found.

'This guy was a frickin' sadist.' Charbonneau picked up his pickle. 'Shot pics of the good times to keep the tingle in his weenie.' Charbonneau finished the pickle, then tipped back his head and drained his soda. 'The shots in his scrapbooks look like amateur mock-ups from the porn gallery. Sick bastard tried to re-create life from his art.'

'Did you find photos of "D"?' My voice didn't sound like my own.

Tight nod. 'One pretty good face shot. Luc's circulating it in Canada and south of the border.'

'Where were the home videos?' Ryan asked.

'Mixed in with the porn tapes.'

'Got them with you?'

Charbonneau nodded.

'Your place or ours?'

'Our unit's piece-of-crap VCR is busted again.' Charbonneau wadded his napkin and chucked it onto his plate.

'There's a setup in our conference room,' I said.

'Let's do it.' Ryan scooped up the bill.

'Bring some sunshine into my day.' Charbonneau pushed back his chair.

My sandwich lay untouched on my plate.

It was worse than I could have imagined. Girls suspended by their arms. Bound wrist to ankle. Spread-eagle. Always hooded. Always passive.

Ryan, Charbonneau, and I watched in silence. Now and then Charbonneau would clear his throat, shift his feet, recross his arms. Now and then Ryan would reach for a smoke, remember, finger-drum the table.

Some footage was jerky, as though taken with a handheld. Some was steady, probably shot from a tripod or some other fixed position.

The tapes were numbered one through six. We'd gotten through most of the first when Claudel walked in.

Three heads swiveled.

'Tawny McGee.' Claudel looked like he'd sucked on a lime.

I hit PAUSE.

'"D"?' I asked.

Curt nod. 'Reported missing by the parents in ninety-nine.'

'Where?' Ryan asked.

'Maniwaki.'

Claudel slid a fax across the table. Charbonneau glanced at it, then handed it to Ryan, who handed it to me.

My scalp prickled.

I was looking at the face of a child. Round cheeks. Braids. Eyes that were eager, curious, always up to something.

Imp. My mother would have called this child an imp.

Like she called me.

Like I called Katy.

I scanned the descriptors.

Tawny McGee disappeared when she was twelve years old.

I swallowed.

'Are you sure this is "D"?'

Claudel slid another fax across the table. I picked it up. On it was the inquiry he'd circulated.

The face in the photo was an Auschwitz version of the one I'd just viewed. Older. Thinner. A hope-lost expression.

No. That was wrong. Tawny McGee's face showed nothing at all.

'Have you gotten anything on the bastard that had her?' I asked, my voice taut with anger.

'I'm working on it.'

'Have you called the McGee family?'

'Maniwaki's handling that.'

'Where the hell's Stephen Menard?' My pitch was rising with each question. 'Could Menard be in on this? Could Menard and this guy have been working a tag team? Did SIJ find other prints in that house?'

Claudel tipped back his head and slid a look down his nose.

Charbonneau got to his feet. 'I'm on Menard.'

When they left I punched PLAY, biting a knuckle to maintain control.

We were twenty minutes into the second tape when the phone rang. The receptionist announced Dr. Feldman. I mouthed the name to Ryan as I waited for the connection.

'Dr. Brennan.'

'Penny Feldman at Montreal General.'

'How are they?'

'The kid's awake and hysterical. Won't let anyone touch her. Says someone's going to kill her.'

'Anglophone or Francophone?'

'English. She keeps asking for the woman from the house.'

'Anique Pomerleau?'

'No. Pomerleau's in the next bed. I think she means you. Sometimes she asks for the woman with the cop. Or the woman with the jacket. I hate to dope her up before a psychia—'

'I'm on my way.'

'I'll hold off on sedation.'

'By the way, her name's Tawny McGee. The parents have been notified.'

Ryan used the flashers and siren. We were at the hospital in twelve minutes.

Feldman was in the ER. Together we rode to the fourth floor. Before entering the room, I observed through the open door.

It was as though Menard's victims had reversed roles.

Anique Pomerleau lay still in her bed.

Tawny McGee was upright, face flushed and wet. Her eyes darted. Her fingers opened and closed around the blanket clutched under her chin.

Ryan and Feldman waited in the hall while I entered the room.

'Bonjour, Anique.'

Pomerleau rolled her head. Her gaze was listless, her affect dead as petrified wood.

McGee's head dropped. Her gown slipped, exposing one fleshless shoulder.

'It's all right, Tawny. Things will be better now.' I crossed toward her bed.

McGee threw back her head. Cartilage jutted like thorns from her impossibly white throat.

'You're going to be fine.'

McGee's mouth opened and a sob ripped free. The thorns bobbed erratically.

'I'm here.' I reached to adjust the fallen gown.

McGee's head snapped down and her fingers tightened on the blanket. The nails were dirt-packed slivers.

'No one can hurt you now.'

The broken-doll face jerked toward Pomerleau.

Pomerleau was watching us with glassy disinterest.

McGee whipped back to me, threw off the blanket, and began tearing at the IV taped to her forearm.

'I have to go!'

'You're safe here.' I laid my hand on hers.

McGee went rigid.

'The doctors will help you,' I soothed.

'No! No!'

'You and Anique are going to be fine.'

'Take me with you!'

'I can't do that, Tawny.'

McGee yanked her hand free and clawed madly at the tape. Her breathing was ragged. Tears streamed down her face.

I grasped her wrists. She twisted and fought,

desperation firing her with strength I would not have thought possible.

Feldman ran in, followed by a nurse.

McGee grabbed my arm.

'Take me with you!' Wild-eyed. 'Please! Take me with you!'

Feldman nodded. The nurse administered an injection.

'Please! Please! Take me with you!'

Gently prying McGee's fingers, Feldman motioned me from the bed. I stepped back, trembling.

What could I do?

Feeling useless and ineffective, I pulled a card from my purse, jotted my cell number, and laid it on the bedside table.

Moments later I stood in the corridor, jaws and hands clenched, listening as McGee's pleas yielded to the sedative.

Whenever I think back on that moment, I wish to God I'd done what Tawny was asking. I wish to God I'd listened and understood.

33

It was another restless night. I woke again and again, each time tangled in the remains of some barely remembered dream.

When my clock radio kicked on, I groaned and squinted at the digits. Five-fifteen. Why had I set the alarm for five-fifteen?

I palmed the button.

Music continued.

Slowly, awareness.

I hadn't set the alarm.

That wasn't the alarm.

Throwing back the quilt, I bolted for my handbag.

Sunglasses. Wallet. Makeup. Checkbook. Calendar.

'Damn!'

Frustrated, I upended the purse and pulled my mobile from the heap.

The music stopped. The digital display told me I'd missed one call.

Who the hell would call at five in the morning?

Katy!

Heart racing, I hit list.

Anne's cell phone number.

Ohmygod!

I hit option, then call.

'*We're sorry. The party you are dialing cannot—*'

It was the same message I'd been hearing since Friday.

I clicked off and returned to the log. Today's date—5:14:44 A.M.

The call had been dialed from Anne's cell. But Anne's cell wasn't on.

What did that mean?

Anne had dialed, then turned her phone off? Her battery went dead? She moved out of range?

Someone else had used Anne's phone? Who? Why?

Again scrolling through options, I chose SEND MESSAGE, typed in 'Call me!' and hit SEND.

I punched another number. Tom answered after four rings, sounding groggy.

Anne was not there. He hadn't heard a word, nor had any of the friends he'd contacted.

I threw the phone at my pillow. Normally, I leave the phone on my bedstand at night, but the stress of events had broken that routine. I'd left the damn thing in my purse. Make one small mistake and it nails you.

Sleep was out of the question. I showered, fed Birdie, and left for the lab.

Ryan entered my office at a little past eight.

'Claudel won the lottery.'

I looked up.

'The prints taken from the fake Stephen Menard belong to a loser named Neal Wesley Catts.'

'Who is he?'

'Street corner thug. Drifter. Did one bump for peddling weed. That's how his prints got into the system. California's faxing his sheet.'

'Claudel's following up?'

'He intends to know every toilet this punk ever flushed.'

'Take a look at this.' I tapped my pencil on Claudel's MP list.

Ryan circled to my side of the desk.

'I've marked the possibles.'

Ryan scanned the names I'd checked. It was the majority of the list.

'The nonwhites are out.'

'And those who were too old or too tall when they disappeared.'

Ryan looked at me.

'I know. Without lower limits on age and height, I can't really limit the subset that much.' I flapped a hand at the skeletons in my lab. 'These girls could have survived years in captivity.'

Like Angela Robinson, Anique Pomerleau, and Tawny McGee.

'I cut samples for DNA testing on Angie Robinson.'

'The one wrapped in leather?'

I nodded. 'I'm sure it's her.'

'I think you're right.'

'The coroner's office is contacting the Robinson family. We'll need a maternal relative to run mitochondrial comparisons.'

I slumped back.

'Anne called this morning.'

'That's great.' Ryan's face broke into a huge smile.

'No. It's not.'

When I told him what had happened the smile collapsed.

'I've called the taxi companies. They're checking their records for a pickup at your place Friday. Would you like me to contact rental car agencies?'

'I guess it's time,' I said.

'It's only been four days.'

'Yes.'

'If she—' Ryan hesitated. 'If something happened we'd be the first to know.'

'Yes.'

Ryan's cell phone rang. He checked the screen, frowned, then gave me his most boyish of grins.

'Sorry—'

'I know. Gotta take it.'

Ryan had barely cleared the door when my desk phone rang. As per my request, the librarian had found materials on sexual sadism and the Stockholm syndrome.

I was reading an article in the *Journal of Forensic Sciences* when Claudel arrived.

'The dead man is Neal Wesley Catts.'

'*S'il vous plaît.*' I gestured to the chair opposite my desk. '*Asseyez-vous.*' Sit.

Claudel tucked down the corners of his mouth and sat.

'Catts was born in Stockton, California, in 1963. The usual sob story, broken home, alcoholic mother.'

Claudel was speaking English. What could that mean?

'Catts dropped out of high school in seventy-nine, hung with the Banditos for a while, got no invite to patch up. Served one hitch in Soledad on a drug rap.'

'Did he hold jobs?'

'Flipped burgers, tended bar, worked at a window frame plant. But here's a tidbit you'll love. The little pervert liked ogling forbidden grail.'

I listened without interrupting.

'Catts was hauled to the bag several times on peeping complaints.'

'Doesn't surprise me.'

'Cops never had enough to charge him.'

'Voyeurism is a typical first step for sexual predators.'

'One old biddy accused him of snuffing her poodle. Again, no proof, no charges.'

'Where was this?'

'Yuba City, California.'

The name hit me like a blow to the chest.

'Yuba City's right down the road from Chico.'

Claudel's lips did something very close to a smile. 'And Red Bluff.'

'When was Catts there?'

'Late seventies, early eighties. Dropped out of sight in the mid-eighties.'

'Didn't he have to report to a parole officer or something?'

'He was clear with the state by eighty-four.'

When Claudel left to search out LaManche, I went back to my reading. I was on my second trip to the library when I ran into the chief.

'Big day yesterday, Temperance?'

'*Carnival.* You've spoken with Claudel?'

'I've just given him a preliminary on Monsieur Catts.'

'Any surprises?'

LaManche pooched out his lips and waggled his fingers. Maybe yes. Maybe no.

'What?'

'I found no gunpowder on the hands.'

'Were they bagged?'

'They were.'

'Shouldn't powder be present if he fired a gun?'

'Yes.'

'How can that be?'

LaManche lifted one shoulder and both brows.

Charbonneau rounded out my morning's list of callers.

'Menard and Catts knew each other,' he said without preamble.

'Really.'

'I managed to locate one of Menard's former

profs at Cal State–Chico. Guy's been teaching since Truman started redecorating the White House, but his memory's primo. He put me onto one of Menard's old girlfriends. Woman named Carla Greenberg.'

The name meant nothing to me.

'Greenberg's on faculty at some small college in Pennsylvania. Says she and Menard dated their first year of grad school, then she left for Belize. Menard didn't land a job on the dig, or on any other project, for that matter, so he stayed in Chico that summer. When Greenberg got back Menard was spending most of his time with some guy in Yuba City.'

'Catts?'

'Our hero.'

'How did Catts and Menard hook up?'

'They look alike.'

'Come on.'

Charbonneau held up a hand. 'I'm not making this up, Doc. According to Greenberg, people kept telling Menard some pawnbroker in Yuba City was his dead-ringer double. The archaeology students liked to prowl this guy's shop, being as he wasn't overly rigid about laws pertaining to antiquities, if you catch my meaning.'

'And?'

'Menard went for a look-see and the two became buds. At least that's the story Menard laid on Greenberg.'

'That sounds preposterous.'

'Greenberg e-mailed this.'

Charbonneau handed me a color photo printed on computer paper. In it three people stood arm in arm on a pier.

The woman was squat and muscular, with straight brown hair and wide-set eyes. The men flanking her looked like bookends. Both were tall and thin, with wild red hair and freckles gone mad.

'I'll be damned.'

'According to Greenberg, Menard spent less and less time in Chico, eventually blew off the program. She was wrapped up in her thesis that fall and never really gave him much thought.'

'Could you find anyone in Yuba City who remembered Catts?'

'One old couple. Still live in a trailer next to the one Catts rented.'

'Let me guess. Nice young man. Quiet. Kept to himself.'

'You've got it.'

Charbonneau reclaimed Greenberg's picture and looked at it as one might look at a turd on the lawn.

'Luc and I are going to spin down to Vermont, flash the pic, see if we can goose a few memories.'

After Charbonneau left, I dialed Anne's cell. *We're sorry. The party . . .*

I tried working my way through the journals the librarian had pulled for me. *British Journal of Psychiatry. Behavioral Sciences and the Law. Medicine and Law. Bulletin of the American Academy of Science and the Law.*

It was no good. My mind kept wandering.

I phoned Anne again. Her cell was still off.

I phoned Tom. No word from his wife.

I phoned Anne's brothers in Mississippi. No Anne. No call.

I forced myself back to the stack.

One article focused on Leonard Lake and Charles Ng, the California geniuses who'd built underground bunkers to house female sex slaves.

At trial, Ng's lawyers argued that their client was a mere bystander, a dependent personality waiting to be led. According to the defense, Lake's ex-wife was the real heavy.

Right, Charlie. You were a victim. Like poor little Karla Homolka.

In 1991, Leslie Mahaffy, fourteen, was found dismembered and encased in concrete in an Ontario lake. The following year, Kristen French, fifteen, turned up naked and dead in a ditch. Both had been brutalized, raped, and murdered.

Paul Bernardo and his wife, Karla Homolka, were subsequently arrested. Young and blond and beautiful, the press dubbed the couple the Ken and Barbie Killers.

In exchange for testimony against her ex-husband, Homolka was allowed to plead guilty to manslaughter. Bernardo was convicted of murder one, aggravated sexual assault, forcible confinement, kidnapping, and performing an indignity on a human body.

Like Lake and Ng, the Bernardos filmed their little orgies. When the tapes finally surfaced, footage showed bride and groom as equal enthusiasts in the torture and murder. But Karla had already cut her deal.

I was moving on to the next article, when my phone rang again.

'They're gone.' Ryan sounded like he was calling from Uranus.

'Who's gone?'

'Anique Pomerleau and Tawny McGee.'

34

'How can they be gone?'

'When the day nurse checked, their beds were empty.'

'There was no guard?'

'We told Feldman security wasn't an issue.'

'Had they been released?'

'No.'

'Were they alone?'

'No one saw them leave.'

'Had they had visitors?' My voice was too loud. 'A family member?'

'We've yet to locate any of Pomerleau's relatives. McGee's sister flew east from Alberta last night. Sandra something. She and the mother are en route from Maniwaki now.'

Adrenaline surge.

'Menard!'

'I floated his description around the floor. No one spotted anyone resembling him.'

'Tawny McGee was hysterical yesterday. These geniuses are now suggesting she and Pomerleau just pulled on their panties and waltzed out?'

'The head nurse thinks they may have split during a shift change. Or during the night.'

'They didn't have clothes!'

'Two coats and two pair of boots are missing from the staff lounge. Along with seventeen dollars from the coffee fund.'

'Where would two disoriented, homeless women go?'

'Calm down.'

I closed my eyes and willed the adrenaline back to its myriad sources.

'They may not have gone anywhere. General's a warren of tunnels and crannies, the basement's some kind of medieval maze. I'm at the hospital now. If they don't turn up inside, we'll canvass the neighborhood.'

'And then?'

'When the McGees arrive I'll find out if Tawny knew anyone in Montreal.'

'Jesus Christ, Ryan. That poor woman loses her child, probably gives her up for dead, then finally gets word her daughter is alive. Now we have to tell her the kid's missing again?'

'We'll find her.' Ryan's voice was tempered steel.

'I'll call the women's shelters,' I said.

'Worth a try.'

It was a dead end. No one had seen or admitted any woman fitting either of the descriptions I provided.

I went back to my research, but it was worse than before. I couldn't sit. Couldn't read. I was charged with enough energy to blast through granite.

These women had been kidnapped years ago, Angela Robinson in 1985, Anique Pomerleau in 1990, Tawny McGee in 1999. Their abductor was now dead.

So why this growing sense of dread?

Had we blown it? Was Catts the sole abductor? Had Stephen Menard been Neal Wesley Catts's accomplice in his twisted little game, or vice versa? Was Menard still out there?

Were Pomerleau and McGee again in Menard's hands? Had he forced them from the hospital? Had the women gone willingly, still under his spell?

Had Catts killed Menard? When? Why?

Catts should have had gunpowder on his hands. LaManche found none. Was it the other way around? Had Menard killed Catts?

I remembered McGee's pleas to be taken from the hospital.

Had McGee persuaded Pomerleau to leave? Had the women simply fled? Had the unaccustomed environment frightened them into flight? But flight to where?

Why this intense feeling that McGee and Pomerleau were in danger? That I could rescue them if I was just clever enough to sort things out?

Why didn't Ryan call?

I'd squeezed every detail I could from the bones. I'd gone over and over the MP lists. What else could I do?

The videos.

Shoving back from my desk, I hurried across the hall and unlocked the conference room. The tapes lay where Ryan and I had left them the previous afternoon. I hit PLAY and watched scene after scene of hooded young women with goth-white bodies.

By repeatedly rewinding and replaying in slow motion, I was able to distinguish what I thought were three victims. One woman had larger breasts. One had a mole to the left of her navel. One appeared taller in relation to background objects.

The setting never varied, though props came and went. A whip. An electric prod. A glass vial. Occasionally Catts appeared on camera brutalizing or menacing one victim or another.

I was repulsed and sickened. These girls should have been worrying about algebra, falling in love, picking out china. Not hanging by their wrists in a stench-filled basement. This was Canada, not sixteenth-century Transylvania.

Rarely had I felt such overpowering anger.

Be objective, Brennan. Look for associations. Trends.

I began again with the tape marked '1.' As patterns emerged, I made a list.

The women appeared in sequence. The taller of the three could be seen only on the first half of the first tape. The larger-breasted woman showed up in later scenes on that tape, and continued into the tape marked '2.' By tape '3' the larger-breasted woman had been replaced by the woman with the mole.

No scene included audio.

Each scene started and ended abruptly.

Some scenes were smooth, recorded with the camera in a fixed position. Others were jerky, recorded with the camera moving.

Suddenly it hit me.

Was Catts ever in the frame when the footage was jumpy? If so, who was filming?

I'd been viewing tapes for almost three hours when I spotted the scene I was looking for.

The camera cut on and swept the room with a bobbing motion.

A girl lay stretched on Catts's table, wrists and ankles bound by leather restraints. Behind her someone had placed a mirror, rectangular, approximately twelve by twenty-four inches.

Catts was in the frame, back to the lens.

My scalp tingled.

Rocketing to my feet, I hit REWIND, then PLAY.

As the lens crossed a point in its arc, I could see a murky figure reflected in the glass.

Menard?

Reversing again, I inched the tape forward in slo-mo, froze the frame.

My hopes plummeted.

'Shit!'

Though grainy and partially eclipsed, the mirror image of the face squinting into the viewfinder across the room was recognizable.

Anique Pomerleau.

'Very effective, you sick bastard.' My voice rang

bitter in the empty room. 'Force one prisoner to film while you torture another.'

I tried watching more footage, but couldn't sit still. Like a toddler on a Twinkie high, I kept bounding up, checking my office phone, scanning the corridor.

After twenty minutes I returned to my office, nearly nauseous with anger and anxiety.

I began an article on the Stockholm syndrome, but unbidden images sucked my focus from the page.

Anique Pomerleau scurrying past Neal Catts's parlor. Tawny McGee begging to be taken from the hospital. Colleen Stan cowering in a coffin under a bed.

I thought about them, sealed in claustrophobic blackness, petrified, naked, alone. Cameron Hooker had hung and stretched Colleen Stan, whipped her, shocked her with electric wires until her skin blistered. Neal Catts had controlled his victims in identical ways, using sensory deprivation, terror, and pain to break them.

I tried to imagine the ordeal these women had endured. Had they lain in the dark listening to the sound of their own breathing? To the hammering of their own hearts? Had they known day from night? Had they felt terror at each rattling of the lock? Had they abandoned hope? Had memories of their former lives slipped from them with time, like fog slowly evaporating into morning air?

Something hardened inside me. I forced myself to concentrate.

As with the tapes, I began taking notes while reading.

Bondage. Magnification of sexual tension by physical restriction of movement.

Sadomasochism. Generation of sexual excitement by giving and/or receiving pain. In the pathological extreme, kidnapping, imprisonment, imposition of involuntary servitude.

The Stockholm syndrome.

I began an outline of the process, adding points as I moved from article to article.

One. Abduction followed by isolation. Victim confined, stripped, humiliated, degraded.

Two. Use of physical and or sexual abuse. Victim made to feel vulnerable.

Three. Removal of normal daylight patterns. Victim kept in continual darkness or light. Use of blindfolds, boxes, hoods.

Four. Destruction of privacy. Defecation, urination, menstruation controlled or observed by captor.

Five. Control and reduction of food and water. Development of dependency on the captor.

Ryan called at three. They'd searched every inch of the hospital. The women were not there.

I returned to my research.

Six. Imposition of unpredictable punishment. Victim denied explanation or rationale.

Seven. Requirement of permission. Victim must ask to eat, speak, stand, etc.

Eight. Lasting pattern of sexual and physical abuse. Victim becomes convinced of permanence of fate.

Nine. Continued isolation. Captor is victim's sole source of contact, information.

Ryan phoned again at four.

'Mrs. McGee and Sandra are here.'

'You've spoken with them.'

'Yes.'

'How did they take it?'

'The mother was distraught. The daughter was furious.'

'Where are they now?'

'I've checked them into the Delta Hotel.'

'Did Tawny know anyone in Montreal?'

'According to Sandra, Tawny's best friend in Maniwaki had cousins in one of the west island burbs. I'm running that down now.'

An idea.

'McGee and Pomerleau knew Catts was dead. Maybe that house was the one place they felt safe.'

'Great minds, Brennan. But no go. I've had it checked. The place was empty. I'll call if anything breaks.'

I returned to the journals.

Ten. Threats of harm to family and relatives.

Eleven. Threats of transfer to more severe captor.

Twelve. Irrelevant leniency. Victim granted unexplained privileges, gifts, periods of freedom.

Thirteen. Unexpected appearances. Establishment of sense of captor's omnipresence.

At six-thirty my cell phone rang.

The voice gave me that heart-plunge you feel diving on a roller coaster.

'"D" wants you.' Female. Strongly accented English.

'Anique?'

'She needs help.'

'I'm glad you called.' I kept my tone casual. 'We're very concerned about you.'

'"D" wouldn't stay at that hospital.'

'Are you all right?'

'"D" may harm herself.'

'Where are you?'

'Home.'

Where was home for Pomerleau? Mascouche? Pointe-St-Charles?

'You're safe?'

'"D" wants you.'

'Tell me where.' I grabbed a pen.

'De Sébastopol.'

'But we checked the house,' I blurted.

Dead silence.

Stupid! Stupid!

'We were worried about you,' I said.

'Come alone.'

'I'll bring Detective Ryan.'

'No!'

'You can trust Ryan. He's a kind man.'

'No men.' Tight.

'I'm on my way.'

I started to punch in Ryan's number, then stopped.

35

I disconnected and stared at the phone, my mind racing through a million what-ifs.

What if I phoned Ryan? Claudel? Charbonneau? Feldman? I wanted support.

What if I raced to de Sébastopol? These women had to be retrieved.

Pomerleau had requested that I come alone. No men. From all I'd read, that made sense. She and McGee had suffered years of abuse at male hands.

Emotions battled inside me. Anger. Loathing. Compassion. Urgency.

All three detectives would be furious if I went on my own.

He could wait outside.

Again, I started to punch Ryan's number. Again, I stopped.

What if Ryan insisted on escorting me inside?

McGee and Pomerleau obviously had a hidey-hole in that house. Ryan's presence might drive them back underground. Might shatter their trust in me. Maybe they weren't even there, but would provide further instructions only if I arrived alone. A police net around the whole neighborhood would be too obvious.

In my mind, I heard McGee's terrified pleas, felt her grip on my arm, saw the desperate hope in her eyes.

Guilt and self-blame hopped into my thinking.

I'd been unable to calm McGee at the hospital. If anything, I'd increased her alarm.

What if Ryan's presence panicked her again?

I lurched to my feet. Yanked my jacket from its peg.

This time I'd do as she asked. I owed it to her. To them.

A new thought stopped me cold.

What if McGee and Pomerleau weren't alone? What if Menard was still working their heads? What if the call was a trap? Would he really dare to harm me? Why not? He was already looking at life in prison, and he was a malignant sociopath.

'Damn! Damn! Damn!'

Who to phone?

Ryan would go paternal. I couldn't deal with that.

Claudel was out of the question.

Pulse racing, I tried Charbonneau, just so someone would know where I'd gone. A mechanical voice informed me that the subscriber I'd dialed was unavailable, and disconnected without inviting input.

I checked my watch.

Six forty-two. I dialed CUM headquarters and left a message for Charbonneau. He and Claudel were probably still in Vermont, but at least they would know where I'd gone.

Silence surrounded me.

More what-ifs.

What if McGee hurt herself?

What if Menard was maneuvering to add me to his fun house?

What if Menard planned to put a bullet through my brain?

I was scanning the face of each ugly scenario, when my cell erupted in my hand.

I jerked as though burned. The handset flew from my grasp, nicked the wall, and ricocheted under my desk. Dropping to all fours, I scrabbled across the tile, grabbed it, and clicked on.

Another shock.

Without preamble, Anne launched into a rambling apology.

Relief and resentment joined the Armageddon in my head.

I cut her off.

'Where *are* you?'

Anne misread the frantic timbre of my voice.

'I don't blame you for feeling hostile, Tempe. My behavior was beyond selfish, but try to understan—'

Seconds were dissolving. Seconds during which Tawny McGee might be slashing her wrists.

'Where are you?' More forceful.

'I am so sorry, Tempe—'

'Where are you?'

'The Sisters of Providence.'

Anne's voice was opening a small space in my brain. Clear thinking was slipping in.

'The convent at the corner of Ste-Catherine and Fullum?'

'Yes.'

Anne was just fifteen minutes away.

Anne was female.

I made a quick decision.

'I need your help.'

'Anything.'

'I'll pick you up.'

'When?'

'Now.'

'I'll be outside.'

I half walked, half ran to my car, heart beating at a marathon pace.

Was I making a mistake to include Anne? Was she already too emotionally drained? Was I putting her at risk?

I decided to tell all and let Anne decide.

A heavy night cold blanketed the city. The wind was moist, the clouds low and sluggish, as though uncertain whether to rain or snow.

Anne stood shivering outside the old mother-house, luggage mounded at her feet.

Rush-hour stragglers still trudged the sidewalks and jammed the streets. As we drove, traffic and Christmas lights smearing the windshield, I briefed Anne on all that I'd learned in her absence. She listened without interruption, face taut, fingers playing the ends of her loosened scarf.

When I'd finished, a full minute passed. I was certain Anne would ask me to take her home.

'I'm a shoo-in for the world's most worthless goat turd.'

'Don't say that, Anne.'

'While I'm mooning about not heading up God's arrangements committee, these kids have been living a nightmare.' She turned to me. 'What kind of testosterone-crazed dickhead could find pleasure in hurting young girls?'

'Don't feel pressured to go with me. I'll understand if you want no part of this.'

'Not a chance, sweetie. I want at this dogball.'

'That's exactly what you're *not* going to do.' I sounded like Ryan. 'Do you have your cell phone?'

'Piece of crap went dead when I tried phoning you this morning.' Anne patted her shoulder bag. 'But I've got Mace.'

I gestured at my purse. 'Dig mine out.'

As I turned onto de Sébastopol, Anne did as I asked.

I parked opposite the stable. Before cutting the headlights, I saw the mongrel uncurl and slink across the yard, eyes glinting, snout working the air.

Anne and I peered the length of the street. To our right, a lone bulb threw a cone of yellow on the stable doors. To our left, the rail yards yawned dark and empty.

'Stay in the car,' I whispered, depressing the handle on the driver's side door.

'No way.'

'Yes.'

'No.'

'Yes,' I hissed.

I heard a swish as Anne's arms locked across her chest. I turned sideways. Silhouetted in the stable light, I could see her upper teeth clamping her lower lip.

I took Anne's hand, and forced a wasted smile.

'I need your help, Annie. But it has to be from a distance. These women have been isolated for years. The world terrifies them.' I squeezed gently, and softened my whisper. 'They don't know you.'

'They don't know you,' she mumbled.

'They reached out to me.'

'What if this asshole Menard is in there?'

'There's a phone in the house. If I don't ring or signal within ten minutes, call Ryan. He's on my speed dial.'

'If Ryan's not available?'

'Call 911.'

When I alighted, the stable dog trotted to the fence. He followed as I picked my way along the street, rose up and snarled when he reached the end of his enclosure. For reasons of his own, he chose not to bark.

The night air smelled of horses and river and impending snow. Overhead a wire groaned, one bare branch tapped another.

At the turnoff I heard a metallic grinding and

darted into the recessed entrance of the last row house. Frozen in the shadows, I strained to pick out the slightest human sound.

Nothing.

I crept from the alcove and peeked around the corner.

A brown bottle lay on the walk.

Budweiser, some irrational brain cell offered.

A gust nudged the bottle. It rolled, scraping gravel and ice.

Squaring my shoulders, I sidestepped the Bud and headed up the walk, careful not to stumble or twist an ankle. The trees and shrubs were like shape-changers, bobbing and morphing in the darkness around me.

I made the turn. The house loomed black and silent, not a pixel of light seeping from within.

I stepped to the stoop, twisted the bell, waited. I twisted again, body coiled for a backward sprint.

The chain and lock rattled. The door cracked. I moved forward, adrenaline-wired like a soldier in combat.

Death mask face. Wide, blinking eyes.

I felt myself breathe.

'It's Dr. Brennan, Anique.'

Pomerleau's gaze swept over my shoulder.

'I'm alone.'

Pomerleau stepped back and the door swung in. I entered. The air still stank of mothballs and must.

Pomerleau closed and locked the door. She was wearing black jeans and a dark blue sweatshirt.

'Is Tawny all right?' I asked.

Pomerleau rotated with zombie slowness. Behind her the door chain swayed like a pendulum.

'Is "D" all right?' I corrected.

'She's frightened.' Hoarse whisper.

'May I?' I undid my zipper.

Pomerleau circled me as I removed my parka. When she turned toward the hall, I hung the jacket on the knob and flipped the door latch to open.

Pomerleau led me to the parlor Catts had christened with his brains. I followed.

Catts's couch was now draped and shoved against the secretary. A single brass lamp cast the room in pale amber.

Tawny McGee was in one of the armchairs, knees up, head down as when I'd seen her in the dungeon. She was covered by the same blanket she'd clutched that day.

'Tawny?'

She didn't move.

'Tawny?'

The frail body contracted.

I took a step forward, alert for the slightest sign of a third presence. The house was eerily still.

'It's Dr. Brennan, Tawny.'

McGee flinched, nudging the end table. The lamp crystals wobbled, and tiny yellow points danced on her hair.

Kneeling, I laid a hand on her foot. Her muscles tightened.

'You're going to be all right.'

She didn't move.

I reached for her hand. Through the wool, my fingers felt something hard and sinuous.

At that instant, rapid-fire pounding split the silence.

McGee recoiled.

Pomerleau went rigid.

The front door creaked, then a voice carried from the foyer.

'Hello?' Anne called out. '*Bonjour?*'

Pomerleau's lips drew back. 'You lied,' she hissed.

Before I could reply Anne appeared in the hall, cell phone in one hand, car keys in the other.

'What are you doing here?' I snapped to my feet.

'You got a call. I thought you'd want to know.' Anne looked from me to Pomerleau to the catatonic shape cowering under the blanket. 'I thought you'd all want to know.'

'It could have waited,' I said, annoyed past politeness.

Knowing she'd made a mistake, Anne pushed on, eager to rectify. 'Charbonneau left a message at CUM headquarters.' She held up the phone. 'The switchboard phoned your cell.'

I noticed Pomerleau recede into the darkness at the end of the hall.

'Stephen Menard is dead,' Anne continued, her eyes tugging at mine for forgiveness. 'He's been dead for years. Catts killed him.'

A sound rose from the huddled form behind me. Half moan, half whimper.

'I'm sorry,' Anne mumbled. 'I thought you'd want to know. I'll go back to the car.' Anne hurried toward the foyer.

I squatted and placed a hand on McGee's foot.

McGee's back rose and rounded. The blanket slipped and her face came up like a pale winter moon.

McGee's lips were trembling.

'You're safe, Tawny. You and Anique are both safe.'

McGee bucked a shoulder. The blanket opened at her lap.

A rope coiled her wrists.

The image didn't compute. A rope. Why a rope? Was it tied?

I heard the front door open.

I looked up. McGee's eyes were filled with horror. I tracked them.

They were fixed on Pomerleau's retreating back.

My lungs stopped. My heart stopped. I felt the blood drain from my face.

Terror in the hospital.

A face behind a camcorder.

Residue-free hands.

Homolka, a willing participant in her husband's depravity.

I knew!

I shot to my feet.

Pomerleau was moving down the hall as though hot-wired. I heard a sickening crack, then a thud.

I raced toward the foyer. The door was open.

Anne lay facedown with her head on the jamb, legs splayed across the linoleum.

I peered into the night. No sign of Pomerleau.

'Annie!' I squatted and felt her throat for a pulse.

Too late, I heard movement behind me. The door angled inward, jammed the heel of Anne's boot.

Before I could turn, light exploded in my head.

I fell into blackness.

36

Seconds later, or so it seemed, I felt my brain elbowing my skull, aggressively seeking more space. I opened my eyes and moved my head. Particles of shattered glass winged through my vision. I closed my eyes and tried to assess.

My chest burned. I was lying on my left side and shoulder. I swallowed, tried to sit up. My arms and legs wouldn't work. I realized they were under and behind me.

Slowly, awareness crept in. I couldn't feel my hands. My feet. I had to move.

Tightening my abs, I again tried to rise to my knees.

Nausea enveloped me. I vomited.

Using my ankles and hips, I tried to push back from the mess. The effort made me retch again and again until my stomach offered nothing but bile.

I lay a moment, breathing deeply, fumbling for explanations. Where was I? How long had I been there?

Gingerly, I rolled my head. A stab of pain almost caused me to cry out.

Think! one battered neuron screamed.

I tried. My thoughts wouldn't congeal into recognizable pictures.

Focus on the moment!

Smell!

Mold. Ratty fabric. Wood. Something else. A chemical cleaner? Kerosene?

Touch!

Rough fibers scratching my cheek. Grit in my mouth. Dust in my nostrils. A carpet?

Sound!

Wind. A branch striking glass. The creaking and breathing of a house interior.

My pulse hammering in my ears.

Muffled footsteps. A hollow clunk.

Distant. Someone moving. In another room?

I opened my eyes again.

I lay on a very dirty carpet. I could see a carved wooden leg, some cranberry upholstery, and the edge of a tattered blanket.

Recognition! I was in Catts's parlor. The lamp was now off.

A door slammed, then silence.

Armchair ahead. Another slamming sound at a greater distance behind me. My brain was assimilating information with the speed of continental drift.

Had someone used a rear entrance? In the kitchen? Catts's kitchen.

I tried to call up the floor plan from my previous visits. It wasn't there.

I held my breath, listened. Not a sound in the house. The blood in my head hammered on. One heartbeat. A dozen. A thousand.

The rear door slammed again. Hurried footsteps approached. I closed my eyes and lay still, every muscle on fire.

I heard a grunt, then splashing.

The smell jumped all my senses. My fingers clenched in their bindings.

Gasoline!

As my eyelids flew open, I was able to identify two shapes.

Tawny McGee sat swaddled in the armchair.

Anique Pomerleau was dousing the room with liquid from a large can.

Fear short-circuited what little rational thought I'd mustered up. What to do? Talk to Pomerleau? Talk to McGee? Play dead?

My lids clamped down. I listened to the liquid sound of a terrible death.

Seconds later I heard another clunk, receding footsteps, then the slamming door.

I opened my eyes. An empty coffee can lay by the baseboard.

Had Pomerleau gone for more gasoline? Where? An outside shed? How long had her previous trip taken? One minute? Two?

My mind zeroed in on one thought.

Get out!

Strobe images. Anne. Pomerleau. A rope circling Tawny McGee's wrists.

Was McGee tied up? Were her feet bound? I'd stroked one ankle, felt nothing. A shard of hope.

'Tawny.'

Silence.

'Tawny.'

Movement in the chair?

I raised my head. The room was a shadowy pool, the furnishings jagged shapes in the darkness.

'"Q" is going to burn the house. We have to get away.'

An intake of breath?

'I know what "Q" did to you.'

The back door slammed. Feet clumped toward us. I lowered my head.

Through slitted eyes I watched Pomerleau enter with a new can and soak the secretary and couch. When the can emptied, she tossed it to the floor and disappeared for another.

'No one knows we're here, Tawny.'

The silence made the room seem darker, more deadly.

'No one will come for us. We must help ourselves.'

No response.

'If I slide closer, can you untie me?'

Silence.

'Are you able to walk?'

It was like talking to the dead.

Frantic, I struggled with my bindings, bucking

and twisting until my skin felt raw. The knots held.

The back door slammed again.

I relaxed, closed my eyes.

Pomerleau returned with more accelerant.

Dear God. Where was Anne? She wasn't in this room. Could I get Anne and McGee out? Would we die before emergency crews could respond?

Should I talk to Pomerleau? Could I form an argument, craft a thought that might buy us some time?

Did it matter? The house had been searched and found empty. I hadn't told Ryan I was coming. Would Charbonneau get my message?

Tears pushed hard. I ached to rip at my bindings, to spring free and grab Pomerleau, to shut down this impostor for a human being.

I lay still and waited.

The smell of gas was strong now. I tasted bile, felt spasms under my tongue.

Another can hit the floor. I watched Pomerleau's feet round the corner.

This time the rear door didn't slam.

I tracked the footsteps. Hallway. Back room.

'Tawny, we have to move!' I hissed.

It was hopeless. I was going to have to act on my own.

Arching and contracting my back, I strained with every fiber to free my ankles from my wrists. The knots held. I wanted to cry from pain and frustration.

Pomerleau's footsteps echoed again in the hall,

then receded into an adjacent room. Seconds later they were closing in on the parlor.

I settled to the floor.

Too late.

The footsteps hitched, then sped toward the armchair. I heard a mewing, more kitten than human, then the footsteps veered toward me.

'So, my little dormice are both awake.'

It was pointless to remain passive. Summoning all my adrenaline-induced strength, I rolled onto my knees and looked up.

Pomerleau was an ebony cutout in the murky gloom. A cutout holding a coffee can. The room reeked of gasoline.

Fear rocketed from nerve ending to nerve ending.

Empathize? Cajole? Accuse? Beg?

'Where's my friend?' Had Anne gotten away somehow?

Hideous leer from Pomerleau. 'She didn't last. She fell through the looking glass.'

Heartsick, I spat out, 'Catts didn't murder those girls. You did.'

When Pomerleau stepped closer, a single arrow of gray illuminated her face. 'Murder?' Dusky voice. 'Where's the fun in that?'

'You tortured and starved them.'

'They fell through my looking glass.'

'Angie Robinson.'

I felt more than saw Pomerleau tense.

'Tell me why,' I pushed.

'Truth or dare?' Lilting.

'What did you do to my friend?'

'Truth or dare?'

Dear God! The woman was enjoying this!

'You've brutalized Tawny.'

'Another Alice in my Wonderland.' Reptilian smile.

'You killed children.'

'Some last. Some don't.'

'Give me their names.'

'Why?'

'Their families have a right to know.'

'Their families can rot in hell, and you won't be telling them. Fool! You won't be telling anything to anyone.'

'Your parents searched for you.' Pleading tone.

'Not hard enough.' Bitter.

'They miss you,' I lied. 'They want you back.'

'There's no going back.'

'There are people who will help you.'

'The looking glass cracks.'

Flashbulb image. My apartment. Shattered pictures, mirrors.

'All the king's horses and all the king's men can't put the damned back together again.' Singsong.

'What happened to Angie Robinson?'

'Just another lost girl.'

'Lost? Or destroyed?'

'Just so much shoveled dirt.'

Keep her talking!

'When did Angie die?'

'Before my time.'

'I know what happened, Anique. I understand. Catts hurt you, then made you hurt others.'

'Who's Catts?'

'Menard. Catts killed Menard and took his name.'

'Menard. Catts.' Air puffed from her lips. 'Amateur hour.'

'He was evil. He tortured you. He tortured Angie Robinson. You had to play along to please him.'

'I didn't play along.' A finger jabbed her sternum. 'I ruled. I was queen.'

'Q.' Queen of Hearts.

'You did what was necessary to survive.'

'You don't get it. I'm the queen, not the rabbit.' *Go with it.*

'I know. You're the strong one, Anique. You shot Catts.'

'He grew weak.'

'You smothered Louise Parent.'

'A mercy killing.'

Her flippant indifference triggered a helpless, savage anger. Suddenly, I couldn't control myself. Without thinking I abandoned my attempt at dialogue and bucked and twisted. Sweat dampened my face and rolled down my spine.

'You callous bitch!'

Pomerleau laughed and rhythmically rose to her toes and dropped to her heels like an excited child until I sat back, heaving and exhausted.

'The police will find you,' I panted. 'You won't get away.'

Pomerleau hooked one finger under a studded

collar circling her neck. A venomous smile crawled the dead pale face.

'Three bodies were pulled from the ashes,' she chanted. 'But, praise the lord, one victim escaped the flames.'

Upending the can, Pomerleau doused my clothes with gasoline.

My stomach lurched. My heart flew to my throat. *Calm! Stay calm!*

Tossing the can, Pomerleau strode from the parlor. I heard her cross the hall, then move through the kitchen, the back bedroom, and the room beside us, pausing briefly in each. My thoughts shifted to Anne. I'm so very sorry, Annie. So stupid and so sorry. I should never have involved you.

An acrid smell began filling the air. *Dear God!*

'Run, Tawny!' I screamed. 'Get out!'

I wrenched and writhed, chest burning, pain cartwheeling through my head.

In minutes, Pomerleau was back, face etched with, what? Elation? Joy?

'The neighbors will call 911,' I shrieked. 'You won't get far.'

'You'll be dead from the smoke.'

Pomerleau struck a match, and watched the small flame sputter and blossom.

'See you in Candyland.'

Her wrist flicked.

I heard a loud whup, felt heat behind me, then saw the room dance in flickering orange light.

37

The flash of flame withered after the opening burst, but choking black smoke began filling the room.

I couldn't get to my feet. The ropes held me twisted backward, ankles bound to wrists. I rolled back up onto my knees.

My eyes burned. My throat grew raw. Though heat was building, my body shook. This fire would not burn itself out. I had to get away or die.

I tried to think but my mind was drifting, bringing up fearful images from other places, other days.

Chalky white bones in a woodstove. A carbonized skeleton in a burned-out basement. Two blackened bodies in a charred Cessna.

'Cut the crap, Brennan!' I shouted aloud. 'Think!'

I drew a series of shallow breaths, coughed, repeated the litany.

'Think!' I yelled again.

My stomach heaved. I swallowed, spoke loudly again, this time to Tawny.

'Tawny! Can you hear me?'

Fire sizzled and popped behind me. In Tawny's direction, only thickening smoke.

'Tawny!' I yelled again.

Back on my side, flexing and extending my hips and knees, I slithered across the carpet, each thrust wrenching my shoulder and abrading my face.

I was on my third push when a banshee shrieking rose from the armchair.

I froze, every hair upright on my neck and arms.

'Tawny!'

The keening continued, one high-pitched note of panic.

Mother of God! Was she burning?

'Tawny, can you walk?' I shouted.

The wailing faltered, gave way to coughing.

'Steady, soldier,' I said more to myself than to Tawny. 'I'm coming.'

Three more thrusts and my body struck the chair. Gasoline and dust felt thick on my skin.

'Cover your mouth,' I panted, as loudly as I could. 'If you can, get down on the floor.'

The coughing grew frenzied.

Pushing up against the chair with my shoulder, I rolled back onto my knees and tried to rock it again and again.

'Tawny! Get down!' I screamed. 'Now!'

Behind us something whooshed. One wall erupted in flames that rushed the ceiling, washing the room in swimmy orange light.

I felt movement, then Tawny thudded to her knees, drew in her limbs, and collapsed into a knot beside me.

Nausea, pain, and fear were taking their toll. I could barely breathe, barely think. But my sluggish brain had computed what my eyes hadn't seen.

A rope trailed from a dog collar on Tawny's neck. Her hands and feet were unbound!

I swiveled to her.

'Tawny,' I coughed. 'You have to help. You can save us, Tawny. You can save us.'

The human knot contracted.

Think, Brennan, think! Had the spreading fire impelled her? Or had that one barked command worked better than kindness? Was she still programmed to respond to orders?

Nothing to lose.

'Tawny, untie me!' I shouted.

The scrawny neck turtled up.

'Now, Tawny, now!'

Tawny's face came round. When our eyes met, pity jumbled my resolve to be hard.

'You're going home, sweetheart. To Maniwaki. To your mother.'

My chest burned. I coughed uncontrollably.

'To Sandra,' I choked out.

Something flickered in the hollowed-out eyes.

'To Sandra,' I repeated.

Tawny's face slackened as a world she thought dead skittered through her mind. Her mouth opened, trembled, then morphed into an O.

'Sandra,' I repeated.

Without a word, Tawny spun and crawled beneath the smoke toward the rear of the building.

I tried to grab her. The ropes stopped me cold.

'Tawny!' My voice cracked. I coughed until my belly screamed and I tasted blood.

When the spasm passed, I twisted and peered in the direction Tawny had gone.

Nothing but thick black smoke.

My heart shriveled. I'd been left alone to die.

Dear God! Was I alone? Was Anne already dead?

'Tawny!' I called out. 'Please!'

Nothing.

As before, I writhed and thrashed. As before, I collapsed exhausted on the filthy rug, skin raw, lungs in agony.

The room began to recede. I thought hypnotically: I'm going to die. I'm going to die. I'm going to die.

Then I heard scraping and banging, like the hurried opening and slamming of drawers. Seconds later a dark form took shape in the smoke and scrabbled toward me.

Tawny's skin gleamed like alabaster. One hand covered her mouth. The other clutched a long, flat object.

What?

She jerked convulsively. A blade flashed firelight.

A knife!

Tawny's knuckles looked white and bloodless. For a moment she stared at her hand, as if trying to figure why the knife might be there.

Then she pounced and rolled me so my face mashed the carpet.

I felt breath on my neck, weight on my back.

My God, she's going to stab me. 'Q' still controls her.

I waited for the blade.

Instead I felt pressure at my wrists. Sawing.

Tawny was cutting my bindings!

Wrenching my head sideways, I gulped for air.

'Faster, Tawny. Hurry!'

I strained the ropes outward as Tawny slashed back and forth across them. Though my arms were numb, I sensed a loosening as fiber after fiber yielded.

An eon later my hands flew apart. Driving my feet downward, I rolled to my back.

Pain roared up my spine and across my shoulders and hips. My vision blurred.

'The knife,' I gasped.

Two Tawnys reached out, then fell back coughing. I grabbed the knife, dropped it.

I clapped my hands, shook them, banged them on the floor. When I tried again I had enough feeling to grasp the handle.

Within seconds I'd freed my ankles.

I tried to rise, toppled. Beside me, Tawny hacked and gagged.

Groping with one hand, I found a cushion. In two thrusts, I hacked off and bisected the outer covering, placed one half over Tawny's nose and mouth, and pressed her palm to it. The other half I slapped to my face.

An icy tingle was moving from my toes to my feet. I pushed up, slid one knee forward. Moved a hand. Advanced another knee. My limbs were working.

Hooking Tawny's arm, I tugged her to all fours. Together we crawled three-legged from the parlor toward the front of the house where there was less flame.

Six feet up the hall a tendril of night air tantalized my nostrils. Rising to a low crouch, I made a mad scramble to the foyer, threw open the door, stumbled over my parka, kicked it aside, shot outside, and flew down the walk, Tawny in tow.

The night smelled frosty and horsey and sweetly alive. Wind cooled my sweat-slicked face. Pellets of ice stung my cheeks, and ricocheted off my shoulders and head.

I wiped tears from my eyes and looked down at Tawny. She sat cross-legged on the ice, naked, weeping and rocking like a frightened child.

I gazed back at the house.

Smoke seeped from some windows, and billowed in a column from the newly opened front door. Fueled by the influx of air, flames were rising rapidly. Otherwise, not a hint of the nightmare inside.

My chest froze in midheave.

I listened.

No sirens.

No one was coming! Anne hadn't phoned! No one had!

A hand flew to my mouth.

Anne. Could she be alive? 'Q' had talked of three bodies in the ashes. Was Anne inside!

Darting to the stoop, I grabbed my jacket, rushed back, squatted, and wrapped Tawny. Sleet ticked and bounced off the nylon.

'Did you see another woman in the house?'

Tawny continued rocking and sobbing.

I gripped her shoulders and repeated my question.

Tawny nodded.

'Where?'

The bony shoulders trembled.

'Where?' I screamed.

'F-floor.'

'What room?'

She looked up, mute.

'The room, Tawny. What room?'

I shook her, repeated my question.

'B-b-back. Basement. I don't kn-know.' Ash speckled her face. Sweat soaked her hair.

As I stood motionless, undecided, the acrid smell of burning slammed my nostrils, and the size of the orange glow increased.

Anne didn't have time for 911! I had to go back!

But I was soaked in gasoline.

With shaking fingers, I unlaced and yanked off my boots, stripped to my undies, then shoved my feet back into the boots. After wetting my cushion cover with snow, I dashed back to the house, head a vortex of pain. At the open door, I dropped to a squat and duck-walked into the smoke.

Stumbling to the armchair, I snatched Tawny's

blanket, draped my shoulders, and groped my way toward the back of the house.

Again, I tried to recall the layout of the back hall. This time my tortured brain warped up a floor plan. Kitchen to the left. Parlor to the right, study or bedroom beyond. Basement stairs descending from a bedroom straight ahead.

Though flame-free, the hallway was dense with smoke. I felt my way blindly, chest and throat tormented.

My hamstrings screamed in protest. Now and then I winged an elbow or banged a shin. I blundered on, one hand extended, the other clamped to my mouth. I thought only of Anne.

Then my outstretched hand slammed something hard. My stomach lurched. I tasted bile.

I flattened my palm on the door. The wood felt warm. I moved it up. Warmer.

Please! No!

I touched the knob. Hot. I turned it, inched open a peephole.

Flames twisted from the bed and curled the drapes at the back of the room. In the dancing shadows, I saw a shape on the floor.

I flung the door wide.

'Anne!'

The shape didn't move.

'Annie!'

Nothing.

Tossing aside my swatch of fabric, I crawled to Anne, pulled the blanket from my shoulders, and folded it lengthwise in layers beside her.

When I sat back, pain exploded in my head. I forced the throbbing to the basement of my skull.

Mustering my dwindling reserves, I rolled Anne onto the blanket, dug beneath her, and pulled an edge. The blanket unfolded and slid between Anne's body and the floor. I felt my way to an end, wrapped one corner around each hand, and began backing out of the room and down the hall.

Anne weighed a thousand pounds. I tried to reassure her, gagged.

I hadn't taken time to check for a pulse. Was she alive?

Please, God!

I tugged at my homemade travois, gaining inches with each burst. My arms and legs turned to rubber.

I heaved and heaved, coughing and panting, every cell shrieking for air. Now and then I flinched as something exploded or crashed in the house. Backing into the parlor, I twisted my head up and around for a quick assessment. Through the smoke I could see flames working up the walls. Only a narrow path down the center remained fire free.

Hours after setting out, I made the turn into the front hall. My eyes burned. My chest burned. My stomach burned.

Leaning a hand on the doorframe, I bent and vomited more bile. I wanted to sit down, to curl into a ball and sleep.

When my stomach settled, I regripped the blanket. My arms and legs trembled as I lurched backward, blindly pulling with all my strength.

The parlor was now an inferno. Flames crawled the woodwork, devoured the secretary, engulfed the couch. Things popped and spit, sending sparks toward the front hall and foyer. I was past feeling. Past thinking. I knew only to pull, back up a foot or two, and pull again.

The front entrance lay five yards behind me.

Three.

Two.

My mind chanted a mantra, urging my body not to fail.

Get through the foyer.

Over the jamb.

Onto the stoop.

When Anne's legs cleared the doorway, I dropped to the ground and placed my fingertips on her throat.

No palpable pulse.

I collapsed onto Anne.

'You'll be fine, old friend.'

Black dots swirled behind my eyelids.

Sleet pelted my back. The ground felt icy against my knees.

Around me, a cacophony of noise. I struggled to make sense of it.

Sobbing.

Was that Anne? Katy?

The yawing and spitting of flames.

Ticking.

Rain on the magnolia? No. Montreal. De Sébastopol. Sleet on the tankers in the rail yard.

What rail yard?

The rumble of distant engines.
Muted honking.
Coyotes wailing far off in the desert.
Not coyotes. Sirens.
The dots congealed into solid black.

38

I am of the opinion that hospitals are to be avoided. People die there.

Ten hours after arriving by ambulance, I rose, pulled on the sweats Charbonneau had given me at Catts's house the previous night, and left General.

How? I walked out. Like McGee and Pomerleau. Piece of cake.

Unlike McGee and Pomerleau, I scribbled a farewell note absolving my care providers from any responsibility. Tough duty with both hands greased and bandaged.

A taxi had me home in ten minutes.

Ryan was on the line in twenty.

'Are you crazy?'

'I've suffered a few burns and a minor bump. Canadians going south have, on occasion, been more severely blistered by the sun.'

'You need rest.'

'I'll sleep better here.'

'Did your accomplice make a run for it, too?'

The smile felt like shrapnel scoring my face. 'Anne has a concussion. She's not a flight risk.'

'Anne's obviously the brains of the outfit.'

'She'll be released tomorrow. Friday we fly to Charlotte.'

'Where winter is viewed as a passing unpleasantry.'

'No mittens. No shovels.'

'Did she actually do the "get thee to a nunnery" bit?'

'Anne wanted solitude. Cheap. The convent offers clean rooms, decent meals, and all the solitude one could wish.'

Memory rewind.

Sleet on my back. Ice under my belly. Fire. Charbonneau barking orders. Claudel covering me with something warm and soft.

'Any word on Pomerleau?' I asked.

'She won't get far.'

'She could be in Ontario by now, or over the border.'

'We found an old scooter in Catts's shed. That was probably her main means of transportation.'

'How do you suppose she got McGee from General to the Point?'

'Taxi. Bus. Metro. Thumb.'

'Where's McGee now?'

'Back at General.'

'What's happening on de Sébastopol?'

'SIJ found a second false wall in the cellar.'

'Where Pomerleau hid McGee during the follow-up search.'

'Probably. Anne's laptop and camera were stashed there.'

'Pomerleau trashed my condo.'

'Looks that way. Maybe Catts helped.'

'To scare me off the pizza basement case?'

'That would be my guess. She may have spotted the computer and camera while creeping your place, thought they were yours, and figured they held evidence pertaining to the skeletons. She'll roll on the story when we net her.'

'How could she have known where I live?'

'Thanks to *La Presse*, it's no secret what you look like or where you work. Pomerleau had the scooter. She could have waited outside Wilfrid-Derome, followed you to your building, and watched to see which lights went on.'

'I think Pomerleau has a mirror phobia.'

'The lady has issues more serious than glass.'

'Pretty cunning the way she misdirected us.'

'Buckle on a collar, strip, and play the victim.'

'I believed it, Ryan. When I saw her in that dungeon, I wanted to cry.'

'We all fell for it. Did you get the bouquet?'

I turned and looked at my dining room table. The 'bouquet' was the size of Laramie, Wyoming.

'It's beautiful. I'm having Hydro-Quebec run an extra waterline.'

I felt my reserves dwindling. Ryan heard the fatigue in my voice.

'Claudel and Charbonneau have a lot to tell

you when you're feeling up to it. For now, eat something, kill the phone, and hit the rack, hot stuff.'

I did. And slept until midafternoon.

Waking was like crossing an event horizon. I felt zestful. Invigorated. Charged with water-walking, omnipotent vitality.

Until I looked in the mirror.

My face was scraped and blotchy. My hair was singed. What remained of my brows and lashes were crinkly little sprigs.

Showering helped little, makeup even less.

I imagined Katy's reaction on Friday. I pictured Claudel with his razor-sharp styling and advert-perfect creases.

'Bloody hell.'

Rebandaging my hands, I headed to CUM headquarters.

'*Sergeant-détective Charbonneau ou Claudel, s'il vous plaît,*' I requested of the lobby receptionist.

'Busy night,' the receptionist said in English, poker-faced.

'A real pip.'

I pictured myself panty-mooning the sky. Great. Word was out. My PC-challenged male colleagues would have a field day.

Charbonneau came down to escort me through security. He asked how I was, then he led me to the squad room, eyes straight ahead.

I entered to whistling and applause.

Sergeant-détective Alain Tibo dug a bag from his desk, popped to his feet, and crossed to me. He looked the type that would play the bulldog in a Disney flick.

'This ain't Dixie, Doc. It gets real cold in Quebec.' I knew Tibo's sense of humor. If the squad needed a clown, he'd be elected. 'We chipped in and got you some proper gear.'

Tibo offered the bag with solemn ceremony.

The sweatshirt was blue, the wording bright red.

There's no such thing as bad weather, only the wrong clothing.
—Old Scottish fisherman's proverb

Below the proverb, a woman built a snowman in a blizzard of flakes. Her hair was orange, her skin pink. The snowman wore a hat. The woman wore nothing but stilettos, bra, and panties.

Rolling my eyes, I jammed the shirt back into the bag. Charbonneau and I crossed to Claudel, weaving through desks and dodging wastebaskets and outthrust feet.

'Claudel bills you for the overcoat,' said a voice behind us. 'Slide it by the captain as a business chit.'

'The leopard skin a Tuesday motif, Doc?' Tibo asked.

'I hear Wednesdays it's circus day,' another voice answered.

I cocked what remained of one eyebrow at Charbonneau.

He started to speak, but Tibo cut him off.

'Don't worry, Doc. Claudel's got a whole set of

405

boxers with them little smiley-face things. Keeps his ass beaming while the rest of him sulks.'

Scooping a file from his in-basket, Claudel rose, and the three of us trooped to an interview room.

'I see my panties have been entered as evidence.' My voice could have kept ice cream solid for a week.

'Word spreads,' said Claudel.

'Indeed.'

'It didn't come from us, Doc,' added Charbonneau. 'Honest to God.'

Somehow, I believed that.

We took chairs around a battered government-issue table.

'I trust you are feeling better,' Claudel said.

'Yes.' Claudel had sacrificed his pricey cashmere to warm me? 'Thank you for the use of your coat.'

Claudel nodded.

A beat went by.

'Menard is dead?' I asked.

Claudel nodded again.

'How can you be certain?'

Claudel opened his file and slid a photo across the table. 'We discovered this in Menard's house in Vermont.'

The picture was black-and-white, the image off angle on the page, like an amateur, homemade print. Despite some fading, the subject was clear. A tall, thin man in a shallow grave, knees flexed, wrists tethered to ankles. Though distorted in death, Menard's face was unmistakable.

I flipped the print. On the back someone had written the initials S.M., and the date 9/26/85.

'Catts killed Menard in California in September 1985? And kept a photo of the body?'

'The sheriff's going to do some digging around Catts's old trailer,' Claudel said.

'Angela Robinson disappeared in October eighty-five,' I said. 'According to neighbors, Menard returned to Vermont the following January.'

'Only it wasn't Menard.' Charbonneau placed both forearms on the table and leaned forward. 'We're thinking Catts got the idea for his little horror show by following the Cameron Hooker–Colleen Stan media coverage. The shithead was in Yuba City, right down the road from Red Bluff. The press was hemorrhaging stories on "the Girl in the Box."'

'About that same time Catts was getting chummy with Stephen Menard,' Claudel cut in. 'Catts didn't want to repeat Hooker's mistake of remaining close to the scene of the abduction, so Menard's farm was the perfect solution for playing out his fantasies. Catts killed Menard, then waited for his prey.'

'Angie Robinson,' I said.

'Catts abducted Robinson and transported her to Vermont,' Clauel continued. 'Once there, he exploited his resemblance to the Menard kid.'

'Grew flaming orange dreadlocks and beard and stayed clear of the locals,' I said.

'You've got it.' Charbonneau jabbed the air with a finger, then slouched back in his chair.

'Why leave Vermont?' I asked.

'Maybe Catts was getting jumpy. Must have been a few people around who actually knew Menard,' Claudel suggested. 'Maybe Angie died.'

'According to my estimate, Angie lived until she was around eighteen. That would bring us up to 1988, the year Grandma and Grandpa Corneau were killed.'

'Yeah,' Charbonneau snorted. 'We're gonna look into that wreck.'

'Maybe Catts liked the idea of a country without capital punishment. Maybe he thought a border would make him harder to track. Probably figured no one in Montreal knew Menard. For whatever reason, he pulled up stakes and headed north.' Claudel.

'With Angie or her body,' I said.

'The squirrel fools the probate people with his impostor act, goes French, becomes Stéphane Ménard, rents from Cyr, and opens a shop like the one in Yuba City.' Charbonneau.

'Collectibles,' I said.

'The perverted bastard was a collector all right.'

Claudel slid a second picture across the table.

An SIJ label identified the shot as a crime scene photo. The central object was a felt-covered board. The board displayed three human ears, two complete, one partial. The ears had been stretched and mounted like insects on pins.

My stomach soured.

'The sick little twist was keeping body parts from his victims.' Charbonneau.

I recalled the cut marks on the skulls in my lab.

'Souvenir taking may have been Pomerleau's idea.'

'Yeah?'

I pointed to the partial ear. 'Angie Robinson's ear was removed long after she died, when the bone had had time to dry, so Catts initially had not done that. The others were taken while the bone was fresh.'

'You can tell that from the cut marks?'

I nodded, swallowed.

'Nine years passed between the abductions of Pomerleau and McGee. During that time I believe the balance of power shifted between captor and captive.'

'Reverse Stockholm.' Charbonneau shot his hair with one hand.

'Patty Hearst was locked in a closet for eight weeks,' I said. 'Colleen Stan was locked in a box for seven years. Anique Pomerleau was taken in 1990. She was only fifteen.'

We fell silent, contemplating the unspeakable damage possible in that amount of time.

Claudel spoke first.

'Pomerleau was tortured, tried to please Catts, maybe suggested another victim.'

'Or maybe new meat was Catts's idea. Maybe he got greedy and decided to expand his collection,' Charbonneau picked up. 'Pomerleau saw the newcomer as a step up the food chain: by abusing McGee she pleased Catts. Eventually she started getting her own rocks off.'

'The controlled became the controller,' I said. 'Or Pomerleau and Catts just melded.'

Like Homolka and Bernardo, I thought.

'Catts took at least two more captives between Pomerleau and McGee,' I reminded. 'Local girls, according to strontium isotope analysis.'

'We will find out who these girls were.' Claudel's jaw muscles bunched, relaxed. 'You can take that to the bank.'

'I've got a question, Doc.' Charbonneau again leaned onto the table. 'Angie Robinson was Catts's earliest capture. Why were hers the only bones with that grave wax stuff?'

I'd posed that question to myself.

'The tannic acid in leather acts as a preservative, altering the rate of decomposition. And Angie may have been buried elsewhere initially, in a place with more moisture than the pizza basement cellar.'

'That's our thinking.' Charbonneau cocked his chin at Claudel. 'We figure the kid died in Vermont, Catts buried her there, later went back for her corpse. But we've been busting our brains trying to figure out why he'd bother. Your ear thing may be the missing piece.'

'Catts went back for the ear, but ended up bringing the whole body to Montreal? Why?'

'Maybe he felt safer having her right underfoot.'

'But Cyr gave Catts the boot in ninety-eight. If he'd already dug up and moved Angie Robinson once, why leave her and two others behind in that building?'

Charbonneau shrugged. 'Catts's had been skating since he grabbed Robinson in eighty-five. Maybe he'd come to feel invincible. Besides, where else could he bury bodies? He couldn't dig graves in the Corneaus' front yard.'

'And the cellar was otherwise committed,' I said bitterly.

There was a moment of silence as we thought about that. I broke it.

'Who do you suppose Louise Parent saw?'

'Perhaps Pomerleau. Perhaps one of the others. Catts may have kept girls under the pawnshop while preparing his little welcome wagon over in the Point,' Charbonneau said.

'Pomerleau admitted that she'd killed Parent,' I said.

'No doubt she was in it up to her eyeballs. SIJ found Rose Fisher's address in the de Sébastopol basement. But the Parent murder may have gone down at Catts's instigation. He probably told Pomerleau that the old lady had spotted him with captives at the pawnshop. They must have been keeping track of Parent, and when the bodies were discovered they figured they needed to move before she did.' Charbonneau shook his head. 'Ironic, isn't it? They tried to hide everything in the de Sébastopol basement, and that's the only thing that survived the fire.'

'That may be why your friend wasn't down there,' Claudel said. 'Pomerleau probably planned to drag Madame Turnip to the cellar, then changed her mind, fearing the fire wouldn't penetrate that far.'

'Or maybe she just grew tired and dumped her.' I felt my hands curl into fists.

'You were correct about the buttons.' Claudel looked me dead in the eye. 'Undoubtedly Catts dropped them while in the pizza parlor basement. They were unrelated to the bodies.'

I felt no satisfaction at being right, just a deep aching sorrow.

And weariness. My strength was unraveling like the top of an old sock.

I relaxed my hands and laced my fingers. There was one last answer I needed.

'When did you learn I'd gone to de Sébastopol?'

'I retrieved your message on the drive back from Vermont,' Charbonneau said. 'We'd learned from the photo that Menard was dead and that Catts had killed him. We knew that Pomerleau and McGee were in the wind. We knew Catts was dead. Luc and I went directly to headquarters and found a report stating that Pomerleau's prints were on the gun Catts used to blow out his lights.'

'And no prints from Catts,' I guessed.

'*Nada*. And Doc LaManche said Catts's hands were residue-free. We remembered what you'd told us about brainwashing, put two and two together, and hauled ass for de Sébastopol, gambling that we'd get there before you found Pomerleau and came to grief.'

'Thank you.'

'The line of duty, ma'am.' Charbonneau grinned.

I turned to Claudel.

'Thank you, Detective. And I truly am sorry about your coat.'

Claudel nodded. 'You showed great resourcefulness and courage.'

'Thanks again. To both of you.' We all rose and I started for the door.

'Dr. Brennan.'

I turned back to Claudel.

'I have never been an admirer.' The corners of Claudel's mouth quivered toward something verging on a grin. 'But you have given me a new appreciation for leopard skin.'

39

I barely woke when Ryan phoned Wednesday night. Mumbling a number of 'Mm's, and 'Uh-huh's, I dropped back into oblivion.

The next thing I knew sun was streaming through my window, the clock said ten-thirty, and Birdie's face was inches from mine.

And my doorbell was chirping.

Grabbing my bathrobe, I stumbled to the security panel. The monitor showed Ryan wearing a Santa hat with *Le Père Noël* embroidered on the fur.

I did a two-handed hair-tuck, smiling like Claudel's happy-face Skivvies.

Onscreen, the outer door opened and a young woman entered the foyer. Black corkscrew curls. Tall. Earrings the size of croquet hoops.

Ryan hugged the woman to his side. She tugged off his Santa hat.

My hand froze halfway to the buzzer. My smile crumbled.

The prom queen.

An iceberg congealed in my chest.

The prom queen turned. Café-au-lait skin. An expression that suggested she'd rather be elsewhere. Tikrit. Kabul. Anywhere but that foyer.

Ryan smiled and squeezed her again. The woman wriggled free and handed him his hat.

Lord God in heaven! Was the egotistical sonovabitch planning to make introductions?

I caught a glimpse of myself in the hall mirror. Ratty pink terry cloth. Parboiled face. Hair looking like something that fed on plankton.

'OK, buster.' I jabbed the button. 'Bring her on.'

Ryan was alone when I opened the door. The hall behind him was empty.

He'd hidden his teenybopper. Fine. Better.

'Yes?' Glacial.

Grinning, Ryan looked me up and down.

'Entertaining DiCaprio?'

I didn't smile.

Ryan studied my face.

'It's funny about eyebrows. You never really notice them until they go awry.'

Ryan reached out to touch my forehead. I pulled back.

'Or go away.'

'You're here to critique my brows?'

'What brows?'

Not even the hint of a smile.

Ryan crossed his arms. 'I'd like to talk.'

'It's not a good time.'

'You look beautiful.'

I bit back a retort that included the word 'bimbo.'

'Sultry.'

My AWOL brows crimped.

'Smoldering.'

The crimp dived into a full-blown frown.

'If I promise no more fire jokes, can I come back in ten? More than enough time to get yourself beautiful.'

I started to refuse.

'Please?' Lapis-lazuli sincerity.

My libido sat up. I sent it flying into tomorrow.

'Sure, Ryan. Why not?'

Coffee. Jeans and sweater. Teeth. Fresh bandages. Hair? Makeup?

Screw it.

Fifteen minutes later the bell chirped again.

When I opened the door, she was with him.

I stiffened.

Ryan's eyes locked onto mine. 'I'd like you to meet Lily.'

'Ryan,' I said. 'Don't.'

'My daughter.'

My lips parted as my mind processed the meaning of those words.

'Lily, this is Tempe.'

Lily shifted her feet.

'Hi.' Mumbled.

'It's a pleasure to meet you, Lily.'

Daughter? Ohmygod.

I looked a question at Ryan.

'Lily lives in Halifax.'

I turned back to Lily.

'Nova Scotia?' Moron! Of course, Nova Scotia.

'Yes.' Lily took in my frizzled hair and blisters, but said nothing.

'Lily's been in Montreal since the third,' Ryan said.

The day I testified at the Pétit trial.

'Lily and I have been getting to know each other over the past few months.'

Lily shrugged one shoulder, adjusted the strap of her purse.

'I feel the women in my life should also get to know each other.'

The women in his life?

'I'm delighted, Lily.' Jesus! I sounded like a cliché thesaurus.

Lily's eyes slid to Ryan. He nodded almost imperceptibly.

'Sorry about that phone call. I—I shouldn't have said you were dumb.'

The woman at Ryan's place last Thursday had been Lily.

'I understand.' I smiled. 'Sharing your father must be very hard.'

Another shoulder shrug, then Lily turned to Ryan. 'Can I go now?'

Ryan nodded. 'Got your key?'

Lily patted her purse, turned, and walked down the hall.

'Come in.' I stepped back and opened the door wide. 'Dad.'

Ryan followed me to the living room, shrugged off his jacket, and dropped onto the couch.

'This is awkward,' I said, curling into an armchair.

'Yes, it is,' Ryan said.

'I didn't know you had a daughter.'

'Nor did I. Until August.'

The unscheduled trip from Charlotte to Halifax.

'The problem wasn't your niece.'

'It started out with my niece. After the overdose, I flew to Nova Scotia to help my sister get Danielle into a drug rehab program. One of the nurse's aides turned out to be a woman I'd known as an undergrad.'

'A student at St. Francis Xavier?'

Ryan shook his head no. 'I was. She wasn't. I was on a wild ride my first two years at St. F-X. Lutetia was a regular at some of my haunts, hung with a rowdy group of young ladies. Called themselves the Holy Sisters of Negotiable Love.'

I tucked my feet under my bum.

'You know the story. My wild ride ended with a severed artery, a bump in the hospital, and a fresh perspective on the college experience. Lutetia and I went our separate ways. I saw her once, maybe five years after graduation, when I returned to Nova Scotia to visit my folks. Lutetia and I ended up'—Ryan hesitated—'sharing one last religious experience. I returned to Montreal, Lutetia went home to the Bahamas, and we lost track of each other.'

'Lily is Lutetia's daughter,' I guessed.

Nod.

'Lutetia never told you she was pregnant?'

'She was afraid somehow I'd force her to remain in Canada.'

'Did she marry?'

'In the Abacos. Marriage broke up when Lily was twelve. Lutetia moved them both to Halifax.'

Birdie wandered in and rubbed my leg. I reached down and absently scratched his head.

'Why tell you now?'

'Lily had started asking about her biological father. She'd also started pulling some of the same stunts as Danielle. When I showed up . . .' Ryan spread his hands.

'You weren't expecting Lily in Montreal?'

'I opened my door and there she was. The little idiot had hitchhiked.'

Birdie nudged me again. I stroked him, feeling, what? Relieved that the prom queen wasn't a love interest? Disappointed that Ryan hadn't confided in me?

'Why didn't you tell me?'

'Things have been pretty strained between us, Tempe.' Ryan grin. 'Probably my fault. I've been under some pressure lately. Lily. The meth operation.'

Ryan patted his shirt pocket, remembered my no-smoking ban, dropped his hands to his lap.

'But mostly, I was holding off until I was sure.'

'You asked for proof of paternity?'

Ryan nodded.

'How did Lily respond to that?'

'The kid went ballistic, really started acting out.'

The relapse into smoking. The haggard look. Ryan had been under more stress lately than I had.

'I got the DNA report last week.'

I waited.

'Lily is my daughter.'

'That's wonderful, Ryan.'

'It is. But the kid's a pistol, and I'm clueless concerning fatherhood.'

'What have you worked out so far?'

'Lutetia's largely gotten Lily's head straight. Lily loves her mother and will continue to live with her. If she decides she wants another parent in her life, I'll be there for her, whatever it takes.'

I crossed to the couch and sat beside Ryan. He looked at me, eyes boylike. I took his hand.

'You'll be a wonderful father.'

'I'll need a lot of help.'

'You've got it, cowboy.'

I put my face to Ryan's, felt his rough stubble on my cheek.

Ryan held me a moment, then set me at arm's length, and got up.

'Stay here.'

I waited, unsure what was happening. The front door opened, seconds passed. The door closed. I heard rattling. A tinkling bell.

Ryan reappeared wearing the Santa hat and carrying a cage the size of a gym. Inside, a cockatiel clung to an undulating swing.

Ryan placed the cage on my coffee table, dropped next to me on the couch, and wrapped an arm around my shoulders. The cockatiel regarded us as it swung back and forth in decreasing arcs.

'Merry Christmas,' Ryan said. 'Charlie, meet Tempe.'

The swing settled. Charlie checked me out, first with his left eye, then with his right.

'I can't have a bird. I'm away far too much.'

Charlie hopped from the swing to his seed dish.

Across the room, Birdie rose, tail puffed, eyes fixed on the cockatiel.

'Birdie, meet Charlie,' Ryan said to my cat.

Birdie oozed across the carpet, a miniature white leopard on a predawn stalk. Placing forepaws on the coffee table, Bird craned toward the cage, tail flicking only at its tip.

Charlie raised his crown, tipped his head at Birdie, then refocused on his seed.

'He's beautiful, Ryan.' He really was. Soft yellow head, pearl gray body.

Jumping to the tabletop, Birdie placed his paws in a square, sat, and stared at the cockatiel.

'It's a lovely idea, Ryan, but it won't work.'

Bright orange cheek patches.

Birdie settled into his sphinx position, paws curled inward, eyes locked on the bird.

Soft white stripes on his wings.

Birdie began to purr. I looked at him, astounded.

'Bird likes him,' Ryan said.

'I can't commute by air with a cat and a bird.'

'I have a plan.'

I looked at Ryan.

'Live with me.'

'What?'

'Move in with me.'

I was in shock. The idea of cohabitation had never crossed my mind.

Did I want to live with Ryan?

Yes. No. I had no idea.

I tried to think of a suitable reply. 'Maybe' lacked a certain style, while 'No' seemed rather final.

Ryan didn't push.

'Plan B. Joint custody. When you're down South, Charlie bunks with me.'

I looked at the cockatiel.

He really was beautiful.

And Bird liked him.

I stuck out a hand. 'Agreed.'

Ryan and I shook.

'In the meantime, plan A remains on the table.'

Live with Ryan?

Maybe, I thought.

Just maybe.

That afternoon I decided to visit my office. I'd been there about an hour when my phone rang.

'Dr. Brennan?'

'Yes.'

'This is Pamela Lindahl. I'm the social services psychiatrist assigned to assure that Tawny McGee receives appropriate assessment and care. Will you be in your office another forty-five minutes?'

'Yes.'

'I'd like to come by for a brief visit. Would you ask security to pass me through?'

'Certainly.'

As soon as the call concluded I wished I hadn't agreed. Though I recognized the importance of supplying all available information to the care-givers, I didn't feel up to recalling or recounting the depravity, the evil of what I had seen. I thought about phoning Dr. Lindahl back and telling her not to come, then gave in to a sense of duty, contacted security, and began a mental checklist of what I could tell the doctor.

Forty minutes later there was a knock on my door.

'*Entrez.*'

A small, dark-haired girl wearing a trench coat and a brown beret stepped into the room, followed by an older, hatless woman in wool. A moment of confusion, then recognition.

'Hello, Tawny,' I said to the girl, coming around my desk and extending both hands.

Tawny shrank back slightly and did not raise her arms.

I clasped my hands in front of me and said, 'I'm very glad to see you. I wanted to thank you for saving my life.'

At first, no response, then, 'You saved my life.' More hesitation. Then, speaking slowly, 'I asked for this visit because I wanted you to see me. I wanted you to see that I am a person, not a creature in a cage.'

This time when I stepped toward her Tawny held her ground. I enveloped her in a hug and pressed the side of my head to hers. Feelings for

Tawny and Katy and young women everywhere, adored or abused, overwhelmed me and I began to weep. Tawny did not cry, but she did not pull away.

I released her and stepped back, taking hold of her hands.

'I never thought of you as other than a person, Tawny, and neither do the people who are helping you now. And I'm sure your family is very anxious to have you back with them.'

She looked at me, dropped her hands to her sides, and stepped back.

'Good-bye, Dr. Brennan.' Her face was without expression, but there was a depth to her eyes that differed from the blank stare of earlier days.

'Good-bye, Tawny. I am so very happy you came.'

Dr. Lindahl smiled in my direction, and the two women exited.

I fell back into my chair, exhausted but uplifted.

40

The holidays came and went. The sun rose and set on a winter of Mondays.

In one of the dozens of boxes taken from the de Sébastopol basement, investigators found a journal. The journal contained names. Angela Robinson, Kimberly Hamilton, Anique Pomerleau, Marie-Joëlle Bastien, Manon Violette, Tawny McGee.

LSJML-38427 was identified as Marie-Joëlle Bastien, a sixteen-year-old Acadian from Bouctouche, New Brunswick, who'd gone missing in the spring of 1994. Over the years her file had been misplaced, her name deleted from the MP lists. My age and height estimates suggested Marie-Joëlle died soon after her capture.

Dr. Energy's girl was identified as Manon Violette, a fifteen-year-old Montrealer who'd disappeared in the fall of 1994, six months after Marie-Joëlle Bastien. Manon's skeletal age and height suggested she'd survived in captivity for several years.

By March, the bones of Angie Robinson, Marie-Joëlle Bastien, and Manon Violette were returned to their families. Each was laid to rest in a quiet ceremony.

Kimberly Hamilton was never located.

Anne and Tom-Ted plunged full-tilt boogie into counseling. She took golf lessons. He bought gardening books. Together they planted a godzillion azaleas.

I had no further contact with Tawny McGee. She spent weeks in intensive in-patient therapy, eventually moved home to Maniwaki. It would be a long road back, but doctors were optimistic.

Anique Pomerleau's photo went out across the continent. Dozens of tips were received by the CUM and SQ. Pomerleau was sighted in Sherbrooke. Albany. Tampa. Thunder Bay.

The hunt continues.

For Anique Pomerleau.

For Kimberly Hamilton.

For all the lost girls.

FROM THE FORENSIC
FILES OF DR. KATHY
REICHS

For legal and ethical reasons I cannot discuss any of the real-life cases that may have inspired *Monday Mourning*, but I can share with you some experiences that contributed to the plot.

The weather was sunny and shirt-sleeve mild that week in September in Montreal. An Indian summer hiccup before the nine-month freeze.

Friday, September 14, was created for hiking the mountain, playing tennis, or biking the path along the Lachine Canal. Instead, I got a call to report to the lab.

The case was waiting when I arrived, Demande d'Expertise en Anthropologie on my desk, bones on the counter. I went straight to the form and scanned the information.

LSJML number. Morgue number. Police incident number. Investigating officer. Coroner. Pathologist. Description of specimens: fragmentary skeletal remains. Expertise requested: biological profile, manner of death, postmortem interval.

I looked at the three brown paper bags sealed with red evidence tape.

Right.

According to the summary of known facts, the episode began with a backed-up toilet in a pizza-by-the-slice joint. Plunger failing, the frustrated proprietor called in help. While banging pipes, the plumber spotted a trapdoor behind the commode.

Curious, the plucky *plombier* pried, then peered, then plunged underground. When his flashlight beamed up a half-buried long bone, the man surfaced, notified the owner, and the two set off for the local stacks. A copy of *L'Anatomie pour les Artistes* confirmed that the booty in their sack was a human femur.

The pair called the police. The police processed the basement, recovered a bottle, a coin, and two dozen additional bones, and sent the remains to the morgue. The coroner notified the Laboratoire de Sciences Judiciairies et de Médecine Légale. The pathologist took one look and torpedoed my day in the sun.

Sorting and analysis occupied me for several hours. In the end, three individuals lay on my table: a young adult aged eighteen to twenty-four, a middle-aged adult, and an older adult with advanced arthritis. The youngest of the three had sharp instrument trauma on the head, jaw, sacrum, femur, and tibia.

I called the detectives. They informed me that the bottle was new but the coin was old, dating to the late nineteenth century. They could not confirm the coin's association with the skeleton. I told them to return to the basement. I needed more bones.

A week passed.

Bad news. The detectives reported that no cemetery had ever occupied land under or in the vicinity of the pizza parlor building. Worse news. The detectives reported possible mob links for an occupant of the property some forty years earlier.

Again, I repeated my request for reprocessing, and offered to accompany a team back into the basement. Again, a week passed. Two.

Why the reluctance to return to that cellar?

When confronted, the boys had a one-word reply.

Rats!

Compromise. Establish that the deaths had taken place within the last half century, and we'd dig the whole cellar, rodents be damned.

My analysis now focused on the question of time since death. Every bone and bone fragment was dry and devoid of odor or flesh. Only one technique held promise.

After I explained the use of artificial or 'bomb' Carbon 14 in determining postmortem interval with modern organic materials, the Bureau du Coroner authorized payment for testing. I cut and sent samples from two individuals to Beta Analytic Inc., a radiocarbon dating lab in Miami, Florida. A week later we had our answer.

Though the results were complicated, one thing

was clear. The pizza parlor victims had died prior to 1955.

No curtain call with *Rattus rattus*. Cue the archaeologists.

Though the dossier is closed, I still ponder those bones. I am touched by the thought of the dead lying in anonymous cellar graves while the living transact business one floor up.

Pepsi, please, and a pepperoni and cheese to go.

What would they think?

Read on for an exclusive extract from the
new Temperance Brennan thriller

Flash and Bones

Coming in September 2011 from
William Heinemann

1

Looking back, I think of it as Raceweek in the Rain. Thunderboomers almost every day. Sure, it was spring. But these storms were over the top.

In the end, Summer saved my life.

I know. Sounds bizarre.

This is what happened.

Bloated, dark clouds hung low to the ground, but so far no rain.

Lucky break. I'd spent the morning digging up a corpse.

Sound macabre? Just part of the job. I'm a forensic anthropologist. I recover and analyze the dead that present in less than pristine condition – the burned, mummified, mutilated, dismembered, decomposed, and skeletal.

OK. Today's target wasn't actually a corpse. I'd been searching for overlooked body parts.

Short version. Last fall a housewife vanished from her rural Cabarrus County home. A week ago, while I was away on a working vacation in Hawaii, a trucker admitted to strangling

3

the woman and burying her body in a sandpit. Impatient, the local cops had sallied forth with shovels and buckets. The bones were delivered to the Mecklenburg County Medical Examiner's office in a Skippy peanut butter carton.

Yesterday, my aloha tan still glowing, I'd begun my analysis. A skeletal inventory revealed that the hyoid, the mandible, and all of the upper incisors and canines were missing.

No teeth, no dental ID. No hyoid, no evidence of strangulation. Dr. Tim Larabee, the Mecklenburg County Medical Examiner, asked me to have a second go at the sandpit.

Correcting screw-ups usually makes me cranky. Today, I was feeling upbeat.

I'd quickly found the missing bits and dispatched them to the MCME facility in Charlotte. I was en route to a shower, a late lunch, and time with my cat.

It was one fifty p.m. My sweat-soaked T was pasted to my back. My hair was yanked into a ratty knot. Sand lined my scalp and undies. Nevertheless, I was humming. Al Yankovitch, 'White and Nerdy'. What can I say? I'd watched a YouTube video and the tune lodged in my head.

Wind buffeted my Mazda as I merged onto southbound I-85. Slightly uneasy, I glanced at the sky, then thumbed on NPR.

Terry Gross was finishing an interview with Kay Ryan, the US poet laureate. Both were indifferent to the conditions outside my car.

Fair enough. Philadelphia is five hundred miles north of Dixie.

Terry launched into a teaser about an upcoming guest. I never caught the name.

Beep! Beep! Beep!

4

'The National Weather service has issued a severe weather warning for parts of the North Carolina piedmont, including Mecklenburg, Cabarrus, Anson, Stanly, and Union Counties. Severe thunderstorms are expected to move through the area within the next hour. Rainfall of one to three inches is anticipated, creating the potential for flash flooding. Atmospheric conditions are favorable for the development of tornadoes. Stay tuned to this station for further updates'

Beep! Beep! Beep!

I tightened my grip on the wheel and goosed my speed to seventy-five. Risky in a sixty-five mph zone, but I wanted to reach home before the deluge.

Moments later Terry was interrupted again, this time by a muted *whoop-whoop*.

My eyes flicked to the radio.

Whoop!

Feeling stupid I checked the rear view mirror.

A police cruiser was riding my bumper.

Annoyed, I pulled to the shoulder and lowered my window. When the cop approached, I held out my license.

'Dr. Temperance Brennan?'

'Looking somewhat worse for wear.' I beamed what I hoped was a winning smile.

Johnny Law did not beam back. 'That won't be necessary,' indicating my license.

Puzzled, I looked up at the guy. He was mid-twenties, slim, with an infant mustache that appeared to be going nowhere. A plaque on his chest said R. Warner.

'The Concord Police Department received a request from the Mecklenburg County medical examiner to intercept and divert you.'

'Larabee sent the cops to find me?'

'Yes, Ma'am. When I arrived at the recovery site, you'd left.'

'Why didn't he call me directly?'

'Apparently he couldn't get through.'

Of course not. While digging, I'd locked my iPhone in the car to protect it from sand.

'My phone is in the glove compartment.' No need to alarm Officer Warner. 'I'm going to take it out.'

'Yes, Ma'am.'

The numbers on the little screen indicated three missed calls from Larabee. Three messages. I listened to the first.

'Long story, which I'll share when you're back. The Concord PD received a report of a body at the Morehead Road landfill. Chapel Hill wants us to handle it. I'm elbow deep in an autopsy. Since you're in the area, I hoped you could swing by to check it out. Joe Hawkins is diverting that way with the van, just in case they've actually got something for us.'

The second message was the same as the first. Ditto the third, but more terse. It ended with the inducement: You're a champ, Tempe.

A landfill in a storm? The champ was suddenly not so chipper.

'Ma'am, we should hurry. The rain won't hold off much longer.'

'Lead on.' I could not have said this with less enthusiasm.

Warner returned to his cruiser, whoop-whooped, then pulled into traffic. Inwardly cursing Larabee, Warner, and the landfill, I palm-slapped the gearshift and followed.

Traffic on I-85 was unusually heavy for mid-afternoon. As we approached Concord, I could see that the Bruton Smith Boulevard exit ramp was a parking lot.

And realized what a nightmare this little detour of Larabee's would be.

The Morehead Road landfill is back fence neighbor to the Charlotte Motor Speedway, a major stop on the NASCAR circuit. Races would be held there this weekend and next. Tomorrow's qualifying would determine which lucky drivers would make the cut for Saturday's All Star Shootout.

Two hundred thousand avid fans would pour into Charlotte for Race Week. Looking at the sea of SUVs, campers, pick-ups, and sedans I guessed that many had already hit town.

Warner rode the shoulder. I followed, ignoring the hostile glares of those cemented in the logjam.

Lights flashing, we snaked through the bedlam on Bruton Smith Boulevard, past the dragway, the dirt track, and a zillion fast food joints. On the sidelines, the tattooed and tank-topped carried babies, six-packs, coolers, and radios. Vendors sold souvenirs from folding tables beneath improvised tents.

Warner looped the surrealistic geometry of the speedway itself, made several turns, then rolled to a stop outside a small structure whose siding might once have been blue. Beyond the building loomed a series of mounds resembling a Martian mountain range.

A man emerged and issued Warner a yellow hardhat and neon orange vest. As they talked the man pointed at a gravel road rising sharply uphill.

Warner waited while I received my safety gear, then we proceeded up the slope. Trucks rumbled in both directions, engines churning hard going in, humming going out.

When the road leveled I could see three men standing by an enormous dumpster. Two wore coveralls. The third wore black pants and a long-sleeved black shirt over a white T. Joe Hawkins, long-time death investigator for the MCME. All three featured gear identical to that lying on my passenger seat.

Warner nosed up to the dumpster and parked. I pulled in beside him.

The men watched as I got out and donned my hardhat and vest. Fetching. A perfect complement to my current state of hygiene.

'We gotta quit meeting like this.' Joe and I had parted at the sandpit barely an hour earlier.

The older man stuck out a hand. 'Weaver Molene.' Molene was flushed and sweating, and filled his coveralls way beyond their intended capacity.

'Temperance Brennan.'

I'd have skipped the handshake, given the black moons under Molene's nails, but didn't want to be rude.

'You the coroner?' he asked.

'I work for the medical examiner,' I said.

Molene introduced the younger man as Barcelona Jackson. Jackson was very thin and very black. And very, very nervous.

'Jackson and I work for BFI, the company that manages the landfill.'

'Impressive pile of trash,' I said.

'Site's got a capacity of over two and a half million cubic meters.' Molene ran a dingy hanky across his face. 'Friggin' weird Jackson stumbled onto the one square foot holding a stiff. Or maybe not. Probably dozens out there.'

Jackson had mostly kept his eyes down. At Molene's words, he raised then quickly dropped them back to his boots.

'Tell me what you found, sir.'

Though I spoke to Jackson, Molene answered.

'Probably best we show you. And quick.' He pocket-jammed the hanky. 'This storm's coming fast.'

Molene set off at a pace I would have thought impossible for a man of his bulk. Jackson scampered after. I fell into line, paying attention as best I could to the uneven footing. Warner and Hawkins brought up the rear.

I've excavated in landfills, am familiar with the aroma of *eau de dump*, a delicate blend of methane and carbon dioxide, with traces of ammonia, hydrogen sulfide, nitrogen, hydrogen chloride, and carbon monoxide added for spice. I braced for the stench. Didn't happen.

Good odor management, guys. Or maybe it was Mother Nature. Wind swirled dirt into little cyclones and tumbled cellophane wrappers, plastic bags, and torn paper across the landscape.

Our course took us the length of the active landfill, down a slope, then around a series of what appeared to be closed areas. Instead of raw earth, the tops of the older mounds were covered with grass.

As we walked, the rumble of trucks receded and the whine of fine-tuned engines grew louder. Based on the changing acoustics I figured the speedway lay over a rise to our right.

After ten minutes, Molene stopped at the base of a truncated hillock. Though tentative grass greened the top, the side facing us was scarred and pitted, like a desert butte gouged by eons of wind.

Molene said something I didn't catch. I was focused on the exposed stratigraphy.

Unlike the sandstone or shale making up metamorphic

rock, the mound's layers were composed of flattened Pontiacs and Posturpedics, of squashed Pepsis, Pop-Tarts, Pringles, and Pampers.

Molene pointed to a crater in a brown-green layer eight feet above our heads, then to an object lying about two yards off the base of the mound. His explanation was lost to a clap of thunder.

Didn't matter. It was obvious Jackson's 'stiff' had dropped from the mound, probably dislodged by the previous day's storm.

I crossed to the thing and squatted. Molene, Warner, and Hawkins clustered around me but remained standing. Jackson kept his distance.

The object was a drum, approximately twenty inches in diameter and thirty inches high. Its cover lay off to one side.

'Looks like a metal container of some kind,' I said without looking up. 'It's too rusted to make out a logo or label.'

'Flip it.' Molene shouted. 'Jackson and I turned the thing bottom-up to protect the stuff inside.'

I tried. It weighed a ton.

Hawkins squatted and, together, we muscled the drum upright. Its interior was filled with a solid black mass.

I leaned close. Something pale was suspended in the dark fill, but the pre-storm gloom obscured all detail.

I was reaching for my MagLite when lightning sparked.

A human hand flashed white in the electric brilliance.

Dissolved to black.

Virals

Kathy Reichs

Tory Brennan is as fascinated by bones and dead bodies as her famous aunt, acclaimed forensic anthropologist, Tempe Brennan. However living on a secluded island off Charleston in South Carolina there is not much opportunity to put her knowledge to the test. Until she and her group of technophile friends stumble across a shallow grave containing the remains of a girl who has been missing for over thirty years.

With the cold-case murder suddenly hot, Tory realises that they are involved in something fatally dangerous. And when they rescue a sick dog from a laboratory on the same island, it becomes evident that somehow the two events are linked.

On the run from forces they don't understand, they have only each other to fall back on. Until they succumb to a mysterious infection that heightens their senses and hones their instincts to impossible levels. Their illness seems to have changed their very biology – and it's clear that the island is home to something well beyond their comprehension. It's a secret that has driven men to kill once. And will drive them to kill again . . .

WILLIAM HEINEMANN: LONDON

Spider Bones

Kathy Reichs

Dr Temperance Brennan spends her working life amongst the decomposed, the mutilated, and the skeletal. So the two-days-dead body she is called to examine holds little to surprise her. Until she discovers that the man is John Lowery, an ex-soldier who was apparently killed in Vietnam in 1968. So who is buried in Lowery's grave?

The case takes Tempe to an organisation dedicated to bringing home the bodies of unidentified soldiers where she must examine the remains of anyone who may have had a connection to the drowned man. It's a harrowing task, but it pays off when she finds Lowery's dog tags amongst the bones of a long-dead soldier.

As Tempe unravels the tangled threads of the soldiers' lives and deaths, she realises there are some who would rather the past stayed buried. And when she proves difficult to frighten, they turn their attention to the one person she would give her life to protect . . .

arrow books

ALSO AVAILABLE IN ARROW

206 Bones

Kathy Reichs

**'You have an enemy, Dr Brennan. It is in your interest
to learn who placed the call . . .'**

A routine case turns sinister when Dr Temperance Brennan is
accused of mishandling the autopsy of a missing heiress. Someone
has made an incriminating accusation that she missed or con-
cealed crucial evidence. Before Tempe can get to the one man
with information, he turns up dead.

The heiress isn't the only elderly female to have appeared on
Tempe's gurney recently. Back in Montreal, three more women
have died, their bodies brutally discarded. Tempe is convinced
there's a link between their deaths and that of the heiress.
But what – or who – connects them?

Tempe struggles with the clues, but nothing adds up. Has she
made grave errors or is some unknown foe sabotaging her? It soon
becomes frighteningly clear. It's not simply Tempe's career at risk.
Her life is at stake too.

arrow books

Devil Bones

Kathy Reichs

An underground chamber is exposed in a seedy, dilapidated house with sagging trim and peeling paint . . .

In the dark cellar, a ritualistic display is revealed. A human skull rests on a cauldron, surrounded by slain chickens and bizarre figurines. Beads and antlers dangle overhead.

Called to the scene is forensic anthropologist Dr Temperance Brennan. Bony architecture suggests that the skull is that of a young, black female. But how did she die? And when? Then, just as Tempe is working to determine the post-mortem interval, another body is discovered: a headless corpse carved with Satanic symbols.

As citizen vigilantes, blaming Devil-worshippers, begin a witch-hunt, intent on revenge, Tempe struggles to keep her emotions in check. But the truth she eventually uncovers proves more shocking than even she could have imagined . . .

arrow books

Bones to Ashes

Kathy Reichs

Under the microscope, the outer bone surface is a moonscape of craters . . .

The skeleton is that of a young girl, no more than fourteen years old – and forensic anthropologist Dr Temperance Brennan is struggling to keep her emotions in check.

A nagging in her subconscious won't let up. A memory triggered, deep in her hindbrain – the disappearance of a childhood friend; no warning, no explanation . . .

Detective Andrew Ryan is working a series of parallel cases: three missing persons, three unidentified bodies – all female, all early-to-mid teens . . . Could Tempe's skeleton be yet another in this tragic line of young victims? Or is she over-reacting, making connections where none exist?

Working on instinct, Tempe takes matters into her own hands. But even she couldn't have predicted the horrors this investigation would eventually uncover . . . Can Tempe maintain a professional distance as the past catches up with her in this, her most deeply personal case yet?

arrow books

Break No Bones

Kathy Reichs

A decomposing body is uncovered in a shallow grave off a lonely beach . . .

The skeleton is articulated, the bone fresh and the vertebrae still connected by soft-tissue – it's a recent burial, and a case forensic anthropologist Dr Temperance Brennan must take.

Dental remains and skeletal gender and race indicators suggest that the deceased is a middle-aged white male – but who was he? Why was he buried in a clandestine grave? And what does the unusual fracture of the sixth cervical vertebra signify?

But just as Brennan is trying to piece together the evidence, another body is discovered – and before long Tempe finds herself drawn deeper into a shocking and chilling investigation, set to challenge her entire view of humanity . . .

'A brilliant novel . . . Reichs's seamless blending of fascinating science and dead-on psychological portrayals, not to mention a whirlwind of a plot, make Break No Bones a must-read'
Jeffery Deaver

arrow books

Cross Bones

Kathy Reichs

An Orthodox Jew is found shot dead in Montreal, the mutilated body barely recognisable.

Extreme heat has accelerated decomposition, and made it virtually impossible to determine the bullet trajectory.

But just as forensic anthopologist Dr Temperance Brennan is attempting to make sense of the fracture patterning, a mysterious stranger slips her a photograph of a skeleton, assuring her it holds the key to the victim's death . . .

The trail of clues leads all the way to the Holy Land where, together with detective Andrew Ryan, Tempe makes a startling discovery – but the further Tempe probes into the identity of the ancient skeleton, the more she seems to be putting herself in danger . . .

'Reichs is on top form'
Sunday Times

'Reichs is not just "as good as" Cornwell,
she has become the finer writer'
Daily Express

'A rattling good read'
Kate Mosse

arrow books

Monday Mourning

Kathy Reichs

Three skeletons are found in the basement of a pizza parlour.

The building is old, with a colourful past, and Homicide Detective Luc Claudel dismisses the remains as historic. Not his case, not his concern . . .

But forensic anthropologist Tempe Brennan has her doubts. Something about the bones of the three young women suggests a different message: murder. A cold case, but Claudel's case nonetheless.

Brennan is in Montreal to testify as an expert witness at a trial. Digging up more bones was not on her agenda. And to make matters worse, her sometime-lover Detective Andrew Ryan disappears just as Tempe is beginning to trust him.

Soon Tempe finds herself drawn ever deeper into a web of evil from which there may be no escape: three women have disappeared, never to return. And Tempe may be next . . .

'Reichs is not just "as good as" Cornwell, she has become the finer writer'
Daily Express

'Terrific'
Independent on Sunday

arrow books